PRAISE FOR *THE BONES OF MAKAIDOS*

It is fitting for the last book in the Oracles of Fire series to be the best. *The Bones of Makaidos* captured me from the very beginning. Bryan Davis's ability to vividly depict scenes is at its best in the final installment of his bestselling fantasy series. You will not be able to put the book down!

GRANT MILLER

Beloved characters, both new and old, grace the pages of this tale and beckon you to enter their world one last time as they fight against the growing darkness around them. The tapestry masterfully woven is finally complete. But is it really the end?

ANNE K. RILEY

After reading the rest of the Oracles of Fire and Dragons in our Midst books, I find *The Bones of Makaidos* to be a smashing ending. It's so nice to find not one, but two book series that are so enthralling, adventure-packed, inspiring, and God honoring.

REBECCA VATH

I laughed; I cried; I shared with each character's joy and suffering. I could not put this book down, even to go to bed. *The Bones of Makaidos* pulled me in from cover to cover. Bryan Davis has saved the best for last! This book is definitely one you don't want to miss.

SARAH PRATT

This book is absolutely amazing. It's thrilling to join in with all of these characters' adventures once again! I can't keep my hands away from the book. It's sad to know that this will be the last one, but it's great anyway! A must-read for sure!

DANIELLE DIEZ

Bryan Davis has done it again! I knew Mr. Davis was an excellent author, but I was amazed to find myself double-taking and rereading pages as my jaw dropped. You will be up late into the night reading *The Bones of Makaidos* telling yourself, "just one more chapter" over and over again. Possibly Mr. Davis's best yet!

JACOB EGGERT

The Bones of Makaidos is, in my opinion, the best book that Mr. Davis has written yet! The events in this book left me bewildered, and they completely change your outlook on this entire series. It's a work of art!

ANNA BJELLA

The Bones of Makaidos is a tale of love, courage, sacrifice, and redemption; a wonderful end to an awesome series. All I can say is: What a ride!

T. McCARVILLE

In *The Bones of Makaidos,* action will spike your adrenaline; suspense will urge you to read on; sacrifice and salvation will bring you to tears, and the characters will encourage you to trust in God more than ever before.

REGAN HICKMAN

I've cried more in this book than the other seven put together—some were tears of sadness, but most have been tears of joy. Each time you read it, it'll be just as powerful as the first time, if not more. All loose ends will be tied, and when you read the last page, you'll be left with a sense of peace that's hard to describe.

CONNIE WOLTERS

If you don't think the Oracles of Fire series can get any better, then think again. This book outdoes the rest! Prophecies are fulfilled, and any questions from the last seven books are answered. *The Bones of Makaidos* is my favorite of Mr. Davis's books, and I know it will be yours too.

TAYLOR WARD

The Bones of Makaidos is a fitting end to the best series of books I have ever read! In the ultimate battle of good versus evil, I felt joy at surprise reunions and sadness over the loss of loved ones. In the end I was left with a happiness that can only come from experiencing God at work in this world of ours.

RACHEL TETTLETON

"I want you to win my heart. I want you to fight for me, sweat for me, bleed for me. . . ." *The Bones of Makaidos* captures the hearts of readers, brings them into the lives of all the characters, and shows that God is always there, and if you have faith, he will reward you.

KENDRA WILLIAMSON

In *The Lord of the Rings: The Two Towers*, King Theoden said, "If this is to be our end, then I would have them make such an end, as to be worthy of remembrance." Mr. Davis has accomplished this and then some.

HAYLEY COX

The Bones of Makaidos is an epic adventure that brings the wonderful elements of the series together into an ultimate climax. Well done, Mr. Davis!

KENNY DONOVAN

The Bones of Makaidos is my favorite book. There's adventure, excitement, and romance all mingled together. At times I feel like all the characters are real, like I'm going right along with them in their adventures. Most of all, these books have strengthened my faith. Thank you, Mr. Davis!

JENN MORGAN

Throughout the first seven books, Billy, Bonnie, Walter, Ashley, Sapphira, and Elam have grown closer to each other and stronger in their faith in Elohim. Now, together with the rest of the Oracles of Fire, they face their final battle, the fiercest challenge, preceding the ultimate reward.

BRYCE McLEMORE

In this rousing conclusion, Bryan Davis has penned a tale of betrayal and endurance, of faith, hope, and love. Of humor. Of other worlds and of a majestic people in whom the lights of chivalry and honor have not gone out. Indeed, *The Bones of Makaidos* is a masterpiece of Christian literature.

HOLLI HERDEG

Dragons in Our Midst Story World Reading Order

Dragons in our Midst

Raising Dragons

The Candlestone

Circles of Seven

Tears of a Dragon

Oracles of Fire

Eye of the Oracle

Enoch's Ghost

Last of the Nephilim

Refining Fires: The Bones of Makaidos, Part 1

From the Ashes: The Bones of Makaidos, Part 2

Children of the Bard

Song of the Ovulum

From the Mouth of Elijah

The Seventh Door

Omega Dragon

Dragons of Camelot

The Sacred Scales

The Memory Stone

Other Books by Bryan Davis

The Reapers Trilogy

Reapers

Beyond the Gateway

Reaper Reborn

Time Echoes Trilogy

Time Echoes

Interfinity

Fatal Convergence

Dragons of Starlight

Starlighter

Warrior

Diviner

Liberator

Tales of Starlight

Masters & Slayers

Third Starlighter

Exodus Rising

Standalone Novel

Let the Ghosts Speak

The Oculus Gate

Heaven Came Down

Invading Hell

My Soul to Take

On Earth as It Is in Hell

Wanted: Superheroes

Wanted: A Superhero to Save the World

Hertz to Be a Hero

Antigravity Heroes

Astral Alliance

Across Astral Realms

The First Starborn

At the Speed of Mind

Not So Famous Dog Tales

All Dogs Go to 7-Eleven

Mission Impossible

If You Give a Dog a Dictionary

A Series of Unfortunate Dogs

The Wizard of Dogs

BRYAN DAVIS

THE BONES OF MAKAIDOS
PART ONE

REFINING FIRES

ORACLES OF FIRE

BOOK FOUR

wander
An imprint of
Tyndale House
Publishers

Visit Tyndale online at tyndale.com.

Visit the author online at daviscrossing.com.

Refining Fires: The Bones of Makaidos, Part 1

Previously published in 2009 by Scrub Jay Journeys under ISBN 978-1-946253-78-1 as *The Bones of Makaidos*. First printing by Tyndale House Publishers in 2026.

Designed by Jennifer L. Phelps

Published in association with Cyle Young of the C.Y.L.E Agency, LLC.

For information about special discounts for bulk purchases, please contact Tyndale House Publishers at csresponse@tyndale.com, or call 1-855-277-9400.

Library of Congress Cataloging-in-Publication Data

A catalog record for this book is available from the Library of Congress.

ISBN 979-8-4005-0398-6

Printed in the United States of America

32 31 30 29 28 27 26

7 6 5 4 3 2 1

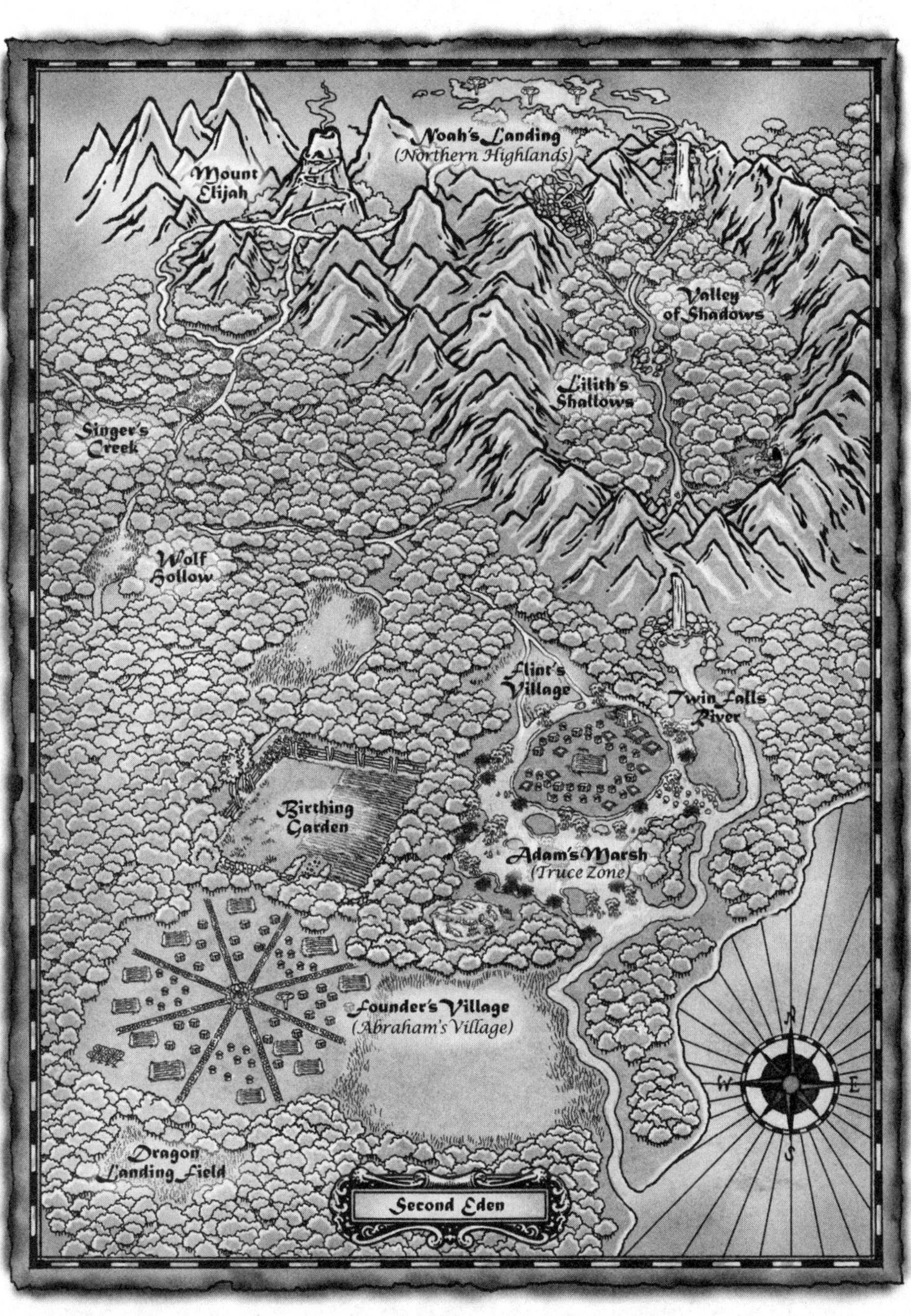
Mount Elijah
Noah's Landing
(Northern Highlands)
Valley of Shadows
Lilith's Shallows
Singer's Creek
Wolf Hollow
Flint's Village
Twin Falls River
Birthing Garden
Adam's Marsh
(Truce Zone)
Founder's Village
(Abraham's Village)
N
W
E
S
Dragon Landing Field
Second Eden

Dragon Lineage

Human offspring are represented on leaves.

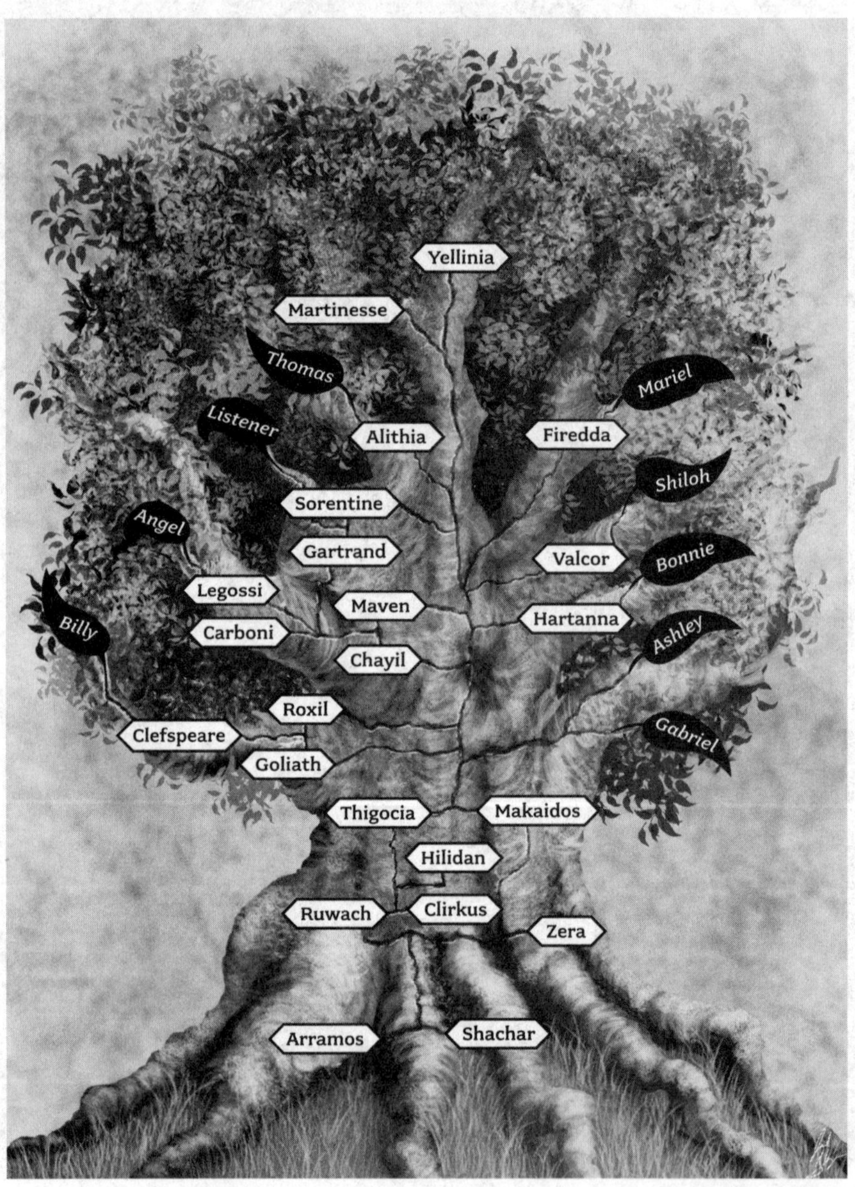

CAST OF CHARACTERS

Abbadon—a powerful angel of the Abyss who takes the form of a dragon

Abigail—the human name of dragon Roxil; previously called Jasmine as a human

Abraham—the human name of dragon Arramos; reborn in Second Eden as the Prophet (not to be confused with the physical dragon form of Arramos later possessed by the devil)

Acacia—an Oracle of Fire; twin to Mara (Sapphira Adi)

Adam Lark—a teenage friend of the Bannisters

Albatross—a dragon of Second Eden

Alithia—a dragon; as a human goes by the name Kaylee

Angel—formerly the wife of Dragon; widowed mother of Candle and Listener

Arramos—a dragon; mate of Shachar; father of Makaidos; grandfather of Thigocia; died in the flood but his body is possessed by the devil while his soul was reborn as Abraham, a human in Second Eden

Ashley Stalworth—daughter of Timothy and Hannah (Makaidos and Thigocia)

Billy Bannister—son of Jared (Clefspeare) and Marilyn

Bonnie Silver—daughter of Irene (Hartanna); previously known as Bonnie Conner

Candle—son of Dragon and Angel

Carboni—a dragon; as a human goes by the name Elise

Carl Foley—a friend of the Bannisters; husband of Catherine; father of Walter and Shelly
Carly Masters—a friend of Bonnie's
Catherine Foley—a friend of the Bannisters; wife of Carl; father of Walter and Shelly
Charles Hamilton—a former teacher of Billy, Bonnie, and Walter
Chazaq—a giant; Mardon's commander
Clefspeare—a dragon; son of Goliath and Roxil; as a human goes by the name Jared
Cliffside—a guard of the birthing garden in Second Eden
Dallas—the human name of dragon Firedda; mother of Mariel
Dikaios—a talking horse
Dorian—the human name of dragon Yellinia
Dr. Whittier—a man who kidnapped Adam's father; also known as Sir Devin, a dragon slayer
Dragon—the husband of Angel; father of Candle and Listener
Elam—son of Shem; grandson of Noah
Elise—the human name of dragon Carboni
Ember—a mare in Second Eden
Emerald—a widow in Second Eden
Enoch—a prophet
Firedda—a dragon; as a human goes by the name Dallas
Flint—Abraham's rebel apprentice
Frank—a villager
Gabriel—son of Timothy and Hannah (Makaidos and Thigocia)
Gartrand—a dragon; mate of Sorentine
Goliath—a dragon; son of Makaidos and Thigocia; mate of Roxil
Grackle—a dragon of Second Eden
Hartanna—a dragon; daughter of Makaidos and Thigocia; as a human goes by the name Irene
Hunter—a false name for Mardon
Jackson—a soldier
Jared Bannister—the human name of dragon Clefspeare; husband of Marilyn; father of Billy
Jordan—the human name of dragon Martinesse

Karen—adopted sister of Ashley; died in battle
Kaylee Saunders—the human name of dragon Alithia; mother of Thomas
King Arthur—king of Camelot
King Nimrod—an ancient king; father of Mardon
Larry—Ashley's supercomputer
Legossi—a dragon; as a human goes by the name Rebekah
Listener—daughter of Dragon and Angel in Second Eden; birth daughter of Tamara; adopted by Mantika after Dragon's and Angel's deaths
Makaidos—king of the dragons; son of Arramos and Shachar; mate of Thigocia; as a human goes by the name Timothy
Mantika—a lowlander; wife of Greevelow; mother of Windor and adoptive mother of Listener and Candle
Mara—an Oracle of Fire; twin to Acacia; later known as Sapphira Adi
Mardon—an ancient scientist; son of King Nimrod and Semiramis; master of the Nephilim; disguises himself using the name Hunter
Mariel—daughter of Dallas
Marilyn Bannister—wife of Jared; mother of Billy
Martinesse—a dragon; as a human goes by the name Jordan
Merlin—King Arthur's wisest counselor
Michael—an archangel
Monique Bannister—adopted daughter of Jared and Marilyn
Morgan—a witch; sister of Naamah
Naamah—a witch; sister of Morgan
Nabal—a cruel giant
Noah—a patriarch who built an ark to save humans and animals from the great flood
Nolan—a bounty hunter
Olsen—a soldier
Paili—an underborn; wife of Patrick; sometimes known as Ruth
Palin—Sir Devin's scribe and squire
Patrick—the human name of dragon Valcor; husband of Paili
Pearl—wife of Steadfast; a medical worker in Second Eden
Raphah—a former slave with Elam

Rebecca—adopted daughter of Jared and Marilyn
Rebekah—the human name of dragon Legossi; mother of Angel
Roxil—a dragon; daughter of Makaidos and Thigocia; mate of Goliath; mother of Clefspeare; as a human goes by the name Abigail
Ruth—an underborn; wife of Patrick; sometimes known as Paili
Sapphira Adi—an Oracle of Fire; twin to Acacia; previously known as Mara
Semiramis—mother of Mardon (Hunter)
Shelly Foley—daughter of Carl and Catherine; sister of Walter
Shiloh—daughter of Patrick (Valcor) and Ruth (Paili)
Sir Devin—a knight; a slayer of dragons; also known as Dr. Whittier
Sir Edmund—guardian to Bonnie and Irene
Sir Winston Barlow—a knight of Camelot
Sorentine—a dragon; mate of Gartrand; as a human goes by the name Tamara
Stacey—adopted daughter of Jared and Marilyn
Steadfast—husband of Pearl; a medical worker in Second Eden
Stout—a villager
Tamara—the human name of dragon Sorentine; mother of Listener before she was sent to Second Eden
The Maid—a fiery teenage girl who lives in the Valley of Souls
Thigocia—a dragon; mate of Makaidos; granddaughter of Arramos and Shachar; as a human goes by the name Hannah
Thomas—son of Kaylee
Timothy—the human name of dragon Makaidos, husband of Hannah; father of Gabriel and Ashley; also called Captain Autarkeia
Valcor—a dragon; son of Makaidos and Thigocia; brother of Hartanna; as a human goes by the names Patrick
Valiant—a village leader in Second Eden
Vlad—a bounty hunter
Walter Foley—a friend of Billy's; son of Carl and Catherine; in the line of King Arthur
Windor—son of Greevelow and Mantika
Yellinia—a dragon; as a human goes by the name Dorian
Yereq—a giant; one of the Nephilim

An Oracle's Call

A tender heart that burns with fire,
A contradicting blend;
With words of heat, I scald the soul,
And with my words I mend.

An Oracle of Fire born
To sacrifice and bleed,
For hungry souls, I spend my life
To meet their every need.

Yet, Oracles of Fire burn;
They pierce, they scald, they sear
Corrupted souls in dark abodes
Who cower there in fear.

The light has come! Begone, you shades,
Who hide in blackest mire!
I free the captives, loose their chains,
And give them holy fire.

While some will carry vibrant light,
The fearful drop the torch;
Courageous souls absorb the fire,
While others fear the scorch.

Yet, flames from God must pierce your breast
To purge the dross of sin
And make your silver wholly pure
And light the flame within.

A bridge awaits, a risky path,
The cross of Christ displayed
A broken body, blood, and tears;
A tomb for us inlaid.

I call you now to cross the bridge,
To take the scarlet key.
To gain the burning, tender heart,
And walk the path with me.

CHAPTER 1

TRANSFORMATION

Mardon stood at the edge of the precipice and peered into the chasm. The sheer rock faces on each side plunged until they seemed to meet in the apparently infinite depths. Stepping back, he turned to a lady draped in a red cloak, Semiramis, her hood lifted over her auburn locks. "Mother, how do you propose that we descend?"

Lowering her hood, Semiramis gazed into the bright sky. "Arramos said he would show us the way during Second Eden's eclipse cycle. Since that eve is upon us, he will fly here soon. He is quite anxious to send us into that world."

A crystalline egg orbited Mardon's head, flashing crimson light from within. As it stopped in front of his eyes, its familiar voice, Sir Devin's voice, penetrated his mind. *Will you trust the instructions of a dragon?* Its eyes, no more than two reddish ovals, blinked. *Arramos is the most devious of the accursed race.*

Mardon stared at the light, concentrating his thoughts on its center. *If you want to gain a new body, I suggest that you withhold your misgivings.*

I put our plan into motion to roust the girl and her dragon friends, so my promise to give you a chance to kill her will soon be fulfilled.

Devin replied, *And my desire to capture her is the reason I put up with you. Although I have bigger draconic prizes in mind, I will mount that demon witch's head on a pedestal so I can see it from anywhere in my leisure room.*

Mardon cringed but said nothing. It was no use talking sensibly to the mad dragon slayer. Their crusades lay at opposite ends. Devin wanted nothing more than to kill all who possessed dragon blood, whether they were full-blooded or merely human offspring of former dragons. He had no spiritual ideals, only a lust for killing.

Shaking his head, Mardon let his gaze follow a narrow footbridge to the other side of the chasm. He sought after so much more than slaying reptiles. Doing away with dragons and their kin was merely a stepping-stone toward the ultimate in spiritual ascensions, the unification of humanity with the heavenly host. Such a feat would demonstrate to all realms that the son of King Nimrod had finally taken his place at the side of the Majesty on High.

As he scanned the skies alongside his mother, Mardon avoided further eye contact with Devin. The cruel slayer might be able to read unguarded thoughts, and if he caught any hint that their purposes differed so greatly, he might cause problems.

Soon, a dragon flew into sight, reddish against the blue sky and carrying something in one of his clawed feet. Seconds later, in a flurry of wings and wind, Arramos set down a bucket and landed several paces from the chasm's precipice. After drawing in his wings, he stared at Mardon with pulsing red eyes. "It is time for your transformation," he growled.

Mardon tried to steel himself, but tremors weakened his legs. "Transformation?"

Laying a hand on the back of his head, Semiramis crooned. "A disguise, my dear. Some of the Second Eden inhabitants know you too well." She turned toward Arramos and nodded at the bucket. "What is this, my lord?"

"Water from the river of the Prism Oracle," Arramos said. "It will help us complete the transformation."

"I see." Semiramis eyed the water. "That oracle has powers beyond what I knew."

Arramos's voice lowered to a rumble. "There is much you do not know."

"Well, if it's just a disguise . . . " Mardon squared his shoulders. "I'm ready."

Arramos snorted twin jets of fire, coating Mardon from his head to his chest.

"Ahhhrg!" Mardon dropped to his knees. Pain ripped across his face. He reached for his mother and tried to scream, but his desperate gasp brought a stream of blazing heat into his mouth and throat, scorching the tender skin inside.

Semiramis grabbed the bucket and poured half of the water over his head. Then, adding gentle splashes with the remainder, she took care to soak every inch of melting flesh. When the bucket ran dry, she slung it to the side and glared at Arramos, her lips pressed tight.

Mardon fanned his face, barely missing Devin's egg as it floated near his cheek, apparently unhurt. "It still burns!" His voice sounded gravelly, like that of a dying old man. "It feels like my skin is melting!"

"Ah, yes," Arramos said with a chuckle. "Fire tends to do that. It will likely torture you for days or weeks to come."

Semiramis shook her fist, her voice spiced with rage. "So this is his disguise? What do you have in mind for me? Mummification?"

"Don't tempt me." His eyes flaming, the dragon's head swayed as he studied her from head to toe. "It is crucial that your beauty remains intact."

Her fingers loosened, but she maintained her violent glare. "My beauty, as you judge it, will be my undoing. The genius dragon girl and the Foley boy will surely recognize me."

"Indeed. Exactly what I hope for. You will appeal to their sense of mercy, and your loving care for this wretched burn victim will be proof of your repentance."

"So my disguise is . . ."

"Righteousness." Arramos tipped his head back and laughed. "The same disguise so many humans use to fool their fellows in every walk of life."

Semiramis lowered herself to her knees. With quick, angry motions, she helped Mardon strip away his smoldering shirt. "Loving my son will not be an act. My goal all along has been to put him on a throne of glory."

"All in good time. Surely ascension to such a throne will include healing. That should be another incentive to ply your trade well."

Clenching her teeth, she wedged her words between short, shallow breaths. "Incentive? After torturing my son, you speak of incentives? Why should I do anything you say?"

"I hold the ultimate dagger over your head, your life and your son's life. I can see to it that you survive in Second Eden in spite of your current state of deadness, but my power will not avail you if you try to enter Heaven. Surely you have wondered how your dead souls would survive. And have you not also wondered how you will be able to defeat the host of Heaven with an army of mortals from the Earth? Compared to them, your army would be a swarm of gnats."

Semiramis turned to Mardon. Her expression gave her away. She had wondered. In fact, those questions had haunted both of them for centuries.

Looking at Arramos again, she murmured, "Go on."

"The Oracles are the key. They have eaten fruit from the Tree of Life, so their makeup has been altered. Unable to die a natural death, they are now like the angels. Since Mardon knows an Oracle's genetic code and her weaknesses, he should be able to learn the secret and pass along her power to the two of you and your armies, thus enabling all of you to become like the sons and daughters of God."

"I see." Semiramis eyed Mardon again. "Can you do this thing? It could be our only chance. If need be, I can temporarily incapacitate an Oracle with a sleeping powder."

Mardon pondered the idea. Since the Oracles originated as plant creatures, they possessed photosynthetic code. Through their eyes, they always had the ability to capture light that could be used for manufacturing energy. He could use tainted light on one of them and confuse her photosynthetic cells, causing them to expend energy rather than produce it, thereby deteriorating her body. In theory, her life-sustaining system would have to respond by battling the photosynthetic cells. She would literally be at war with her own body. Then, by getting samples of cells before degeneration began and after her body battled back, he could figure out how the life-sustaining code worked, reverse engineer it, and replicate it for others.

His throat still on fire, he pushed through the pain. "I have an idea. It would weaken an Oracle at first, but we could use her cellular structure later for our benefit. To begin the process, I must have close contact, at least for a short time."

"One of the Oracles resides in Second Eden," Arramos said to Semiramis. "You will have to gain her trust. Your skill as a deceiver will be put to the test."

Semiramis crossed her arms, her tone softening. "How will I deal with the dragons from Earth? I cannot fool their danger-sensing abilities."

"You are no danger to them. Only Makaidos, king of the dragons, has power great enough to sense danger toward others. Still, you must continue to guard your thoughts well, for the mind reader will try to see past your façade."

"Ashley?" Semiramis shook her head. "She will not be a problem. I have learned how to block her mental penetration. Her inability to see past my defenses will make her suspicious, but there will be no proof she can use against me."

"Very good." Arramos spread out his wings. "Let us fly now to Second Eden."

"Fly?" Semiramis asked. "How so?"

"The portal the Nephilim used remains open, though it is only a one-way passage to those who lack my power. It has been very useful for transporting new allies and one very old . . . shall we say . . . crystalline weapon for our eventual confrontation. I have been given permission to move parts of two circles of Hades to Second Eden, the great abyss that once imprisoned the Watchers as well as the village of the sixth circle where Morgan held Shiloh prisoner. That village now resides in Second Eden as a buffer between here and there. I can take you as far as Morgan's prison, and, from that point, you are on your own." Arramos lowered his head to the ground, creating a staircase. "The eclipse is upon us. Let us make haste."

"Very well." Semiramis took Mardon's hand and helped him climb the spiny steps.

As soon as they settled between two tall spines, Devin's crystal flashed in front of Mardon's eyes. "I warned you about dragons," the slayer said. "And this one has betrayed you. Will you trust me now?"

Still racked with pain, Mardon nodded at the egg and spoke to it with his mind. *Let us make our plans in secret. Perhaps we both can achieve our goals and thwart those of the dragon. Trust me. My mother is not pleased with this plan, and she has already told me how she will bring you back to life in a way that will surprise everyone, perhaps even Arramos.*

CHAPTER 2

HIDDEN GEMS

Bonnie looked down at the magma far below. As the slow-moving river boiled, heat rose from the depths and warmed her skin, a refreshing change from the chilly air that normally filled the tunnels and chambers in the nether regions of Hades. If she stayed here much longer, she would have to take her sweatshirt off. Her long-sleeved T-shirt and jeans would be enough to keep her warm.

While small whirlpools spun in slow rotations, huge gas bubbles erupted on the surface and popped, spewing ash and steam upward in swirling clouds of sulfur-permeated air. The entire stream churned from right to left, at half the speed of a normal walking pace.

Standing between Sapphira and Shiloh on the rocky ledge, Bonnie unfurled her wings and rested a tip on each girl's shoulder, ready to pull them back should they lose their balance. Shiloh, Bonnie's nearly identical cousin, matched her height, but Bonnie had to reach down a few inches to cover Sapphira, the petite Oracle of Fire. Both companions wore matching outfits, sweatshirts and jeans, perfectly suitable for exploring the sometimes narrow caves. Shiloh also wore a ring with a red rubellite, making her ready to pretend to be Bonnie, just in case.

"I don't understand how it could ever have been harmless," Bonnie said as she fanned her face with her hand. "It's scalding even way up here."

"Oh, it's deadly now." Sapphira picked up a fist-sized stone and tossed it into the chasm. The moment it struck the current, a plume of steam shot from the contact point, sending reddish black fragments high into the air. "When most of the portals closed a long time ago, it turned into normal molten rock."

"Normal?" Taking a step back, Shiloh blew a strand of dampened hair from her face, her British accent as pronounced as ever. "As if anything's normal in this place."

"You're sweating," Bonnie said. "What are you wearing underneath?"

Shiloh lifted her sweatshirt, revealing a T-shirt with a lion on the front. "It's the Narnia shirt you gave me in the sixth circle. It's too warm for two layers and too cold for just one."

Bonnie shielded her eyes from the river's glow and scanned the other side of the chasm. Rising heat warped her view, making the rocks on the opposite wall hard to define. As undulating light from the restless source below created strange shadows all across the sheer rock face, one shadow seemed constant, a protruding lip of stone. "What's over there?" she asked, pointing. "I think I see another ledge."

Sapphira pulled back her stark white hair and tied it with a rubber band. "There *is* a ledge. When there was a portal nearby, my eyesight was sharper, and I spotted a tunnel opening on the other side. Even now I sense something, as if a weak or distant portal is around, but I don't know where it could be. Anyway, I never figured out how to get across the chasm to check it out."

Flipping Sapphira's ponytail with the tip of her wing, Bonnie grinned. "Now we have a way to get there."

"I wouldn't try it," Shiloh said. "The updrafts from that crazy pot of stone soup could toss you around like a feather in a storm."

Bonnie let her wings droop. "I guess it'll have to stay a mystery." She looked again at the opposite ledge. Shadows continued to stalk its surface, so real they seemed alive. But, of course, they were the result of the odd light, nothing to worry about. With Yereq guarding the only entrance to the mines, no one could intrude on them.

"Speaking of mysteries. . . " Sapphira turned toward an opening in the wall behind them. "The only place left to show you is the kiln level, where Elam used to make magnetite bricks with Raphah. I've never even been there myself."

"Why not?" Shiloh asked. "If you were here for centuries, you had plenty of time."

"It was a forbidden zone for years and years, and after everyone left, Chazaq wasn't around to lower the platform in our elevator shaft. It's a long drop, much farther than what we climbed to get to this level, so if I went down there, I thought I might never get back up. And now the rope's not even long enough to go that far. When Bonnie's fully healed, maybe we can give it a try. She might be able to boost us with her wings."

Bonnie nodded. It had been about a month since her mother left with Acacia through a portal to Second Eden. They had used a section of the elevator rope Sapphira had cut to climb through the cross-dimensional hole. Bonnie and Shiloh had also tried to climb, but the portal collapsed, and rocks fell through, sealing the hole and injuring Bonnie's shoulder. Fortunately, as an anthrozil, the photoreceptors in her blood helped her heal quickly, though not as quickly as she would have healed in the sunlight.

Sapphira lifted her hand and whispered, "Give me light." A blaze erupted in her palm, a small fireball, bluish white and sparkling. "Ready for the climb back up? I think it's only about a half hour until Gabriel's supposed to come."

"About twenty-five minutes," Shiloh said, looking at her watch. "We can make it, if Bonnie's up for the climb."

Bonnie rubbed her shoulder. "It feels good, but I could use another dip in the hot springs after Gabriel leaves."

Sapphira touched a pouch that had been sewn to her jeans waistband, perfectly sized to hold Enoch's ovulum, a crystalline egg at least five times the size of a hen's egg. "Let's go. I left the ovulum in our hovel. I'm kind of nervous about being without it."

As Sapphira led the way toward the tunnel, Bonnie followed, looking back as she walked. The fireball cast an azure glow across the chasm, though not enough to see the other side clearly. As the light shrank away from the expanse, a strange shadow took shape, growing larger by the second.

Bonnie turned and spread her wings. "Sapphira! Shiloh! Run!"

As the two looked back, Bonnie grabbed each of them around the waist and lifted off the ground. Beating her wings, she scooted through the exit passageway and into the tunnel. The moment she lowered them to the floor, Sapphira jerked free. She stepped back toward the passage, spread out her arms, and shouted, "Ignite!"

Her body burst into flames from head to toe, her hands ablaze in white hot tongues that shot three feet in front of her. "Who's there?" she called, her voice deeper than usual.

In the light of Sapphira's flames, the shadow vanished. A human male walked through the exit, his hands raised to block the heat. "Hey, Sapphira! Cool your jets!"

Bonnie laughed. "It's Gabriel!"

"In the flesh." Dressed in a long-sleeved flannel shirt and khaki cargo pants, he nudged Bonnie's side. "Your wings look awesome. Did you never lose them, or did you get them back?"

"I'm not supposed to tell. I'm not even sure you're supposed to know I have them."

"Oh, well," Gabriel said, shrugging. "Cat's out of the bag . . . or the backpack, I guess."

Sapphira lowered her hands and let the flames dwindle to a fireball in one palm. "How did you get here without us seeing you?"

Gabriel pointed toward the chasm. "I flew across that crazy lava river. Quite a ride, that's for sure."

"I lived here for multiple millennia," Sapphira said, "and I never found a passage to that side."

"Leave it to me to get lost looking for you." Grinning, he gave her a wink. "Actually, there's a way to get there from the lowest level. It's kind of a steep climb, though."

Shiloh elbowed his ribs. "Okay, mystery boy, spill the story. How did you get to the lowest level?"

He walked back toward the ledge. "Come on. I'll fly you over there one at a time, and we'll talk. Yereq's there, too, and a few other surprises you'll have to see to believe."

"Yereq's there?" Sapphira said as she and the others followed. "Who's guarding the entrance?"

"Walter's dad." Stopping close to the edge, Gabriel looked into the depths. "You should see him. He looks pretty cool with an assault rifle, and Walter's mom is there, too. She had a pump-action shotgun. Anyway, since we couldn't find you in the hovel or the springs, Yereq hung a new rope in the elevator shaft and lowered us to the bottom. He's stronger than a gorilla and climbs like one, too. I told the others to wait while I checked out the tunnel that led up here."

Bonnie reached over with a wing and tapped his shoulder. "How about if I carry Sapphira and you carry Shiloh?"

"Sure." Gabriel shrugged. "If they're not queasy about a rough ride."

Shiloh raised her arms. "Lock and load, Batman. I'm ready for anything."

As Gabriel wrapped his arms around Shiloh, Sapphira copied her pose. "Bonnie, are you sure you can carry me?"

"That's why I picked you." Bonnie slid her hands around Sapphira's slim waist and pressed her chest against her back. "You're the lightest one here. I once carried Billy from our schoolyard all the way to the top of a mountain. He probably weighs almost twice as much."

Gabriel pointed a wing at Bonnie. "I learned this the hard way. The heat will push you higher, so keep your webbing at an angle, almost like you're descending, and you can glide most of the way across. Maybe three wing beats will do it."

"Got it."

Gripping Shiloh tightly, he flapped his wings and lifted toward the chasm. Almost instantly, a rush of air thrust him higher, but he quickly corrected and glided away.

"Last one there has to kiss Morgan," Shiloh sang out.

Bonnie followed, keeping her wings tilted forward. At first, she dropped, raising a gasp from Sapphira, but when she adjusted to catch more of the rising air, she ascended toward the opposite ledge, flapping slowly to compensate for the inconsistent surges from below. The heat dried her eyes and cheeks, delivering a painful sting, and her wings felt weak, having had so little exercise in the caverns of Hades.

Boosted by a final thrust of rising air, Bonnie flew over the wall's protruding lip and released Sapphira, who jogged to a graceful stop. Bonnie flapped again to keep her balance and managed not to stumble.

Gabriel extended an arm toward a low-clearance hole in the wall. "Follow me, ladies." He ducked under the arch and disappeared, Shiloh staying one step behind him.

"They'll need light." Sapphira created another fireball and hurried through the opening.

As soon as the glow faded, Bonnie took another draw from the sulfur-rich air. If only Billy could see this place. He'd be amazed. But he was probably seeing even more amazing things himself, going on adventures in Second Eden she could only dream about. Of course, being with him would be awesome beyond words, but staying here for now would have to do. After all, that's what God wanted. Nothing else mattered.

"Aren't you coming?" Gabriel called, his head sticking out through the hole.

"Sorry. I got lost in thought." Collapsing her wings and ducking low, she hustled under the arch and followed Gabriel as he walked, hunched-over, toward a light in the distance.

"Don't stand straight yet," he said. "The ceiling's pretty low for a while."

Keeping her eyes on Gabriel's wings, Bonnie scrambled along the pebbly floor until they reached Sapphira. The petite Oracle stood without bending, while Shiloh and Gabriel remained stooped. "Now you see why Yereq didn't follow me." He pointed into the darkness. "Sapphira, if you please. There aren't any hazards between here and there."

Sapphira marched ahead, her fireball now brighter than ever. Shiloh kept two steps behind, while Gabriel took Bonnie's elbow, slowing her pace as they followed. "Are you doing okay?" he whispered.

"My shoulder's healed, if that's what you mean."

"That, too, but I was wondering about staying down here. Sapphira's used to it, and Shiloh stayed alone for forty years, so she can handle it."

Bonnie smiled. Images of Gabriel's past appearances ran through her mind. When she was only six years old, he appeared to her in the form of radiant energy, and she thought he was an angel. "My guardian angel is a wonderful, caring young man."

"Young? Do you know how old I really am?"

"Sixty, maybe?"

Gabriel laughed under his breath. "Older, but nice try."

"And how old is Shiloh?" Bonnie asked. "Fifty-five?"

"Something like that."

"Hmmm . . ." Bonnie pressed her lips together, trying to hide a grin. "Close enough, I think."

"Close enough?" Gabriel squinted at her. "What are you suggesting?"

"Suggesting?" Bonnie tried to read his eyes, but shadows blocked her view. "What were *you* thinking?"

"Never mind."

This time, Bonnie let her smile break through. Everyone knew of Gabriel's attachment to Shiloh, but he was too embarrassed to admit it.

Finally, the ceiling angled up, allowing her to stand upright. The tunnel widened into a well-lit chamber, a square room about thirty feet across. Freestanding ovens lined each of three walls. Their chimneys rose toward holes in the ten-foot ceiling, though they came short by various distances. Their crumbling tops, likely penetrating the ceiling holes at one time, revealed their age and lack of recent use.

Flickering lanterns sat on the floor. A person crouched or stood near each one, most of them women, except for Yereq and an old man wearing sandals and a forest-green medieval tunic that overlapped dark, knee-length breeches.

Bonnie eyed the elderly gentleman. With a bright white aura surrounding him, he seemed ghostly, even semitransparent. For a moment, he would be solid, then a shimmer would pass across his body, allowing a split-second view of the rock wall behind him. With scattered white hair covering his ears and bright sparkling eyes, he seemed familiar. In a way, he resembled Professor Hamilton, her former teacher who passed away after a battle with Devin the dragon slayer. Yet, since she missed him so much, every lively old gentleman brought back thoughts of her beloved professor, though they didn't really look alike.

Bonnie followed a trail of light from his aura to one of the women. She carried the ovulum in her cupped hands. Like a movie projector, it seemed to create the aura and the man within.

Gabriel gestured toward each person in turn. "Bonnie, Shiloh, and Sapphira, I would like to introduce you to Rebekah, formerly Legossi; Dallas, the woman holding the ovulum, was once Firedda; Elise, also known as Carboni; Dorian, who once flew the skies as Yellinia; Kaylee, who, when dressed in scales, answered to the name of Alithia; Jordan, known to the dragon clan as Martinesse; and Tamara, affectionately dubbed Sorentine by her fire-breathing family members."

He took a deep breath and exhaled heavily. "Whew! I practiced that for hours."

"Excellent!" The elderly man clapped his hands. "And I am Enoch, prophet of the Most High. And of course," he said, motioning to a giant man sitting near a corner, "you already know Yereq."

Gabriel let his wings sag. "Sorry. I was going to introduce you next."

"It's quite all right. Sapphira and Shiloh already know me." Enoch reached for Bonnie's hand, but his fingers passed right through hers. "And Bonnie saw me from the window of her motel room."

"I *thought* I recognized you," she said. "It was dark that night, so I didn't get a good look."

"Nor I at you. And although we can now see that you have wings, you and everyone here must guard that secret. A day may come when we can use the ignorance of others to our advantage. And plans for the future are why I arranged this meeting. I am in my viewing room at Heaven's Altar where I can see almost anything I request, and I can project my image if the Lord so allows. The ovulum is very useful as my hologram-generating device."

Sapphira laid a hand on her empty pouch. "How did the ovulum get here? I left it in my hovel."

Gabriel pointed at himself. "I found it there. When I picked it up, it started talking. Scared me half to death."

"I apologize for the scare." Enoch began pacing in a small circle near the center of the room, glancing at each person as he made the circuit. "The people in the land of Second Eden are preparing for a great battle, and they are woefully unprepared. They have only recently had to take up arms to ward off infrequent attacks from small bands of shadow people, who are relatively weak compared to the forces that will someday come against them. The enemy will eventually include the entire race of shadow people as well as another tribe of humanlike creatures that has no name, as far as I know. A cadre of Nephilim will join them, and one of the mightiest of all dragons, Goliath, will surely enhance their power and strategic maneuvers."

Tamara, a slender brunette who now sat cross-legged near a kiln, hissed, then quickly covered her mouth. "I . . . I am sorry. Old . . . um . . . habit."

Bonnie smiled at her. Obviously some of the former dragons didn't speak English very well. Wearing a long dress and smock, and her hair tied in pigtails, Tamara looked like an overgrown child, complete with a cute smile and dimples.

Enoch waved his hand. "Some habits die hard, and some we must retrieve and again make our own. Each one of you dragons, for one reason or another, has chosen to take part in the human race. Yet now I am asking you to return to your draconic states and join the battle in Second Eden, at least as many of you as possible."

A low rumble sounded from somewhere above, making the ground tremble. Enoch looked up, his bushy white eyebrows scrunching down. "Yereq, will you please investigate?"

When Yereq climbed to his feet, his head rose to within inches of the ceiling. He bowed to the prophet. "Shall I take a messenger who will send word in case I become involved in a battle?"

Just as Gabriel raised his hand, Rebekah shot to her feet, her waist-length blonde tresses swaying as she rose. "Send me. The winged boy will be of greater use here if escape is necessary."

Enoch nodded at her. "Then make haste. We will fill you in on the details later."

Rebekah stripped off a zippered jacket, revealing a long-sleeved baseball-style jersey tucked into loose-fitting camo pants. She jerked up a lantern and swung toward Yereq, fire in her eyes. "Let's make tracks!"

As soon as the giant and former dragon disappeared into another tunnel, Enoch continued, his pace of delivery much faster now. "You cannot transform into dragons until you arrive in Second Eden, and the available portals are dangerous, so we must get you there by way of a new kind of transport. Marilyn Bannister, the human wife of Clefspeare, is building a device called Apollo that will, in combination with Sapphira's power, create an entirely new portal opening."

Sapphira raised her hand. "Father Enoch?"

"Yes, my child." His tone seemed patient, but his eyes kept glancing at the ceiling. Even though he wasn't actually in the chamber, somehow he could perceive direction of sound.

"What about the portal in the museum room? I sense that it's still there, but when I try to reopen it, I see that the passage is blocked by rocks."

"The portal is still there. Apparently, someone has again plugged the hole at the top of Mount Elijah, so the inhabitants of Second Eden must break through in order for us to use it again. I have no way of knowing why they have not done so, because my viewing portal to that world was limited to the ovulum. Even I cannot travel there at this time."

Forming her hands into a cradle, Sapphira took the ovulum from Dallas. Enoch's projection drifted with the egg's movements. "Maybe we should try to get this to Second Eden. It would be more useful in their hands than in mine."

Another rumble sounded, louder this time, followed by a stronger tremor. Bonnie and Gabriel flapped their wings to steady themselves, while Enoch stood upright, unaffected.

When everything settled, Enoch scanned the chamber's inhabitants. "I heard the quake, and by your reactions, I assume the tremor was powerful."

"Yes, Prophet," Gabriel said. "A real shaker."

Enoch sat down. As his body hovered just above the stone floor, he stroked his chin. "This is quite unexpected. I have no idea what is causing the seismic disturbances."

Sapphira stood next to him, her head only inches higher than his. "Shall I try to go to the surface?"

"Alone?" Gabriel asked. "Without a weapon?"

Enoch chuckled. "Sapphira Adi, the Oracle of Fire, *is* a weapon."

Sapphira blushed. "Then shall I go?"

"No, child. We will await word from Rebekah. Let us rest and have faith."

She sat down and crossed her legs. "I have several questions, if you don't mind."

"Then ask." Enoch glanced again at the ceiling, listening. "My meeting agenda is on hold until we learn what is afoot."

Sapphira began counting on her fingers. "When will the Apollo device be finished? Does this mean Bonnie and Shiloh and I don't have to stay here? And . . ." Her cheeks flushed a deep cherry red. "Will I get to see Elam soon?"

Enoch patted her hand, though, again, he made no real contact. "I am a prophet, dear one, but I do not have all the answers. Regarding Apollo, without Ashley there to help, Marilyn has only Larry to guide her, so I cannot guess when it will be finished. I arranged for helpers to come to her aid, but it remains to be seen how much benefit they will be. So, while I evaluate the dangers on the surface, you will stay here, at least until we test Apollo. The purpose of this meeting was to gather all the former dragons in a safe place and inform you of our plans."

"That makes sense." Sapphira bit her lip before continuing. "And what about Elam?"

"Ah, yes, my old friend, Elam." Enoch gazed at her, pausing for a moment as a faraway look passed across his eyes. "It is difficult to know how God will bring people together, or if he will at all, so I cannot answer. I hope the two of you will be united at last, but I think divinely arranged marriages are relatively rare."

"Like Billy and Bonnie?" Gabriel asked.

Enoch smiled at Bonnie before shifting to Gabriel. "Merlin's prophecy seems to indicate an eventual union between two people of similar characteristics, but they are not named. And the poem also does not reveal when, where, or how it will take place."

"But isn't Bonnie closely related to Billy?" Gabriel asked, scratching his head. "Something like second cousins or first cousins once removed? I can never figure that out."

Enoch laughed gently. "They are related through their dragon lineage, and God's laws allow for unions between closer dragon relations than they do for human ones. Billy and Bonnie, however, are quite safely within the limits for both species." He pointed at Gabriel. "On the other hand, take for example you and Shiloh. Although she is your niece, which would disqualify a union between the two of you in the code for humans, since that relationship is of draconic origin, you could be married."

Gabriel's cheeks turned even redder than Sapphira's had. "Yeah," he said, running his shoe along the floor. "I get it."

Bonnie sneaked a glance at Shiloh. Her face, too, had flushed, and a barely perceptible smile bent her lips.

Dallas stood up. "I hear footsteps."

Rapid clops sounded from the tunnel. Seconds later, Rebekah burst into the chamber, her lantern swinging. Breathless, she bent over and laid a hand on her chest. "Explosions. . . . Men with jackhammers . . . Two with guns."

With a beat of his wings, Gabriel glided to her side. "How about Mr. Foley? Is he okay?"

After taking a deep breath, Rebekah straightened and shook her head. "He's wounded, as is his wife. Yereq put them in a safe place before he began fighting the invaders."

"Did Yereq collapse the entrance tunnel?" Sapphira asked. "That was our plan in case of attack."

"He said he was going to, but I left before he could do it."

"We gotta get up there," Gabriel said. "With my wings helping, I can climb that rope in a heartbeat."

Sapphira leaped to her feet. "I'll go. I'm the lightest. Gabriel can use the rope to pull me from the upper level, and I can help with hauling up the others."

"Count me in," Bonnie said, raising her hand.

As Shiloh and the former dragons chimed in with their calls offering to help, Enoch waved his arms. "Come together! Hurry!" When they gathered around, so close they penetrated his aura, he spoke with a solemn tone. "Do not act in haste. You are the reason the invaders have come. If you pop out of your hole, they will pick you off. Go in stealth, and proceed with caution."

"Understood." Gabriel picked up a lantern. "Follow me!" He exited through the tunnel, the glow of his lantern bobbing with his quick march.

Sapphira gave the ovulum to Bonnie. "You stay at the back of the line and use this for light." Carrying a ball of fire in her hand, Sapphira hurried to follow Gabriel. Shiloh went next, then Rebekah and the other former dragons, some carrying lanterns. When the last one filed out, Bonnie looked at Enoch. With only two weak lanterns on the floor, the glow from the prophet's hologram seemed brighter than ever.

"I have to catch up," she said, "but something's been bothering me." She touched the side of her waist, as if gripping a belt. "It feels like something's tied to me, but when I try to grab it, I can't feel anything. Even when I take off my clothes to bathe in the springs, I think it's still there."

Enoch leaned close. "I cannot try to feel it for you. Have you asked Sapphira?"

"She can't feel it or see it. Neither can Shiloh."

"Hmmm..." His eyes brightened, as if energized by his drilling stare. "I have an idea about what this might be, and it could be of grave concern, but while I ponder it, you should hurry and join the others." The hologram faded along with the aura. "I hope to see you again soon."

Bonnie picked up one of the lanterns, blew out the other, and rushed into the tunnel. Ahead, light appeared. As it grew brighter and closer, a voice sounded in the distance. "Bonnie, is that you?"

"Yes, Shiloh." Flapping her wings to give herself a push, Bonnie scooted toward her. "Thank you for waiting."

"No problem." Shiloh's eyes sparkled as she winked. "I figured we'd better make like twins before we showed our faces."

Bonnie nodded. It was time to get their backpacks on, just in case.

CHAPTER 3

HELPERS

Sliding his sword from its scabbard, Edmund edged close to the door. "Stay hidden, Madam. I will investigate."

Marilyn smiled at the noble knight. Dressed in a pair of Jared's jeans and one of Billy's West Virginia sweatshirts, he seemed out of place with his sword and shield. "Don't worry, Edmund. The Caitiff wouldn't ring the doorbell."

"Ah! You are right." Keeping the sword behind his back, he opened the door. "Yes? May I help you?"

A low "ahem" sounded, then a hesitating voice. "Uh . . . don't the Bannisters live here?"

Marilyn peeked around Edmund. The teenager standing on the porch seemed very familiar. Could it be? Adam Lark?

"Yes, they live here. I am Edmund, knight of the—"

"Adam!" Marilyn called, pulling the door fully open. "Come on in!" She patted Edmund on the shoulder. "It's okay. He's . . . a friend."

Adam wiped his feet on the welcome mat and stepped inside. Flashing a grin, he nodded at Edmund. "What's with the sword?"

"Young man," Edmund said, bowing, "I am protecting this house while the other men are away."

Adam pulled up his T-shirt, revealing a handgun in a waist holster. "My Glock is better than a sword, at least for me. I had to shoot one of those monsters just yesterday."

Edmund cradled his sword in his palms. "Yes, my good fellow, but a blade is more effective with these creatures, because—"

"It's okay, Edmund," Marilyn said. "I'm sure you can talk later."

"That would be a pleasure." Edmund bowed and backed out of the way.

Giving Adam a warm smile, Marilyn closed the door. "What brings you here?"

Adam pulled an envelope from his back pocket. "This note." He handed it to her. "Check it out."

Marilyn withdrew a folded letter and read the beautiful script out loud.

DEAR ADAM,

As you are well aware, not all is right with our world. While the number of Caitiff has certainly decreased, more and more souls long thought dead are appearing at their former homes, frightening the current residents. Not only that, people claiming to be infamous scoundrels—Hitler and Stalin, to name only two—have surfaced, and DNA tests have proven their claims.

The situation is dire, Adam, and it is time for you to step up and be the hero God has recently called you to be. Because you are acquainted with the Bannisters and are aware of Billy's, shall we say, special gift, I am asking you to go to his house and offer your services. Tell Mrs. Bannister that you have considerable skills in electronics and can help her with the Apollo project. Please arrive at five in the afternoon on the date you receive this letter.

SINCERELY,
ENOCH, PROPHET OF THE MOST HIGH

Marilyn refolded the note and slid it back into the envelope. "Well, that's quite a surprise."

"Yeah." Adam nodded at the letter. "Is it some kind of joke?"

"It's not a joke." Marilyn guided Adam farther inside and lowered her voice. "So you know about Billy's . . . uh . . . gift?"

Adam shrugged. "I figured it out. When Dr. Whittier kidnapped my father and started preaching about slaying dragons, I kind of put two and two together. I never told anyone and kind of laid low until all the dust settled. But when I got that letter, I decided to go ahead and check it out."

"And you have skills in electronics?"

He nodded. "Ever since my father came home, he's been teaching me. Dr. Whittier's a creep, but I think he sobered my dad up. Things've been a lot better lately."

She laid a hand on his back. "Well, let me show you what we're doing. We—"

The doorbell rang.

"I will get it," Edmund called.

This time he opened the door without hesitation. A teenaged girl stood on the porch. Wearing glasses, an old "Pittsburgh" sweatshirt, and a long flowing skirt, she peered inside. "Is this . . . the Bannister residence?"

Edmund gave her a half bow. "It is, indeed. Won't you come in?"

Shivering in the draft, she extended an envelope to Edmund. "I got this letter, and—"

Edmund nodded toward Marilyn. "If you please, Miss, give it to the lady of the house, Mrs. Bannister."

As Edmund swung the door closed, the girl again extended the envelope, her arm still shaking. "Mrs. Bannister, I think this will explain why I'm here."

"A message from Enoch?" Marilyn asked as she took the letter.

The girl's eyes grew wide. "How did you know?"

Marilyn winked at Adam. "It's happened before." She opened the enclosed note and again read out loud.

DEAR CARLY,

I write to you with an urgent request. Your dear friend Bonnie Silver is in grave danger, and you might be able to make a difference in the outcome of her trials. At this very moment, she is hiding in a secret place, but forces of great evil stalk her constantly.

From the moment the two of you met on a bus in first grade, she has entrusted you with many secrets, including her greatest secret, and her recent letters to you have described some of her circumstances, using, of course, the code the two of you developed for such messages.

I ask you now, Carly, to go to the Bannister home at 1545 Cordelle Road in Castlewood, West Virginia. I am well aware of the dangers of solitary travel for a young lady such as yourself, but the situation is grave, and I am sure you will want to help your dear friend.

Please tell Mrs. Bannister that you are skilled with computers and can help her with the Apollo project. Be sure to arrive at five in the afternoon on the date after you receive this letter.

SINCERELY,
ENOCH, PROPHET OF THE MOST HIGH

"So, you're Carly," Marilyn said.

"Yes." Carly offered her hand. "I'm glad to meet you."

"Any friend of Bonnie's is a friend of mine." Marilyn shook Carly's hand gently. "How did you get here?"

"I took the bus from Pittsburgh and transferred in Morgantown. Then I walked from the Castlewood bus station. That's why I'm a little late. I didn't know how far it was."

"It's five miles to the bus station!"

"Yes . . . I know that now."

Marilyn shook her head. "You poor thing. No wonder you're shivering so."

Carly touched her sweatshirt. "I have layers underneath. I thought I'd be warm enough."

"Your parents must be worried sick. Would you like to call them?"

Carly dipped her head low. "Uh . . . Neither of my parents wanted me, so I live in a group foster home. I often go for long walks, so they might not miss me until dinnertime."

"Oh, Carly! And you came by yourself, even with all the Caitiff lurking!" Marilyn took her into her arms and hugged her close. "We'll have to get in touch with someone at your home, but you're welcome to stay here as long as you want."

"Thank you." Sniffing, Carly drew back. "I appreciate it."

Marilyn set a hand on her hip. "Well, I wonder how many more helpers will be coming."

After glancing at a clock on the wall, Edmund peered out a window next to the door. "It is ten past five, and I see no one else."

Adam extended his hand toward Carly. "Adam Lark, friend of Billy Bannister. If you know Bonnie, I'm sure you've heard of him."

"Nice to meet you," she said, shaking his hand. "And, yes, Bonnie goes on and on about Billy in her letters."

"Figures. Everyone knew she and Dragon Breath were crazy about each other."

Carly tilted her head. "Dragon Breath?"

"Never mind. I'd better get used to calling him Billy."

Marilyn glanced toward the rear of the house. "Shall I introduce you to Apollo and my project team?"

"Sure," Adam said.

Carly nodded. "Yes, thank you."

"And I will patrol the perimeter," Edmund said, sliding his sword into its scabbard. "If there is trouble, I will sound the usual alarm."

Marilyn winced. Edmund meant the trumpet he had found at the Foleys' home some months back. She gave him an uneasy smile. "A shout will be fine, thank you."

Opening the door, Edmund nodded, disappointment clear in his expression. "As you wish, Madam."

Marilyn led the new helpers through a hallway and stopped at a closed door near the back of the house. "Just to let you know in advance, you're about to meet Shelly and Larry. Shelly is our neighbor, and Larry is . . . well, you'll see."

She swung the door open, releasing a low-pitched hum from the room. Inside, the drone of cooling fans pushed against them like a sonic wall, and the breeze from an air conditioner made Carly push her hands into her sweatshirt's front pouch.

Shelly, dressed in dark gray sweats, sat in a swivel desk chair just outside a glass-enclosed chamber, typing at a keyboard while watching a display mounted on the chamber's exterior. The transparent walls took up most of the rear half of the computer room. The walls made up the housing for a ceiling-high box of metal and plastic—Larry the supercomputer. Covered with notched dials, flashing diodes, and plasma monitors, to Adam and Carly he probably looked like something straight from the Starship Enterprise.

As the trio walked in, Shelly spun in her chair and stood up. Flashing a nervous smile, she pulled Marilyn's sleeve, drawing her close as she whispered, "So . . . why are you letting Adam Lark in on our secret? And who's the girl?"

"Take a breath, Shelly. It's okay." Spreading out an arm, Marilyn turned in a slow circle. "Adam and Carly, this is Larry's abode."

Carly's eyes grew wide as she and Adam surveyed the room. Marilyn followed their gazes. From flowcharts on the walls to the monitors on Larry's panels to flashing lights, animated graphs, and beeping speakers on his control screen, the work area was definitely impressive.

Marilyn stepped between Adam and Carly and set a hand on each of their shoulders. "Larry, I would like for you to meet Adam Lark and Carly . . . uh . . ."

"Masters," Carly said.

A voice, a blend of computerized and normal human speech, sounded from the mounted screen.

"Greetings. I have recorded Carly's voice and will store it for future security use. My database already contains an entry for Adam Lark. Hmmm . . . Billy's notes are not exactly flattering."

"Yeah." Adam shifted his weight from foot to foot. "We kind of didn't . . . I mean—"

"Erase that entry," Marilyn said, "and create a new one. We're starting with a clean slate."

"Old entry deleted. New record stored, complete with voiceprint."

"Now . . ." Marilyn led them to a ten-foot-long wooden table abutting the wall opposite Larry. "This is our workspace for assembling Apollo."

Carly used a pair of tweezers to lift a silicon chip about the size of a thumbnail, one of the many computer parts scattered across the table. "What exactly is Apollo?"

Marilyn picked up Apollo by one of its foot-long dowels. Except for the rectangular shape of its inner glass enclosure, Apollo, a virtual twin of its predecessor, looked more like an old-fashioned hourglass than a cross-dimensional portal device.

As she tilted it, a glass door swung open on tiny hinges, and a cat's-eye marble rolled out onto her palm. "It's supposed to be a portal opener. The original one created a flash of light made up of exactly the right wavelengths to create a window to another world." She showed them the marble. "This is exactly the size and weight of something we want to transport to another realm, so we keep it in there for our tests. So far, it hasn't worked."

Adam's eyes bugged out, but he stayed quiet. Obviously the talk about another realm had given him a shock.

"So," Marilyn continued, "we want to send a gem called a rubellite. It's needed to increase the power of Excalibur, the legendary sword. We're hoping to get it to Billy and Walter so they can install it in the sword's hilt."

Carly touched one of the four dowels. "Bonnie wrote to me about this. Sometimes I wondered if her stories could possibly be true, but seeing this makes them come alive."

"Did she include her adventures in Hades?" Marilyn asked.

"If you mean the Circles of Seven," Carly said. "Yes, she did."

Marilyn closed Apollo's glass door. "Well, that's related to what's going on here. Hades has combined with Earth, and the appearance of strange creatures and the resurrection of dead people are the result of the merging. Billy and Walter are in another realm called Second Eden. For some reason, that place is the key for getting everything back to normal."

Adam pointed at the floor. "So all the chaos in the world can be traced to what's been going on in this house?" He let out a whistle. "This is getting cooler all the time."

"Cool, yes, but dead serious, too. We're going to help them by any means we can, and if sending the rubellite works, we'll try to open a portal big enough to send people."

"So what do we do?" Carly asked.

Marilyn set Apollo down. "Building this much was easy. The hard part has been getting the electronics to work. They're housed in a cap that snaps on to Apollo's top . . ."

For the next few hours, Marilyn explained the device and how her tests had failed to this point. She even replicated the failures three times to give her two new helpers hands-on experience. With her adoptive daughters, Stacey, Rebecca, and Monique, away at a church function, she had plenty of time to recount many of their adventures. Finally, after eating a late dinner, they returned to the worktable.

"So," Marilyn said. "Any ideas? Adam? Carly?"

Adam ran his fingers through his scraggly shock of dark hair and leaned over the table. As his Castlewood Valley High School T-shirt rubbed against the edge, he peered into Apollo's glass enclosure. "The flash wasn't very bright, nothing like the wattage you're supposed to be getting."

"If that's the case . . ." Carly smoothed out a schematic, a collection of printed pages taped together, and pointed at a microprocessor symbol near the bottom of one of the pages. "I think this one's the culprit."

"Could be." A few inches taller than Carly, Adam looked down at her, gesturing with his hands as he spoke. "Since Apollo flashed, it must've gotten the signal from Larry, but the flash was too weak. Something must have told the generator the wrong electromotive force."

Carly pointed at the microprocessor symbol again. "Since that chip has the math coprocessor, and since the coding calls for higher precision, we might have a rounding problem somewhere in the calculations. Rounding might not matter sometimes, but precision is crucial in this case. If one of the earlier numbers is wrong, the error gets worse and worse with every line of math code."

"So, the processor calculated the wattage wrong?" Marilyn asked.

"Well, voltage," Adam said. "That drives the wattage. But, yeah."

Carly tapped a finger on Apollo's top. "If we can swap out that chip, we can test Adam's theory right away."

Crossing her arms, Marilyn gave Adam and Carly an admiring gaze. Adam had changed so much since his bullying days at Castlewood Middle School. And Carly's computer skills had already been a godsend. "Okay!" Marilyn said. "Let's give it a shot."

Carly's eyes darted from one side of the table to the other, searching across scattered chips, diodes, and resistors. "Do we have another one here?"

Marilyn looked back at Shelly. She was sitting once again at Larry's control panel. "Do we have any more of Ashley's zeta chips?" Marilyn asked.

"Probably." Shelly stared at a flat monitor mounted on a wall panel as she pecked on a keyboard. "I'll check inventory."

"You may use verbal inquiries, Shelly. My parsing engine has fully integrated your voiceprint as well as your biography—Shelly Foley, twenty-one-year-old daughter of Carl and Catherine, sister of Walter, and one-time hostiam for—"

"Stifle it!" Shelly pointed a rigid finger at the monitor. "Just tell me if we have—"

"Any of Ashley's zeta chips?"

Shelly rolled her eyes. "Give me a break, Larry. If you already knew what we wanted, why'd you give me such a hard time?"

"To allow time for background processing. I wanted to check our usual suppliers for the raw materials. Our inventory shows zero zeta chips, but an epsilon chip would likely suffice. It is an older generation but quite functional for this application, though it lacks Ashley's newer communications protocol."

"Will that be a problem?" Marilyn asked.

"Only in that it will make transmissions a few milliseconds slower."

Shelly jumped up from her seat and headed for the hallway door. "I'll get the chip." She stopped, twirling her shoulder-length brown hair as she looked back. "Need anything? Drinks? Cookies?"

"I don't." Marilyn touched Adam's shoulder. "How about you?"

"The pizza made me thirsty. Anything non-diet."

"Water would be great," Carly said.

Marilyn nodded at Shelly. "Water for everyone, thank you."

Adam picked up Apollo's top, a black disc about the size of a hockey puck. "You think Ashley might hire someone like me? I mean, after I graduate, of course."

"Maybe she could take on an intern before you graduate. You certainly have the skills." Marilyn let out a silent sigh. With Adam and Carly around, they would probably eventually get Apollo working. But what would that mean? So many events had to fall into place. Who might find the rubellite once they transported it to Second Eden? How would that person know to give it to Billy? Leaving so much to faith felt like jumping into a dark pit, but what choice did she have? Somehow she had to provide a path for her men to march home . . . her men . . . Jared and Billy.

Marilyn clenched her fist. They had to come back. They just had to.

While Carly and Adam pored over the schematic, whispering to each other, Marilyn sat in the control desk chair. "Larry, I hope you don't mind if I ask again, but—"

"I am a computer, Marilyn. I do not get weary of questions. I constantly monitor the communication ports, both conventional and cross-dimensional, especially Ashley's tooth-transmitter protocol, and there are no messages."

Marilyn rested her chin in her hand. No word from Jared or Billy in a month. Were they all right? If so, what could they be doing in Second Eden that would prevent them from returning? Did they have a way to return at all?

Shelly popped back into the computer room, a small plastic bag pinched in her fingers. At the bottom of the bag lay a tiny black chip. "Found it!"

"Perfect!" Carly said, reaching for the bag.

Adam slid Apollo closer to her. "Let's fire it up again."

"I'll get the water now." Shelly hustled out of the room.

As Marilyn rose from the chair, a phone on the desk chimed. She jerked it up. "Hello?"

"Mrs. Bannister?" The voice was deep, almost like a lion's growl, yet drowned in static.

"Yes. Who is this?"

"I am Yereq."

She glanced at the caller ID number—Carl Foley's cell phone. "Yes, Yereq. Is something wrong?"

Again the voice seemed weak, as if submerged in water. It broke up at times, creating gaps between words. "Mr. Foley is hurt, and I cannot . . . I am unable to get help. I pressed a button on this . . . and your name appeared . . ."

Marilyn swallowed and tried to keep her voice calm. "Yereq, where is Mrs. Foley?"

"She . . . also hurt . . . breathing . . . not talking."

"She's unconscious but alive?"

"Yes."

"Listen carefully. After we're finished, press the end button. Then push nine, then one, then one again and the send button. It's probably green. Do you see those?"

After a few seconds, he said, "Yes. I understand."

"Good. That's the number for emergency calls. Tell the operator where you are and that you need an air ambulance. Do it now." Marilyn hung up the phone and exhaled loudly, feeling a sudden loss of energy. Just staying calm for Yereq had drained her reserves.

Shelly walked back in, carrying four bottles of water. "I heard the phone."

"It was Yereq. He says your parents are hurt."

Shelly dropped two of the bottles. "Did he say how bad?"

Marilyn jumped up and collected the bottles. "Only that he couldn't get help. With all the static it was hard to hear him."

Shelly's voice squeaked. "Can you call him back?"

Marilyn shook her head. "Yereq had a bad signal, and he's probably trying to call nine-one-one right now, so I don't want to confuse him with a call-waiting beep. We can hunt down the hospitals in the area and contact them."

"I am printing out a list of hospitals within a hundred miles of that location. The closest major health center is in Kalispell, Montana."

Shelly jerked the sheet from Larry's output bin and grabbed the phone. "I'll start calling. Maybe someone can tell me if an ambulance was dispatched."

While Shelly punched in the first number, Marilyn joined Adam and Carly at the table. "Will you two be able to do this by yourself?"

"Sure," Adam replied. "It'll be a breeze."

"Good." She rolled the marble into his hand. "How long do you think?"

"I have to take out a circuit board." Holding Apollo by one of its dowels, he set the marble inside the glass enclosure. "Probably about ten minutes."

"That might give us enough time to get news on Walter's parents." Crossing her arms over her chest, Marilyn walked toward Shelly as she waited with the phone against her ear, apparently on hold.

Marilyn sighed. On hold. With her husband and son off in another world, her life had been "on hold" for so long! Were they safe? Were they even alive? And what could she do once she arrived in Montana? Of course, she would have to find someone to look after Stacey, Rebecca, and Monique before she took off, but that wouldn't be a problem. They had stayed at friends' houses before.

She watched Adam as he feverishly worked on Apollo, Carly looking on. That strange device was their only hope for piercing the curtain of questions, and the answers couldn't come soon enough.

CHAPTER 4

THE VACANTS

Billy stopped on Mount Elijah's steep incline and wrapped his cloak tighter around his body. The frigid wind tore through the woolen material, chilling his skin. Elam had warned him that the higher elevations were much colder than the valleys, but with the potential for battle looming, he had declined to wear more layers. A swift march up the slope would have to be enough to keep him warm.

Looking back at Walter, he raised a battle shield to block the wind and pressed a finger against his lips. "Let's keep it down."

Puffing white streams over his own shield, Walter joined him, whispering. "How much farther?"

Billy pointed. "You can see the top. The path will switch back twice more before we get there."

Walter angled his head to see the pinnacle. "Is that a fire?"

"Looks like they're trying to stay warm." Billy reached under his cloak and withdrew Excalibur from a belt scabbard. "Get ready."

Walter opened his cloak, revealing the hilt of a sword. "I've got your back."

"But who has our front?" Billy scanned the cloudy twilight skies. From the stories Valiant told, Second Eden had never experienced such overcast conditions, but ever since Angel's lie a month ago, rain and snow had come to the land in regular cycles. With no need for the watering mists and with the next eclipse due, would the fountains erupt and flood the Valley of Shadows as before? If so, what effect would the rising water have on Abraham's wall of fire, the protective shield that kept Flint, Goliath, and their armies from attacking the villages?

Billy grabbed Walter's sleeve and pulled him close. "When we get to the north face again, we'll hold there until Pegasus rises. It looks like the sky's clearing in that direction, so maybe we'll see the eclipse, and we can listen for the fountains. But whether we hear them or not, when it gets totally dark, that's when we run the rest of the way to the top and attack. Excalibur's light should scare them half to death. And if it doesn't, the dragons will."

"If they show up on time." Walter looked up at the darkening sky. "No sign of them yet."

"Dad will wait until the last minute. No use letting themselves be seen too soon. He and Hartanna know what they're doing."

"Yeah, but Valiant's description of these goons makes me wonder if your father has ever faced anything like them before. And what if they really have candlestones?"

Billy nodded. Walter was right. Valiant had called them "Vacants," empty of soul, emotions, or capacity for pain, humanoid creatures Abraham had once mentioned as if from a fairy tale. The villagers had spoken of altered tribes, but most of them had seen only the shadow people. Now, as if resurrected from ancient history, this tribe had returned to Second Eden. Why? No one knew. But since they stalked about the woods and mountains north of Founders Village but hadn't attacked the village itself, they seemed content to keep Abraham's people close to home, forcing Elam, Valiant, Sir Barlow, and others to maintain as many guards as possible.

Still, they had accosted the village's patrol, making the path to Mount Elijah dangerous, so the band of Vacants guarding the top of the volcano would have to go, and with only a narrow access trail available, it seemed best to Elam to send two warriors for a surprise attack. With Acacia now fully rested, she could try again to open the portal in the volcano's throat, if it still existed at all. Clefspeare had tried to clear the Vacants out once before but grew weak as he approached. Could that mean these creeps had a candlestone? Who could have given it to them? And how could they know that it weakened dragons?

Pointing with Excalibur, Billy whispered, "Let's move. Remember, we'll stop at the next switchback. That'll be the north face."

Soft-stepping on the gravelly path, they eased around the mountain and out of its shadow. Pegasus came into view, barely visible over the horizon. Although partially veiled by thin clouds, it shone a swath of yellowish moonlight across an array of peaks and valleys, creating a stunning portrait of a river-fed landscape, the western side of each mountain shrouded in shadows.

As a sliver of darkness passed over the edge of the huge moon, wind pummeled their bodies and flapped their cloaks. Billy pulled up his hood and pressed his back against the mountain. The rocky wall didn't shield him from the wind, but at least it held his cloak in place.

Walter joined him at his side and pointed toward a valley. "The fountains are supposed to be somewhere over there."

"I see bubbles in the river," Billy said. "I'll bet that's where they spring up."

"Yep. They're about to blow, all right."

"Perfect. The noise should help."

Leaning his head against the mountain, Walter looked at Billy. "You ever think back to how all this started? I mean, how we teamed up?"

Billy nodded. "When did you first know I was different?"

"When you breathed on your Pop-tart on the bus, and it toasted on the spot."

"That soon? I didn't know you noticed."

"I didn't know your breath would turn into fire, but I noticed."

Walter pulled out his sword. "And I'm glad I did. Life's been awesome ever since."

The shadow crossed the moon's halfway point, further darkening their surroundings. "Are you ready for another battle?" Billy asked.

"Fire up that sword, and I'll follow the glow."

"Just a couple more minutes, I think." Listening for a rush of water, Billy kept his gaze locked on the skies. Just a hint that his father lurked nearby would be a big help. These Vacants sounded as bad as the Nephilim, maybe worse. And with Excalibur acting in an unpredictable manner, who could tell how effective it would be? Still, it had always provided at least a bit of light, and the blade was as sharp as ever. If necessary, he could also use his fire breathing, but that would have to wait until they engaged the Vacants in close conflict. He didn't want to accidently scorch Walter.

When the last slice of Pegasus drained away, Billy summoned a bare glow from Excalibur, just enough to see the path in front of him, a path wide enough for the two of them to march side by side. He stepped away from the mountain and whispered, "Ready?"

Walter sidled up close. "Let's do it."

Craning his neck, Billy listened for the fountains. Although the wind whistled past his ears, a sudden rush burst through. Water raged somewhere in the distance.

Billy threw off his cloak and charged ahead, Excalibur leading the way. With Walter in the darkness behind him, he concentrated on the path, resisting the urge to summon a brighter light. The closer they could get without alerting the Vacants, the better.

As he rounded the final switchback, a shout reached his ears, then another. Excalibur's glow covered the mountaintop, revealing several scurrying shadows on its flat surface. Two shadows charged down the path, both with blades reflecting the glow, but before they could reach Billy, a blast of fire ripped across the sky and doused the pair with flames, fanned by beating wings that rushed by in the darkness above.

Billy and Walter hopped over the writhing, burning bodies and ran on. Another stream of orange splashed onto the very top of the mountain, energizing the Vacants' campfire. With flames now illuminating the scene, Billy made a quick count. About five of the goons remained. Not a problem.

All five charged, swords bared and spears raised. Billy waded into them, slashing with all his might, shooting fire from his mouth, and blocking their blows with his shield. After dismembering one and setting another ablaze, he burst through to the other side and swung around. Walter battled two Vacants, swiveling back and forth to meet their swords with his, while a third approached from his rear.

As Billy set his feet to attack again, dizziness flooded his mind. Nausea boiled in his stomach. Was a candlestone around? No matter. He had to fight.

"Walter! Behind you!" Walter spun, but too late. The Vacant stabbed him in the side with a spear. As Walter slumped to his knees, Billy charged, again slashing with Excalibur, but this time only smoke spewed from his mouth.

After crashing into one of the Vacants and knocking him down the slope, Billy lopped the head off the one who stabbed Walter and kicked its body off the side of the mountain. In the distance, a shadow fled away, probably an escaping Vacant.

His shoulders now sagging, Billy faced the final opponent, a tall brute of a man. With a spear uplifted and ready to throw, the Vacant held something in his other hand, something that emitted a dim beam of light.

Billy gulped. His arms wilted, unable to lift his sword and shield. He couldn't fight. He couldn't even run. His legs refused to budge.

Just as the Vacant slung his spear, a voice bellowed from above.

"Son! Drop to your belly!"

Billy threw himself to the ground. The spear swished over his head. A thud sounded, then a ripping noise. Soon, only the rush of water and the whistling wind reached his ears. With strength returning to his muscles, he pushed up to his hands and knees and turned toward Walter. "You all right, buddy?"

Now on his stomach, Walter clawed the path, groaning. "Nope. Guess again."

"I'm coming." As Billy crawled toward him, a sudden wind beat his hair into a frenzy. A dragon landed on the volcano's flat top, its wings outstretched.

"Son!" Clefspeare called. "Are you wounded?"

"I'm okay, but Walter's pretty bad."

Clefspeare raised his head and trumpeted. When his call died away, he shuffled his body toward Billy. "I signaled Hartanna. She carried the candlestone bearer to his doom, but she is now weak. I will take Walter to our healers, and she will carry you back to the village as soon as she is able."

"I'll check out the hole," Billy said. "That's what we came for."

"It is dark. Be careful. We will return with Acacia in the daylight." With a beat of his wings, Clefspeare rose into the air, passed over Billy, and picked up Walter in his claws. Rising and falling in the whipping wind, the great dragon disappeared in the darkness.

Billy climbed to his feet and, clutching Excalibur, staggered toward the portal hole on the mountain's flat top. He summoned the brightest glow the sword would give and passed the light across the volcano's throat. A pile of boulders plugged the hole. The Vacants must have torn down the remnants of the wall that once arched over this circular floor and rolled them in.

He leaned against the pile. There was way too much debris to dig through by himself, and Acacia would be needed to open the portal. No use wearing himself out before she arrived.

As he searched the dark skies, a sliver of Pegasus appeared from behind its eclipsing shadow. Light seeped out and spread across the starry canopy, turning it purple and magenta. The rush of water eased, a sure sign that the eclipse had reached its waning minutes.

He looked at the river's source. Fountains still pushed water well above the surface, breaking off chunks of ice as the flow surged past the edges of a glacier. With light continuing to clarify every detail, he walked to one of the dead Vacants and used the flat of his blade to turn the creature's head face up. Although his facial features somewhat resembled that of humans—two eyes, one nose, one mouth—their sizes and positions differed. The mouth sat lower, near the chin, much smaller than normal, more like a guppy's mouth. Its eyes, still open, were also lower, one on each side of a central nose, if you could call it a nose. It looked more like a doorknob with breathing holes. And the eyeballs? As big as ping pong balls yet as dark as coal, they reflected the moon, seemingly without a defined iris or pupil.

As the glow from Pegasus continued to brighten, he moved the sword to the Vacant's arm, the site of his fatal wound. Covered with a metal-reinforced sleeve, an elbow-length stub oozed dark blood. Was the blood black, or just dark red?

Billy looked away. Just two years ago this sight would have made him gag, but now it brought a sense of heaviness—so much fighting, so much bloodshed, so much evil in every realm. And now he was a warrior, called to battle on every front. Sure, he had become strong, and he had courage. And, yes, he could handle a sword with the best of them. But what good was all of that when his primary reason for wielding his sword was far away in another world? Would he ever see Bonnie again?

As he walked back to the volcano's throat, he looked again at the massive moon, as bright as two Earth moons now that its time of darkness had slipped away. This place was so different—shadow people, Vacants, odd swamp folks, and a peaceful group of humans training for battle while a protective wall of fire slowly ebbed.

Yes, it was different . . . and dangerous, even to the point of death, especially now for Walter. Would he even survive his wound?

Billy picked up one of the stones plugging the hole and heaved it down the slope. At least he could move some of this stuff out of the way while he waited. It would take his mind off Bonnie and Walter.

After a minute or so of hauling rocks, he sat down on one of the larger ones. He was wrong. Images of his friends stayed locked in his mind. He looked up at the sky. Hartanna couldn't show up soon enough.

* * *

After stopping at their hovel to put on their backpacks, Bonnie and Shiloh ran side by side through the main corridor, Bonnie carrying a flickering lantern. Because of the delay, they had to hurry to catch up with the others.

Bonnie stopped at the mouth of the escape tunnel to her right, a narrower passage that ascended at a sharp angle. "Lights out?"

"Probably a good idea," Shiloh said. "Sapphira can always relight it with her patented, 'Ignite.'"

Lifting the glass, Bonnie blew out the flame. Now in darkness, she whispered, "A little slower now."

The two scurried up the incline, feeling the walls on each side as they climbed. Soon, shouts and a clamor of metal on rocks echoed through the passage.

"The girl's on fire! What is she, a demon?"

Craning her neck to listen, Bonnie slowed her pace further. That was a male voice, strained and unfamiliar.

"Sapphira!" someone else called. "Get back! He's got a gun!"

Bonnie grabbed Shiloh's arm. "That was Gabriel!"

As they dashed ahead, a bright glow came into view and guided their way. When they neared the source, they crept close to the wall, staying in the shadows. Sapphira stood at the center of the tunnel, completely ablaze in white flames that spread from one wall to the other. Behind her, Gabriel shielded the former dragons with his wings.

Three men stood on Sapphira's far side, one with a rifle poised at his shoulder. A pile of rubble blocked the way beyond them, dust swirling from an apparent collapse. The rushing air proved that a vent somewhere still allowed passage to the outside.

"Vlad," the tallest man shouted. "Shoot her! Just shoot her!"

"I can't!" Vlad's rifle trembled. "She's just a girl, Nolan! I can't shoot a girl."

Her white hair streaming in the flames, Sapphira formed a fireball in her hands. "Do you want to see me throw like a girl?"

A short, bearded man climbed up the pile of rubble. "She's a demon, I tell you. I'm outta here." He disappeared through a hole in the rocks.

Sapphira threw the ball against the pile. White-hot flames splashed all around. "That was a warning," she said as she fashioned a new ball. "The next one will roast your flesh."

Nolan snatched the rifle. "If you won't do it, I will!"

Gabriel burst through the wall of flames and leaped for the gunman. The moment he reached for the barrel, the rifle went off with a loud pop.

Sapphira's body snapped back and dropped to the ground. Her flames dwindled as the gunshot's echo reverberated in the tunnel.

"Sapphira!" Bonnie scrambled toward her.

Nolan kicked Gabriel in the groin, then smacked the side of his head with the barrel, sending him crashing against the wall. Gabriel slumped and slid to the floor, out cold, or worse.

Now with only lantern flames lighting the tunnel, Nolan turned the rifle toward Bonnie, Shiloh, and the others as they huddled around Sapphira. "Vlad, find the one they call Bonnie and get her out of here."

Bonnie angled her face toward the shadows. She had to protect her secret and get to Second Eden. If she couldn't hide or escape from these intruders, all would be lost.

"I'm Bonnie," Rebekah said, rising to her full height. "Take me, and leave the others alone."

Nolan jerked a photo from his shirt pocket. Holding it close to his eyes, he glanced between it and Rebekah. "Liar!" He handed the photo to Vlad. "Use this to find her. I'll cover you."

Bonnie kept her head low, listening to Sapphira's rapid breaths. Blood spilled from a shoulder wound, and her eyelids fluttered. "I'm okay," Sapphira whispered. "Let him get close, and I'll—"

"I'm Bonnie." Shiloh stood and stepped into the lanterns' glow, faking an American accent. "Now put down that gun, and I'll go without a fight."

Vlad set the photo close to Shiloh's face. "She's the one, all right."

"Get her in the chopper and tie her up," Nolan said, waving the rifle toward the exit hole.

Vlad pulled a dagger from his belt and pressed the tip against Shiloh's chin. "Get moving."

As Shiloh climbed the rubble, Nolan lowered the barrel. "Now that we have what we came for, the rest of you stay here for ten minutes. Then you're free to go."

After looking back at Gabriel, Shiloh disappeared through the hole, followed seconds later by Vlad.

"Where are you taking her?" Rebekah demanded.

Nolan smirked. "To someone who pays very well, but I'm sure he would be rather angry with me if I revealed his identity or his whereabouts." He backed toward the rubble, a hint of unsteadiness in his step. "Now, if you'll excuse me."

Sapphira reached for Bonnie's hand. "Help me up," she whispered. "I hear pain in his voice. It's happening."

"What's happening?" Still angling her face away from the gunman, Bonnie locked wrists with Sapphira and hoisted her to her feet. "What are you talking about?"

"You'll see." Sapphira faced Nolan as he climbed the pile, the rifle still pointed her way. "Feeling bad, Nolan?" she asked.

He paused at the edge of the hole and squinted at her. His head lolled like that of a drunken man. "I . . . I feel fine."

Sapphira reached to her shoulder, smeared blood onto her palm, and showed it to Nolan. "He who spills the blood of an Oracle of Fire will surely die."

Heaving shallow, choking breaths, Nolan clutched his shirt as he gasped his words. "You *are* a demon . . . or some . . . some kind of witch."

Sapphira's hand ignited from the heel to the tips of her fingers. The blood sizzled and burned away. "Tell us where your partner is taking Bonnie."

With sweat streaming down his three-day beard, Nolan gagged, barely able to speak. "Will you . . . let me . . . live?"

"Tell us!" Sapphira shouted. "You are in God's hands now."

Nolan stared at his hands with wide eyes. The fingers touching his rifle smoldered, as if on fire. Then, sparks erupted from the tips, like holiday sparklers—white and orange. He threw down the gun and shook his hand, but the flames ate away his fingers, faster and faster.

The fingers on his other hand ignited, then his feet and lower legs. As he burned, he screamed. "Curse you! Curse you all, dragons and demons alike!"

Bonnie turned her head. It was awful, just too awful. Flickers of light from his engulfed body painted the wall, and his fading screams and the odor of burning flesh assaulted her senses. Soon, all was quiet.

Turning back, Bonnie looked for him but found only a heap of bones, charred and smoldering.

Rebekah picked up the rifle and pointed it at the escape hole. "I'll need three to come with me. The rest of you stay here to help our wounded. Alithia, check on Gabriel."

One of the former dragons, a short, stocky lady, ran to Gabriel's side and pressed her fingers against his throat. "He's alive."

After Rebekah climbed through the hole, Dallas and two others followed. Then, when all three had disappeared, Rebekah poked her head back through. "Hide the bones. I'll send someone back with a report as soon as I can."

Bonnie stooped beside Gabriel and touched his caretaker's arm. "Does he need a doctor?"

"I am a doctor . . . Kaylee Saunders, M.D." She pulled Gabriel's eyelids up and peered in. "He's unconscious. Let's get some water."

Rotating her wounded shoulder, Sapphira looked at Bonnie. "Can you lead them to the spring?"

"Of course." Bonnie peeked at Sapphira's back but saw no blood, no obvious exit wound. "And you'll need to soak, too. Maybe Dr. Saunders can get that bullet out."

"I'd like to wait for word on Shiloh," Sapphira said, "and the Foleys and Yereq."

Bonnie picked up a lantern and held it close to Sapphira's shoulder. Blood dampened a splotch the size of two hands. "No way. We have to clean that wound and stop the bleeding. Besides, those guys might come back for their partner."

"So we have to make sure they can't." Wincing, Sapphira glared at the hole in the rubble. "I'm still well enough to stop them."

Dr. Saunders looked up at one of the other former dragons. "Dorian, hide the bones and stand guard. If someone comes through besides one of our own, come and warn us."

"How will I find you?" Dorian asked. "I know not the path to the spring."

Bonnie pointed into the darkness. "Go to the end of this tunnel. Turn left, then right again when you hear the sound of water."

"Very well." Dorian bowed her head. "If they pursue me, I will lead them away from your refuge and then return and warn you."

While the other former dragons carried Gabriel, Sapphira and Bonnie led the way, Sapphira with a weak ball of fire in her hand and Bonnie with a lantern in hers. Whenever they jostled him, Gabriel mumbled a few indecipherable words.

Bonnie kept a close eye on Sapphira. At times, her gait wobbled as she negotiated the descent, but she always managed to straighten again. With her white eyebrows bent low and her red lips pursed, she seemed to be battling intense pain. That bullet had likely damaged more tissue than she had let on.

When they reached the passage to the spring, the sound of falling water and a rush of wet air filled the tunnel. After traversing a short path, they entered an enormous chamber. Their lights flashed into the upper reaches, revealing a cathedral-like ceiling.

Steamy springs cascaded from three holes near the top of a flowstone wall, dropping down a stair-step array of flat rocks before joining into one stream. At each level, water collected in pools behind and around the rocks, some neck-deep and some barely deep enough to scoop up a handful. Overhead, stalactites dripped cool limestone water, making the chamber feel like a storm had just passed as the sodden branches of imaginary trees trickled their excess on passersby.

Bonnie set her lantern by one of the deeper pools, her favorite place to sit and soak. The rocks within the stream formed a bench, perfect for relaxing. When she sat in this pool, the surface reached up to her neck, and a waterfall poured a hot shower just beyond her feet, sending a warm current her way.

The former dragons laid Gabriel gently on the stone floor. Tamara sat next to him and propped his head on her thigh. "His breathing is good," she said. "He's still mumbling, but his eyes are closed."

"Then Sapphira is our priority." Dr. Saunders eyed her shoulder. "If I cut the bullet out, am I subject to the Oracle's curse? You will certainly bleed more."

"No worries," Sapphira said. "Paili once removed a splinter from my foot. I bled, but she was fine. Apparently, if the blood-letting is for healing rather than for harm, you're safe."

"That's good enough for me." Dr. Saunders reached for Sapphira's shirt. "Let's get this off and have a look."

Sapphira glanced at Gabriel. "Okay, but—"

The doctor followed her line of sight. "Don't worry. He's unconscious. I think he'll see only stars for quite a while."

As she pulled up the bottom hem, Gabriel called out, "Wait!"

Dr. Saunders lowered Sapphira's shirt. "Ah! You're awake!"

Gabriel sat up, holding a hand against his forehead. "I might be seeing stars, but I don't want to risk seeing any other heavenly bodies."

"Ladies," Bonnie said with a smile, "we have a true gentleman among us."

Sapphira pointed at a plastic basin near a lower pool. "There's a sponge in that basin. Someone can take that and help Gabriel back to the tunnel."

Bonnie stepped down the stony staircase, filled the basin with cooler water from an estuary pool, and she and Tamara supported Gabriel as they walked to the outer passage. After helping him sit with his wings spread comfortably behind him, Bonnie mopped the back of his head with the sponge. "There's some blood here."

"Yeah, I felt it. I don't think it's too bad." Opening his eyes fully, he looked at Bonnie. "So . . . what happened to Shiloh?"

As she wrung out the sponge, Bonnie tightened her jaw. "They took her," was all she could manage.

Gabriel's wings fell limp. "I see."

Bonnie swallowed down a painful lump. For some reason, Shiloh's sacrifice brought feelings of shame. Why didn't the real Bonnie stand and say, "I'm Bonnie"? But what choice did she have? Enoch had told her to stay hidden, to keep her wings secret. And now this very event might have been the one Enoch had planned for, to use Shiloh as a decoy to keep the real Bonnie safe.

But that didn't help much. Poor Shiloh now sat in the clutches of a stranger who promised to take her to some unnamed person who obviously didn't have her best interests in mind. What would he do if he discovered she wasn't the real Bonnie? How long could Shiloh keep up the charade?

Again dabbing his head wound, Bonnie told Gabriel what happened during the moments he lay unconscious. Although the events themselves seemed to transpire in slow motion, unfolding in the span of several minutes when they occurred, retelling them took far less time.

"So," she said, wringing out the sponge again, "we're waiting on word from Rebekah, and those guys might come back to find out what happened to Nolan."

"I don't think they're worried about retrieving a hack like him, but if they figure out Shiloh's not who she says she is . . ."

"That's what I was thinking."

"Then we need to set a trap," Gabriel said, "something that'll keep them from ever returning."

"Like what?"

"We'll ask Sapphira." Gabriel leaned on one hand and reached for Bonnie with the other. "In the meantime, help me up. I want to go outside and see if I can help Rebekah."

Bonnie shook her head. "No way. You might have a concussion. I'm sure Rebekah can handle it. She seems like a ball of fire."

"Did someone mention my name?"

Bonnie turned toward the voice. As the lantern light grew closer, the silhouettes of two females took shape, and their faces clarified. "Keep going, Bonnie," Rebekah said, smiling. "I was enjoying your conversation."

"It's nothing I wouldn't say to your face. You're a real go-getter." Bonnie raised her eyebrows. "So what did you find out?"

Rebekah gestured toward the escape tunnel. "I saw two helicopters taking off. One looked empty except for the pilot, and Vlad sat in the front passenger seat of the other one. I thought I saw Shiloh in the back, but I wasn't sure. There were two dead guys on the ground, pretty much mangled, like a wild beast had torn into them. I guess Yereq did that before he left. I saw a lot of blood, but no sign of anyone else."

"So Yereq must have taken the Foleys somewhere to get help," Bonnie said. "And he tried to block the tunnel before he left."

"And we finished the job." Dallas pointed at herself with her thumb. "Dorian and Elise are still back there sweeping up bones."

"So we're trapped?" Bonnie asked.

Gabriel managed a pain-streaked smile. "If Rebekah is as smart as I think she is, she made sure we have a way out."

Rebekah grinned at Dallas. "What did I tell you?"

Dallas rolled her eyes. "You were right, as usual."

"So you did?" Bonnie said. "How?"

"Oh, you'll see soon enough." Rebekah stooped next to Bonnie. "So how's the hero?"

Gabriel ran a hand through his hair. "Singed a few follicles and put a new dent in my head, but with all these brilliant ladies taking care of me, I'll be as good as new in no time."

"And Sapphira?" Dallas asked.

"I think the doctor wanted to do surgery, but I'm not sure how she can. We have a razor blade, and I'm sure Sapphira can sterilize it, but without anesthesia . . ."

A shrill cry sounded from the springs, followed by a muffled moan. A pain-filled lament filled the tunnel, its echo repeating several times before it faded away.

Tears flooded Bonnie's eyes. With Shiloh in trouble, Gabriel hurt, Yereq missing, and Sapphira suffering through surgery, everything seemed to be going wrong all at once.

She looked around at her three companions, each face darkened by worry and the dimness of the tunnel. In many ways, this place felt like the candlestone, a dark prison that forced its captives to wait for outside help while trusting in friends in higher places.

She took Gabriel's hand, barely able to speak. "Will you sing a prayer with me?"

"You bet." Gabriel slid back against a wall and rested his head. "What song?"

"The one you taught me when I was six years old, remember?"

"How could I forget?" Gabriel let out a long sigh. "I've sung it a hundred times since then, especially while you were in the candlestone."

"I was just thinking about that place. How did you know I was in there?"

Gabriel caressed her hand. "I saw you. I was with you."

"You were? If you were light energy, why didn't I see you? I could see everyone else in there."

"You didn't see me? I surrounded you when you first got there, when Devin tried to grab you."

"You were the cage of light?"

He nodded. “Apparently, God allowed me to become visible when you needed me most.”

“Like in the bedroom when I was six.” Bonnie again imagined that day long ago when Gabriel first appeared to her. She had been devastated by her father’s cruel remarks about her wings, and Gabriel comforted her with a song.

“Right,” Gabriel said. “And when Palin was ready to cut you open on your thirteenth birthday. My energy field somehow lit up a poster of a guardian angel, and the glow let Palin see you. I think when he figured out that you were a girl, he couldn’t kill you. So he just left. I guess he never told Devin.”

“That’s amazing! I didn’t even know that happened!”

Gabriel smiled. “I wish I could tell you all the ways God protected you. Maybe now that we’ll be together for a while, I can. But I think when you were six, that was the most special time.”

“Me, too. The prayer has stayed in my mind ever since.” Now on her knees, Bonnie gave him a hug and kissed his cheek. “I don’t think I could’ve made it without you, but . . .”

“But what?”

“I feel so ashamed. When you never became visible again, I kind of forgot about you. I started wondering if you were just in my imagination, you know, the hopeful dream of a six-year-old. Then, when I turned thirteen, I saw Sapphira. She told me you were there, so that’s when I started hoping again, hoping I really had a guardian angel, but I never told anyone, not even Billy. I wasn’t sure anyone would believe me.”

A tear dripped down Gabriel’s cheek. He looked at her for a moment, his chin trembling. “I think—”

Another shriek sounded from the springs chamber, long and sharp, then a series of halting wails.

Bonnie covered her mouth and breathed her words through her fingers. “Poor Sapphira!”

Gabriel straightened. "We'd better start singing." He looked up at Rebekah and Dallas. "Care to join us?"

Both ladies sat on the floor, cross-legged. "If we don't know the words," Rebekah said, "we'll hum along."

Bonnie settled beside Gabriel and clutched his hand tightly. Everything seemed so dark, so hopeless. When she was in the candlestone, her song always made her own body brighter and created a shield that protected her from Devin. Now it felt like she needed a shield more than ever, and a cascading waterfall of light to chase away the shadows.

She took a deep breath and sang, Gabriel joining in on the second word.

Whither shall I go from thy spirit?
Or whither shall I flee from thy presence?
If I ascend up into heaven, thou art there:
If I make my bed in hell, behold, thou art there.
If I take the wings of the morning,
and dwell in the uttermost parts of the sea;
Even there shall thy hand lead me,
and thy right hand shall hold me.
If I say, Surely the darkness shall cover me;
even the night shall be light about me.
Yea, the darkness hideth not from thee;
but the night shineth as the day:
The darkness and the light are both alike to thee.

Exhaling heavily, Bonnie looked at each of her fellow singers in turn. All eyes glistened. In each face, sadness blended with hope. Despair had fled away.

Still holding Gabriel's hand, Bonnie loosened her grip. They had done all they could do here. It was time to add action to their prayers.

She stood and helped Gabriel to his feet. "Let's set that trap we talked about," she said. "I'm ready to catch a few kidnappers."

CHAPTER 5

THE HEALER

Billy slid down Hartanna's flank and landed flat-footed on the grass. "Thanks for the ride!" he said as he adjusted his scabbard belt.

With Pegasus now high overhead, Hartanna's features were clear in the bright moonlight. "Please bring back a report as soon as possible. Walter is very dear to all of us."

"Don't worry. I will." Billy sprinted toward the village as fast as his mail, cloak, and scabbard would allow. Since they had landed in the field near the birthing garden instead of the dragon landing area, he would enter the village from the north, nearer Abraham's former home. Since Elam didn't want to assume too much, he had declined the villagers' offer to have him live there, choosing a less prestigious hut instead. It lay vacant because of the deaths of the couple who once lived there, both victims of the rampage by Goliath and the Nephilim when they entered Second Eden a month ago.

The villagers later converted Abraham's house into a triage station for wounded soldiers. With the firewall keeping their main enemies at bay, only a few troops had need of it, those who had suffered minor injuries from skirmishes with the Vacants who had ventured too close to the villages.

When Billy arrived at the triage hut, he paused next to one of two dragons painted on either side of the door. Now warm from his run, he shed his cloak, tucked it under his arm, and pushed the door open.

Inside, Walter lay on a raised cot near the back, well away from the cold draft breezing in from the street. Ashley and Steadfast stood on either side, Ashley with her back to the door and both leaning over Walter's body. Neither one looked up to see who had come in.

After easing the door closed, Billy walked closer. "How is he?"

"If you have an extra hand," Ashley shouted, "get it over here now!"

He dropped his cloak and ran across the floor, dodging a row of cots as he loosened his scabbard belt and let it fall. With a hop over the last cot, he joined Ashley. She and Steadfast had both hands inside a gash in Walter's chest.

Ashley spat out her words. "Alcohol on the table! Douse your hands and come back!"

On a table near the wall, Billy found a glass bottle, poured a splash into his palm, and washed. "Okay!" he called, leaping back. "What now?"

Keeping her fingers in place, Ashley pulled aside Walter's skin with the heel of her hand. Blood flowed freely and dripped down Walter's ribcage. "See what I'm holding?"

Billy peered inside. "A vein?"

"An artery. Grab it."

Praying for a strong stomach, Billy reached in and pinched the wet artery. "Like this?"

"Perfect." Ashley let go and dashed to the table. Blood spewed from her other hand's release point, spraying Billy's shirt. Two seconds later, she jumped back with a needle attached to a long strand of thin black thread. "Okay, just keep holding it until I say so."

Billy bit his lip hard. So much blood! And the wound looked awful. But it didn't matter. Duty called.

Ashley poked the needle into Walter's artery and began stitching around it. Apparently the Vacant's spear had sliced through it, and now she had to splice the loose ends together. As she worked, the delicate artery seemed to line up and seal itself effortlessly, as if the combination of her stitching and her healing touch cauterized the vessel.

Ashley looked up at Steadfast. "Doing okay over there?"

"Yes." A bead of sweat trickled from Steadfast's forehead down to his clean-shaven cheek. "These veins are not leaking badly. I am able to hold them until you are finished there."

"Good. This won't take long." Ashley blew hair out of her eyes. "I hope it works. I helped stitch up Valiant, but it was nothing like this. And every stitch seems to wear me out."

After another minute or so, she tied the thread and cut it with a small knife. "Okay, Billy. Take a breather and wash up." She gestured toward the door. "You'll find a pitcher pump out back."

Billy pulled his hands from Walter's warm body. His fingers, now dripping blood, felt cold and cramped. He paused, staring at Walter's nearly motionless body. Nausea churned. A blanket of heaviness weighed down his shoulders. What would happen? After all the dangers they had faced, would a stupid monster from another world bring Walter's life to an end?

"Billy!"

Ashley's sharp voice shook him out of his daydream.

"What?"

"Get washed up," she said, her tone now calm. "I'll need your clean hands again in just a minute."

Billy ran to the door, pushed the latch button with his wrist, and forced the door open with his foot. With the great moon still bright, and lanterns lining the street, finding the pump in the back proved to be no problem. After scrubbing his hands and then his face, he hurried back, finding Ashley tying off another stitching job.

He showed her his hands. "What now?"

Ashley nodded toward the table again. "See the little bottle, the brown one?"

"Uh-huh."

"Put one drop of that stuff on your finger and smear it under Walter's tongue."

Billy stepped over to the table and pulled a cork from the tiny bottle, no bigger than an eye dropper bottle. "What is it?"

Steadfast, two fingers still in Walter's wound, looked his way. "An elixir Angel created. It discourages blood loss."

"Probably some kind of clotting enhancer," Ashley said. "We have to do something more to stop the bleeding than this patch-work job I'm doing."

Billy let a drop leak onto the tip of his index finger. Pressing Walter's cheeks together with one hand, he pushed the medicated finger into the opening and rubbed the tip under Walter's tongue.

Walter jerked his head and bit down lightly on Billy's finger before settling down. Billy withdrew his finger and shook out the pain. "Done."

"Thank you." Ashley snipped a thread and reached for a bloodstained rag. "Steadfast will close the incision. I have to check his pressure."

She picked up a makeshift blood pressure cuff from the supply table. As she wrapped Walter's arm with the sleeve—a bladder, of sorts, constructed from rabbit gut—she looked at Billy. "When your father brought Walter here, we weren't sure how badly he was hurt. He was conscious, but when his blood pressure kept dropping, we knew he must have had internal bleeding. Then he conked out, and we knew we had to go in."

She pumped up the sleeve with a bulb, also made from some kind of animal gut. "He stayed kind of delirious. He kept trying to get up and charge back into battle, so Steadfast knocked him out with another one of Angel's home brews."

Releasing the air, Ashley watched a needle move across a bleached leaf painted with hand-numbered pressure readings. "I didn't have time to look for my stethoscope, but with my sensory gifts, I can feel the pulse changes." She closed her eyes for a moment, then unwrapped the sleeve. "Eighty-five over fifty. We might need some blood."

Billy rolled up his sleeve. "I'm O positive."

"Same here, but I don't know what Walter is. Steadfast says Angel had a way of knowing who was compatible with whom, but it's based on matching their companions somehow. Since that won't work with Walter, we'll stick with what we know. O is a universal donor, but if Walter's a negative, our RH factor could be a big problem."

Billy looked again at Steadfast, now stitching Walter's skin closed. After Angel went up in flames with Abraham, the poor guy was called into service as a surgeon after being little more than a medical orderly. Still, he knew enough to help, and between him and his Eve, Pearl, they worked nonstop.

"So, we'll chance the RH factor if we have to," Billy said. "I mean, giving him our blood beats bleeding to death."

"Right." Her hands red, Ashley brushed her tangled hair back with her forearm. Dressed in blood-dappled white T-shirt and a pair of jeans that were obviously slept-in, she looked exhausted from head to toe. "Steadfast is really good at stitching. I think the process drains my healing power, so it's best to let him take over on the less-critical ones."

Billy looked past Ashley. Steadfast, a thirtysomething male, just like all the other patriarchs in the village, meticulously worked the needle and thread. A nearly transparent egg floated close to his ear, its barely visible eyes looking on and wobbling, as if nodding approval at Steadfast's work. At the other end of the thread, Walter's skin lifted, still bloodstained, as two flaps joined tightly together. His chest raised and lowered in time with his breaths, shallow and gurgling.

Even with his shirt off, Walter looked warm enough. Glistening with sweat, his body, more muscular and hardened than Billy had ever seen it, glowed in the light of the lantern's dancing flame. "So, how bad was the damage?"

Ashley looked back at Walter, concern sagging her brow. "The spear sliced a gash in his lung."

"Sliced a lung?" Billy laid a hand on his chest. "Ouch!"

She nodded. "Thank God it missed his heart, but it cut enough blood vessels to kill him. We patched him up the best we could, so we'll just have to monitor him for more bleeding."

He looked back at the door and lowered his voice. "Are you up for a full-blown healing?"

She matched his tone. "When Walter was passing out, I didn't have time to get Acacia to try it. But now he might be out of danger, and you know what Elam said."

Nodding, Billy replayed the recent event in his mind, their first discovery of the Vacants. Valiant had been patrolling alone in the woods to the north and came upon at least a dozen of them. They attacked, and Valiant fought . . . well . . . valiantly. After killing three of their party, he managed to escape, but he suffered multiple spear wounds.

He staggered back to Founder's Village, where Ashley attempted a healing with Acacia providing the fire. It worked, at least for Valiant, but Ashley nearly cooked. Her temperature spiked to 106 and stayed above 104 for three days. Now, a full week after she was finally able to get out of bed, she still tired easily. And Acacia seemed drained as well. She didn't feel fully recharged until yesterday. Elam gave both a stern command not to try any further healings unless someone would surely die without the attempt.

"We could ask your mother to try again," Billy said. "Just because her healing power hasn't worked on humans here, it doesn't mean it'll never work."

Ashley touched his arm. "Billy, it's all right. Trust me. If I thought Walter was about to die, I'd do it in a heartbeat."

"Should we fly him up to the hospital, then?"

"That won't do any good. We brought the heart and lung machines down yesterday. Cliffside's going to land the entire hospital soon. No sense in keeping it flying around up there when the worst of the bad guys are trapped behind the wall of fire."

Billy looked again at Ashley's hands, slender and strong. A ring decorated one of her fingers, a red gem shining from its mount. "How'd you learn so much about surgery?"

"Doc taught me. Bonnie's father, I mean. Since we kept quite a few animals, we sometimes had to do some minor surgery. Instead of taking them to the vet, Doc showed me how. He went to medical school, but after he got his MD, he didn't like seeing all the suffering and death, so he turned to pharmacy."

Billy offered a sympathetic nod. Ever since Dr. Conner died heroically after their battle against Devin in the underground laboratory, he had often wondered about how great an asset Dr. Conner would have been. Now his talents seemed wasted. "I guess we could really use him."

"You bet." Ashley crossed her arms over her chest and huffed a sigh. She glanced at Walter before shifting back to Billy. Her brow drooped again, along with her sad eyes. "How are you doing?"

Billy picked up his sword belt and fastened it around his waist. "Okay, I guess. No wounds."

"No, I mean—" She laid a hand on his chest. "I mean here. It's been a month with no contact."

"Yeah. I knew what you meant." He clutched Excalibur's hilt and massaged its smooth surface. "And I think you already know the answer."

Pressing her lips together, she nodded. "When I'm tired, I can't control this mind-reading thing very well. Sorry for butting in on your emotions."

"No big deal." He glanced at her hand, still pressed gently against his chest. She was obviously tired and mentally drained. "Emotions are all I have left," he said, "and I'm kind of wearing them on my sleeve."

"I know. Me, too." Pulling her hand back, she looked at Walter again. Steadfast had covered his torso with a sheet and was now checking his pressure. Since he lacked Ashley's sensory powers, he was using her makeshift stethoscope to listen for the heartbeat. "I see you found it," she said.

Steadfast nodded, his eyes trained on the meter. "It was next to the laundry bin."

"Sorry. I remember now. I put it there this morning." Looking more exhausted than ever, she turned back to Billy and lowered her voice to a whisper. "You know, I like the people here, and I know how important our work is, but sometimes I just want to go home. Do you know what I mean?"

"Sure. I think about that a lot."

"How badly do you miss home? I mean, I know you must really miss Bonnie, right?"

Heat flowed into Billy's cheeks and ears. "When you butt in, you really butt in."

She clenched her fist and scolded herself. "Get with it, Ashley! Don't be such a relational clutz!"

"Don't worry about it. I shouldn't have said it that way. I mean, I do miss Bonnie . . . a lot . . . and I miss my mother, too. But we've been so busy here, the only time I think about it is when I go to bed. But that doesn't last long. I'm so exhausted, I conk out right away."

"I know. You and Walter have been training constantly. Either that or out on patrol."

He pointed at her. "Look who's talking—Miss Never Sleeps. You're either a doctor, a mechanic, or an inventor. If you don't rest more, you're going to have a breakdown."

Looking at the floor, she nodded. "I know, I know. But who else is going to do those things?"

"I can't argue with that." Billy glanced at Walter again. Steadfast had finished taking his pressure. He probably would have reported anything unusual. "Speaking of inventions, any news on your radio project?"

As a weak smile appeared, Ashley's voice perked up. "My tooth transmitter still works. It's not nearly strong enough to call home, but it's perfect for communicating locally. And I altered Merlin's radio frequency without a problem."

"Any luck with that?"

She shook her head. "I can't get anywhere with the magnets. The field they create isn't strong enough to make a crack in the dimensional wall. Without at least a tiny opening, Larry wouldn't be able to hear me even if I sent a megawatt signal."

Billy painted a picture in his mind—his mother operating Larry's console. Without communications, their only hope was to find a portal. Acacia would have to try again at Mount Elijah, the sooner the better. "If Walter seems out of the woods in the morning," he said, "I'll take Acacia and Listener up to the volcano and see what we can see."

"Okay, check back here first thing. I'll let you know how he's doing."

"You're staying here? Doesn't Steadfast have this shift?"

"He does." She dragged a cot close to Walter's and sat down. "I just want to be here in case he needs me."

Billy sat next to her, adjusting his sword to make room. "I don't need to be a mind reader to know that something's up between you two."

Her cheeks flushing, Ashley suppressed a smile. "That noticeable, huh?"

"Your sleeve is covered with it."

She brushed her sleeve and let her smile break through. "Walter and I are like this, Billy." She slid closer, hip to hip. "We're friends, partners, fellow warriors, but not lovers. Ever since we worked together to help you and Bonnie navigate the Circles of Seven, we've fought together and bled together. But you know what? We trust each other so much, it's like we're building a foundation for something else later on."

"You mean when Walter's old enough."

She nudged his side. "Who says you're not a mind reader?"

"When would that be? Three years? Five years?"

"It's hard to tell. This place has changed us so much, it's like we're maturing at double the normal speed. He already looks more like a man than a boy."

"Yeah. I noticed. Maybe it's something in the air here." Billy rose to his feet. "I'd better get to bed. Gotta climb a volcano tomorrow."

Ashley showed him her bloody hands. "I'll get cleaned up and then sack out."

"Want me to bring you a change of clothes?"

"No. I don't want you to wake Emerald. She's an early riser. I'll be fine."

Billy walked to the head of Walter's cot and gazed at his friend's ashen face. Still gurgling as he breathed through his open mouth, Walter's eyes darted under his lids. Whatever Ashley had used to put him under didn't slow down his mind. He was likely fighting even now, probably skewering a few more of those Vacants.

Gripping Walter's shoulder, Billy whispered, "Get well soon, buddy. I need you at my side."

As he turned to leave, Ashley caught his pant leg. "Will you pray for Walter?"

"Sure. When I get back to the hut, I'll pray until I fall asleep."

"No. I mean now." Her brow arched up. "Please?"

"Uh, yeah, sure." Taking her by both hands, he lifted her to her feet. As they faced each other, she closed her eyes and tilted her head upward. Billy traced a tear stain from the point it exited her eye, through her cheek's contours, and down to her chin. This would be hard. Although he found praying easy and liberating, doing so out loud in a way that would comfort someone else seemed out of reach. But he had to give it a try, just pretend Ashley wasn't there and say what was on his mind.

Compressing her hands lightly, he spoke in a low tone. "Father, you know how much we both love Walter. He's such a good friend—brave, loyal, and always trying to make people smile. If he dies, we know he would go to a better place, but . . ." He paused. With his throat narrowing and his voice breaking up, this was getting even more difficult than he imagined.

Ashley's fingers tightened around his, and she broke in, her voice just as tremulous. "But we really need him here . . . so if you don't mind . . . please let him stay for a while, at least until . . ."

Her hands began to pull away, but Billy held them fast. It seemed that their physical connection helped her thoughts and feelings flow. Now the mind reader had become a mind writer. He knew exactly what she wanted to say.

"So please let him stay," Billy continued, "at least until we can tell him how much we love him."

As he opened his eyes, he let her hands slide away. After dabbing new tears with her shirt sleeve, she kissed him on the cheek and whispered, "Thank you."

On the way to the door, he picked up his cloak and slung it over his shoulder. Then, pulling the door open, he looked back. Ashley sat once again on the cot, her eyes wide and wet. He gave her a nod, hoping she could read the brotherly love pouring from his heart. "Good night, Ashley."

She replied in a weak voice. "Good night, Billy. I'm glad I can count on you."

Adding a wave as he kept an eye on Ashley, Billy called out, "Good night, Steadfast. Take good care of both of them."

Steadfast wiped his bloody hands on a rag and waved back. "I will. You can count on that."

After once more glancing at Ashley, Billy walked out and closed the door. Something was wrong. Ashley seemed to want something, but what? Could her ability to sense emotions also transmit messages somehow, or were they both so tired that every little twitch and change in body posture seemed to communicate more than it was meant to?

Now out in the cool breeze again, Billy pushed his arms through the cloak sleeves, fastened the collar clasp, and pulled up his hood. He looked toward the birthing garden. Now that it was likely well past midnight, his father would have relieved Thigocia and settled down for his turn as the birthing garden's watch dragon.

Billy strolled that way. Wearing a black cloak and hood, he probably looked like a ghostly shadow wandering through the midnight wind. It was a good thing the village folk slept deeply at these hours, even Cliffside, who normally guarded this field. With dragons taking over that duty, Elam put him on daytime woods patrol, a responsibility he relished. Actually marching out to possible battles definitely beat standing on the garden periphery night after night with nothing to do but whistle all-clear signals to his fellow guards.

While marching across the grassy meadow between the village and the garden, Billy caught sight of a pair of glowing dots, scarlet and pulsing—Clefspeare's eyes shining red. Even with the beams turned off, the fiery pupils were easy to see. "Dad," Billy called. "It's me."

"Yes, son," came a deep, rumbling voice. "I know, though your scent is not quite the same."

Billy brushed his hands together. "Probably Walter's blood. I was deep in it for a while."

"And how is our valiant soldier faring?"

With his snout now close, the dragon's breath caressed Billy's face with warmth. "Not great, but Ashley's taking good care of him. He—"

"Mercy!" The plaintive female voice came from the field's western border, close to the twin fir trees, Hilidan and Zera. "O virtuous dragon, I beg for mercy!"

Clefspeare's eyebeams flashed and locked on a feminine form staggering toward them with another figure, probably male, at her side. "Who goes there?" Clefspeare growled.

Now within three or four paces, the woman dropped to her knees, her hands clasped. "O mighty dragon, I beg you not to breathe on us with your punishing flames. Another dragon, Arramos by name, has hurled his fiery wrath at my son, and he would not survive another blow."

The man, still standing at her side, covered his face with his hands.

"Step out of the woman's shadow," Clefspeare ordered, "and show yourself."

Trembling, the man took a step and stopped again. With Pegasus as bright as ever, his details sharpened. Shorter than average and dressed in a typical villager's garb—cotton long-sleeved tunic and woolen trousers—he slowly lowered his hands from his face, revealing the telltale marks of recent burns.

Billy grimaced. With swollen cheeks, charred eyebrows and scalp, and practically no lips, this guy was a pitiful mess.

"Where did you see Arramos?" Clefspeare asked.

Rising to her full height, the woman stepped into the moon's glow. A lovely angular face and smooth complexion made her seem too young to have an adult son. Yet, with a hood covering her hair, any possible grayness stayed hidden. She pointed toward the western border. "We saw him out there, beyond that wall."

A growl rose from Clefspeare's gullet. "I sensed no danger."

"Great dragon, I know so little about your kind, so I do not know how your danger sense operates. How far does it extend? We were at least a thousand paces away, well into the prairie."

"I see." Clefspeare extended his neck, bringing his head close to the woman. She cringed but stayed still while he sniffed her face, then her hands. "I sense no danger from her, and her words carry the ring of truth. If Arramos has come to Second Eden and yet lurks nearby, our danger has increased a hundredfold."

The woman clasped her hands again. "Good dragon, do you have a doctor in this village? My son requires care."

"We have no doctor, but perhaps we can help." Clefspeare turned to Billy. "Has either Ashley or Steadfast cared for burn victims?"

"Not that I know of, but I'm sure they can do something. They have some pain relievers and an ointment that'll take down swelling."

The woman grasped Billy's hand and kissed it. "Thank you. Please lead us to these medicines. I have no money, but I will work for you."

"From what village do you hail?" Clefspeare asked. "And what is your name?"

"We come from a faraway land not yet known to these people." She swept back her hood, revealing shining hair that fell to her shoulders. "And my name is Semiramis."

CHAPTER 6

ELAM'S JOURNAL

Her right arm in a sling, Sapphira knelt and touched the floor of the tunnel with her free hand. She rubbed her finger along the cracked stone, squinting at the surface in the light of three lanterns carried by Bonnie, Rebekah, and Dallas.

Bonnie edged close and looked over Sapphira's shoulder, careful not to cast a shadow. What could she be looking for? While Gabriel and the others had gone on a journey outside to search for Yereq and the Foleys, Sapphira had said she would stay and set a trap for any future invaders. For some reason, she had chosen this spot, a point where the escape tunnel intersected at right angles with one of the main tunnels.

In one direction, this passage led to the living quarters, and in the other, it split into two wide corridors. Following the left passage would lead someone to the growth chamber section and another trio of tunnels, and wandering through the one on the right would surely get a person lost. It led into a honeycomb of narrow shafts that funneled into more rooms that Bonnie had not had time to explore.

On her one journey into that section, it had taken her three hours to find her way back. Probably only Sapphira could walk through that maze without losing her way. After so much time alone in these caves, she likely had the entire network mapped out in her mind.

Finally, Sapphira pointed at the floor. "There should be a cavity below us, and the rock layer here is no more than a foot thick all along this tunnel. That's why Morgan put the girls' living quarters that way." She pointed in the direction of the hovels. "The giants had no reason to go there, so there was no risk collapsing the floor."

"But hasn't Yereq been walking through here when he brings you supplies?" Dallas asked.

"He has. That's why this intersection might work for setting a trap." Sapphira again passed her hands along the floor surface. Her fingers rippled with tiny flames. "The cracks are bigger than before. It's almost exactly the same as the layer that covered the abyss Paili and I found thousands of years ago. It's fragile and close to breaking."

Bonnie joined Sapphira on her knees. The cracks, indeed, had widened since the first time she had noticed them, now a few millimeters across in some places. The light from Sapphira's hands plunged deeply into the fissures, like sunshine in a narrow canyon.

"So our plan," Sapphira continued, "is to break through the floor and cover the hole. I should be able to heat the rocks enough to loosen them, but we'll need something heavy to punch through. One of us could look for a shovel or a pick on the mining level, but they might be too brittle to use by now."

"Let's get the rope from the elevator shaft," Rebekah said, "and tie it to an anchor. Once you get it heated up, one of us could jump on the spot while hanging on to the rope."

Sapphira raised a finger. "One item I forgot to mention. The cavity leads straight to the magma river. If you can't hang on to the rope, you're done for."

"Then can you just heat it up slowly?" Bonnie asked. "To test how weak it gets?"

"I suppose so. If it starts collapsing, I can probably get away in time."

Bonnie stripped off her backpack, releasing her wings. "I'll hold on to you just in case."

Pressing a palm on the floor, Sapphira took in a deep breath. "Stand clear."

As Rebekah and Dallas backed away, Bonnie stayed close and clutched Sapphira's shirt. The Oracle's hand suddenly blazed. As fire shot out from under her palm, redness crawled along the floor, as if blood were seeping from wounds in Sapphira's hand.

Soon, the heated area spread out in a three-foot-wide circle, orange at the perimeter and red changing to white closer to her hands. When the widening arc reached Sapphira's denim-covered knees, she scooted back to avoid the superheated stone.

A cracking noise blended in with a chorus of hisses and sizzles, sounding like a bonfire fueled by green wood. Sapphira lifted her hand and slid back farther. "I think it's pretty weak now."

Rebekah pushed a flat rock with her foot and slid it past the perimeter of heated stone. "Try hitting it with this."

Still holding Sapphira, Bonnie pushed the rock over the hottest spot, then, unfurling her wings, she stepped on it, careful to keep most of her weight on her other foot. More cracks sounded, but the floor didn't give way. How much pressure could she add? Of course she could jump back in time, even fly if she had to, but should she risk it? Probably not. It wasn't worth it to—

Suddenly, the entire tunnel shook. Unable to brace herself, Sapphira toppled forward and smacked her head against the floor. The weakened stone collapsed, swallowing Bonnie and Sapphira.

As they slid into the hole, Bonnie lurched forward and wrapped her arms around Sapphira's waist. Now falling freely in a cavernous chamber, she unfurled her wings and flapped, slowing their plunge.

Shouts sounded from above. "Are you all right? Can you fly back up here?"

Bonnie couldn't answer. Not yet. Her wings billowing with warm, rising air, she had to orient herself and figure out which way was up. Flying in a slowly ascending circle, she found the hole above. Rebekah and Dallas crouched at the edge, looking down.

"I'm all right," Bonnie grunted.

Gasping for breath, Sapphira managed, "I'm all right, too."

Rebekah reached down. "Can you get her up here? Dallas and I can catch her."

"I can't hover," Bonnie said. "But I'll see what I can do. Get ready."

While Rebekah and Dallas looked down from the hole in the flat ceiling, Bonnie flew in a wider circle, dipped for a moment, and then zoomed up, flapping madly as she boosted Sapphira toward four outstretched hands.

Rebekah latched on to the wrist of Sapphira's good arm. Bonnie's momentum drove her into the ceiling, smacking her head. Dazed, she fell again, but managed to twist her body back into flying position. Again riding the drafts, she looked up at the hole. While Rebekah pulled Sapphira's arm, Dallas grabbed the back of Sapphira's jeans and hoisted her the rest of the way.

Rebekah reached down again. "You're next."

Rubbing her head, Bonnie eased higher. Her wings brushed against the ceiling, and she passed just out of reach of Rebekah's hands. As she circled again, Sapphira shouted from the hole. "You could land on the chasm floor next to the magma river and then hike to the overlook back where we met Gabriel. From there, flying up with the rising air shouldn't be too hard."

"I'll give it a try," Bonnie said.

Sapphira pointed. "When you get to the bottom, make sure you walk in that direction. It'll be hot, but there should be room on the chasm floor to stay clear of the river."

"Got it."

Letting herself fall into a circling dive, she surveyed the chamber. At least twice as big as the springs room, the gap between the bare rock walls narrowed at the lower levels and converged into a fissure about six feet across.

Bonnie aimed for the crack and pulled in her wings. She plunged through, tears streaming as hot dry air whipped across her face. Once she came out into the open, the gap widened again, revealing the chasm and channel she had seen from the precipice, though at a different point on the river.

After orienting herself again, she flapped her wings and headed in the direction Sapphira had told her, flying well above the churning magma. She grimaced at the blistering heat. Why not just fly all the way to the ledge? It would be better than walking. No use getting too close to the river.

The channel, now about fifty feet from one wall to the other, veered to the right, then back to the left, narrowing as it continued. Soon, Bonnie approached a place where the walls jutted out, creating a pinching point, too narrow to fly through, though near the ground it widened, providing plenty of space for walking.

This had to be the reason Sapphira suggested going on foot. Maybe with her enhanced vision she had seen this tight passage from her vantage point on the ledge. If so, maybe the destination would soon be in sight.

As she descended, Bonnie winced at the scalding heat. There was no way she could land without getting cooked.

She angled back up and made a slow circle. When Sapphira walked down there, back when the river acted as a portal to another world, the floor level wasn't as hot. In her hurry, she likely hadn't thought about that.

Bonnie looked up. The tight fissure she had dropped through loomed above, much too narrow for a return flight. Somehow she would have to build a lot of speed, shoot the channel's gap with her wings folded, and catch an updraft before crashing into the river.

After flying up to the narrow gap in the ceiling, she angled her body toward a spot in the fissure about halfway between the ceiling and the river. Then, half falling and half gliding, she zoomed toward it.

Again searing heat stung her eyes and instantly dried the sweat dripping from her pores. The gap between the protruding walls drew closer and closer, apparently deeper from the fissure's front entry to its rear exit than she had thought. When she pulled in her wings, would her momentum get her through before she dropped too far? Maybe, maybe not. But there seemed to be no other choice. She had to go for it or be stuck there flying in circles forever.

Just before slicing through, she jerked in her wings, leaving them out enough to catch a little bit of updraft. Now plunging at a sharp angle, the tips of her wings scraped the side walls. The air grew hotter. The magma drew closer, singeing, scorching, blistering.

As her lips cracked, Bonnie screamed, "Help me!"

With one mighty flap, she shot through the fissure's exit, then expanded her canopy. Beating her wings furiously, she fought the dive. Pain roared through her mainstays. Heat seared the membranes. She felt like she was on fire.

After swooping within five feet of the river, she leveled out and began a slow climb, too slow to keep the heat from baking her skin. The magma boiled and popped below. A droplet splashed on her sleeve, instantly setting it on fire.

Crying out, she flailed her arms and beat out the flame. Her wings now scraped and weary, and her body dehydrated and half-cooked, it was all she could do to ascend even a few feet. Soon, however, she rose above the danger point, out of reach of the bubbling soup. Now it was time to look for the ledges leading to the tunnels. Either side would do.

Still flapping with all her might, Bonnie looked up. There, maybe a hundred feet ahead, both ledges jutted out into the chasm. She aimed for the one on her right, the ledge leading to the brick kiln room. It looked slightly lower and closer.

She summoned a burst of energy, flapped her wings, and shot upward. The rising air buoyed her effort, but a swirling air current swept her to the side and slammed her against the wall.

Fluttering her wings to stay in place, she clawed at the wall until she caught hold of a rocky lip. She pushed the toes of her shoes against the slick face, but they slipped, unable to find solid footing. Something hurt down there, something hot.

Twisting her neck, she looked down. Her pant leg smoldered at the cuff, stinging her ankle. Would a blaze spring up? Hanging on with all her might, she slowed her wings, not wanting to fan the flame.

She rubbed her sweaty face against her upper sleeve. Now what? Push off and try to fly again? That might work, but another slap against the wall could knock her out. Then she'd be nothing more than a quick flash of fire and a puff of smoke.

She looked up. Fifty feet to climb with no other protrusions to grab. It was impossible.

Licking her dry lips with a dry tongue, she set her feet against the wall and—

"Bonnie! Catch this!"

A rope fell across her shoulder. Grabbing it, she looked up again. Rebekah stood at the ledge holding the other end.

"I've got you," Rebekah shouted. "Use your wings to help."

Pressing her feet against the stone, Bonnie spread out her wings, flapped slowly against the rising air, and scrambled up the wall. When she crested the ledge, she fell forward to her knees and slapped her palms on the ground, panting.

Rebekah patted her on the back. "You look like you had a rough ride."

"I did." Bonnie flopped backwards to her seat and batted at her pant leg to snuff the sparks. "Let's not try that again."

"We don't have to. The hole you made is perfect. Sapphira's working on covering it up." She waved across the expanse and called, "I've got her, Dallas. We'll meet up top."

Bonnie looked that way. Barely visible as she stood on the opposite ledge, Dallas waved in return and disappeared in the shadows.

"So," Rebekah said as she wound the rope into a coil, "it looks like you should visit Dr. Saunders."

"Probably." Bonnie smacked her dry lips. "I need some water before we do anything."

Rebekah hoisted the rope coil over her shoulder, rings of perspiration dampening her shirt at the underarms and chest. "We'll have to wait for Dallas to drop us a line. We brought the only ropes, so she and Sapphira will have to figure out how to fish it up to the top level first."

Heaving a sigh, Bonnie climbed to her feet. Her mouth and throat were so parched, she had to drink something soon. Her sweat had dried, and no more emerged in spite of the heat.

When they entered the low tunnel, Rebekah picked up a dim lantern and led the way. Feeling dizzy now, Bonnie spoke, hoping to shake away the daze and forget about her terrible thirst. "Did you find out what made the tunnel shake?"

Rebekah slowed to let her catch up. "No. We didn't have anyone available to go up top to find out."

"So is Sapphira alone?"

"Until Dallas gets back, yes. But I don't think we have to worry about her. She should be registered as a lethal weapon."

Bonnie stayed quiet. Even with Rebekah's reassurances, thinking about Sapphira up there alone felt awful. Getting shot made her seem so much more fragile, and her loss of blood had weakened her quite a bit.

When they arrived at the kiln room, Rebekah headed straight for the other exit tunnel and stopped at its opening. "You look like you're ready to drop."

Bonnie blew out a tired breath. "I can make it."

"Rest here for a while." Rebekah pointed at a raised part of the floor. "Have a seat, and I'll check on the elevator shaft and come back for you when Dallas drops the rope."

"Great. Thanks."

Rebekah picked up a dark lantern next to the door, lit its wick using hers, and left it at Bonnie's side.

Lowering herself while stretching her pain-filled wings, Bonnie sat on the foot-high step and tried to swallow, but with her throat so dry, the motion felt like shoving down desert sand. Her head swam, as if an ocean's surf ebbed and flowed from one side of her head to the other. If she didn't get something to drink soon, she'd pass out for sure.

She leaned over and rested her head on the step, bracing herself with her hand, her fingers overlapping the edge. As she gripped it, something moved underneath her fingertips. She peered under the ledge and looked at the face of the step. A loose section of stone had shifted, revealing a hollow space behind it.

What could it be? With her vision blurred and swirling, everything seemed like part of a dream—hazy, out of reach, incomprehensible. It was probably broken by centuries of natural crumbling, but, even in her foggy vision, the dividing line between the movable stone and the surrounding fascia seemed distinct, not a random crack.

Pushing in one side of the section, she opened it further. Something lay inside. A book? She reached in and withdrew a small volume, about the size of a diary, but another object lay in there as well. Reaching farther, she grasped a glass vial, small enough to enclose in her hand. A handwritten label wrapped around its middle, bearing an odd script.

ὃς δ᾽ ἂν πίῃ ἐκ τοῦ ὕδατος οὗ ἐγὼ δώσω αὐτῷ, οὐ μὴ διψήσει εἰς τὸν αἰῶνα.

She peered into the bottle. Sealed with a corklike stopper, it seemed about a third full of liquid of some kind, transparent and more viscous than water.

She tried to swallow once more. Just looking at liquid made her throat ache more than ever. Feeling dizzy again, she turned her attention to the book, hoping to distract herself. She opened the cover, feeling its supple leather and the rough twine that tied the pages together at its spine. It had to have been put there recently, certainly not millennia ago when Elam lived here. It would have rotted by now. Still, maybe Hades made things age differently. Who but Elam could have stored a book in a room that had been abandoned for so long?

She studied the first page. It held more strange letters, yet they differed from those on the bottle. She thumbed through the pages and stopped at the last one. What was this? English words?

Drawing the book closer, she read the text.

I believe my time here is short, so short that I wonder if I will have opportunity to finish this entry and bind it with the others. And I wonder if it matters at all. If I make a hurried escape or am dragged to a death sentence, who will ever read this missive, this journal of tortured body and tortured thoughts? Only God knows.

Because of my refusal to betray Mara, Morgan is losing her patience with me. I think she is likely to kill me, but she is a hard one to predict. Yet, no matter what tortures she brings to bear, no matter how much flesh she rips from my back, I will never, never betray my beloved Mara. She who brought food to my starving body, carried in the most precious of vessels, I could never betray, nor even entertain an unkind thought. Once a lump of coal, she is now a gem. The pressures of her slavish strife have fashioned a polished diamond—pure, strong, and of infinite value.

Friend, I hope you are able to read my hastily scrawled letters. It is a strange occurrence that as I rub the juice of the fruit of the Tree of Life on its pages, hoping its properties will preserve it for whoever finds it as an antiquity, the words transform into odd characters that I cannot fathom. Is it a miracle? Perhaps. I can only hope that God will use it for good and carry my thoughts of love to a generation that needs them, for although my story is one of heartbreak and pain, a glimmer of light persists. My faith in God has never died. No matter what happens to me, I know that one day I will stand unashamed in his presence, and I hope that my beloved will stand with me.

Until that day, the fetters I bear are but a passing annoyance, for I know that the coming Messiah will deliver me from the chains of this realm and take me to a higher plane. Yet, I look forward to giving my body and soul to Mara in the bonds of marriage, the shackles of unconditional love, and in breathing this prayer, I am content to let God's will be done.

Bonnie rubbed her eyes, but in her dehydrated state, no tears flowed. These words of Elam's were so beautiful, so full of faith! What a treasure of a man he must be—another diamond forged by the trials and tribulations of never-ending hardships.

She closed the journal and hugged it to her chest. Obviously Elam meant for this to be read by anyone, so she could show it to Sapphira. She would be able to read any of the languages.

Looking at the vial of liquid again, Bonnie imagined Elam pouring out drops and rubbing them over the pages. At first it seemed so strange, but was it really? The same fruit that kept him and Sapphira alive and young for centuries might also maintain parchment, but how could it translate written words into a more modern language? A miracle? Why not? Wasn't it already a miracle that fruit from the Tree of Life could keep the book intact? And weren't words associated with eternal life? Didn't Jesus say, "The words that I speak unto you, they are spirit, and they are life"?

With her throat again aching, Bonnie eyed the liquid. Was she allowed to drink it? Why not? There was nothing saying she shouldn't. She picked at the label, a thin strip of parchment. Might this text be a warning of some kind?

She pulled out the stopper, poured a drop on her fingertip, and smeared it across the label, making sure to cover the entire text. Within seconds, the words transformed into:

But whosoever drinketh of the water that I shall give him shall never thirst.

Bonnie tried to swallow, but the grit in her throat wouldn't let the muscles finish the motion. The liquid in her grasp would soothe her aching throat and end her torture. But was she allowed to take it? Did finding this vial mean that God would allow her eternal life on earth?

As she continued staring at the liquid, so clear, so desirable, an image appeared in her mind, the first circle of Hades where she argued with the dragon. He had tempted her to look into a pond to see the scales she had felt on her face. The temptation to acquiesce was so strong! While she fought the urge, it felt like snakes were biting her. Yet, that time, she had received a solemn warning not to look into any mirrors, so giving in wasn't a real option. As a child of God, she had to obey her one and only master.

But what about this time? There had been no command not to drink the liquid. This water of life would not only soothe the pain that was every bit as bad as the striking serpents, it would also likely give her long life and maybe even . . .

Healing? She looked at a burn on her hand where a splash of magma had taken a bite out of her flesh. Raw and swelling, it hurt like crazy, but still nothing like the desperate thirst that ravaged her entire body.

Again applying a single drop to her finger, she swabbed her burn. It stung at first, but within seconds, the welt shrank and disappeared. The patch of skin, now smooth and pink, looked healthier and younger than the surrounding area.

Bonnie held the vial in her open palm and stared at this priceless treasure. There was no longer any doubt. She knew what to do. Standing up, she put the stopper back in the bottle and slid it into her pocket. She would give it to Sapphira and heal her shoulder.

CHAPTER 7

VISITORS

"Semiramis," Clefspeare said. "The name is familiar to me, but I cannot place it."

She lowered herself to her knees again. "I have nothing to hide, great dragon, and I will tell you my story, but I beg you to let us be on our way to any medical aid you can supply. My son is in great need."

Billy looked at his father, waiting for a signal. With all those burn wounds, this poor guy needed help, and fast, but he wasn't about to offer help before the two newcomers passed his father's scrutiny.

Clefspeare nodded. "Son, take them to triage. When both have had sufficient rest, I want to talk to them further."

"Yes, sir." Billy grasped the man's arm. "Do you need support?"

"I would be glad of it, young man."

His voice seemed raspy, like shoes dragging across sandpaper. Billy pushed his shoulder under the man's arm and helped him walk. "I'm Billy Bannister. What's your name?"

"Hunter. My companion believes I am a hunter, but I have yet to prove it."

Out of the corner of his eye, Billy caught a glimpse of Hunter's companion floating near his neck. It was slightly bigger than most, and a bluish light shone from within, making its egg shape clear.

Semiramis helped from the other side. "Let us hurry, Master Billy. I fear that infection might soon set in."

When they arrived at Abraham's hut, Billy pushed the door open and peered inside. Ashley lay sleeping on her cot next to Walter's, which had been lowered to a normal level. Steadfast sat on a short bench with the blood pressure sleeve hanging over one of his slumped shoulders.

"We have a new patient," Billy said, keeping his voice low.

Steadfast jumped up and hurried toward them. "A burn victim?"

"A wicked dragon spewed his hellish fire," Semiramis said. "When my son is well, he will hunt that beast and fulfill his destiny."

Steadfast helped Hunter lie down on a cot and knelt at his side. "Billy," Steadfast said, pointing at the equipment table, "please fetch that lantern. It is my brightest one. And the jar of salve. It should be labeled, 'Healing Ointment.'"

"Will do." Billy grabbed the lantern and jar and brought them back. "Can you help him?"

"Help? Yes." Steadfast pried a rubber lid from the jar. "Heal? I have my doubts."

While Semiramis eyed him carefully, Steadfast dipped his finger into the jar and smeared yellow ointment on Hunter's cheek.

Hunter cringed but didn't cry out. Still, his entire body trembled.

Steadfast dipped into the jar again. "He reacts with pain. Shall I continue?"

"My son is brave," Semiramis said. "Do not spare the healing ointment."

Steadfast applied the salve and rubbed it in from Hunter's scalp to just below his charred lips. With every push on his skin, Hunter jerked but stayed silent.

As he put the lid back on, Steadfast looked at Semiramis. "I can give him something to help him sleep."

"Yes," she said, nodding. "I think that would be best."

Steadfast pointed. "Billy, there is a clear crystal vial near the back of the table."

"Got it." Billy retrieved a tiny oval bottle with a flat bottom. Inside, the medicine was so clear, it seemed invisible.

Steadfast pulled out a stopper and poured a drop into Hunter's mouth. Within seconds, his trembling stopped, and his breathing grew heavy and easy. "Now," Steadfast said as he handed the bottle back to Billy, "we can talk about his condition."

"Good doctor," Semiramis said, laying a hand on his arm, "do me the kindness of a blunt word. It is not a service to tell me less than all you know."

"First, my good lady, I am not a doctor, so blunt or not, my word may well be little more than the chittering of a monkey. Yet, I will give you my opinion. His burns are not life-threatening, but they are irreversible. He will wear his scars for the rest of his days."

"I see." She drew her hand back. "With all these fine potions and ointments, surely there is someone in this village who possesses more medical knowledge."

"We had a doctor with considerable skill, but she is no longer here." He nodded at Ashley, still sound asleep on her cot. "I have, however, extraordinary counterparts, this young lady as well as my Eve. We also have a man named Patrick and his wife, Ruth. Patrick has no formal medical training, but he is quite adept at first aid, while Ruth was once a nurse."

Semiramis looked at Ashley, her eyes widening. "Oh!" She quickly covered her mouth.

"Do you know Ashley?" Billy asked.

Lowering her hand, she nodded. "In the land where I live, I was the guardian of Zeno's Chasm. I saw her there."

Billy searched for her companion but found none. "The land where you live? You mean, you're not from Second Eden?"

"No, but my son is."

"Then how did you—"

"Oh, Master Billy, that is a long story, and I will gladly tell you when I am summoned again to the good dragon outside, but since I fear what Ashley will tell you when she wakes, I will give you a summary. You see, I was in service to the dragon who burned my son's face. The wretched lizard betrayed us, curse his name, and banished me to this world. But while in his service, I tried to prevent Ashley and her company from crossing a most dangerous bridge. Not only did I fear for their lives, I knew the dragon Arramos would surely destroy them for making the attempt. He sent giants to shake them from the bridge, and I was powerless to stop them. My fear is that Ashley will think I was in league with those giants and claim that I am your enemy."

"Maybe not," Billy said. "It's tough to fool her."

"Yes, I knew right away that she has a gifted mind, but as I watched those giants deal so treacherously with her and her friends, I sensed an intense anger . . . a righteous anger, mind you, but truly intense."

"Well, don't worry too much. I'll talk with her. She can't deny the evidence. I mean, it's obvious Hunter's no friend of Arramos."

"Very true, Master Billy." Semiramis stifled a yawn. "I apologize. Ours has been a very long journey."

Billy looked at Steadfast. "Any vacancies in the village?"

"Since Ashley is here, her bed at Emerald's home is likely empty. We can find a more permanent option when daylight comes."

"I'll escort her." Billy took off his cloak and offered it to Semiramis. "Ready?"

"Ah!" Semiramis said, taking the cloak. "This village is populated by gentlemen."

As Billy guided her along the dark street, Semiramis said nothing. She just sighed now and then as she glanced at the moon. After waking Emerald and her father and making the bedding arrangements, Billy turned to go.

Semiramis caught his sleeve. "Wait."

He spun back. "Yes?"

"Your cloak." She let it slide off her sleeves and then slowly down her body. "The night is long and cold."

"Thanks," he said, reaching for the cloak. "You're right."

As she released it, she let her fingers glide along his forearm. "And I take it that you have no Eve to keep you warm?"

His cheeks heating up, Billy drew back and shook his head. "It'll be a while before I'm ready for that."

"I see." Semiramis bowed her head. "Good night, Master Billy." With that, she closed the door.

A shiver ran up and down his spine. Was it really that cold? Or was Semiramis's manner just a bit too friendly? The females of Second Eden had been more affectionate than those at home, apparently innocently oblivious to how a lingering touch might affect most males of the species, at least those from Earth. And Semiramis's touch seemed more powerful than most—electric, sensual, something that aroused his sense of wariness.

He pushed his arms through the cloak sleeves, raised the hood over his windblown hair, and hurried toward Elam's home. With only a few hours till daylight, there wasn't much time to sleep. Not only did he have to get up early to take Acacia to Mount Elijah, Elam would want to know all the details about the newcomers, Semiramis and Hunter.

Now exhausted, Billy shuffled to the door and eased it open. Inside the one-room hut, Elam lay sleeping on a straw-stuffed mattress near the left wall. After slipping off his shoes and cloak, Billy tiptoed to a mattress on the opposite wall, watching for any sign of Elam awakening. With darkness covering Billy's movements, Elam would likely sleep on. The warrior chief had worked on training the troops with Sir Barlow all day, and the exercises he had put himself and the others through were often brutal.

Billy and Walter had joined the regimen during the past four weeks and collected blisters and calluses on hands and feet. But it wasn't all bad. The expanding pectorals and bulging biceps, as well as their newfound quickness and agility, made it all worth it.

As Billy lay down, he let out a quiet sigh. Every muscle seemed to sigh with him, as if deflating after another grueling day. Even his brain seemed to leak, too tired to spark anything more than the simplest thoughts. There was so little time now for reflection and prayer. If only—

"Billy?"

He turned toward Elam. With the door closed, darkness shrouded the gap between them. "Yes. I'm here."

"You're back so late. Is everything all right?"

Billy imagined Elam's form, perhaps propped on an elbow. "Well . . . no. But it's all under control."

"What happened on Mount Elijah? Did you find Vacants?"

"A few. Walter and the dragons and I cleared them out. I'll tell you about it in the morning."

"Sounds good. Thanks."

Billy settled again and stared into the darkness, listening to the marsh peepers raising a racket from a nearby pond. *Sounds good,* Elam had said. But was it good? Not really. With Walter hurt so badly and a pair of strangers in town, everything felt as dark as the room, heavy somehow, stifling. Something was definitely wrong, but what? The feeling wasn't exactly like danger sensing, more like an uneasiness in the pit of his stomach. Could it be from the hideous burns on Hunter's face? Semiramis's electric touch? The sight of Walter's blood spewing from his sliced-open body?

As Elam turned, crackling the straw in his bed, Billy looked his way. The warrior chief seemed restless. No wonder. With so many pressures on his shoulders, anybody would lose sleep. But this guy, the grandson of Noah himself, surely had more wisdom than anyone else around, so he probably felt the uneasiness in the air.

Billy closed his eyes and let the weariness take control. The dawning of a new day would likely bring answers to his questions, for good or for evil.

* * *

With Rebekah supporting one side and Dallas the other, Bonnie staggered into the springs chamber. Water splashed and licked at the stones as it rushed downward, but the sound was pure torture. Relief lay close by, but not close enough. Her feet dragged, as if slogging through sticky clay.

Finally, the two women lowered her to her knees near one of the cooler pools. Bonnie set down Elam's journal, dipped her hands into the shallow rock basin, and splashed her face. Then, taking another double scoop, slurped the water as fast as her swollen tongue would allow.

Ah! It was so good! How could sulfur-tinged water carry such a rich and delicious flavor? It was heavenly!

As she continued to drink deeply and wash her parched skin, a whispered conversation drifted past her ears.

"Oh, thank God Bonnie's okay."

That was Sapphira's voice. She seemed shaky, upset about something. Bonnie slowed her drinking and glanced their way.

"Did you learn the reason for the tremor?" Rebekah asked.

Sapphira, now dirty from head to toe, braced herself on Rebekah's elbow. "Our exit tunnel caved in even more, so I think the collapse caused the shake. Nobody was around, so I don't know if the others got buried or if they're safe on the other side. I tried digging through, but the rocks are way too heavy."

"Especially with one shoulder out of commission," Dallas said.

Tucking the journal under her arm, Bonnie rose to her feet and pulled the vial from her pocket. "Put this on your wound."

Sapphira took the vial and lifted it close to her eyes. As a rippling fire spread across her fingers, the liquid inside seemed to carry a phosphorescent glow. "What is it?"

"Juice from the fruit of the Tree of Life. It has healing properties. I put a little on one of my burns, and it disappeared."

Sapphira pulled the stopper from the top. "Where did you find it?"

"Hidden in the brick kiln room." Bonnie showed her the journal. "It was next to this. I couldn't read much of it, only the last page, but I'm sure it's Elam's."

"Elam's?" Her hands now jittery, Sapphira gave Rebekah the vial. "Would you apply it, please?"

Rebekah slid Sapphira's shirt down her shoulder and began stripping off the blood-soaked bandage. "This will probably hurt."

"It's worth it." Wincing, Sapphira took the journal and opened it to the first page. "It's written in Hebrew."

As her eyes moved back and forth across the text, her lips quivered, and her voice trembled. "It's Elam's journal. He . . . he's writing about how he feels after meeting me through the hole in the wall. Before that, he never had a reason to write, because every day was the same, just one day after another of baking bricks, getting whipped by Nabal, and searching for food until he fell asleep on the floor. But now that he met me . . ." Sapphira choked on her words. "He has a reason to live . . . and he wants to leave a lasting record of his love for me . . . and the secrets he learned that he wasn't allowed to reveal until someone discovered this journal."

"Secrets?" Bonnie asked.

Sapphira nodded. "I suppose I'll have to read it one page at a time to find out what he—"

Rebekah made a shushing sound. "Now hold still for a second. I'm going to pour this directly over the stitches."

"Shouldn't you take them out first?" Bonnie asked.

"And open the wound?" Rebekah's brow furrowed. "I should say not. Her bleeding would be profuse."

Bonnie touched a hanging strand from one of the stitches. "Wouldn't it be easier to pull them now than later when her skin is healed?"

"Hmmm. . . ." Rebekah said. "I see your point."

"Our first-aid kit is still on that rock." Sapphira pointed at a large, flat stone near one of the bathing pools.

Dallas hurried to the rock. "I'll get it."

Soon, Rebekah began cutting and pulling out the stitches, applying a little of the juice after each one. "This is working splendidly. Blood pours out. I sprinkle a few drops. The cut seals."

"Thank you." Sapphira read the journal, cringing at every cut and pull.

Bonnie looked over her other shoulder and scanned the ancient text. Some of the words had been set in stanzas as if arrayed in poetic lines.

"This makes sense," Sapphira said, running a finger from right to left on a line. "Elam says he's going to rearrange the pages. Hebrew works start at the back and go to the front, but he received a prophecy that told him to start at the front for future readers."

"Elam received prophecies?" Bonnie asked.

Sapphira nodded. "Enoch once told Elam that he was a prophetic heir, sort of like the way Elisha took Elijah's mantle and became a powerful prophet."

"Are any of the prophecies written in the journal?"

Sapphira pointed at the page again. "This might be one. It's a poem, so if I translate it, it will lose its rhyme and meter."

"I still remember Hebrew," Rebekah said, "but no use wasting time reading it in both languages."

Sapphira pressed her finger on the page and moved it along each line, pausing between them as she translated. "Elam says there's a dark world . . . a realm below all others . . . reserved for neither good nor evil . . . a valley of dead souls who cannot ascend to Paradise . . . or descend into the Lake of Fire . . . because they yet have a purpose in the land of the living . . . to escape this valley, they must be called by name . . . into the world in which their purpose is to be fulfilled. . . . A day will come when a king will plunge into that valley . . . and wait for his resurrection call . . . but it can come only when precious blood is freely given . . . by one who is as white as snow. . . . Two maids will offer their blood . . . one to make a warrior invincible . . . and one to resurrect a king."

Sapphira lifted her finger from the page and looked at the others. "And there is a way to enter that realm from the magma river view."

"Well, my dear," Rebekah said. "Your skin is as soft as a baby's backside."

Sapphira rotated her shoulder. "It feels perfect."

Rebekah slid Sapphira's shirt back in place. "I saved a few drops for

Bonnie's burns and scrapes, and then we should see if the four of us can clear a path to the outside."

"And then . . ." Sapphira closed the book and rubbed the cover lovingly. "Maybe we can see if there's a king in that valley of souls."

* * *

Marilyn jogged across the grass. The edge of a deep pit was now in sight. After flying with Shelly on a commercial airline to Kalispell, she borrowed a small private plane from a friend of Jared's and flew it to the hilltop where Ashley's home once stood. With the bad weather and such a small ground strip, the landing had been rather harrowing, so feeling solid earth beneath her feet boosted her energy.

She stopped at the edge of the pit and looked down. High winds whipped her hair, and the depth made her head swim. Thousands of feet below, people moved, looking more like animated toys than real humans. She checked the pistol in her shoulder holster. It was firmly in place.

She pulled a phone from her pocket and read the signal meter. Nothing. Not a surprise, though. The static-filled call from Yereq had let her know that mobile phone service was lousy in this area and probably even worse at the bottom of the pit.

"So," she murmured, "we'll execute plan B."

She withdrew a makeup compact from her jacket, opened it, and searched for sunlight. With clouds racing overhead, the sun peeked out intermittently, providing a bright ray for only a second or two at a time. She angled the mirror and caught the sun in the reflection. A shaky circle of light danced on the grass. As she turned the mirror, the circle dove into the pit and instantly reappeared on the floor.

Another cloud blocked the sun. The circle vanished. Marilyn tapped her foot, keeping the mirror at the same angle as she waited. Soon, the sun flashed another beam. She guided the light toward the people and waved it across them, but it lasted for only a moment. Again the sun hid behind a cloud, this one larger and denser. There would be no more rays for a while.

A flicker of light caught her eye. She looked at the people below, all now standing still. The light flashed again. They had seen her.

Waving both arms, she shouted, "It's Marilyn! I need transport!"

She lowered her arms. Of course, her voice might not have carried that far, but the signal proved that they likely knew who she was. Gabriel would probably fly up, but with thousands of feet to ascend, it might take a while.

Hugging her jacket close, she looked toward Kalispell and replayed Shelly's recent phone call. Shelly had rushed to the hospital in a taxi, and Marilyn was getting the smaller plane ready for takeoff when Shelly's call came in.

* * *

"Dad's in critical condition. He took bullets in his chest and back, and he lost quite a bit of blood."

"Is he going to be all right?" Marilyn asked.

"The doctor thinks so. I donated blood, and so did Mom. We're all the same type."

"Then your mother must have recovered."

"She woke up when Yereq carried her out of the pit. Then he went back and hauled Dad out. That's when Dad lost a lot of blood. It's not an easy climb."

"I can imagine."

"Then he carried Dad to the highway, and Mom waved down a guy driving a flatbed truck. When he saw a ten-foot-tall man carrying a bloodied body, he wasn't exactly keen on giving them a lift, but Mom talked him into letting them all ride in the back."

"It's a good thing she was there."

"You bet. And Yereq, too. If not for him, Dad would be dead for sure. He's not out of the woods, and he's still unconscious, but his vitals are pretty strong. By the way, Yereq's probably already back at the pit. He was pretty anxious to return and protect Sapphira."

* * *

Marilyn touched her cell phone, now in her jeans pocket. If only she could call for an update. Shelly had sounded fairly confident, but a hint of worry darkened her voice.

Soon, Gabriel came into sight, his wings beating against the fierce wind. After a few more minutes, he rose above the rim, and with a final surge, he landed next to Marilyn.

"Whew!" He laid a hand on the back of his head. "That knock on the noggin I took is still throbbing."

Marilyn touched his hand. "Are you sure you can carry me down?"

"Yeah." He brushed dirt from his jeans and long-sleeved T-shirt. "You're a pilot, so you won't puke if it gets bumpy, right?"

Lifting her arms, she laughed. "Let's go, flyboy. Don't spare the speed."

"You asked for it." Standing behind her, Gabriel slid his arms around her waist and leaped into the hole. As they dropped, Marilyn's stomach pushed into her throat, taking her breath away. The wall of rock zoomed upward, and the floor rushed toward her so fast, the objects below blurred.

Soon, Gabriel unfurled his wings, slowing the plunge. His hands pushed into Marilyn's abdomen and squeezed out her last gulp of air. As he glided to the ground, the pressure eased, allowing her to take in a breath as well as the sight below. Several women stood with hands on hips peering into a hole in the wall, some dressed in jeans and others in long skirts, all covered with dirt.

Gabriel landed in a trot, releasing Marilyn as he slowed. "Is Yereq ready?" he asked.

"Almost," one of the women said. "It's the last of the dynamite, so he's making sure it's placed perfectly."

As the woman pushed back her tangled hair, Marilyn recognized her smudged face—Dorian, once called Yellinia. These former dragons had all gathered in Castlewood before traveling to Montana and had spent enough time in Marilyn's home for everyone to become acquainted.

Marilyn quickly scanned the others—Elise, Kaylee, Jordan, and Tamara. "I take it Rebekah and Dallas are still inside with Bonnie and Sapphira," she said.

Gabriel nodded. "It looks like the collapse was pretty massive, so we might not be able to blast through it, but Yereq says he'll dig it out eventually. We're just trying to give him a head start."

"What is that?" Dorian asked, pointing toward the sky.

Marilyn looked up. A gleam reflected one of the sun's passing rays, blinding her for a moment, but when another cloud blocked the light, the object became clear—a helicopter.

"Chopper," Gabriel said. "And it's heading this way."

"Shall I find Yereq?" Tamara asked as she leaned toward the tunnel entrance.

Dorian touched Tamara's hand. "Call his name as you feel your way along the wall and watch for his lantern."

Tamara nodded, ducked under the low arch, and disappeared.

As the helicopter, a large transport unit, descended, Gabriel waved toward the tunnel. "Take cover in the dark. Out in the open, we're fish in a barrel."

The other four dragon women skulked into the cave while Marilyn stayed at Gabriel's side. "I'm packing a Glock inside my jacket," she said.

Gabriel stared at the chopper. "How many rounds?"

"If that helicopter's full of bad guys, not enough."

"Got a plan of action?"

Marilyn touched one of Gabriel's wings. "I think you'd better stay out of sight and be ready to fly out of here with one of the women."

"But I should stay and—"

"What are you going to do, slap them with your wings?" She gripped his taut bicep. "Save the heroism for the escape flight."

Folding his wings tightly, Gabriel backed toward the tunnel. "I'll watch. If you get in trouble, I'm flying you outta here first. Yereq can protect the others."

As he faded in the tunnel's darkness, the helicopter settled to the ground, raising a cloud of sand. A muscular man stepped out from the pilot's seat, and a tall sinewy woman emerged from the back passenger door, both dressed in army camouflage, complete with high boots and caps that shadowed their eyes. Each carried an automatic rifle tucked under an arm.

Marilyn patted the outside of her jacket and felt the shape of her weapon. With that kind of firepower approaching, her pistol seemed no more than a toy.

The man stopped within ten paces of Marilyn, set his feet, and spoke in a commanding tone. "If you surrender peacefully, no one will get hurt. Tell your company to come out of the cave and file quietly to the helicopter."

Shouting over the din of the beating chopper blades, the woman waved at someone inside the passenger compartment. "Get out before I use you for target practice!"

A hairy little man hopped out and looked all around, confused and scared. Another followed, then a third. Soon, at least ten of the creatures had gathered, the whipping wind tossing the hair on their bodies about. One of them dragged an old backpack on the ground. Dressed only in ragged gray loincloths, they looked more like diapered chimps than men.

Marilyn tensed her jaw. The Caitiff. Why had the soldiers brought those foul beasts here?

The man waved his gun toward the helicopter. "Get on board. If no one comes out from that hole, I will count to five and start shooting into it."

Marilyn walked as slowly as she dared. Would Gabriel swoop out and jerk her off the ground? Or was he thinking they'd both get shot out of the sky?

The female soldier marched toward her, gesturing for the Caitiff to follow. She patted down Marilyn's jacket and pulled the Glock from the inner holster. "You got any other surprises in there, honey?" she asked as she slid the gun behind her belt.

Marilyn shook her head. "Where are you taking me?"

"You'll find out soon enough." She looked at the male soldier. "Jackson, let's clear them out."

Jackson raised the rifle to his shoulder and fired a round into the cave. A muffled shriek erupted from near the entry, then silence ensued.

"Wait!" Gabriel called. "Hold your fire." He emerged, cradling a woman. As blood trickled down her dangling arm, he scowled at Jackson. "What kind of idiot would shoot into a dark cave?"

Jackson pointed the rifle at Gabriel. "A soldier who wouldn't mind putting a hole through your head, freak."

Gabriel didn't flinch. "If I wasn't carrying an innocent woman you just shot, I'd salute you for your courage."

"Cut the bravado." He aimed toward the cave again. "How many more dragon-kind are in there?"

"Just one." Gabriel turned that way. "Might as well give it up, Dorian."

As he set the wounded woman on the ground, Marilyn peeked at her. It was Tamara. Her eyes closed, she breathed through her mouth, her chest rising and falling in rapid, shallow bursts. Keeping her eyes on Jackson, Marilyn began edging closer to Tamara, hoping to offer some help, but how could she do anything with armed thugs around?

Dorian emerged from the tunnel, her head low and her hands in the pockets of her denim jumper.

"Any others?" Jackson asked.

Keeping her stare low, Dorian shook her head.

"We'll see about that." Jackson fired at least a dozen more rounds into the tunnel, spraying them from side to side. Then, pulling a flashlight from a belt clip, he nodded at the female soldier. "I'm going in, Olsen."

As he waved the beam, Jackson kept the rifle at his hip, a finger on the trigger. When he disappeared inside, Olsen barked at the Caitiff. "Take another sniff to remind yourselves of the dragon scent."

The one carrying the backpack lifted it to his nose and sniffed. Then, like a pack of anxious dogs, the others gathered around and did the same, each one fidgeting and scratching himself after his turn. With every second, their agitation grew. As they jumped in place, they looked more like monkeys than ever.

"When I give you the signal," Olsen said, "go in there and find the dragons."

"Dragons," they echoed, jumping even higher now. "Dragons!"

Olsen called into the tunnel. "Jackson! Is it clear?"

A shrill whistle sounded from within. Olsen furrowed her brow and stalked toward the entrance. "What's going on?"

Dorian withdrew a clenched fist from her pocket and pressed something with her thumb. An explosion boomed from the cave, sending out a shock wave that knocked Olsen to her seat.

In a flash of wings, Gabriel zoomed to her, snatched the rifle, and kicked her in the face, knocking her flat. One of the Caitiff grabbed his wing and jerked him to the ground, and two jumped on his back. The others rushed into the cave, whooping, the lead one carrying a flashlight.

Marilyn tackled one of the brutes and beat his hairy body with her fists. Dorian wrestled the one clutching Gabriel's wing and slung him away. As Gabriel fought off the third, a loud voice boomed from the cave. "Gabriel! Marilyn! Dorian! Let them go and stay down!"

Marilyn flattened her body. Shots rang out, and the three Caitiff flopped to the ground. As soon as the gunshot echoes died away, she jumped up and looked at the tunnel. Yereq stood at the entrance, Jackson's rifle at his shoulder, ready to fire. The Caitiff writhed in pools of dark blood, and Olsen lay on her back, apparently unconscious.

Tamara rose to her knees and pushed her hair back, smiling. "My acting good?"

"You certainly fooled me," Marilyn said. "The blood looked real."

"Blood real." Tamara pointed at her arm. "Cut on stone."

"The tunnel is open," Yereq said, "and some of the Caitiff went through. I was unable to stop them."

Gabriel brushed sand from his clothes. "Let's go. If Sapphira set the trap, maybe we can help the Caitiff fall in." He handed Olsen's rifle to Dorian. "Keep an eye on her."

Marilyn retrieved her own gun from Olsen and pointed it at one of the wounded Caitiff, but she didn't have the heart to shoot the struggling beast again. "Bullets only slow them down," she said to Dorian, "so be careful."

"We should go now." Yereq picked up a lantern at the entrance and led the way through a haze of swirling dust. Soon, he stopped at a deep cleft in the wall. "While we hid in this alcove, the gunman walked into our trap, and he is now no more."

Kaylee and Elise stepped out from the recess, followed by Jordan. "Was anyone hurt?" Kaylee asked.

"Yes." Marilyn pointed toward the exit. "Take Jordan and Elise, and see what you can do out there."

"The Caitiff," Gabriel said. "Did you see them?"

Kaylee nodded toward the tunnel's down slope. "They passed us by. One paused for a second and sniffed around, but he took off again."

Marilyn pushed her gun back to her holster. What could that mean? If Bonnie and Shiloh exchanged clothes and backpacks, maybe those beasts had Bonnie's scent in their nostrils and had picked up her trail.

She patted Yereq on the arm. "Let's get back to the mines. There's no telling what damage those little devils might do before we can get there."

CHAPTER 8

THE RIVER PORTAL

"Well, so much for that." Rebekah tossed a splintered pick handle to the ground. "Save your hands, ladies. We'll have to come up with another plan."

Bonnie sat on a boulder and looked at her palms. Dirty and blistered, they weren't tough enough, nor was any of her party strong enough to dig through the tons of stone in the collapsed tunnel. Although she could have healed her hands with the two or three drops she saved in Elam's vial, it wasn't worth it. Better to keep it for an emergency. "Gabriel knows we're here," she said. "He and Yereq will figure out a way to get in."

"And what if they try to blast through?" Dallas asked. "Another collapse?"

Rebekah kicked a rock across the floor. "My guess is they won't risk it for a while. They know we have food and water, and now we're safe from outside interference. But they might try to communicate, maybe with tapping noises."

"I agree." Sapphira picked up a lantern. "May I suggest that you and Dallas stay here while Bonnie and I look for the portal Elam wrote about?"

Rebekah took the lantern and extinguished the flame. "After a water break, sure. We can come back here and listen."

"And we'll relieve you when we come back." Sapphira snatched up the pick handle, set it ablaze, and led the way as the four walked to the end of the escape passageway. She stopped at the mouth of the larger tunnel and used her bare foot to sweep dirt over an exposed corner of the blanket that concealed the hole in the floor.

Dimming her flame, she turned to the others. "It looks pretty natural, don't you think?"

Bonnie stooped and touched the covering with a finger. "Only if it stays this dark. Someone with a bright lantern might notice and—"

An ear-splitting bang shot through the tunnel, and the ground shook violently.

Bonnie jumped away from the trap. "What was that?"

As grit rained down from the ceiling, coating their heads and shoulders, Rebekah held up her lantern. "Sapphira, give me some light."

Sapphira pointed at the wick. "Ignite!"

As a lively flame erupted, Rebekah extended her arm into the escape passage, creating an orange halo in the dusty air. "Maybe someone is blasting their way in."

"That's fine if it's Gabriel," Dallas said. "But how can we safely find out?"

Rebekah lifted a finger to her lips. "Shhh. Let's listen for a minute."

Folding her wings in tightly, Bonnie eased into the tunnel. Echoes of tapping sounds reached her ears, small rocks falling to the floor, then the clinking of metal—picks or shovels striking stone.

Rebekah pointed at Bonnie. "Your wings are exposed, so you and Sapphira stay here. Dallas and I will check it out."

"You don't have a weapon," Bonnie called as they marched up the dim tunnel's incline.

"If it's Gabriel, we don't need one. If it's someone else, we'll be back in a hurry." Soon, the light faded away.

Sapphira handed Bonnie the pick handle, now burning with a small flame. "This will give us a chance to look at Elam's journal." She pulled it from behind her jeans waistband and opened it to a page she had marked with an old lantern wick. The ovulum, now back in its pouch, bobbed with her movements.

Bonnie held the flame closer to the page. The handwritten letters were thick and bold in one entry but weak and barely readable in another, probably reflecting Elam's exhaustion when he wrote it. Still, bold or not, none of the odd characters made sense.

"This Hebrew poem," Sapphira said, running her finger along the text, "is cryptic. We'll have to figure out the symbolism. It talks about liquid fire, which is probably the magma river, and water stirred by an invisible oar, which might be the whirlpool Elam and I went through to get to Dragons' Rest."

Bonnie nodded. "That makes sense, but it's obviously too hot down there now."

"Right, so we have to figure out the rest. It says to obey the command Moses neglected, and Nebuchadnezzar's dream will awaken. Yet, fear not, for he who . . ."—she squinted at the words—"made alive, I think would be the best way to say it. He who made alive Balaam's lowly servant can do the same for a face of granite."

"Balaam's lowly servant," Bonnie repeated in a whisper.

Sapphira looked at her. "I've read the story of Balaam, but I don't remember a servant."

"Balaam had a donkey that spoke to him. Maybe that's what it means by making his servant alive."

"I suppose a donkey could be a servant. What about the other parts?"

Bonnie blinked at the text, still a mess of indecipherable marks. "Well, the command Moses disobeyed was to speak to a rock that gave them water in the wilderness. And Nebuchadnezzar had a dream about a statue made out of gold and silver and clay. Then a stone crushed the statue and became a mountain."

"I remember that." Sapphira kept her finger on the page. "So it sounds like we have to speak to a face of granite."

"Have you seen any granite that looks like a face?"

"The cliff that overlooks the magma river is granite. When I was down at the side of the river where Elam and I waded in, I tried to find a place to climb up, but I don't remember anything that looked like facial features."

"Was that when Paili fell from the cliff?" Bonnie asked.

"Right. I guess I didn't notice anything but her."

The sound of running footsteps clopped toward them. Bonnie turned and looked up the incline. A light bounced in the distance, getting closer in a hurry.

Rebekah's voice broke the silence. "That blast punched a hole through the rubble." When she arrived, she stopped and gasped for breath.

Dallas joined her a half second later. Puffing, she pointed back into the tunnel. "A bunch of strange creatures are gathering on this side of the debris."

"Strange creatures?" Sapphira asked. "What did they look like?"

"Covered with hair, more like monkeys than men, but they wore loin cloths and spoke to each other, so they couldn't be monkeys."

"Did they see you?" Bonnie asked.

"I'm not sure. They didn't seem to. They just sniffed and snorted and jumped up and down."

"They had a bright flashlight," Rebekah said, "so I kept the lantern behind me. I would guess there were at least six of them, but they were still coming through the hole. They'll probably head this way as soon as they're all through."

Bonnie pointed at the hidden trap. "Maybe the first few would fall in, but it couldn't possibly catch them all. They'd have to be pretty stupid."

"If you saw them," Dallas said, "you might be more confident. They make monkeys look like Einstein."

"We can't fight that many." Rebekah nodded toward the springs chamber. "Should we hide at the waterfall?"

Sapphira sidestepped the trap. "You and Dallas hide there. Near the ceiling where the springs come out, you can climb behind the falls. When you swim under the rock, you'll come out in an air pocket with enough room for both of you. There's a vent, so you should have plenty of air."

Rebekah forked her fingers at Bonnie and Sapphira. "What about you two?"

"We'll head down the shaft and then the river overlook," Sapphira said. "If they show up there, I should be able to send a few over the edge."

"What if there are more than just a few?" Dallas asked.

"Then we'll have to deal with that." Sapphira tucked the journal behind her waistband. "You and Rebekah go. It might take you a little while to get hidden. I'll stay here until the last second."

Rebekah gave her an inquisitive look. "Why?"

"If they're just creeping along, they'll see the hole. So I'm going to make sure they're in a hurry."

"Bait the trap?" Rebekah gave Sapphira a thumbs-up. "Good idea."

As soon as the two former dragons left for the springs, Sapphira took the pick handle from Bonnie and crept a few feet into the escape tunnel. As she crouched, she appeared to be listening, her white hair shining in the glow of her flame.

Bonnie tiptoed in and crouched next to her, careful not to make a sound.

"If they figured out that Shiloh's an impostor," Sapphira whispered, "they're probably coming for you."

Bonnie nodded, holding her breath as she listened. The fire on Sapphira's stick dwindled, now barely the size of a match flame. In the dim light, the sides of the passage seemed to get narrower, funneling the slightest sounds from the depths—a scratching noise, a click, a tap.

Were they even real? Or were they figments, tricks her anxious mind played to get her to run?

Soon, a whisper pierced the silence, then another, though the words seemed foreign, more like guttural chatter than human speech. A circle of yellow light came into view, distant, yet growing by the second.

Sapphira clutched Bonnie's wrist and whispered, "Get ready."

Bonnie tightened her leg muscles. She mentally traced a path to the elevator and imagined the climb down, already difficult enough without strange monkey men chasing her. But there wasn't another option.

As Sapphira rose slowly to her feet, Bonnie did the same. Sapphira pressed the stick into Bonnie's hand and whispered, "When I say run, you go first. Don't worry about me."

Bonnie nodded. "Don't take too many chances."

Suddenly, the stick blazed. "Bonnie!" Sapphira shouted. "Someone's out there! We have to hide! Run!"

Bonnie turned and, dodging the hidden hole, sprinted toward the elevator shaft. With her wings giving her a boost, she zipped along, but as she neared the shaft, the breeze blew out her flame. Now in darkness, she groped for the opening in the wall, looking back for any sign of a white-haired girl with a ball of fire riding on her palm.

Finally, her hand passed across a gap. She reached in, grabbed the rope, and looked back again. More shrieks erupted in the darkness. Had some of the creatures fallen into their trap? Was Sapphira trying to increase the number of victims somehow?

A hand touched her shoulder. "Let's get going!"

"Sapphira? How did you—"

"I know my way around in the dark. Climb down! Hurry! I'll be right behind you."

Bonnie swung out into the shaft and let the rope slide through her hands, braking with her shoes only when the burning sensation in her fingers grew too painful. Within seconds, she felt the breeze from the next level's opening and swung to the floor, then quickly backed away to make room.

The sound of bare feet slapping the stone followed. A fireball appeared. As it grew to the size of a baseball, it illuminated Sapphira's palm and face. She whispered, "Come on," and ran through the tunnel.

Bonnie dashed after her, again propelling herself with her wings. "How many of the ape men were there?"

"I think four fell in the trap," Sapphira called back, "but there were at least six more. I'm not sure if they saw which way I ran."

As they jogged along the stony path, they passed by a tiny spring pouring from a one-inch-wide hole in the wall. A bucket collected the water, but it had long since overflowed. The excess spilled to the floor and ran down a network of shallow cracks.

When they reached the entry arch to the magma river overlook, Sapphira stopped and set a hand on her chest. "Whew! That's the farthest I've run in centuries."

Bonnie looked back. "I think I hear something, that chatter those creatures make."

"Let's get out of sight." Sapphira snuffed out her fire and guided Bonnie through the entrance. When they neared the ledge, the river provided all the light they needed.

Stretching out her wings, Bonnie looked over the side. "You came here to try to find the face, didn't you?"

"We couldn't all fit in the other hiding place anyway, and this was the first alternative that came to mind."

"So if the face is on the cliff underneath us, do we speak to it from up here or from down there?"

"We might as well try from up here first," Sapphira said, "but what do we say to it?"

Bonnie looked back at the tunnel. The sound of monkey chatter drew closer. "Moses was supposed to get water from his rock, so maybe we should ask this one for water."

"It's worth a try." With Bonnie holding to her shirt, Sapphira leaned over the edge and shouted at the wall below. "Would you please give us some water?"

No reply came, only the low rumble of partially molten rock grinding against the walls on either side of the river.

As Bonnie pulled Sapphira back, a light appeared on the tunnel wall just outside the entryway. Bonnie spread out her wings. "They're coming!"

"Fly me to river level," Sapphira said. "We could ask the wall from down there."

"It's too hot to land." Bonnie looked out over the chasm again. "Maybe we could fly in front of the cliff and find a face. If it has ears, we can talk into one. If all else fails, we'll head to the other ledge."

"It's worth a try. But it will be faster and safer if you search without me. Remember the updrafts."

Two hairy men crept toward them, one bearing a thick club and the other a flaming torch.

Bonnie pointed. "You can't stay here with them."

"I'll fend off the monkey men." Sapphira stepped back from Bonnie and spread out her arms. Her entire body erupted in flames, sending their attackers scurrying. "Now hurry. I can't do this for very long."

Flapping her wings, Bonnie leaped out over the chasm. A surge of hot air pushed her higher, but she quickly adjusted and angled down toward the cliff wall. Flying in a tight oval, she scanned the granite surface. Two deeply set clefts near the top could easily be eyes, and a rugged protrusion just below them made for a crooked but passable nose.

She flew lower. After flapping once, she let the upwelling breezes keep her in a glide. A deep hole, round and craggy, made the face seem like it was trying to blow out a flame. Yet, with the wall staying flat as far as she could see, there seemed to be no place for ears anywhere.

As she swept closer to Sapphira, she shouted. "No ears. I'm going to ask as I pass by the mouth."

Sapphira, still in flames, kept her arms spread wide, while shadows jumped up and down nearby. "Okay, but I'm running out of energy."

Bonnie flew back to the face. Just before reaching the circular mouth, she shouted, "Please give us water!"

Nothing happened. Bonnie passed by the mouth, made a tight

one-eighty turn, and flew toward it again. Suddenly, water gushed out in a geyserlike surge. It blasted against her side and thrust her across the chasm and into the far wall. Her wing bent painfully against the rock, but its strong mainstay cushioned the impact, allowing her to push off with her feet and fly toward the precipice.

Now dripping wet from her waist down, Bonnie had to beat her wings hard to stay aloft. The hot updrafts had vanished, and her right wing faltered, likely bruised by the impact.

Her flames dwindling, Sapphira grunted as she flung fireballs at the approaching monkey men, now several in number. "You can do it!" she called. "You're almost here!"

With a final thrust, Bonnie lunged back to the ledge and stopped just short of Sapphira's flames. The attackers ran away, the last one with a flashlight in his grip. As they retreated in the inner tunnel, the glow dwindled for a few seconds before steadying. Quiet chatter echoed from wherever the hairy beasts had stopped.

"I guess they're regrouping." Sapphira shut off her inferno. "Good thing. You can't fly me anywhere until I get cooler." She touched Bonnie's shoulder. "Are you all right?"

Bonnie shook her wings, throwing off streams of water. "Just a bruise, I think." She hustled back to the edge and looked down. A three-foot-wide column of water shot from the face's mouth and plunged into the river. Huge plumes of steam rocketed upward, filling the chamber with a misty cloud.

"Whew!" Bonnie waved a hand at the vapor. "I got back just in time. That steam would have cooked me."

Sapphira fixed her gaze on the river. "And now we might have another problem."

Bonnie joined her. Below, at the point where the water struck the magma, the river solidified. As the hardening magma piled up behind it, the flow of molten rock rose with the growing wall.

"How high can it go?" Bonnie asked.

Sapphira pointed at the far wall. "I think it will eventually seep around the sides of its own barricade, but with the water flowing faster than the magma, it's hard to tell."

Bonnie stared through the rising vapor. "It looks like the waterfall's making a pool, and it's swirling."

"I noticed," Sapphira whispered. "That must be our portal."

Bonnie glanced back at the entry. The flashlight's glow stayed steady. The monkey men still lurked, but they seemed to be coming no closer. "So do we go through it?" she asked, matching Sapphira's low tone. "Or do we fly to the other ledge and warn Rebekah and Dallas about the rising magma?"

"I can't see it rising all the way up here. Once it gets higher than the water source, there's nothing to dam it up."

"Will our new portal stay open if the magma creeps around the sides? I mean, if hardening magma caps it off, we might not get back."

"It's hard to say, but considering the prophecy, I think we have to see what's there." Sapphira touched the wounded wing. "Are you able to carry me down?"

Bonnie pulled her wing to the front and massaged a bruise on the outer part of the mainstay. "I think so. Going down should be easier than crossing the chasm."

A shriek sounded from the tunnel. In the shadows, a line of hunched men drew near, snarling. One of them carried the bucket Bonnie had seen in the tunnel.

"The monkey-man fire department is here." Sapphira pulled Bonnie toward the edge. "Let's fly!"

A wave of water flew over them. Her hair dripping, Bonnie wrapped her arms around Sapphira's waist. Just as one of the creatures leaped, she vaulted into the air. The beast's momentum carried him over the side, and he plummeted, his hairy limbs flailing.

"When we get down there," Sapphira shouted, "I'll let you know if I sense a portal."

A loud bang sounded in Bonnie's ears, then another. "Did you hear that?"

"Gunshots? Did those freaks get reinforcements?"

"Maybe. Let's hurry." Staying close to the near wall, Bonnie flew around the column of steam and drifted downward from the cooler side. As they closed in on the whirlpool, the swirling water grew clear. It spun downward at least ten feet, guarded by a wall of steam and mounting rock that separated the pool from the oncoming magma.

"I can feel it!" Sapphira yelled. "The portal!"

"Do we just dive right in?"

"What's the worst that could happen? We'd get wet."

Bonnie grimaced. The words *we could drown* came to mind, but she decided it would be better to stay quiet. Elam's prophecy had come true so far, so this portal had to lead somewhere. But to a dark world beneath all others? Would that be worse than drowning? Yet, with her injured wing aching, there seemed to be no other option.

As she neared the mouth of the whirlpool, she folded in her wings, held her breath, and plunged in feetfirst. The water, hot enough to sting her skin, sucked them down. Then, like a slide at a theme park, it zipped them along a twisting path. With her eyes closed, she could only feel the sensations—bubbles brushing past her face, a sense of coolness as the water tempered, Sapphira's warm body in her arms, and a continued downward pull into a seemingly endless coil.

Her lungs now begging for air, and the rush of water slowing, she opened her eyes. Darkness blinded her. Thousands of bubbles continued to blow past, but not enough to allow her to catch a gulp of oxygen. Within seconds she would have to try, or else faint.

Just as she opened her mouth to gather bubbles, she burst out of the water. Her shoes struck soft turf, and she tumbled into a somersault, flying over Sapphira and sliding to a stop on her back.

Blinking, she sat up and looked behind her. Sapphira had already risen to her knees. In the dimness, she appeared as a dripping gray shadow against a darker background.

Bonnie climbed to her feet and helped Sapphira get up. "Can you call for some fire?" Bonnie asked.

Sapphira shook her hands, slinging droplets. Then, raising a palm, she whispered, "Give me light."

Nothing happened.

She added a hint of sternness to her voice. "Give me light."

Again, nothing happened.

"Are you too wet?" Bonnie asked.

"I don't think I'm any wetter than I was at Morgan's swamp." She blew on her hands. "Maybe I flamed out scaring those monkey men. I'll try again in a minute."

A low voice rumbled from somewhere nearby. "You have no power here, dread Oracle. At least, not yet."

CHAPTER 9

A NEW DRAGON

Churning her arms and legs as fast as she could, Marilyn puffed. If Yereq didn't slow down soon, she would have to fall back and follow his lantern light instead of his sprinting body. Sure, it was easy enough for Gabriel to keep up. He had wings to give him a boost, while she had nothing but weary legs. Following these two was like trying to compete with Superman and the Flash.

Finally, Gabriel and the giant slowed to a stop. Marilyn caught up and braced her hands on her knees as she tried to catch her breath. The two were looking down into a hole at the intersection between the escape and main tunnels.

"What happened?" she asked.

"It's the trap," Gabriel said. "I see the light from the magma river way down below. I hope some of the beasts fell into it."

Marilyn peered over the edge. "Where do we look for Bonnie and Sapphira?"

Gabriel set a finger on Yereq's stomach. "You know the mines better than we do. What do you think?"

"I will search this level," Yereq replied. "It has the most rooms and mazes, and I know them well. I suggest that you and Marilyn go down the elevator shaft and check the next level. You need only search the magnetite channels and the magma river overlook. If you do not find them, you can go to the brick kiln level where we met them earlier."

After picking up another lantern near the wall and lighting it, Yereq left it on the floor, sidestepped the hole, and headed toward the springs chamber in a quick march.

Gabriel handed the new lantern to Marilyn. "Hang on to this. We'll take a shortcut straight down. If they're at the overlook, this has to be the fastest way."

"Let's split up," she said. "Since you'll have light from the river, I'll go down the shaft with the lantern. That way we'll cover more ground."

"Do you know how to get there? Won't you need protection?"

"Don't worry. Just give me directions." She patted her holster. "I have a protector right here."

"Right." He pointed into the darkness. "Follow the tunnel until you see an open doorway cut into the rock wall to your right. There's a rope that'll lead you to the next level down." He touched the lantern. "Can you climb while holding that?"

She looked at the narrow handle on the top of the lantern. "I'll hold it in my teeth if I have to."

"Good. After we search that level, I'll fly you back up. See you at the overlook." Folding in his wings, Gabriel leaped into the hole.

Marilyn didn't bother to watch his progress. She had to hurry.

Jogging in the direction he had pointed, she waved the lantern from side to side to illuminate every cleft in the dark walls. Staring past the flickering light and trying to pick up a nondescript black hole seemed impossible, but soon it came into sight.

She set the lantern handle between her teeth, grabbed the rope, and, braking with her shoes, climbed down hand over hand. It was hotter in the shaft, and the work raised a quick sweat. Within a few seconds, a draft cooled her skin. Had she reached the next level? With the lantern's glow blinding her eyes, she couldn't see an exit hole.

She pushed a foot against the far wall, hoping not to crash into anything. As she swung, her hair brushed against something, probably the top of the lower doorway. She dropped to solid ground, released the rope, and pulled the lantern from her mouth.

"Whew!" She mopped her forehead with her sleeve. "Now to find the overlook."

Again holding the lantern out in front, she passed by a dark chamber. She stopped and lifted the lantern close to a sign on the wall next to the gaping entrance. The strange lettering probably revealed exactly what was inside, at least to someone who could read the language.

Extending her light, she stepped in. Her shoe pushed something heavy, making a scraping noise. She set the lantern on the floor and touched a wooden handle with curved metal on the opposite end. It looked like a rusted pick. As she lifted it, the handle crumbled in her grasp.

"The mines," she whispered.

Trying to quiet her pounding heart, she turned the lantern's brightness up and tiptoed in. When Yereq mentioned searching the magnetite channels, she had imagined a network of trenches with sweating girls driving their picks into hard rock while a brute of a man ripped their backs with a barbed whip. Of course, the girls were gone, but as she stepped down into a trench, it seemed that the pain of every lash pierced her mind, and the anguished cries of little slave girls drifted through the stale air.

She stooped and picked up a flat glass disk. On the inside, black particles covered the bottom. They looked like iron filings, the kind she had used for magnet experiments in school. A scrap of an old dress lay nearby, torn and bloodied. She snatched it up and clutched it tightly in her fist. Those poor girls! The torture they endured must have been the worst of nightmares!

As she let the scrap fall, she straightened and looked into the darkness. This place had to be massive, far too big to search thoroughly.

Maybe if they were close, they would respond to a call. If not, she could come back after checking the overlook.

"Bonnie!" she shouted.

The name echoed in the chamber, fading with each reverberation.

"Sapphira!"

Again, the name echoed. The sound seemed to travel along multiple corridors, as if conducting a search in the deep recesses of the mines.

Marilyn listened. Besides the sound of her own breathing and a slight trickle of water somewhere in the distance, nothing reached her ears.

After calling each name twice more, she climbed out of the trench and returned to the tunnel. As she hurried on, strange sounds emanated from the darkness in front of her, a combination of running water and . . .

She squinted. "Monkey chatter?"

Creeping slowly now, she passed a fountain springing from the wall, explaining one of the sounds. As she continued, the shrieking clamor heightened. A light appeared to the right, revealing another arched passage. The light danced, seemingly in time with the chanting beasts.

Marilyn set the lantern down and pulled out her gun. Even if bullets just slowed the Caitiff down, a few well-placed shots might be enough to send a monkey into the magma river.

With her back against the wall, she slid closer, listening. A girl somewhere within the adjacent chamber called out, "Let's fly!"

Extending the gun with both hands, Marilyn leaped in front of the opening. Behind a wall of jumping Caitiff, two with flaming torches, Bonnie vaulted from a ledge with Sapphira in her arms, both dripping wet. One of the Caitiff fell in their wake and disappeared.

"Back off!" Marilyn shouted as she stalked toward the other Caitiff. "Get out of my way!"

The hairy men, now about seven in number, turned as one. Snarling, one leaped toward her, but with a quick aim she shot it through the chest. As it dropped to the ground, she turned the gun back on the others. "Who's next?"

One of the Caitiff threw a bucket. She ducked, but it glanced off the side of her head, making her stagger. Squealing, the Caitiff lunged. She fired shot after shot. One fell, then another. But three made it through her hail of bullets. A hairy hand grabbed her gun. Two others latched on to her wrists and bowled her over. A torch fell beside her ear, something metal struck her head and flashed a light in her eyes, and an arm covered her mouth.

She yelled into its smelly skin, her voice muffled. "Get off me, you disgusting ape!"

Just as one of the beasts turned her gun toward her, it flew backwards into the darkness. A second disappeared, releasing her wrists. Finally, the one covering her mouth jumped off and backed away slowly.

Marilyn grabbed the torch and leaped to her feet. Extending the flame, she illuminated the area. Gabriel, his wings spread wide, pointed another torch at the Caitiff. "If you don't want to follow your buddies into the chasm, then get out now!"

The lone Caitiff turned and sped out through the passageway.

Marilyn ran to the edge of the precipice. "Did you see where Bonnie went?"

"Bonnie? You saw her?"

"She jumped off with Sapphira in her arms."

She looked down into the depths. Water poured from a hole somewhere in the wall, but with the magma river's glow dying from the cooling effect, and steam rising in a billowing column, she couldn't see anyone.

Marilyn cupped her hands around her mouth and called out as loudly as she could, "Bonnie!"

Gabriel threw down his torch and beat his wings. "I'm going in."

"Be careful!"

He leaped straight out, then dropped. As he fanned his wings, he slowed his descent and disappeared into the plumes of white.

Marilyn continued her calls, shouting for Bonnie and Sapphira again and again until her voice grew hoarse. With the roar of water and the loud hiss of venting steam, her cries seemed to hit a barrier and die away.

After a few minutes, Gabriel flew back to the ledge, soaking wet and puffing. With a shake of each wing, he cast off hundreds of droplets. Some splashed on Marilyn's cheek, hot and stinging.

"Sorry about that."

She rubbed her cheek. "It's okay. I've had worse burns."

"I know what you mean. Flying here through the channel nearly fried me."

"Any sign of them?"

"Not a trace." He turned back toward the chasm and looked down. "The water's rising like crazy, and I didn't have a light."

She pushed the torch into his hand. "Then try again. We have to find them."

"Not with this," he said, pushing it back. "That steam will put it out in a heartbeat."

"Then maybe . . ." Waving the torch near the ground, she scanned the area. "I felt something hit me, something metal that flickered in my eyes."

The firelight raised a sparkle a few feet away. Gabriel leaped toward it and snatched up a flashlight. "This should do it."

"Any sign of my gun?"

"Nope. I think it went into the soup with the first one I yanked off you."

"Okay." She rubbed her head where the flashlight had hit her. "Better get going."

"I'm on my way." With a leap, he dove into the chasm again.

Marilyn shuffled back to the tunnel, her head aching. She searched for her lantern, but it was nowhere to be found. With a huff, she murmured, "The Caitiff must have taken it."

Now with only a dwindling torch, she hurried back to the edge and waited. The beast that escaped might return soon, and who could tell if there were any others in the matrix of tunnels?

After several minutes, Marilyn sat down in a shadow near the wall. No use yelling for Gabriel. He probably couldn't hear her anyway, and she didn't want to alert anyone else to her presence.

The flames at the end of her torch wilted, then died away. Probably all for the best. Now to anyone walking by, she would be undetectable.

Soon, lantern light appeared in the tunnel again. Marilyn froze. She glanced back and forth between the chasm and the passageway. How many of those monsters were coming? Where was Gabriel now?

A massive figure lumbered onto the ledge, his lantern illuminating his bearded face.

Marilyn jumped up. "Oh, Yereq! I'm so glad to see you!"

He offered a smile, but his expression quickly turned serious. "Where is Gabriel?"

She nodded toward the chasm. "I'm pretty sure I saw Bonnie fly Sapphira down there, so he's trying to find them."

"Since I was unable to locate anyone on the upper level," Yereq said, "I tried to climb down to the kiln chamber, but it was flooded, so I decided to find you."

Marilyn kept her gaze fixed on the white clouds rising from the boiling water below. They jetted upward only a few feet in front of her, vanished into the darkness above, and reappeared in swirling streams that rocketed down, then back up again after bouncing off the swelling river. "This place will be like pea soup in a few minutes," she said. "Gabriel had better hurry."

The magma's glow continued to weaken, and with thick vapor filling every cubic inch of air, the chamber grew darker and darker. Pops and sizzles diminished until only the sound of falling water reached their ears.

Soon, another sound drew near, flapping wings and heavy grunts.

"It's Gabriel!" Marilyn stepped as close to the edge as she dared and searched the sea of white fog. "I can't see him anywhere."

Yereq knelt, reached over the precipice, and hoisted Gabriel up to the ledge, a handful of shirt in his huge hand. After setting him upright,

Yereq raised the lantern near Gabriel's face. "Did you see them?" Yereq asked.

Water streamed from Gabriel's soaked hair and down his reddened cheeks. "No sign of them," he said, puffing quick breaths. "I thought I saw a swirl in a pool, so I dove in. It didn't lead anywhere, and the water was scalding, so I climbed out." He took a deeper breath and let it out slowly. "Magma was spilling in, and while I was flying around, it hardened over the first pool and now the sideways geyser is making a lake over the new layer."

"So will it keep making layers of rock and water until it fills the chasm?" Marilyn asked.

He nodded, slinging water up and down. "Looks that way, at least for a while. The cooling magma built a wall a little ways upstream, so it overflows, cools down, and keeps building the wall."

"So where could Bonnie and Sapphira have gone?"

"Nowhere down there, unless there was a portal. When I was in an energy state, I could sense a portal, but not now." He nodded toward the other side of the chasm. "I'm going across to check the brick kiln room."

She grabbed his drenched sleeve. "Yereq already went there. It's flooded."

"Then I'll search the tunnel. Maybe they're hiding out in between." He took the lantern from Yereq, then, with a quick flap, he leaped into the vapor and disappeared, leaving Marilyn and Yereq in the darkness.

"If he doesn't find them," Marilyn said, "we'll have to leave and come back as soon as possible with search lamps and maybe even scuba gear."

Yereq kept his gaze locked on the fog. "I have heard of such equipment. Are you trained in its use?"

"I'm certified, but not for cave diving. If this chamber fills up, it'll be very dangerous. I'll have to find an expert."

For a few minutes, silence ensued, save for the constant splashing from below. Then the familiar beating of Gabriel's wings drew near, and lantern light pierced the fog. He landed in a graceful walk, stepping between Marilyn and Yereq as he folded in his wings.

"I struck out." Water streaming down his worried face, Gabriel nodded toward the chasm. "It's filling up pretty fast. We'd better go topside."

Marilyn touched his arm. "We'll get search equipment and come back."

He paused, looking forlornly at the rising steam. "If there's anything to come back to."

After climbing to the first level and hurrying through the escape tunnel, they rushed out into the daylight. Blinking, Marilyn looked around. Dorian sat cross-legged on the ground next to two dead soldiers, the rifle in her lap. Kaylee, Tamara, Elise, and Jordan were all at the helicopter, Kaylee studying the controls and the others standing just outside the pilot's door.

"To preserve my life, I had to shoot the woman," Dorian said. "She is no longer among the living. The man is dead, as well."

Kaylee called from the pilot's seat. "Marilyn, this is not my field of expertise. Have you ever flown a helicopter?"

"Not one this big, but I should be able to handle it." Marilyn marched toward them. "We'll need it if we're going to get search equipment down here."

After everyone except Yereq boarded the helicopter, Marilyn started the blades rotating. Yereq stooped at her side, the shining lantern again in his grip. "If you see them," she shouted as she passed her cell phone to him. "Push number three and hold it down for two seconds. It will dial the phone Gabriel has."

Gabriel reached into his pants pocket. "If it's not too wet."

"And if that doesn't work," she continued, "dial nine-one-one like you did before. You might have to climb to the top to get cell service."

"I understand. I will continue searching until you return. At the very least, I should try to find the last Caitiff. If he is still prowling, Bonnie and Sapphira are not safe."

She touched her holster. "Do you need a weapon?"

"I have my sword, and the dead soldiers left their rifles. I know how to use them."

"Great. We'll be back as soon as we can." She lifted the helicopter into the air and guided it slowly upward. The surrounding walls seemed closer than before. Of course, it was an illusion, but with the swirling wind, it wouldn't take much of a gust to sweep them close enough to brush the tail against the rocks. The higher they rose, the more susceptible they would be to the winds at the surface.

Soon, however, they had flown safely above the crater's lip and were rising still higher. The mountain's bald top came into view, the borrowed airplane still parked near the forest's edge.

Marilyn wrapped her fingers around the cyclic stick. Flying the plane would be a lot easier, but the helicopter had more passenger room, and transporting people and equipment from one vehicle to the other would be too time consuming. Experienced or not, she would have to make do.

"Okay," she said as she turned the helicopter toward town, "let's get everyone up to date and plot our strategy."

* * *

Bonnie swung toward the voice. Dread Oracle? Who could have said that?

She whispered to Sapphira. "Did you hear a voice?"

"I heard, but I didn't like the tone."

Bonnie cleared her throat. "Who's there?"

The voice returned, this time with a low echo following each word. "The guardian of the expectant ones, the warden who watches the fruit of unopened wombs, the caretaker of the forsaken but not forgotten. So you see, I am all three."

She narrowed her eyes. Something moved out there, something large and dark. But how far away was it? Everything was warped. The man's reply, if it was a man at all, seemed to beg her to ask what his strange words meant. Should she play along? Or should she go straight for the heart of the matter?

"Who are you?" she asked.

"A guardian."

Sapphira clutched Bonnie's arm and whispered, "Wait. Let me."

"I was hoping you would."

"Guardian," Sapphira said, "you speak in riddles. Are you able to tell us plainly who you are and where we are?"

"Some now, some later." The voice carried no hint of friendliness or malice. "The learning ladder is better climbed a rung at a time rather than in leaps and bounds."

Darkness faded. Like dawn on a cloudy day, muted light illuminated their surroundings. Behind them, a head-high waterfall fed a swiftly flowing brook, shallow by all appearances. To each side, a wall of black mountains sealed them in, perhaps a mile or so away, though their height likely skewed the distance. In front, a verdant field lay before them with human-shaped statues dotting the landscape, one within reach.

A column of white mist swirled around the statue, dressing the polished black stone with a semitransparent veil. With every orbit around the stony face, the vapor seemed to animate the features, giving life to the eyes, nose, and mouth. Wrapped in fog, an arm stretched slowly toward Bonnie and Sapphira. Starting at the tips of its fingers, stone morphed into flames, making a crackling sound as the transformation inched along. Muscles rippled on the forearm, and a fiery sleeve took shape over the bulging bicep.

Bonnie latched on to Sapphira's elbow and backed away. "I don't think it wants a hug."

"Not likely." Sapphira raised her free hand. "Give me a fireball!" She looked at her uplifted palm. Nothing appeared.

Now engulfed in flames from its waist up, the figure took a step. As if breaking the façade away with its crunching weight, the stony boot crumbled, revealing more flames.

"It's too slow to catch us," Bonnie said, her retreat keeping pace with the statue's advance. "I wonder what it is."

"Once it's finished transforming, it might be a lot faster, so we'd—"

"You are solid rock!" The voice seemed to thunder across the land. The flaming man stopped in mid-step and hardened to stone again.

Bonnie looked up at the ash gray sky, searching for an airborne creature, something large enough to bellow such a resounding command, but nothing appeared.

A low voice droned. "It is wise to my eyes to avoid the citizens of this valley. You are likely not prepared to face them or displace them."

Bonnie again looked for the speaker of the rhyming words. A large red dragon stood near the brook, maybe a dozen feet away, the end of its tail flicking the water.

Pushing back her wet hair, she narrowed her eyes again, trying to get a good look at the dragon. This scene was so much like the first circle in the Circles of Seven, even the heaviness, a dragging weight that was worse than the effect of her saturated clothes.

"Do you fear me?" the dragon asked, his voice low but not unpleasant.

"Well . . ." Bonnie peeled her sweatshirt over her head and began wringing it out. Maybe it would be best to show confidence in spite of their circumstances. "*Should* I fear you?"

The dragon's eyes flashed dark blue, and his voice lowered to a growl. "Only my enemies need fear me. My friends revere me."

"Hmmm. . ." Bonnie squinted at him. He didn't answer the question, very much like the deceitful dragon in the circles. During that encounter, the dragon had tried to get her to look into a pool, in violation of a command to avoid reflections. If this one was trying to play games with her mind, she would have to be on the alert.

Sapphira stepped ahead of Bonnie. "What's your name? And how did you know to address us in English?"

Extending his neck, the dragon brought his head closer and spoke in what sounded like an old and lovely language.

Sapphira set her hands on her hips. "No, I don't prefer ancient Hebrew. I'm just trying to figure out who you are and where we are."

"You two are inquisitive for a pair of intruders." The dragon shuffled toward them and stopped within a wing's reach. "Tell me, if two alien beings barged into your home and demanded answers to their inane questions, would you be pleased or pestered?"

While Sapphira aimed a suspicious stare at him, Bonnie pondered his words. With only the dragon and statues in this land, a human could be considered alien, yet the statues seemed human enough. Apparently hewn out of some kind of black rock, they were roughly shaped and indistinct, though the faces carried more detail. "I would be pestered," she finally said.

"Why did you hesitate?" the dragon asked. "Is truth so precious in your land that you must speak it sparingly? Do you consider the cost of truth before you spend it? Or do you merely lend it at your leisure?"

Bonnie looked at Sapphira. With her hands still on her hips and her brow bent low, Sapphira seemed unwilling to play this dragon's game. Bonnie copied her pose, hoping to show her distrust, but for some reason, her arms and legs felt heavy and stiff. She had to raise and lower her feet as if marching in place to keep her blood circulating. And she had to answer. This dragon represented their only source of knowledge.

"It's fair to say that truth is precious in my world," Bonnie said. "There are many liars, as well as those who would use our words against us, making us hesitant to reveal all we know. Yet, among friends, we are glad to speak truth without reservation."

The dragon let out a long "Hmmm," then added, "Is that so?"

Sapphira dipped her knee as if offering a curtsy and flavored her tone with a lovely formality. "Please pardon our intrusion and our many questions, but since we all find truth to be valuable, is it not reasonable for us to seek it and for you to dispense it?"

The dragon gave them a slow nod. "Reasonable to ask? Yes. Reasonable to expect answers? Not necessarily. For the one bearing answers is sometimes obligated to hold his tongue. For some, truth is an incisive sword, a light in low luminance, a path to protection, yet, as the other lass has already indicated, in other hands, truth is a divider, a stone hurled to inflict injury, a club to beat down those who lack opportunity to light lamps of their own."

Bonnie let his words soak in. They seemed profound, more straightforward than those of the dragon in the Circles of Seven. And this dragon alternated between lovely prose and abrupt, in-your-face declarations, sometimes alliterating and sometimes speaking with rhymes. He was definitely not the evil dragon from the first circle.

"It is wise," the dragon continued, "to learn in what manner someone will wield a sword before equipping her with one. Quite often this discernment requires a test to prove both worth and wisdom, and those of integrity never fear the light that such a test would bring, for light is the key to every locked door."

"Very well." Sapphira bowed her head. "Since we have no opportunity to prove our worth, may we have leave to explore this land . . . to light our own lamps, as you say?"

"Have you grown weary of conversing with me?" Twin lines of smoke rose from his nostrils. "Do you think that I am unable to light your lamps? Ask me a question. I will give you a truthful answer."

Bonnie looked down at her legs. Her jeans were caked with dried mud. She stamped her foot lightly, making it break away and relieving a buzzing tingle.

"A truthful answer?" Sapphira spread out her arms. "What is this place, and who are you?"

"I invited a singular question," the dragon replied, "and you have offered a pair of puzzlers. Is requiring only one a reasonable request?"

"It's reasonable. I just wanted to save a little time."

"Ah, yes. Time. A tantalizing topic." The dragon set his head near Sapphira's and drilled his shining stare at her eyes. "Tell me, do you believe that God exists within a time framework, or is he outside of time, able to see every past and future event as if they were present?"

"Why does that matter?" Sapphira asked. "I'm just trying to figure out where we are."

Bonnie glanced once more at her heavy legs. As before, mud covered her pants from knees to ankles. She stomped both feet, loosening the dirt again.

"Explaining where you are," the dragon said, "is dependent on your understanding of time."

As the dragon droned on, Bonnie looked at Sapphira's legs. They, too, were coated with drying mud, and her feet seemed locked in place. Bonnie took Sapphira's hand and pulled her to the side, forcing her to move her feet. The mud cracked and flaked away.

"Why did you do that?" Sapphira asked.

"Just trust me." Bonnie shifted back to the dragon. "It's been nice talking to you, but we really need to go and learn about this place ourselves."

"Has it *really* been nice talking to me?" he asked. "Or is this an idiomatic pleasantry by which you are hiding the truth of the matter?"

Keeping hold of Sapphira's hand, Bonnie walked back the way they came. "We're going."

"You may go," the dragon said as daylight waned. "But you must begin without a flame or a flicker. As you discover the truths of my realm, your vision will be restored."

Bonnie wheeled back toward the dragon. Darkness blanketed everything in sight until only a pair of pulsing blue eyes floated in the midst. "I will provide you with a few of truth's precious gems," he continued. "First, you who claim to cherish the true treasures have neglected to secure a most precious valuable. Since the waterfall was your source of entry, I suggest you search the river. Second, you have no reason to assume that the creatures you meet in this place will tell you the truth. And third . . ." The eyes drew so close, Bonnie could feel the dragon's hot breath on her cheeks. "There is only one way to escape. That truth you must also learn on your own, but it might be a terrible truth that you will be unable to bear."

The eyes vanished, leaving Bonnie and Sapphira in complete darkness. A shiver ran along Bonnie's soaked skin. She checked for her necklace. It was gone, likely stripped over her head by the rushing water, but would the dragon be aware of that? "Do you know what valuable he was talking about?" she asked.

"Maybe . . ."

Bonnie waited, listening to the swish of Sapphira's wet clothes. A low groan followed.

"The ovulum and Elam's journal are gone!"

CHAPTER 10

A REUNION

Where did you last remember having them?" Bonnie asked.

"The ovulum was still in my pouch when we were on the ledge, and the journal was tucked behind my waistband, so they must have dropped out in the whirlpool. Since I was so wet, I guess I didn't notice the change."

"Come on." Bonnie groped for Sapphira's hand. "He said to search in the river."

As soon as she felt Sapphira's grip, Bonnie led her toward the sound of running water. "I don't think it's deep, and won't the ovulum glow? It should be easy to find."

"It doesn't always glow, and when it does, it's usually when I'm holding it. And the journal's probably waterlogged somewhere."

"True," Bonnie said. "We'd better concentrate on the ovulum." She thought about mentioning the journal's protective coating, but would that also protect it from water? She decided not to bring that up and raise potentially false hopes.

As their feet sloshed into the edge of the river, Sapphira drew back her hand. "I don't trust that dragon. Everything he said about truth being precious to him might have been a lie."

"I know what you mean," Bonnie said. "I've dealt with a lying dragon before, but he might be telling the truth about where the ovulum is. It's worth a try." She waded into thigh-deep water. At least she wouldn't have to worry about mud collecting on her clothes in here.

When it began getting shallower again, she moved back to the deepest section, stooped, and searched the sandy bottom with her fingers. "Do you know if it floats?"

Sapphira splashed next to her. "I don't remember it ever being in water."

"If it sinks, then it's likely to be in the middle instead of the sides, but if it floats, then the current might take it past us."

"And it might have already floated beyond this point."

Bonnie grimaced. Sapphira was right. This search might be a fool's game, but what else could they do? Consulting Enoch about this place and how to escape might be their only hope.

As she shuffled forward, listening to the sound of the nearby waterfall, the cold current chilled her skin, making her shiver again.

"It's getting colder," Sapphira said.

"I noticed." Bonnie had to clench her teeth to keep them from chattering. "I wonder why. I thought we might get used to it after a while."

A gentle laugh arose, far away and drifting on the wind. It sounded wonderfully alive and carefree.

"Did you hear that?" Bonnie asked.

"A woman laughing?"

"I think so."

"Just a second ago," Sapphira said, "I thought I heard a man talking. It's almost like he told a joke, and the woman laughed."

Bonnie shuddered, yet not from the chill of being wet. The feeling that someone was watching never seemed so real before. It felt like cold, curious fingers petted her bare forearm, raising a thousand new goose bumps.

As they pressed on, the sound of falling water grew louder. The riverbed descended, signaling the deeper pool dredged out by the plunging force. Strangely enough, a sense of warmth flowed across Bonnie's skin.

"Feel that?"

"I do." Sapphira ran a slippery finger across Bonnie's arm. "And the water feels oily, like it has some kind of petroleum in it. If there's a spring at the bottom, then this pool might be really deep. And if the ovulum sank, then—"

"It is quite deep, ladies."

Bonnie stopped. A male voice? Where did it come from?

"Who's there?" she asked.

"Bonnie, don't you recognize my voice?"

The sound came from the riverbank to her right. She turned that way and replayed the words in her mind. The voice was familiar, but hearing it in total darkness made it seem heavy, frightening. "I'm sorry," she said. "I don't—"

Sapphira grabbed Bonnie's arm and whispered, "Remember what the dragon said? Don't give away truth so fast."

"Right." Bonnie pressed her lips together. The voice still buzzed in her brain. It was so tantalizing, like a cry from her past, a call she couldn't possibly ignore.

Sapphira cleared her throat. "May I ask who is addressing us?"

"I am Dr. Matthew Conner, Bonnie's father."

A new chill ran up Bonnie's spine. "My father? But he died. I saw him die."

"So did you, Bonnie, and now you breathe the breath of life."

Bonnie stood upright, now in waist-deep water. The voice did sound like her father's, though younger, more like the father she knew when she was about six years old. "How did you come back to life?"

"I did not say that I came back to life. I only mentioned your resurrection, not mine."

Sapphira clutched Bonnie's wrist. "He's being evasive, Bonnie. I don't think—"

"The other water wader speaks again." He chuckled in a friendly manner. "May I suggest that the one standing on solid ground might be the one making more sense right now?"

"We might as well get out," Bonnie said. "If the ovulum sank, we won't find it until we have some light."

As the two trudged over to the bank, Bonnie felt a strong grip on her hand and a helpful pull. She didn't bother to resist.

The man released her and continued. "Do you know where you are, Bonnie?"

"We've been trying to figure that out, but the dragon—"

"The dragon wouldn't tell you, right?"

Bonnie let a laugh flavor her reply. "He's not exactly free with information."

"It took me a while to learn that lesson." The man's voice grew warm and caring. "Think about it, Bonnie. You saw me die at the hands of Devin, but when you visited Heaven, did you see me there?"

Bonnie's heart sank. Remembering the city of ivory and the streets of shimmering gold should have sparked joy and anticipation, but now, like every time she thought of that holy place, her emotions seemed torn. No, she hadn't seen him there, and ever since that visit, she forced herself to sweep away every thought that her daddy had instead been condemned.

"Your hesitation speaks volumes," he said. Fingers combed back her wet hair, and his voice trembled, filled with sorrow. "Sweet daughter, did you think I had gone to Hell?"

Bonnie swallowed hard. Sweet daughter? It was like an echo, a long lost dream. The words bathed her ears with fresh joy, the joy her images of Heaven should have kindled with every thought. How old was she when her father last uttered that phrase? Four? Five? When her wings started growing, the terms of endearment ended, replaced by . . . "Freak of nature," she whispered out loud.

The fingers pulled back. "What did you say?"

Bonnie pressed her lips together again. With tears welling, her voice cracked as her words poured out. "Daddy, you called me a freak of nature. I heard you. I was only about six, but I remember. I was playing with my dolls, and . . ." She felt smaller, vulnerable and weak. "You . . . you said it to Mama. It hurt. It really hurt a lot. And you never called me your sweet daughter again."

Her tears burst forth. Strong arms wrapped her up. A hand stroked her head and another rubbed her shoulder. "Oh, Bonnie! I'm sorry. I'm so, so sorry!"

She laid her head on his chest and wept. Her hands curled into fists, begging to pound his chest, yet her arms ached to hug him in return. She tried to speak, but her words came out in spasms. "Daddy . . . I . . . I love you. But . . . but you hurt me so bad. When I didn't see you in Heaven . . . I wasn't sad . . . not really. I just . . ." She threw her arms around him and pressed closer. "Oh, Daddy, I love you so much!"

The hands continued stroking her head, and his familiar voice, that tender voice from long ago, whispered in her ear. "I love you, too, sweet daughter. Never again will you fear the hateful words that imprisoned you. They are gone forever."

She blinked. Although tears blurred her vision, his shirt came into view. The darkness had faded, not much, but enough to see the man in her arms. She looked up at his face. Yes, it was Daddy. His face was the youthful one she remembered from her younger days. Although tears streamed down his cheeks as he gazed back at her, his eyes sparkled with delight.

"Bonnie," he said, his voice now weak and forlorn, "will you please forgive me?"

She tightened her grip and again pressed her head against his chest. "With all my heart."

As she pulled back, a brisk warm breeze freshened the air. She felt lighter, as though gravity had decreased by half. Even her clothes had given up their dragging effect. Had the breeze dried them that quickly?

With her hand still clutching her father's, Bonnie turned to Sapphira. "Look! It's my daddy!"

Sapphira stood at the edge of the waterfall's pool, her hair and clothes still dripping. "Bonnie, I can't look. It's still dark."

"Dark?" Glancing at her father, she walked to her and waved a hand in front of her eyes. She neither flinched nor blinked, and her pupils stayed dilated. "Very strange."

"That's one of the odd characteristics of this place," her father said. "The residents here have differing perspectives based on what they've learned, or allowed themselves to learn, and their perspectives become reality."

Bonnie looked downstream. The dragon was nowhere in sight. The statue that had nearly come to life stood motionless near the river's edge, and other stony figures marked the landscape both near and far. "Like those statues?"

"So it seems. Most were here before I arrived, but one man showed up later. He soon turned to stone."

"Why didn't you become a statue?"

"I did become one. I met the dragon, and we had a long discussion about truth and how the space-time continuum works. By the time we finished, I couldn't move. Then, when the other man arrived, I was able to listen to the conversation between him and the dragon. It wasn't long before he, too, became a statue, but it seemed as if his arrival somehow allowed me to break free. The dragon shouted for me, but I escaped before I could solidify. My feet began to catch on fire, so I ran through the edge of the river. Ever since, I've just stayed out of the dragon's sight."

"I don't blame you." Bonnie took Sapphira's hand. "Now if we could figure out how to get Sapphira to see, we might be able to search the pool for the ovulum."

Sapphira rubbed one of her arms. "The water is oily, Dr. Conner. Do you know why?"

"I hadn't noticed." He touched her skin and raised his finger to his nose. "It's a strong odor. Could it be camphor?"

After Sapphira smelled the back of her hand, her voice sharpened. "I think you're right!"

"Why the alarm?" Bonnie asked.

"It's the odor of Morgan's witchcraft. I smelled her brews so many times, I couldn't possibly forget. And it's the same thing I smelled when Goliath called to Roxil, back when Gabriel and I were trying to rescue her from Dragons' Rest."

Bonnie's father crossed his arms over his chest. "It seems that I have much to learn about this girl, don't I?"

Setting a hand over her mouth, Bonnie grinned. "I'm sorry. You were never introduced."

After Bonnie explained who Sapphira was, including a rapid-fire sketch of her life as an underborn and her most important adventures, she finished with a loud exhale. "And now we're looking for the ovulum to see if Enoch can tell us what's going on."

"Very interesting." Bonnie's father sniffed his finger again. "Sapphira, you might not be aware of this, but I am trained in pharmacy. It's no wonder Morgan used camphor in her spells. It has many analgesic properties, and, as she and other witches likely believed, it supposedly has spiritual properties. It was used to exorcize an evil spirit and to reduce certain bestial urges."

Blinking again, Sapphira reached for Bonnie. "I can see better now. It's still pretty dark, but I can tell it's you standing there."

"Revelations of truth are opening your eyes." Bonnie's father stroked his chin. "I'm learning as much by your visit as you are."

Sapphira stepped into the pool. "This feels like a portal. My eyesight is getting really sharp." As she lifted a hand, a ribbon of fire sprouted from her palm and spun into a fireball. "Look. My flames are back."

"But you can't light a transporting fire in the water," Bonnie said.

"No, but the camphor oil has a source in this world." Sapphira waded farther out. "With my portal eyesight, maybe I won't have to go very deep to figure out where it's coming from. And maybe the ovulum's down there, too."

"You're diving in?" Bonnie asked.

"Sure. I was hoping you'd come with me." Sapphira blew out the fireball in her palm. "Do your wings keep you from swimming?"

"Actually, they help me, but—"

"Then we should go together, just in case."

"Just in case what?" Bonnie asked as she stepped into the pool.

"I have no idea, but trouble is better faced in twos."

"Or threes." Bonnie's father waded in with the girls. "I have seen strange shadows in this pool. Maybe it was my imagination. Then again, maybe not."

With a jump, Sapphira dove in. Bonnie followed. She opened her eyes and found the Oracle gliding effortlessly downward, her body undulating as if she were a white-haired mermaid.

Bonnie angled her wings and pushed against the water. Like two massive flippers, they shot her forward. Holding her nose, she equalized the pressure and looked back. Her father gave her an "Okay" sign. He couldn't move as quickly, but he could see well enough to follow.

Now about fifteen feet down, she caught up with Sapphira. With bubbles rising from her nose as she hovered, the Oracle pointed into the darker depths. A faint glow pulsed, red in a sea of black.

Bonnie thrust with her wings and shot toward the glow, continuing to equalize pressure as she dove. With her eyes burning and the slimy sensation increasing, the water felt like cooking oil. When she reached bottom, she found the ovulum lodged between two rocky knobs. Tiny bubbles percolated from dozens of pores in the pumicelike floor, popping as they rose toward the surface.

Grabbing the ovulum, Bonnie pulled, but the knobs held it fast. With her lungs aching, she couldn't afford a delay. She pulled again. Still no movement.

Her father lunged past her and grasped the egg. Flexing his muscles, he jerked it free. Bubbles poured out, thousands, big and small. Sapphira joined them, frantically waving her arms and pointing toward the surface.

A shadow loomed over them. As it drew closer, light from above faded. Red pinpoints appeared in the shadow, bright and angry.

Sapphira waved an arm, shouting a warped cry. Her own bubbles blended with the chaotic mix. As her palm swept through the effervescence, sparks erupted. Then, like lightning arcing across the sky, the sparks leaped from bubble to bubble, igniting the gas within.

With rising bubbles feeding the storm, a web of electrical pulses surrounded the swimmers. Every popping bubble that struck Bonnie's skin felt like a hornet's sting. All three batted at the swarm. Above, the shadow continued to hover, as if waiting to pounce should the victims swim out of the hive.

Sapphira waved both arms around her body and swept the water in a circle. Bonnie did the same, touching her father with her foot to get him to join in. Soon they created a vortex. As the web of sparks swirled around them, Bonnie's chest felt like it was about to explode. Her body demanded oxygen. She had to breathe . . . now!

The orbiting web of sparks blurred into long, fuzzy streaks. Soon, everything went black. The oily wetness streamed down her arms and legs, like slippery worms sliding across her skin. She sucked in air. Finally! Although saturated with camphor and garlic, it was the sweetest breath she had ever taken.

Blinking, she searched for her father and Sapphira. She dared not whisper. Who could tell what evil lurked in this dark place? A dripping sound reached her ear, multiple streams hitting a solid floor. She craned her neck. Wet clothes? These weren't her own wet clothes. The drips came from about five feet away.

Taking a step, she reached out and touched someone, a shorter person, soaked, yet warm. Grabbing a handful of wet material, she pulled the person close and whispered, "Sapphira?"

"Shhh," came the reply. "Enoch is speaking to me." As Sapphira turned, the ovulum's glow appeared.

"I'll be quiet," Bonnie said, "as soon as I find my father."

"I don't think he came with us."

"Then he had to face that dark creature we saw?"

"I think so." Sapphira shushed Bonnie again and lifted the ovulum close, still whispering. "Bonnie's here, Father Enoch. Please repeat what you told me."

The prophet's low voice emanated from the crystalline egg, stirring the red mist within, but static blended with the voice, as if the signal came from a distant radio station. "Sapphira asked why the ovulum glowed," Enoch said. "I have been calling you from my viewing room at Heaven's Altar, and my call brought light to the ovulum's inner mist."

The radiance darkened, then sparked with life again, the shifts in power coinciding with the surges of static. "Sapphira told me," Enoch continued, "that your father is present in your current realm."

"Yes," Bonnie said. "There's no doubt about it." Now that her eyes had adjusted to the ovulum's light, she looked around the room. A square of stone walls surrounded them, the closest one maybe four feet away, while the others stood at least five times farther. The near wall displayed rows of ornate columns with indistinct murals in between. The red glow dispersed above, revealing no cap on this stony box of a room, but the lack of moving air gave evidence that some kind of roof sealed them in.

"Very interesting," Enoch said, his voice still distant and scratchy. "Since your father and I never crossed paths at Heaven's Altar, I wondered what became of him, so a few months ago I consulted the Prism Oracle. Dr. Matthew Conner stood in the Oracle's spray without hood, crown, or walking stick, indicating that he had, indeed, passed from life on Earth. But it also means that he was neither in Heaven nor in Hades. I searched the Bridgelands and as much of Second Eden as I could, but I found no trace of him."

"Is there any way you can find out if he's okay?" Bonnie asked. "I mean, did Sapphira tell you about the creature in the pool?"

"She told me. Since your father is already dead, yours was the greater danger. Only those in Hades need fear the second death. My guess is that he escaped unharmed."

"Then where are we?" Bonnie asked. "Another afterlife realm of some kind?"

"As one who lives in Heaven's Altar rather than Heaven itself, I have very little access to those who know more than I do. Occasionally I have the opportunity to speak to a passing angel, but they are usually in a great hurry, and my inquiry about Dr. Conner pales in importance to whatever task the angel has been called to accomplish. Still, a Seraph paused for a moment to tell me about a place your father might be, a realm called the Valley of Souls."

"The Valley of Souls," Bonnie repeated in a whisper.

The ovulum's light faded to a bare hint of a glow, diminishing Enoch's voice further. "I had never heard of it. I consulted my books but found no such entry, and I had no further opportunity to consult an angel."

Sapphira breathed another shush. "I hear something." She pushed the ovulum back into her pouch, covering its light.

A dragging sound filtered in, each slide followed by a thump. The noise grew louder by the second, and a throaty grunt punctuated the thumps.

A tiny flame sprouted from Sapphira's finger. "We'd better hide," she said, pulling Bonnie toward the wall. They crouched behind one of the Ionic columns, not quite wide enough to hide them both. Sapphira blew out her flame and whispered "Shhhh." They crouched and peered around the marble pillar, straining to listen.

Slide. Clump. Oomph. Slide. Clump. Oomph.

In a distant hallway, a flicker of orange light appeared. As it expanded, a shadow expanded with it. Draconic in shape, the shadow stretched upward and arched along the curve of a domed ceiling. Below, the creature casting the shadow took shape, a dragon, the same dragon they had seen by the river, carrying a lantern with one clawed hand and a chain with the other.

After each step, it jerked the chain, and a trailing object thumped against the floor. As he drew closer, his lantern illuminated a large stone table at the center of the room. About four feet in height and at least ten feet long, it looked like a place for a large family to gather.

The dragon set the lantern on the table. The light danced across an array of three-legged wooden mounts. They looked like stands that might hold a display, maybe a book or a framed photo, but they were empty. A taller mount sat in the middle of the table, also empty. Stubby candles surrounded the central mount, their colors indiscernible.

Giving the chain a final jerk, the dragon brought the trailing object into view—a statue, human in shape and size, apparently one of the figures they had seen near the waterfall's river. The dragon set it upright, carefully balancing it next to the table. With his hands raised, the petrified man seemed to be singing, as if lifting up a psalm of praise.

After looking it over, the dragon breathed a stream of fire and covered the statue in flaming tongues from top to bottom. Like mud streaming from a filthy child, the statue's black coat washed away, leaving behind a flaming man, still frozen in his worship position.

As if thawing from a deep freeze, the man began to slump, his limbs as fiery as Sapphira's when she kept the monkey men at bay. The dragon caught him with a foreleg and picked up a small bottle from the table. After taking out a stopper with his teeth, he poured a single drop on top of the man's head. Dense fog crawled along the man's scalp and filtered down over his face and shoulders. Soon, the fog enveloped his entire body, veiling him and the dragon's limbs completely.

For a moment, all was silent. Then, a huff sounded, and the fog blew away. An egg-shaped crystal about the same size as the ovulum sat in the dragon's cupped hand. He placed it gently on the center mount, picked up a hefty stylus, and scratched something down in a huge open book.

After putting the bottle on the table and picking up the lantern, he turned. He sniffed the air. Blue beams, much wider than the narrow lasers other dragons used, swept slowly across the wall adjacent to where Bonnie and Sapphira hid. They crouched low and squeezed behind the column.

The beams passed the corner and began tracing their wall, pausing as they met each column. When the beams reached the girls' hiding place, they paused again, then moved past.

The blue lasers flicked off. Frowning, the dragon turned again and shuffled into the hallway. Soon, with the sound of the dragon's sliding steps dying away, the lantern's aura shrank.

With the dying light still enough to guide them, Sapphira tiptoed out and crept toward the table. Bonnie followed, peering down the hallway. No sign of the dragon.

Sapphira relit her fingertip and touched it to the wick of one of the candles. As its flame sparked, she snuffed her own flame and slid the candle close to the book.

"What about the ovulum?" Bonnie whispered. "Is Enoch still with us?"

Sapphira opened her pouch and peeked at the egg. It was completely dark. "I think we lost the signal."

"Then we're on our own." Bonnie studied the book. Thousands of oddly shaped symbols covered the parchment, more like tiny cartoon characters than letters or numbers. With no apparent rows or columns, the symbols seemed random, a mosaic of scattered shapes.

"I can't read this," Sapphira whispered. "It's a language I've never seen before."

Bonnie touched one of the characters, a birdlike creature. "Maybe it's like hieroglyphics. The pictures represent—"

A string of whispered words rose from the page, strange and guttural. Bonnie jerked her hand away and stepped back. "What was that?"

"It's an old language." Sapphira narrowed her eyes. "Roughly translated, it said, 'Dragon essence recognized. Language recognized. Translation in progress.'"

"Dragon essence?" Bonnie pointed at herself. "It detected that in me?"

"That's my guess. Maybe it's like a password. Only a dragon is allowed to see what all this stuff means."

Bonnie squinted at the page. The symbols darkened and lifted from the parchment, growing and morphing as they elevated. The bird transformed into a dragon with purple scales. Two humans rode on its back, a man and a girl strapped into seats, the girl apparently the pilot as she slapped the dragon's neck and whistled.

Backing away with Sapphira, Bonnie looked at the corridor again. Would the dragon hear the commotion and return? She froze in place, unable to hide. The sight was too mesmerizing, almost hypnotic.

The dragon, about the size of a human hand, flew several inches above the book, which had become a valley scene, a forest with a river running through it. As soon as it landed, the man slid down and helped the girl dismount. After speaking quietly for a moment, they looked up at the sky. Another dragon approached, a white one, also carrying two riders.

The man scooped up the girl, ran into the forest, and stopped at a cave. Trembling, he shouted into the cave's opening. "Oracle! I have come with the sacrifice. Are you there?"

A brilliant light poured from the cave, and someone answered, but the rush of the river and the beating wings of the approaching white dragon drowned out the voice.

The man leaped away from the blazing light. Caressing the girl's cheek, he spoke to her, but again, the surrounding noise made the words impossible to hear.

Sapphira tugged Bonnie's sleeve. "I know that man," she whispered. "He's Makaidos, king of the dragons. That's his human form. I met him in Dragons' Rest."

"Enoch told my mother that Makaidos sacrificed himself to save Roxil and Ashley, and now his bones have the power to regenerate." Bonnie edged closer to the scene. "With all the fire and fog, I couldn't tell for sure, but that man looks like the statue the dragon brought in here. If he's Makaidos, his human name is Timothy."

Sapphira joined her. "I thought he looked familiar, too. They're probably one and the same."

"If so," Bonnie said, "it would make sense for the dragon to have the book open to his page."

"But he looked younger when he came out of the statue, maybe early twenties."

"Shhh!" Bonnie pointed at the scene. "Look!"

Timothy held a dagger against the girl's throat. A woman shuffled toward him on her knees, her hands clasped, while another man looked on. Suddenly, Timothy pushed the girl toward the woman and dashed into the cave. The light transformed into a rush of flames. As cries of "Timothy! No!" rang out, the scene crumbled and fell to the page.

Bonnie tiptoed back to the table and touched the book. "Could this hold the stories behind all the people here?"

"That's what I was thinking."

Bonnie studied the page again. Near the bottom, an English entry, penned in lovely script, read:

Makaidos, also known as Timothy. Scheduled to be recalled from the Valley of Souls to Second Eden. Implanted in ovulum. Mounted in transport position. First attempt failed when residents did not call upon him by name. Goliath, also known as Dragon, transported in his place from an alternate ovulum mount. Because of the freedoms granted to Goliath, if he resurrects as a dragon, he will likely retain his memory of his time here and remember that his son also dwells in the valley. Makaidos will also remember this place, but only if those in Second Eden are wise enough to learn of the necessary sacrifice. Otherwise, he will not survive.

She looked at the array of wooden mounts on the table, one holding the egg the dragon had made. Were the others the "alternate" mounts? Could this place be a resurrection portal of some kind? She nudged Sapphira and whispered, "Is your eyesight sharper here?"

"I think so. And I feel a heaviness. It's a portal, for sure."

A flicker of light caught Bonnie's attention. She looked down the hallway. Nothing but darkness.

She lowered her voice even further. "Should we see where that corridor goes?"

Sapphira matched her tone. "I'm thinking the book might tell us. It's safer that way."

"I wonder if it has an index of some kind." Bonnie marked the page with one finger, pressed another finger behind the last page, and flipped to the back of the book. As before, dozens of odd symbols covered the parchment, but these seemed more organized, as if lined up in two columns. She touched a symbol at the top that appeared to be one of the column headings, larger and darker than the entries beneath it.

The book's voice returned. "Destination Earth."

She touched the other heading. Again, the voice rose. "Destination Second Eden."

"Look." Bonnie pointed at the first column. "This list is a lot shorter than the other one."

"I think I'm getting the picture." Sapphira set her finger on a symbol in the Earth column. "Try this one."

As soon as Bonnie touched the entry, the voice responded in monotone. "Lazarus of Bethany. Called back to Earth by the Son of God."

She moved her finger to another line.

"Dorcas, otherwise known as Tabitha. Called back to Earth by Peter, the apostle."

Bonnie stared at Sapphira. "This is a list of resurrections!"

"No wonder it's short. There probably haven't been that many bodily resurrections. How many are listed here? Fifty, maybe?"

"Looks like it." Bonnie touched a symbol closer to the bottom, a small bird.

"Bonnie Conner, otherwise known as Bonnie Silver. Called back to Earth by Ashley Stalworth, dragon healer."

Now staring at the mounted egg, Bonnie swallowed through a lump. What could it mean? Had she come to this place? Had she been a statue, dragged to this room by the dragon and placed inside an egg? But how could that be? She had traveled to Heaven. She had seen Jesus and rested in his embrace. Could it all have been a dream?

She touched the entry again. "I wonder how we can find the right page that will tell what happened to me."

The parchment bent. As Bonnie withdrew her hand, the pages flipped and stopped at a point near the back of the book. She touched one of the symbols, a humanlike figure, and, as before, the characters rose from the page and painted a scene, the quaint village in the sixth circle of Hades, complete with the street, the pitcher pump, and the building where Bonnie and Shiloh tried to escape through an electrified doorway.

In the image, Bonnie, less than a twentieth her normal size, pushed her wing into the doorway, blocking the light. Shiloh leaped through and disappeared. The charge slung Bonnie away, and she tumbled across a road, her limbs and wings flopping wildly. She came to rest in a cloud of dust, gasping for breath.

A man appeared out of nowhere, a tall man walking slowly toward her. An aura of light surrounded him from head to toe, much brighter around his face, blurring his features.

The miniature Bonnie called out, "Jesus, help me!"

The man drew closer and sang out, "Contentment holds eternal keys to days of peace that never pass."

As her breathing eased, Bonnie whispered, "Contentment," and closed her eyes.

The man leaned over, scooped her spirit effortlessly into his arms, leaving her dead body behind. He kissed her forehead. "Come, my child, my beloved lamb, and see what awaits you in your final resting place."

As the man held her aloft, the village faded away. Seconds later, a new scene took shape, a dazzling city with streets of gold, gem-coated ivory buildings, and a lush tree heavy with enormous fruit. People strolled along the streets, singing and talking, each one with a brilliant smile.

The man covered Bonnie's mouth with his own, a kiss of sorts, but much more than a kiss, the passing of breath from one soul to another. As he pulled his head back, she gasped and inhaled. As gentle as a first-time father with a newborn, he set her down feetfirst. She looked all around, her eyes wide. The man pointed at various people, whispering to her, as if telling her each person's name.

Finally, she turned and gazed at him, her eyes sparkling. "Jesus?"

"Yes, little lamb," he said, extending his arms.

She leaped into his embrace and disappeared for a moment within the light. When he released her, she bounced on her toes. "Am I in Heaven?"

His voice, fine and resonant, seemed peaceful, unhurried. "You are at Heaven's boundary so that I may give you this glimpse of what awaits you. Remember what you have seen, for you will need this vision to encourage another child of mine in the near future."

"So I'm not staying?" Her head drooped a fraction.

Smiling, he set his finger under her chin. "After one of my angels leads you on a brief tour, I will take you to the Valley of Souls where you will await your resurrection to Earth. When you rise, you will not remember that valley at all, for it is a land between the worlds where all events are lost, save for what is recorded in Abaddon's log book."

As if blown by the majestic voice, the book's projected image faded away.

"Abaddon?" Sapphira asked. "That name sounds familiar."

Bonnie rolled her eyes upward as she tried to recall the Scriptures. "In Revelation, Abaddon is the angel of the abyss. In the Old Testament, the name was used side by side with Death and Sheol."

"Do you think he's the dragon?"

"Maybe." Bonnie touched her chin, repeating the words from the vision. A land between the worlds, a place to await a resurrection. So she really *was* here!

After finding Makaidos's page again, she kept her finger there and flipped back to the index. "Let's see what the other column is all about." She touched one of the symbols near the center of the list.

"Unborn hybrid," the voice said. "Daughter of Tamara, the former dragon. Killed in the womb."

Bonnie touched the name again. The book flipped back to the appropriate page, but this time, instead of characters, English words spelled out the logged entry.

This is an unusual case. The female child came to me as a hybrid, part dragon and part human, as if an incomplete metamorphosis had taken place. Although she was weak and malformed, the spirit in her pulsed with a radiance I have rarely seen. Because of her dual

natures, I decided not to give her a rubellite ring as I had given the human child who became Angel, that is, the unborn offspring of Rebekah, the former dragon. Instead, I assigned two companions to her, one of dragon essence and one of human essence, and they seemed at odds with one another immediately. I granted one the right to name the child, and it decided immediately, much earlier than the usual one-year standard. Why it chose "Listener," I do not yet know. I then sent the child to Second Eden.

"What about my father?" Bonnie turned back to the index. "If he's in this place, maybe Abaddon wrote about him."

Sapphira set a hand on Bonnie's arm. "I thought I saw something, a flash of light down the hall."

Bonnie looked that way. "I saw it earlier. I'll hurry."

She touched several entries in the first column in rapid succession, listening to each name the book announced, but none seemed familiar. Then, beginning at the bottom of the second column, she touched those entries until it said, "Matthew Conner. Killed by Devin the dragon slayer."

When she touched the entry a second time, the book flipped back a few leaves of parchment. Again, the page contained only words.

After I received Matthew Conner and used my rhetoric to turn him into stone, he escaped, and I have not been able to locate him. Because the land of Second Eden cries out for his medical expertise, he was scheduled to go there at this time of danger. I will continue to search for him, for the days in that land continue to darken. Without him, many could die.

Sapphira jerked Bonnie's arm and hissed, "Someone's coming."

Bonnie flipped the book to Makaidos's page and ran with Sapphira back to the column. As they hid behind it, Bonnie tried to settle her breathing, but to little avail. Knowing now that the dragon was probably the dreaded Abaddon, a powerful angel, her heart thumped wildly.

As before, lantern light drew close and filled the hallway, ushering in the draconic shadow. The new light played on the walls, but something was different, a tiny competing shadow.

Bonnie looked back at the table and gulped. The candle! It was still lit!

She grabbed Sapphira's knee and pointed. With a wave of her hand, Sapphira whispered, "Extinguish." The candle's flame withered and disappeared.

The dragon shuffled into the room and set the lantern on the table along with a large hourglass. His scaly brow arched down. Picking up the candle, he stared at a thin string of smoke rising from the wick.

His blue eyebeams flicked on again. "Intruder," he said with a calm voice, "if you insist on snooping and stealth, then you are proving your lack of love for truth. Those of high character live in the light, unashamed of being seen no matter where they go. I entreat you, in the name of integrity and incorruptibility, make the choice to show yourself, and your punishment will not be pitiless. If you ply a treacherous trade in this domain, you will surely fail, and the injury will come upon your own head. So I will not seek for you. The choice is yours."

CHAPTER 11

ABADDON'S LAIR

Bonnie measured the dragon's words. Of course she wasn't being treacherous, but she didn't want to suffer punishment, severe or not. Yet, if he was Abaddon, he was really an angel, but was Abaddon a good angel or a fallen angel? She couldn't remember if the Bible made that clear.

She looked at Sapphira, who was now staring straight at her. Sapphira raised her hand, as if conveying a stop sign. Silently they agreed to take their chances and wait where they were.

The dragon flicked off his beams and let out a long, "Hmmm."

Turning back to the table, he flipped over the hourglass. Sand trickled through the pinched glass and collected in the lower half, each grain sparkling as if electrically charged.

"The time of resurrection approaches," the dragon said. "When the last grain falls, the ceremony in Second Eden will commence, and those on the table who are called from that realm will rise to resume life there. But what brings life to them will bring strife to others. If you are in this chamber when the table is energized by power from on high, and you are unprepared, you will die." Breathing a spark-filled stream, the dragon turned and walked toward the hall.

When the lantern light died away, Sapphira rose and lit up one of her fingers. "Should we try to open the portal here? That would be the quickest way out, and maybe we could help the people of Second Eden."

Bonnie scooted to the table and eyed the hourglass. At the rate the sand fell, it looked like they had at least several minutes. "We have to get my father to give himself up to the dragon. Second Eden needs a doctor."

"But we'd have to find both your father and Abaddon before time runs out." Sapphira touched the bottle of liquid the dragon used to put Timothy into an ovulum. "We could try to do it ourselves."

"Should we follow the dragon?" Bonnie asked. "Maybe he would help us if he thought I could talk my father into going."

Lighting a fireball in her hand, Sapphira looked around the room. "I don't see any other way to get out, so following him makes sense."

"Then we'd better take this." Bonnie picked up the hourglass. From top to bottom, it was about the size of her head. "That way we'll know how much time we have."

"Fair enough. He probably left it here for us anyway."

Sapphira led the way through the hall. With their wet shoes squeaking on the stone floor, they had to soften their steps. Even the weakest squish echoed in the cavernous corridor.

A warm breeze blew past. Although permeated by camphor and garlic, it felt good as it swept through their wet clothes. Bonnie touched her sweatshirt, merely damp now. The humidity in this place had to be extremely low for it to dry that quickly.

As Sapphira's fireball washed the hallway in pulsing light, Bonnie scanned the surroundings. Vibrant frescoes decorated each side wall—men and women rising from coffins and hospital beds, babies hatching from plant sacs, and a man walking out of a cave, bound like a mummy in linen wrappings.

At the border of each mural, a painting of an open door ushered in the next fresco. The doors were old and wooden with hinged iron knockers, and a dragon ducked his head to pass through. Each dragon at each door carried a lantern at eye level, the glow extending behind him halfway across the previous mural and also forward to meet the glow from the next dragon's lantern. The series of dragons seemed to be a guide to passersby as they walked through the corridor in this museum of resurrection.

Bonnie looked from side to side, trying to find any of the biblical accounts of resurrection. One might have been Lazarus coming out of his tomb, but without labels it was impossible to tell for certain.

Soon, a new arc of light came into view far ahead. As the flickering aura bobbed up and down with the dragon's now familiar gait, Sapphira blew out her fireball. They slowed their pace further.

After a few more seconds, Bonnie spotted the dragon. An old wooden door swung out on its own, and he disappeared through the opening, leaving her and Sapphira in the retreating light of his lantern.

A shiver ran across Bonnie's skin. She felt like a character in one of the murals, or a lost museum patron trying to find the exit. It seemed that Abaddon was leading them along. He had even left the door open. They had to keep following. They didn't have much choice.

Still pressing their shoes down quietly, Bonnie and Sapphira kept pace. After traversing another long hall, this one without frescoes, they stopped at a second door. This one was closed, and the dragon's lantern hung on a hook attached to the ceiling. A long shepherd's hook leaned against the wall next to the doorjamb. With the warm breeze still flowing, the lantern swung lazily from its perch.

Sapphira grasped a metal handle and pushed the door, then pulled, but it wouldn't budge. "Should we look for another exit?"

"It doesn't make sense," Bonnie said. "I think Abaddon was leading us. He even left a lantern here, so why would he give us a dead end now?"

"A test?" Sapphira asked.

"He did talk about a test to prove wisdom."

Sapphira knitted her brow. "Just what we need. We're in a hurry to save lives, and this dragon wants us to solve a puzzle."

"But to him we're intruders. Why shouldn't we have to pass a test?"

Sapphira blew out a sigh. "Okay. Time's running out. What could the test be?"

"Do you sense a portal?"

Sapphira furrowed her brow for a moment before shaking her head. "It seems normal."

"A secret word, maybe?"

"I have no idea what it would be. I doubt that 'Open sesame' is going to work here."

Bonnie glanced at the hourglass. It looked like about a fourth of the sand had drained to the bottom. "How about a series of knocks? You know, the six, nine, thirteen combination you told me about."

"How would Abaddon know about that?"

"It can't hurt to try, can it?"

"It *can* hurt." Sapphira lowered her voice a notch. "He'll know for sure that we're here."

"I think he already knows."

"Okay. I guess it's worth a try." Sapphira stepped up to the door and tapped six times with her knuckles. After a moment's pause, she tapped nine times, then thirteen.

Nothing happened. It seemed that the door glared at them impatiently.

Sapphira picked up the shepherd's staff. "Should I knock with this?"

Bonnie touched the curved end. What could it be for? There weren't any sheep around, and knocking with a staff wouldn't be any different than knocking with a hand, would it?

As she thought, a slight squeaking sound made her look up. The lantern continued to sway in the breeze.

"I have an idea." She set the hourglass down, took the staff, and reached the curved end toward the lantern. With a deft twist, she looped the end through the handle and lifted the lantern from the hook. As she brought it down, she backed away from Sapphira, allowing her to take it.

"I remember now," Sapphira said, holding up the lantern. "The dragon said something about light being a key."

"A key to every locked door." Bonnie put the staff back in place and picked up the hourglass. "I guess we just walk toward the door."

Extending the lantern, Sapphira waved it across the door from left to right. With a low creak, the heavy panel swung toward them. Daylight spilled in, though still muted by the gray overcast.

Bonnie shielded her eyes and stepped out into the valley they had left behind. As her vision adjusted, she scanned the scene—grass under her feet, a river only fifty or so paces away, and several statues standing at various places.

Sapphira joined her. "Now to find your father."

The rusty hinges sounded again. Bonnie spun back, but there was no wooden door, just a rectangular hole in the scenery that led into the hallway. When the panel closed, the gap filled in, leaving no sign of the passage to the resurrection chamber.

She tried to touch the invisible door, but her hand passed right through. "How are we going to find this place again?"

"With this." Sapphira set the lantern on the grass. "If we find the lantern, we find the door."

"That might be a big *if*."

"We'll make a sign at the riverbank."

The two ran to the river's edge. Sapphira fished a grapefruit-sized oblong stone from the bed and drove it far enough into the soft ground to make it stand on end. "That ought to do it," she said, clapping her hands together.

Bonnie nodded upstream. "Let's go. The sand is almost half gone." Holding the hourglass steady, she took off in a trot. As they ran, she searched for Abaddon, but he was nowhere in sight. Within a minute, they arrived at the waterfall. Bonnie stopped at the edge of the pool.

"Daddy!" she called. "It's Bonnie!"

Sapphira looked into the deep water. "No sign of him down there."

Bonnie scanned the sandy edge for footprints. She found tracks leading in but nothing leading out.

"Look!" Sapphira pointed at a long indentation closer to the waterfall. "Something was dragged away from here."

Bonnie and Sapphira followed a trail of flattened sand and grass that ran parallel to the waterfall's cliff. It led into a sparse forest of skinny pines and a few oaks. Since needles coated the ground, the trail was easy to follow. Finally, they rounded a massive oak and found his body sitting upright against the trunk.

"Daddy?" Bonnie dropped to her knees next to him. His clothes felt damp, and his eyes were closed. "Are you all right?"

"He is alive," a female with a French accent replied, "but he is unconscious."

Bonnie turned toward the sound. A teenager sat on a knee-high boulder only a few feet away. With waist-length blonde hair, a long white dress overlaid with a brown tunic, and a sword scabbard attached to a leather belt, she seemed to have stepped out of a medieval storybook. A shield leaning against the boulder completed the portrait.

"Who are you?" Bonnie asked.

The girl slid down. As soon as her feet touched the needle-strewn path, her body burst into flames.

Bonnie gasped and stepped back, but Sapphira held her ground, staring.

The girl walked toward them, her beaming face still clear through the flames. Although her feet blazed, the needles didn't catch fire. "I am a sojourner, like your father, yet I am not a fugitive from the dragon." With her hands folded behind her, she leaned to the side as if trying to look behind Bonnie. "May I ask who you are? I have never seen a winged maiden before."

Trying not to tremble, Bonnie drew a wing around to her front and touched the tip. "I guess you could call me a sojourner, too. I'm from West Virginia in the United States."

"I see. And as you have likely guessed, I am from France." She added a gentle laugh, the same laugh Bonnie heard during their search for the ovulum. "I have been told that my English carries my native land's flavor."

Bonnie looked at the hourglass. Two-thirds of the sand had spilled into the bottom. "We have to get him to the resurrection table. Can you help us?"

The girl gazed at Bonnie's father. "I have watched this one. He fears Abaddon's enchantment and has hidden for quite some time. But all who will rise from the table must willingly come under the dragon's control."

"What about you?" Sapphira asked. "You're not one of the statues."

"Until it is my turn to rise to new life, I have been assigned to watch over the reluctant ones. I am here to show them what they must become, spirits enflamed by an indwelling passion to serve God with body, soul, and mind. You might say that I am an illustration." She withdrew a sword from her scabbard and rested it on her shoulder. "Your father was attacked by the pool's guardian, a stingray of sorts. I rescued him and purged the water from his lungs, but he now suffers from the stinger's poison."

"Poison?" Bonnie reached into her pocket and withdrew Elam's vial. After jerking the stopper out with her teeth, she pushed the top between her father's lips and tapped the bottom, forcing the last drops into his mouth.

She pushed the vial back into her pocket and drummed her fingers against her thigh, watching for the slightest hint of change as she spoke through clenched teeth. "Come on. Come on."

Her father blinked his eyes. As he looked at her, his brow shot up. "Bonnie?"

"Daddy!" She hugged him briefly, then grabbed his arms, grunting as she pulled him up. "Come on! We have to resurrect you from the dead."

* * *

Billy felt a nudge. Was it part of his dream? Maybe.

Then again, maybe not. He turned his head. More sleep. He just needed a little more sleep.

The nudge came again. "I'm sorry to wake you, but we have a lot to talk about."

Forcing his eyes open, Billy looked up from his straw-stuffed pillow. "Elam?"

Elam stood next to his bed, dressed in his new battle uniform, an orange short-sleeved tunic over two shirts—a thick, silver shirt with sleeves almost to his elbows and a red one with sleeves reaching to his wrists. "I talked to Ashley. It sounds like you and Walter had quite a night."

Billy scanned the room. Sir Barlow and Candle stood near the open door, their hands loosely gripping the hilts of their swords. Candle's companion rushed through the boy's dreadlocks, making them sway.

"Yeah, we did," Billy said. "How's he doing?"

Elam touched the front of his tunic where a red dragon marching on his hind legs was superimposed over a circle divided into twelve sections, emblematic of the twelve dragons who were called to become humans in the time of King Arthur. "The chest wound is still pretty bad, but thanks to some heroic surgery by Ashley, Steadfast, and you, it looks like he'll be all right, though he'll be laid up for a while."

Billy rose to a sitting position and focused on Elam's face. Although a smile dressed his lips, his eyes seemed far more serious. "What time is it?"

"Almost second hour. That's why I woke you. You said you were going to test the portal with Acacia, so you need to get started. Also, Candle would like another flying lesson, and we have some other business to discuss before the ceremony tonight."

"Other business?"

Elam turned and nodded at Barlow and Candle. "Go ahead and gather the men and horses. I'll be at the training field in a few minutes."

"Valiant and Windor gathered them," Candle said. "Dikaios and Ember are already at the field. I thought you knew—"

"Ahem!" Sir Barlow grasped Candle's arm. "Very good, warrior chief," Barlow said. "We will see you at the training grounds." He turned and hustled Candle out the door.

As they departed, Barlow's powerful voice carried back to the hut, fading as they grew more distant. "Never *remind* a commanding officer of something both of you already know. That was just his way of telling us that he wanted to speak to William in private. It is important to learn . . ."

Smiling, Elam reached down, locked wrists with Billy, and hoisted him to his feet. "Emerald told me about her guest, the woman who brought her son, the burn victim."

"Right. Semiramis." Billy stretched his stiff back. He wasn't quite accustomed to sleeping on straw. "Her son was pretty bad off. I didn't know what else to do."

Elam patted Billy on the shoulder. "You did fine. Apparently she tells a convincing story."

"You think it's not true?"

"I'm not saying that, but after encountering her at the bridge, I'm not sure what to believe. She tried to get me to go another way, and that would have been the wrong choice."

Billy picked his cloak off the floor and put one arm through a sleeve. "Being wrong about something doesn't make a person evil."

"Trust me. I know. I've been wrong plenty of times. And her story about being betrayed by Arramos makes sense, too, but there are holes she needs to fill." Elam rested his hand on the hilt of a sword protruding from a scabbard at his hip. "Why does she live in the Bridgelands while her son lives in Second Eden? If she has a son who looks about fifty, why does she look no older than twenty-five? Why hasn't anyone here ever heard of the village he's supposedly from? Yet, Hunter has a companion, so it's hard to dispute that he's a true Second Eden resident."

"And she doesn't seem to pose any danger," Billy added. "Clefspeare didn't detect any."

"Neither did Thigocia or Hartanna. They talked to her this morning."

"How about Ashley? Could she pick up anything?"

Elam shook his head. "But that doesn't really prove much. Back when they first met at the bridge, Ashley didn't detect Semiramis's presence.

And since Semiramis is somehow able to block her thoughts, Ashley doesn't trust her. If Semiramis didn't have anything to hide, she wouldn't be putting up a shield."

"Makes sense, unless Semiramis doesn't trust Ashley."

Elam tightened his grip on his sword, and his voice lowered. "You weren't at the bridge. If you had seen her that day, you would know that my low regard for Semiramis needs no further proof."

They stared at each other for a moment. Billy firmed his chin and gave Elam a nod of surrender. Obviously this thousands-of-years-old warrior had a lot more experience. "I'd better check on Walter." Billy finished putting on his cloak. "Maybe a good pep talk will cheer him up."

Elam grabbed his arm. "Do it when you get back. Acacia and Listener are already waiting at the dragon launching field. And Listener made breakfast for you, so after you wash up, you can get started."

"I guess you're right." Picking up a basin and Excalibur, Billy headed to an area behind the hut, filled his basin from a pump, and hurried to the men's bathhouse, one of two in the village. Although it was little more than a five-station outhouse with wooden tubs for bathing, it had everything anyone really needed. After a quick face wash, he hustled toward the dragon launching field.

As he ran, it seemed that something pulled him back. So many needs beckoned him. How was Walter feeling? What was Semiramis up to? Did anything change in the garden during the night? With Ruth's next attempt to resurrect Makaidos at hand, would the Vacants try to disrupt it?

Billy heaved a sigh. Others would have to take care of those issues. He had his own job to do.

When he arrived at the field, Acacia and Listener had already buckled two seats on Grackle, the purple dragon, and one on Albatross, the white. Listener, wearing a rabbit-hide tunic with a belt that held her spyglass in place, patted Grackle on his flank. "You and Acacia can take him, and I'll lead the way with Albatross."

Billy held out his arms. "Hugs first!"

Listener leaped into his embrace, her twin pigtails flying. As he pulled her close, he relished the delightful warmth, even the tickle of her companion as it nuzzled his cheek. In less than a month this sweet little girl had become like a sister, so loving, so innocent, pure joy in a feminine little package.

"So how's the best dragon pilot in all of Second Eden doing this morning?" he asked as he let her down.

She grinned. "Valiant's the best flyer. Everyone knows that."

"Okay. Second best." Billy reached for Acacia and gave her a hug from the side. "Ready to open a portal?"

"I'm not sure." Acacia laid a hand on her forehead. "I woke up dizzy this morning."

He cocked his head and looked into her vibrant blue eyes. "Any idea why?"

"I had an unusual dream. I saw Mardon shining a strange light in my eyes. It had many colors—red, blue, purple, yellow. Even in the dream, I felt dizzy. Then I felt a sharp pain in my scalp, and I woke up. It seemed that someone ran away from me, but my head was swimming so much, I couldn't tell for certain. The dizziness has lessened, but it never went away."

"Are you sure you should go? If you're feeling weak, we wouldn't want you to catch a cold or something."

"I'll be all right." She tightened a belt that wrapped her tunic, jostling a coiled rope dangling from a clip. "I think I'll be warm enough in this."

"I know what you mean." Billy said, giving his arms a flap. "I'm getting used to the cold here. Just a cloak is enough. I think the fireproofing stuff Ashley put on it makes it warmer."

Listener looked up at the cirrus-scattered sky. "It's the clouds. We never got clouds here before, and now it's warmer. But the season of death starts tonight, so everything could change very soon."

"Speaking of cold," Billy said, "did you pack extra clothes in case we get some visitors through the portal?"

"Yes, sir." Listener nodded toward Grackle. Two garment bags had been tied behind his rear seat.

Billy scanned over the village roofs and locked his gaze on the trees bordering the field leading to the birthing garden. "Where's the rest of our firepower?"

"Thigocia was meeting with Clefspeare and Hartanna," Acacia said. "Something about the lady in red and her son."

"What's your take?" Billy asked. "Can we trust her?"

"When I saw her with her son, her love seemed convincing, but I'm not sure." Acacia folded her arms over her chest and looked skyward. "I think we should keep her far from the birthing garden during the ceremony. I'm suspicious about her showing up the night before."

Billy nodded. She was right. The last time they tried to bring Makaidos back, a deceiver prevented it from happening. Semiramis's arrival seemed too coincidental. "My dad will keep an eye on her," he said, "and I'll watch her with both eyes when we get back."

Listener reached into a shoulder bag on the ground and handed Billy a fist-sized roll. "It's berry bread. I baked it this morning."

"Thank you." He raised the warm roll to his nose and drew in its aroma—rich grain, ripe fruit, and something sweet, maybe honey. "What kind of berries do you use?"

"We call them pucker berries, because they're so tart when you first pick them. If you let them ripen on the vines, the birds get most of them, so we pick them early and wait for them to get sweeter before we eat them. Walter says they look like the raspberries from your world."

Billy bit into the roll. "Mmm, good," he said, muffled by his mouthful.

"There's Thigocia!" Listener pointed toward the village. A beige dragon flew over the treetops, casting a shadow on the village's huts. With a flurry of wings, she settled down next to Billy. The other two dragons, about a fourth smaller, bowed their heads. Albatross seemed nervous, shuddering his wings and even spilling ice pellets from his nostrils. It hadn't taken the dragons of this world long to assume a subservient position to the dragons from Earth, yet their only negative reaction was a hint of fear rather than resentment.

Listener trotted up to Thigocia and touched a stitched portion of her wing. "How does it feel today?"

"I am perfectly well, thank you." Thigocia curled her neck and set her eyes near the wound in her canopy. "I considered asking the seamstress to remove the stitches, but she is so busy making military uniforms, I had not the heart. I would have pulled them out myself, but my wing bonded with the stitching material, so I need the assistance of skilled hands."

Billy touched one of the stitches. "I can probably do it. Mom made me learn how to sew."

"Perhaps later. I can fly well enough, so I will have no problem completing this mission."

"Sounds good." Billy pointed toward the northern forest. "When we get to the highlands, we'll scan the area for Vacants. If all is clear, Grackle and Albatross will drop us off on the plateau and we'll hike up the volcano while all three dragons patrol. Once we're there, our return plan depends on whether or not Acacia is able to open the portal."

Listener whistled a sharp note. Albatross lowered his head to the ground, making his neck into a staircase. Picking up the shoulder bag, she scrambled up to the seat and strapped in. "I've never been to Mount Elijah through the air. This should be fun."

"I agree," Acacia said as she climbed aboard Grackle in the same fashion. She settled into the rear seat. "We can bypass the skunk lizards."

Billy laughed. A month ago, when he went with Acacia, Listener, and her brother, Candle, to Mount Elijah, Candle led Acacia home and took a shortcut through a swampy area inhabited by four-foot-long lizards that sprayed a foul liquid on intruders. Acacia wasn't quick enough and suffered the consequences.

After strapping into Grackle's front seat, Billy wolfed down the rest of the berry bread as he scanned the darkening skies. Clouds rolled in from the east. Though not yet ominous, they might soon obscure the mountain. Traveling by dragon rather than by airplane, however, would simplify matters. They could buzz across the tops of the trees and follow the footpath until they reached the lava field that signaled the approach to the volcano. Once there, they could land anywhere they chose.

Listener had warned him, however, that although the ice-breathing dragons were adept at landing on areas as small as the top of Mount Elijah, the volcano frightened them, so it was much safer to disembark close to the base.

Listener whistled again and slapped Albatross's flank. Beating his wings, the white dragon lifted into the air. Grackle followed, apparently not needing a command. As soon as they rose above the tree line, the top of Mount Elijah came into view far away, its decapitated profile obvious in spite of thin fog veiling the landscape and the miles between them and the volcano.

As expected, Listener kept Albatross on a low trajectory as she leaned over and peered through the thick tree canopy below. Grackle stayed a few feet higher but still close enough to the trees for his wings to fan the tops as they raced by.

Listener extended her finger downward, apparently pointing out a skinny dirt trail through the underbrush, but the rushing wind kept Billy from shouting his understanding. She had found the path and would stick to it for as long as possible.

Billy looked back. Thigocia trailed them, flying much higher as she skimmed the bottom of the thickening clouds.

After nearly half an hour, the trees thinned out, giving way to gray and black lava fields dotted with scrubby trees. With sparse pinelike needles and twisted trunks, they looked like they rarely benefitted from the eclipse-cycle mists that once watered the land.

As light drizzle dampened their faces, the terrain gradually sloped upward, signaling their approach to the highlands, but with the cloud-bank now obscuring the mountaintops, and the trail imperceptible in the lava beds, Listener took Albatross down for a landing. Grackle again followed and came to a stop nearby. Both dragons beat their wings and scattered droplets over everyone. Apparently they had not yet learned how to politely carry riders in this kind of weather.

Billy dismounted, and after helping Acacia down, he searched the sky. "Do you see Thigocia anywhere?"

Listener snatched the spyglass from her belt. Peering into the eyepiece, she swept the tube slowly from one side of the horizon to the other. After a few seconds, she pointed. "Over there. I think she's showing us the way to Mount Elijah."

"Okay," Billy said as he tightened his scabbard belt. "Let's hoof it from here."

Listener stroked Albatross's neck. "If Vacants show up, go ahead and leave without us. We'll all ride Thigocia if we have to."

Albatross spat a spray of ice on the ground and blew a series of whistled notes, low and chaotic.

Listener giggled. "That's a challenge to fight. He's telling me he's not afraid of the Vacants."

"Good for him." Billy nodded at the sky, his hair now dripping. "Better keep track of Thigocia. The rain's getting heavier. We don't want to lose her."

Listener raised the spyglass again. "We won't. I can see her red eyebeams."

"Perfect." Billy set a hand on Listener's shoulder. "Keep watching and lead the way. I'll make sure you don't fall."

With Acacia following, Billy and Listener marched across the lava field—furrowed rock that made for good footing as the rain fashioned crooked rivulets in the gaps. Soon the terrain steepened, and the field narrowed. The surrounding mountains funneled wet wind that bit through their inadequate clothes.

Now shivering, Listener stopped and lowered the spyglass. "I lost her. Maybe she's not blowing fire anymore."

Billy pulled her closer. "Thigocia's around somewhere. She would never—"

A sudden burst of wind made them turn. Thigocia landed behind them and shook out her wings. "The path to the volcano is clear," she said, "but the wind is fierce as you go higher. Once you reach the top, a firestorm might be impossible. Perhaps another day would be better."

Billy looked at Acacia. "What do you think? Are you feeling okay?"

She pushed a strand of wet white hair from her eyes. "I don't think my dizziness will affect my fire. I once created a firestorm in a swamp, so I don't think wind will stop me. As long as we have plenty of time to get back to the village before evening, I think we should try."

"Very well," Thigocia said. "I noticed an encampment of Vacants on the far side of the mountain to your left, but they seem hunkered down for the weather. I will keep an eye on them."

"It's good to have you around." Billy shielded his eyes as he surveyed the misty landscape. "How far to the base of the volcano?"

"The upward path becomes clear about a hundred paces in the direction you were heading, so you should have no trouble."

Billy nodded. "I'll recognize it when I see it."

"Would you like a Sahara treatment before you continue?" Thigocia breathed a stream of dry air that bathed his face in warmth.

"It feels great, but we'd be wet again in just a few minutes. No use wasting time."

"As you wish." Thigocia beat her wings and lifted into the air. After flying in a low, tight circle, she ascended toward the clouds. "I will be watching."

CHAPTER 12

A NEW LAKE

Billy withdrew Excalibur an inch or two from its scabbard, then slid it back. Even without a shield, they would have enough protection—his sword, his fire-breathing, and a dragon's flames from above, not to mention the firestorms Acacia could whip up.

With a wave of his hand, he nodded forward. "Let's climb."

After a minute or so, a steep path came into view, smoother than the surrounding lava field. It switched back and forth across a vertical rock face, obviously cut intentionally to provide an easy way to climb the volcano. Although he and Walter had already climbed it before, the misty gloom made it look like a path through the unknown. They could see only several paces in front of their feet, not exactly a comforting view.

Without a word, the trio ascended the path, Billy leading the way as they pushed against the wet incline, and Acacia trailing, one hand on Listener's back.

When they reached the vantage point where he had first seen the Vacants on the volcano's top, he halted. As fog streamed past his eyes, he searched for the flattened cone above, but it was shrouded in clouds. An odd pinch in his gut sounded a weak alarm. Was it danger? To this point only one of his former dragon traits had returned, his fire-breathing, but a tingling sensation hinted that another trait was trying to live again.

"Is something wrong?" Acacia asked.

"Maybe." The cloud at the peak thinned, allowing a veiled look at the top. Nothing. Just the heap of stones still plugging the volcano's throat. He nodded forward again. "I guess it's safe. We can trust Thigocia to watch over us."

When they reached the top, Billy stood at the edge of the rock pile. Although he would have to carry the larger stones himself, most were small enough for the females to carry and throw down the slope. There was no need to call on Thigocia or the native dragons for help. As she had warned, a bitter wind cut across the peak. This would be a pain-filled job.

He detached Excalibur's scabbard from its belt and laid it on the ground. "Okay. Let's get to work."

Acacia set down the rope as well as a hammer, an iron spike, and a small roll of mesh, while Listener added her spyglass to their pile. Then, retying their outer cloaks and keeping their gloves on, the trio began clearing the stones.

While they labored in the cold rain, now mixed with snow, Thigocia appeared below the clouds from time to time, her eyebeams bright. During one of her visits, she reported on the encampment of Vacants. They seemed to be stirring, as if getting ready to break camp, so she would keep an eye on them.

After a few minutes, only a few stones remained jammed in the volcano's throat. Hot air rose through the gaps and transformed into streams of white mist as the cold breeze swept it away. Although the wind had diminished somewhat, and the hard work had warmed their bodies, the air brought a piercing chill.

Billy picked up the scabbard and withdrew Excalibur. "Better stand clear." He pushed the sword's point into one of the gaps between the stones.

While Acacia and Listener backed away a few steps and huddled close in the frigid wind, Billy dislodged the stones. They dropped silently for a moment, then a plume of steam burst forth, a brief but vivid surge of white.

Billy scanned the valley. Did the Vacants notice? Would the steam be a signal that might rouse their curiosity?

Gesturing for the girls to rejoin him, he looked into the hole. "See anything?"

Listener peered down with her spyglass. "Yes. I see the tree I saw last time."

"That's good enough for me," Acacia said. "I'll try to open the portal."

While she created a swirling column of fire within and over the hole, Billy drove the spike into the ground and tied the rope to its exposed head. The wind whipped the cyclone of flames but not enough to blow it away from the volcano's throat.

"We're ready," Acacia called. "The portal's open. I can see the tree now."

"Just a second." After stretching the rope between the spike and the firestorm, Billy selected a spot near the hole and wrapped the rope with the roll of mesh—a fibrous, asbestos-like netting—covering a three-foot section. He tossed the remaining coil through the wall of fire and into the volcano's throat. When it tightened, the mesh sizzled in the flames, but it seemed to stay intact.

"You first," Acacia said. "Then Listener. Then me."

"You bet." After refastening Excalibur, Billy pinched the fringe of his cloak. "I hope the stuff Ashley painted on these cloaks works."

"It will," Listener said. "She tested it."

"With normal fire, not Acacia's." Billy raised his hood, grasped the rope, and faced away from the hole and its surrounding fire. Listener did the same at a spot two paces in front of him.

"Let's do it," Billy said.

Ducking low, he backed through the fire and began sliding down the rope, glad for the thick gloves protecting his skin. Just a foot or so above, Listener followed. With her spyglass back in its harness, it dangled only inches from Billy's eyes. Obviously this little girl had spent many hours climbing the vine-covered trees of Second Eden. She kept pace with Billy effortlessly, apparently unafraid of the flames that swirled all around them.

As the heat dried his clothes and warmed his skin, he looked down, trying to find a place to set his feet. The fire illuminated the chamber below, the museum room Acacia had told him about. The cylindrical wall of flames enclosed the Tree of Life. Still on fire but not burning up, it would likely be too hot to stay close to it. They would have to move fast.

As soon as they reached bottom, the rope reeled up and disappeared. Billy and Listener burst through the wall of flames and hustled to the museum room's bookshelves. They grabbed one of the tall ladders, and when they pulled it away from the shelf, a scroll of parchment fell to the floor and rolled through the wall of flames, stopping at the base of the Tree of Life. An edge of parchment near one of the scroll's dowels caught fire.

Carrying the ladder, Billy and Listener punched through the vortex and pushed the top of the ladder toward the portal opening.

"It reaches!" Listener shouted.

"Shhh!" Now sweating, Billy leaned the ladder against the edge of the hole above. "Let me get that scroll before it burns up."

Wrapping his fireproof sleeve around his hand, he reached under the lowest branches and grabbed the unlit end. He batted the flames away and hurried back in time to help Listener support the ladder for Acacia.

When Acacia climbed down with the rope coiled over her shoulder, she looked at the scroll. "Why are you carrying that?"

"It fell from the shelf." Billy ran a finger across the scroll's skin. A thin film of white residue coated his fingertip. "This stuff is strange."

"It glows," Listener said.

Billy peeled back the scroll's edge. "Maybe we'd better take a look at it."

"You should move the ladder first," Acacia said, taking the scroll. "It will fall when the firestorm dies away."

Billy pulled the ladder down and dragged it toward the shelves. "Better get away from the tree," he called back. "Your cloak won't keep you from roasting."

As the portal flames dwindled, Billy walked with Acacia and Listener through the museum's exit, a partially broken doorway. When they emerged into cooler air, he mopped a sleeve across his brow. "That plan worked perfectly."

Acacia's brow dipped down. "If I had thought of the ladder last time, we could have avoided a lot of trouble."

"Don't be so hard on yourself. I thought the rope would work, too." With light from the flaming tree illuminating their surroundings, Billy took the scroll and pulled the parchment out several inches. "Most of it is blank, but there are a few lines written in a strange language."

Acacia looked on. "It's in Hebrew. When Sapphira and I took turns going on scavenger hunts in the world of the living, sometimes we were able to pick up scrolls and books that had been discarded." She pointed at a line near the edge. "This says it's from the book of Jeremiah. It must be a Bible text that a scribe was copying. He likely threw it away because he made an error."

Billy touched the ragged edge with a finger. "It's burned up to this point. Can you make out the rest?"

"I'll do the best I can." Squinting, Acacia read, pausing at times as she translated out loud. "Is there no . . . ointment in Gilead? Is there no . . . doctor? Why then is not the health of the daughter of my people . . . restored?"

"Any idea what it means?" he asked.

"Maybe," Acacia said. "It's already damaged. Why don't you tear off that part, and we'll talk about it later."

"Right. We're wasting time." After stripping off the section of parchment and folding it into his pocket, Billy scanned the area. The huge chamber was exactly the way Acacia had described it—big, empty, and lonely.

Acacia reached up and removed a lantern from the sill of an open window. With a nod, she ignited the wick. "Not much oil in this one, but it should last."

"Right again." Billy took the lantern. "Let's make this quick."

Acacia dropped the rope at the door and pointed into the dim chamber. "The exit tunnel is that way."

After adjusting Excalibur in its belt scabbard, Billy lifted the lantern high and strode ahead. He passed under an arch and entered a tunnel, high enough to navigate without ducking and wide enough for all three to walk together. The light flickered on the side walls, revealing dark clefts and caves that gave no hint as to what lay inside.

All three stayed quiet, more from instinct than from fear. It would be senseless to make a lot of noise when they didn't know who or what might be lurking around the next bend.

After passing through another chamber and two more tunnels, they reached a hole in the floor.

"Strange," Acacia said. "This wasn't here before."

Billy stooped. As he peered into the hole, cool air dried out his eyes. At least fifty feet below, a river flowed from left to right, illuminated by the glow of what looked like hardening magma on either side. "An underground spring?"

Setting a hand against the floor, Acacia knelt next to him. "That's very strange. The springs feed a reservoir, but we never learned where it flows out. We had a magma river down there that ran much farther below, and this new river seems to be running in between volcanic residue."

"Maybe the reservoir sprung a leak," Listener said.

"If so, then the water level might be rising." Acacia rose to her feet. "We'd better hurry."

Billy lifted the lantern again. "So what's that way?" he asked, pointing beyond the hole.

"Our hovels and the springs."

"That sounds like a good place to look." Billy stepped around the hole and continued marching along the corridor. Calling for Sapphira and Bonnie, they checked the hovels and the springs to no avail. Further searching revealed a massive collapse in another tunnel.

"No way we can move that many rocks," Billy said. "What next?"

"The mines level." Acacia started back the way they came. "This way."

When they reached a shaft embedded in the wall, Billy grabbed a dangling rope and looked down. "I can't see anything, but I hear water."

Acacia shivered. "I have a bad feeling about this."

Billy spread an arm around her and pulled her close. "Sapphira knows what she's doing. I'm sure she and Bonnie and Shiloh managed to get out. I mean, they're not here. They wouldn't have gone below and let themselves drown."

Acacia let her shoulders sag. "You're right. But now we have to go back to Second Eden without any dragons."

A new voice broke through from the darkness behind them. "Not exactly."

Billy pushed the lantern toward the sound. "Who's there?"

Two women walked into the light, both so saturated, water streamed down their faces, their clothes stuck to their bodies, and their hair dripped. One of the women extended her hand. "I am Rebekah, also known as Legossi." She nodded toward the other woman. "This is Dallas, formerly Firedda, daughter of Makaidos and Thigocia."

Billy took her hand, noting a ring on her finger with a white mounted gem. "Oh, yeah. We met back in Maryland. Sorry I didn't recognize you."

"Our meeting was brief." Rebekah pulled her soaked shirt away from her skin. "And we didn't look like this."

"I was wondering about that. What happened?"

Before Rebekah could reply, Acacia piped up. "Have you seen Sapphira? Or Bonnie or Shiloh?"

"Not lately," Rebekah said. "Shiloh was kidnapped, but that's—"

"Kidnapped?" Acacia raised a hand to her mouth. "By whom? Where did they take her?"

"As I was about to say," Rebekah continued, "that's a long story. The rest of us were being chased by intruders, so Dallas and I hid in the springs.

Sapphira was going to find another hiding place for her and Bonnie. She said something about the magma river overlook. When you came into the springs chamber, we heard you calling, but we didn't want to answer until we were sure who you were. It took a while for us to get out of our hiding place, but . . ." She spread out her dripping arms. "Here we are."

Acacia pointed at the elevator shaft. "The river overlook is on the mining level."

"I'm going down," Billy said.

Acacia grabbed the rope. "I'm with you all the way."

He handed the lantern to Rebekah. "Keep an eye on Listener, okay? She can fill you in on what's going on in Second Eden, and you can tell us about Shiloh when we get back."

Rebekah nodded. "Will do."

Acacia climbed down the rope and out of the lantern's glow. Billy followed, glad once again he had kept his gloves on as the rope slid through his hands. Now in darkness, he listened for a signal from below, but only the sound of splashing water filled his ears. Finally, he felt a tug on his pants.

"Swing out here," Acacia said.

Billy obeyed. A flash of light erupted in Acacia's palm, a new fireball, shedding a bluish white glow all around.

"This way." Acacia broke into a trot.

As Billy followed again, he watched Acacia's lithe body glide along effortlessly. With white hair and petite frame, she seemed more like a phantom child than an ages-old oracle. He couldn't help but admire her. With unfailing love and steadfast purpose, she seemed so . . . so perfect.

Soon, they turned through an archway to the right and stopped at a lake. They stood on a dark beach, a slab of solid rock. Acacia walked to the water's edge and let the tiny waves lap over her feet.

"Does this lake have a name?" Billy asked.

She looked back at him, her brow bent with concern. "It's not supposed to be a lake. This used to be an overlook, and the river of magma flowed way down below."

Billy stooped and touched the water. "It's warm. Real warm."

"Can you tell if it's still rising?" She held her ball of flame higher.

Squinting, he scanned the shoreline. By fractions of an inch the water crept higher. "Nothing to make us run out of here, but it's gradually moving up."

Acacia bent over and squinted. "Do you see something sparkling over there?"

"Yeah." He stepped to the water's edge and picked up a string of beads from the shallows. As he drew the string close to his eyes, they reflected Acacia's fire in an array of rainbow colors.

"A necklace?" she asked.

Billy had to swallow hard before he could speak. "It's Bonnie's."

Acacia touched the necklace. Her voice fell to a whisper. "That doesn't mean they didn't get away, you know."

"I know, but she wouldn't have taken it off and laid it here. It's not broken. Something must've pulled it over her head."

Billy stared at the water. A rushing flood could have easily done the job. If Bonnie had been caught in a sudden rush, it might have taken her away in the flow and stripped the necklace off.

Cupping his hands around his mouth, he shouted, "Bonnie! Can you hear me?"

A distant echo replied, *Hear me. Hear me.*

Acacia joined in. "Sapphira!"

Sapphira. Sapphira.

A wave of cold chilled Billy's skin and penetrated his heart. His legs trembled, and his arms fell limp. Again, he had to swallow through his tightening throat. "Do you think they drowned?"

Acacia sat down. Now an inch of water covered what had recently been a stony beach. She pulled Billy down to join her. "Rest for a minute, and we'll talk."

As he lowered himself to a sitting position, the warm water soaked his pants. It felt soothing, like soaking in a luxurious bath. He pulled his sword belt around to keep Excalibur out of the rising lake.

Acacia blew out her fireball and took his hand. All was dark. Only the sound of running water and the gentle lapping of waves against his body gave a hint that anything existed at all.

Still hot from the flames, her skin radiated warmth into his. "Billy, I have been alive for thousands of years. I have seen toil, torture, and cruelty more times than I could ever count. I was even thrown over this very precipice, and I plunged into a river of magma.

"As I fell, complete despair washed over me. Although I was a slave girl, I still had hopes and dreams. Sapphira and I used to read about the upper lands and daydream about going there someday. We would draw pictures of us dancing together under that strange light the people up there called the sun. 'Can you imagine?' we would ask. 'How could a ball of fire hang in an endless sky?'"

She compressed his hand. Her touch felt comforting, soothing.

"Billy," she continued in a lamenting tone, "we had never seen the sky. To us it was a fantasy that someone invented in a storybook. We wanted to believe it. Oh, Billy, we wanted to believe it so badly we would talk about it for hours on end. But when I was falling toward the magma, I remember thinking that I would never see it. There must be no sky, no sun, no upper lands at all. These mines are all there is, and I'm just a slave girl, forsaken and lost. And nobody cares."

Billy felt a tear trickle down his cheek, but he didn't bother to brush it away. "That . . ." He cleared his throat, trying to steady his voice. "That must've been awful."

"Worse than awful. But I think you know how it feels. You lost Bonnie once before. You carried her dead body through the seventh circle of Hades. It doesn't get much worse."

"I can't argue with that. That was the lowest I ever felt." Finally wiping the tear, he added, "But it turned out all right."

"That's what I'm trying to say. You have a prophecy that says you'll get married. You have to hang on to that."

"Well, that's how we interpreted it. We're not completely sure. Maybe our union won't happen till we get to Heaven."

"Prophecies are often like that. Sometimes they have spiritual fulfillments." She pulled his hand up to her lips and kissed his knuckles. "I trust that yours will come to pass with a physical kiss."

Warmth again radiated through his body. It was a good warmth, a holy warmth. This girl was as pure as an angel.

Again steadying his voice, he said, "I hope so."

She let go of his hand. "Sapphira and I are also the subjects of prophecy. I believe she is destined to wed Elam, son of Shem." With a sudden burst of energy, she clapped her hands. "Oh, that will be a glorious day! She has longed for that day for centuries!"

"What about you?" Billy asked. "Is there a husband in your future?"

Her voice lowered to a whisper. "My lot has always been to serve others. I cannot hope for the blessings of a journey beyond maidenhood, or the adventure a husband and children would bring. I believe I will not see the end of suffering before I pass on to the next world."

"But you've already suffered so much. Doesn't it make sense that God would allow you to have a little bit of joy before you die?"

"Why should we assume this, Billy? To serve is to live. To suffer is to serve better. Why should I hope for more? If God is pleased with my humble efforts, then I am fulfilled. There is nothing else."

Billy shook his head. "It just doesn't seem right. No one has suffered more than you have."

"Not so, Billy." A tiny fireball, no bigger than a dime, formed in Acacia's hand, illuminating her lovely face. "No one has suffered more than Sapphira. No one, save our Lord Christ. And when she takes Elam's hand in marriage, her journey of loneliness will finally come to an end."

Billy gazed into her sparkling eyes, so rich, so filled with mystery. They were pools too deep to fathom, yet he longed to dive in, to gain the ages-old wisdom this fairylike maid had to offer. "You said you were the subject of prophecy, too."

"Just a hint, really." Her brow lifted. "Shall I sing it for you?"

"Please do."

Her eyelids lowered, hiding the deep pools. As she touched the water with a fingertip, her ivory throat vibrated, and a beautiful voice trilled from her pursed lips, seeming to blend with the sound of running water.

Sapphira bends, but will she break?
Depends on Elam's safe return.
For if he fails to bring the ark,
Her life is chaff and soon will burn.

She set the little fireball between herself and Billy. "What do you think?"

Locking on her gaze, he played the words over in his mind, but the song was so cryptic it didn't make much sense. "I . . . uh . . . I didn't hear your name mentioned."

"I am the ark," she said, pointing at herself. "That's why God made sure I was named Acacia. The ark of the covenant was made of acacia wood, and just as it carried the word of God, I brought Paili to Second Eden to bring a word from God."

"So what does the song mean?"

"Elam asked Enoch about it, but, as prophets sometimes do, he avoided answering. So Elam thinks he has to bring me back to Earth for some reason. Since he's from Earth, it makes sense that a return would be to Earth, and if he doesn't do it, Sapphira's life will burn like chaff."

"Sapphira's life? I thought it meant the ark's life."

"The ark's life?" Acacia lowered her gaze. Her lips moved, as if replaying the words in silence. Finally, she looked at him again. "I see what you mean."

Billy tried to read her expression. She seemed puzzled. She had believed an interpretation of a prophecy that had been guiding her thoughts and motivations, hoping somehow to be used by Elam to save Sapphira's life, but now that interpretation crumbled, leaving her without a foundation.

"Well," he said, trying to build her up again with a livelier voice, "one thing I've learned about prophecies is that sometimes you just have to wait and see what happens. No sense in banging our heads against the wall trying to figure them out."

"I suppose that's true." As a tear traced down Acacia's cheek, her voice trembled. "Will you pray for me?"

He took her hand in both of his. "Of course. What do you want me to pray about?"

"That God will give me the courage to do what I have to do."

He rubbed his thumb across her knuckles. "What do you have to do?"

"I cannot tell you. I think I know the prophecy's meaning. Your question has brought it to light."

"My question? How?"

"Please." Tears dripped to her lap as she squeaked, "Please don't ask me again."

"Okay. I won't." As he looked at her, wave after wave of emotion crashed over him. This great prophetess, packaged in a diminutive body, was breaking his heart. She had asked him to pray, but how could he? Praying with Ashley hadn't been so hard; she was a friend, a fellow Earthling. But Acacia? She was a thousands-of-years-old Oracle, an otherworldly creature that transcended understanding and even mortality, almost like an angel. And how should a regular guy pray for an angel?

Finally, he decided. The best prayer would be a short one, straight from the heart.

Caressing her knuckles again, he looked into the darkness above and spoke clearly. "Father, you have watched your faithful servant Acacia for thousands of years. No one needs to remind you of what a brave, noble, and sacrificial person she is. She has served you faithfully in Hades, on Earth, and in Second Eden. Now, after listening to your voice from three different worlds, she believes she knows how she's supposed to fulfill a prophecy, and the thought of it makes her heart quake. Please let her know if she's right or wrong. Help her to clearly see the next step she should take. And I ask that she not become chaff to be burned, because . . ." His throat tightened, pitching his voice higher. "Because we would . . . *I* would miss her terribly."

After swallowing, he breathed a quiet "Amen."

Acacia leaned forward and kissed him on the cheek. "Thank you, warrior, for lifting your sword for me." Her whisper was weak, yet it carried a hint of relief, as if a burden had been lifted from her shoulders.

"It's an honor." He forced a tone of resolve into his voice. "Let's get back to the others. They'll be worried about us."

"Okay."

Still holding her hand, he rose to his feet and helped her up. "Before the night is over, we should have three new dragons in our army, Legossi, Firedda, and Makaidos."

She took the necklace from Billy and, using her non-fiery hand, pushed it over his head. "And who knows?" she said, touching one of the beads now dangling just below his throat. "Maybe a certain dragon girl will show up, too."

CHAPTER 13

SAND IN THE HOURGLASS

Bonnie pushed her shoulder under her father's arm on one side while Sapphira helped from the other. He seemed groggy. Although he stood well enough, his weight sagged their shoulders a bit. Since his eyes wandered, he probably hadn't fully recovered his wits.

Bonnie looked at the girl who had rescued him. Although flames created a fiery aura all around her body, her face shone through, peaceful, joyous. Bonnie nodded toward the hourglass sitting on the ground. "Will you get that for me?"

The girl glanced at it. Now only a fifth of the sand remained in the top half. "I see no reason for carrying a time-keeping device," she said. "If watching it would increase your speed, then your passion for completing your task is based on a wisp, an illusory figment called time, something you can neither capture nor contain. And time is a wicked taskmaster."

Bonnie narrowed her eyes at the girl. Blonde, lithe, and beautiful, she seemed far calmer than the situation demanded. "Look," Bonnie said, trying to keep her voice steady, "if we don't get to the resurrection chamber before the sand runs out, it will be too late. Abaddon said so."

"That is easily solved." The girl knelt and pried the top off the hourglass. Then, looking up at Bonnie and Sapphira with a coy grin, scooped a handful of sand and poured it into the top half. "There," she said, pushing the top back in place. "The sand will not run out soon."

Heat surged into Bonnie's ears. What was wrong with this girl? She didn't appear to be a simpleton. But what could they do now? Their way of telling time was ruined.

The girl stood and, flashing a bright smile, showed Bonnie the hourglass. "Do not be dismayed. In this realm, solutions to problems are not what you would expect. My action was a prayer for more time, and if it had not been granted by our Lord, I would not have been able to do it." She set the hourglass in front of Bonnie's feet. "Go in peace, Bonnie Silver. You have proven your faith while inside the candlestone, and you will be tested even more severely in coming days. Yet, you are precious in God's sight, so the sands of your hourglass will not run out before the purposes of God are fulfilled."

Bonnie squinted at her. Not only did this girl rescue her father and apparently buy them more time, she seemed to know everything about her. "Who *are* you?"

The girl curtsied. "You may call me The Maid."

"Thank you . . . uh . . . The Maid." Bonnie tried not to frown. Calling her that name was clumsy, to say the least. "I appreciate your help in rescuing my father, but if you knew who I was, why did you ask earlier?"

"Revelation comes to me in strange ways." As she tilted her head slightly upward, her fiery hair swayed at her waist. "If you stay here long enough, you will learn."

Sapphira grunted under the increasing weight of their load. "Do you have a litter or something we can transport him on?"

"Perhaps." The Maid hurried back to the boulder and picked up her shield. She laid it on the ground and waited at a distance while Bonnie and Sapphira lowered Bonnie's father to a sitting position on it. Laying a gentle hand on his head, Bonnie looked into his eyes. "Can you sit here okay, Daddy?"

His head still wavering, he whispered, "Yes, I think so."

The Maid spread out her arms. The flames made a whooshing sound as she moved. "Remember, he must surrender to Abaddon willingly, for only the dragon can prepare him for the journey that lies ahead."

Bonnie nodded. "I understand, but how will we find Abaddon?"

"I do not know." Smiling, she touched the base of the hourglass with her toe. "Remember the lesson of the sand, and let wisdom guide you."

"I see." Bonnie studied the shield. There was no rope to pull it, and no way to tie a rope to the shield even if she had one. She could try to fly while holding him, like she did with Billy and a few others, but her father was taller and more muscular, probably too heavy. There seemed to be only one option. "If we push him, your shield will slide easily on the ground, correct?"

"Oh, yes, Bonnie. You really *do* understand, don't you?"

"And once we get back to the river," Bonnie continued, "the shield will float, even under my father's weight."

The Maid clapped her hands. "Excellent! I had not even thought of that."

Smiling, Bonnie locked gazes with The Maid. Sincerity poured forth from her youthful face, along with a blend of complete confidence and deep faith. This was a girl after her own heart, yet The Maid's exuberance wasn't as contagious as her confidence.

Bonnie sighed. "It doesn't work that way in our world, at least not all the time."

"Sadly, no." The Maid drew close and hovered her flaming hand over Bonnie's cheek. Warmth flowed over her skin. "Enjoy it while you are here. There will come a day when every desire of your heart will be granted without even a prayer, for you will be in the Messiah's presence, and his light will fill the temple."

"Does that mean Sapphira and I can leave this place just by wanting to?"

The Maid laughed again. "Oh, that prayer won't be so easy to act out. It is not the same as pouring sand in an hourglass or sliding a shield. If it were, I would have departed long ago. Still, I am content to stay and serve in whatever way I can. Abaddon and I have a working relationship you might call . . ." She rolled her eyes upward, searching for a word. "Tolerable, I suppose. Since I work for him, I thought he might stop trying to turn me into a statue."

"How did you keep from changing into one?" Sapphira asked.

The Maid's brow wrinkled. "Why would you ask me such a question? Since you have also escaped that fate, surely you know."

"We didn't die to come here," Sapphira said. "I thought that was the reason."

The Maid laughed gaily. "Oh, no. That is not the reason. But if I tried to explain the method, surely my words would endanger you, for the seeking of this knowledge would handicap your efforts."

"But you know the method," Sapphira said, "and you're not a statue."

Bonnie looked down at Sapphira's feet. Mud again caked her legs from her knees downward. She grabbed Sapphira's arm and pulled, forcing her to move. As before, the mud crumbled away.

"We should leave now," Bonnie said. After setting the hourglass in her father's lap, she laid her hands on his back and pushed. At first, he budged only a few inches, but when Sapphira joined in, the shield glided easily through the woods and out to the river.

When they stopped at the river's edge, Bonnie stepped around to the front and looked at her father. His head had stopped wobbling, but his eyes looked glassy. "Are you all right?" she asked.

Blinking at her, he whispered, "Bonnie?"

"Yes, Daddy. It's Bonnie."

"Is your mother home yet? I made lunch. Grilled cheese sandwiches and tomato soup."

Shaking her head, Bonnie dipped a cupped hand into the river and drew out some water. She washed his face with it, though much of the water dribbled down his shirt.

Sapphira carried two handfuls of water and splashed his face. He shook his head hard, slinging drops all around. Then, looking up at Bonnie, he gasped. "The pool! You got out!"

"Welcome back!" She kissed him on the forehead. "Yes, we found a portal that led us to a chamber where dead souls are resurrected from this realm, and we need to get you on the schedule right away."

"The schedule?"

"To get resurrected."

Giving her a confused look, he picked up the hourglass. "What's this?"

"I'll tell you about it in a minute." Bonnie grabbed his wrist and hoisted him to his feet. He staggered for a second but quickly gained his balance.

"So . . ." He kept his focus on the sand running through the hourglass. "If I get resurrected, where would I go?"

"To Second Eden," Bonnie said. "They need a doctor there, so the dragon wants to transport you."

"A doctor?" He gave his head a rapid shake. "I haven't practiced in years, since before you were born."

Taking his hand, she gazed into his eyes as she spiced her voice with a lamenting tone. "But they need you there. At least you'll be better than no doctor at all."

"I'm not so sure of that. Sometimes a bad doctor is worse than no doctor."

She hooked her arm around her father's and leaned her head against his shoulder. "Did one of your medical decisions hurt someone?"

He lifted his head and gazed at the sky. For a moment it seemed that he wouldn't answer at all. Finally, he looked at her, his eyes glistening. "A little girl died. I thought she had the flu, so I sent her home with the usual liquids and bed rest regimen, but it turned out to be bacterial meningitis. Of course, I went to her funeral, and when I walked to the front to express my condolences, her parents wouldn't even look at me, much less speak." Shoving his hands into his pockets, he let out a sigh. "I quit my practice the next day. I couldn't take it. But I swore that I would dedicate the rest of my life to finding ways to stop suffering and somehow cheat death."

Bonnie looked at the hourglass. There was still plenty of sand at the top. "And that vow led to your experimenting with dragon blood."

He pushed a hand into his pocket and nodded. "I thought we had found the key to a long and pain-free life, but it wasn't until the day of my own death that I saw how much suffering I caused you and your mother. I could never make that up to you."

"Maybe you can." She pulled him forward. "Come on. This will be a chance to redeem yourself."

He followed with halting steps. "What do I have to do?"

"When we find the dragon," Sapphira said, "you have to surrender to him."

He stopped in his tracks. "And become a statue?"

"If need be." Sapphira hooked his other arm, and the two girls forced him to continue. "Maybe he won't have time to turn you into one."

As they followed the river's gently meandering shoreline, he gathered his strength and regained his senses. He provided more details about the girl who died and continued lamenting about how much suffering he had caused.

Bonnie listened patiently. It was probably better to let him vent than to try to talk him out of his sorrows.

When they reached a shallow stream, a tributary for the larger river, he hopped over it in a single bound before reaching out from the other side to help the girls. His chatter grew livelier for a while, but when Bonnie explained The Maid's way of giving them more time, he became silent and stayed that way for the rest of the journey.

Soon, they arrived at the spot where they had set the oblong stone. Turning toward the ridge of highlands, they walked to where the door should have been and searched for the lantern in the ankle-high grass, but it was nowhere in sight.

Bonnie stopped at a point that looked familiar. Although the grass was uniform in consistency and color, this spot seemed a little flatter than the surrounding area. Maybe this is where they had jumped out of the corridor. "I'll bet Abaddon found the lantern," she said. "Maybe he took it back inside."

"Probably." Sapphira brushed her foot along the grass. "It was his lantern, so why not?"

Bonnie set her hands on her hips and looked at the hills in the distance. "There's got to be a way to figure this out. If adding sand to the hourglass bought us more time, this place must allow for the most unusual solutions. We should be able to solve this new puzzle."

"So how does it work?" Sapphira asked. "I'm not very good at coming up with illogical solutions."

"Maybe it's like this. Think of the simplest way to solve the problem, something that doesn't seem like it would work. Then give it a try."

Bonnie's father raised a finger. "You mean like a child's solution?"

"That's exactly what I mean. If you have to get to the resurrection chamber before the sand runs out, add more sand."

"So what do we do if we have to find an invisible door?" Sapphira asked. "That doesn't seem quite as easy."

Bonnie's father set the hourglass on the ground. "My guess is that once we solve it, we'll wonder why it seemed so hard, just like adding sand does now."

"How about if I just open it?" Bonnie reached into the middle of the air, hoping to grasp a knob, but found nothing. "Well, so much for that idea."

"Light from the lantern opened it last time." Sapphira lifted a ball of fire in her palm. "Let's see if my light will work."

"But if we don't even know where the door is, how will your light open it? We had to stand close to the door before it opened last time."

Sapphira waved her ball of flames back and forth. She painted the grass with a wash of yellow light, easy to see under the dismal sky, but no door opened.

Bonnie stepped in front of Sapphira and into the fireball's light. Her shadow appeared on the grass, a winged girl shrouded in black. She whispered, "I think I know how to find the door."

"How?" Sapphira's firelight dimmed. "Should I—"

"No!" Bonnie waved a hand at her. "Keep it going! Stronger, if you can."

New light blazed, arcing over Bonnie and clarifying her shadow. Off to the left and several paces away, another shadow loomed, not as dark, but still recognizable as a rectangle, skewed into a diamond shape by the light's angle.

"We find the door by locating its shadow." Bonnie stepped toward the dark diamond, curling her finger to signal for Sapphira to follow. As she neared, the shadow straightened in the moving light. When it drew a perfect rectangle on the grass, Bonnie raised her hand.

Sapphira halted, stopping the light's progress.

Bonnie set her toes a few inches in front of the shadow's edge and reached out. Her fingers passed through where she thought the door would be, but her hand's shadow disappeared. "It's here. Bring the light."

Holding the hourglass once again, her father walked with Sapphira to the spot. As the light closed in, it drew a yellow circle on and around Bonnie's hand.

Bonnie eased her hand back. A low creak sounded as the door swung away from them.

For a few seconds, the hinges continued squeaking a half-hearted complaint, then, all was silent as the three stared at the doorway that had appeared out of nowhere.

Bonnie stepped inside and nodded toward the ceiling. "The lantern's not there."

Her father and Sapphira joined her in the narrow corridor. Sapphira's flame blazed and painted the ceiling and walls with Bonnie's larger-than-life shadow. Her silhouette looked like the dragon guide who haunted the museum's frescoes.

She glanced back at the hourglass in her father's grip. If they hadn't put more in, the sand would have run out long ago, but even now it seemed dangerously low. Although The Maid had added a good deal more sand, she hadn't filled it beyond the bottom glass's ability to capture every grain. Overfilling it would probably have violated the rules of this place. Still, it would run out soon, and there would be no sand to gather here.

Now walking abreast, they passed through the hall of frescoes. Strangely enough, the dragons in the murals were again walking in the same direction they were, opposite of the way they were facing during their previous visit.

Bonnie shivered. This was all too weird to believe, like the creepiest nightmare of all time coming true.

Soon, they passed by the mural depicting the mummified man walking out of a cave. Sapphira blew out her light and whispered, "We're close to the chamber."

As darkness shrouded them, the trio crept along, Bonnie's father leading the way. A light appeared in the distance, reddish and flickering as it moved from left to right across their field of vision.

When they reached the end of the hall, they crouched and watched the scene in the chamber. Abaddon carried the lantern to the table in his clawed hand. With a red flame burning inside the smoky glass, the glow looked more like thin mist than light, as if fog had settled into the room and created a blood-tinged haze.

As soon as he set it down, his blue eyebeams flicked on. They knifed through the red mist, creating purplish rays that scanned the wall adjacent to the exit corridor. When they moved to the corridor itself, the beams sliced through the darkness above Bonnie's head.

She held her breath. Should they just stand up and announce their presence? If her father was going to surrender to him, maybe that would be the best plan. Still, it wouldn't make sense to reveal everyone. If Abaddon meant them harm, it would take only one of them to find out. The others could escape.

She touched her father and whispered, "Stay here and watch closely."

He grabbed her wrist. "I can't let you face that dragon without me."

"Just trust me, please. I've dealt with a lot of dragons."

Pulling away from his grasp, she picked up the hourglass, rose to her full height, and marched forward, letting the blue lasers strike her chest. "I am Bonnie Silver, and I am surrendering myself to you, Abaddon, and to your mercy. The first time I came, I was an unwilling intruder, drawn here by a portal at the bottom of a pool. This time, I have come, not as an intruder, but as a wanderer seeking counsel. As a lover of truth, I am sure you understand my motivation."

Abaddon's eyebeams turned off, and he gave a deep, throaty laugh. "Well, well, the winged wonder has shown herself. Why did a lover of truth forsake asking me for counsel during her first foray here?"

"I was confused, scared, and soaked to the skin. I wasn't sure what to do. I thought you might be angry."

"Ah, I see. You projected your own feelings upon me, judged my character, and deduced my response to your innocent intrusion." His brow lifted. "Are those just actions? Are they in keeping with the truthfulness you cherish? Are you not a hypocrite for casting such shadows upon me?"

Bonnie took a step closer to him. "I hope you will pardon my boldness, but I have been in the company of dragons before, one in particular who did everything he could to get me to doubt my character. I will not be tempted to do that again."

Twin plumes of smoke rose from his nostrils. "If you speak of Arramos, indeed, he is a crafty creature." His ears rotated, as if alerted by a sound. "As you must have noticed, I am not he."

"I apologize for any lack of respect." Bonnie dipped her knee as if offering a curtsy. "If I have understood your book correctly, you wish to prepare Matthew Conner for resurrection."

He again raised his scaly brow. "Ah! So you have also intruded upon my personal journal. You who are so confident in your character, how do you rationalize your rashness?"

"You left it open. I assumed it wasn't private."

"Private? If you left a diary open in your bedroom, would you consider it a violation if someone walked in without warning and pried into your prose?"

"I would never write anything that I wouldn't allow others to see. My mother has read every word I've written in my diary."

"Your mother? Not your father?"

Bonnie's cheeks burned. She ached to look back and see her father's expression, but she dared not.

"Your silence speaks truer than trumpets, and since you already know my name, you must have read more of my writings than what you saw on the open page. Indeed, I am addressed as Abaddon. As one who is a serious student of the Bible, you must have heard of me."

Bonnie offered the slightest of nods. "I have."

"Many think of me as an evil being, a crafty creature, especially those who believe in tall tales." He spread out his wings, broad, thick, and muscular. "I am the fifth angel of Revelation. I hold the key to the abyss, and I am the king of the punishers that lie therein. One day I will leave this place and bring God's wrath upon the wicked people of the Earth." His blue eyes flashed. "I am destruction."

Bonnie swallowed. Had any dragon ever looked so strong, so noble? Maybe he really was an angel of some kind, an avenging angel. She cleared her throat and spread out her own wings. "Excuse me for not understanding who you are. Since we've never met, I—"

"Oh, but we have met, my pet. Did you not find the entry in my journal that spoke of you? Did you resist the temptation to mollify your meddlesome nature? If so, then perhaps I have misjudged you."

She fidgeted. She was losing ground to this dragon, and losing it fast. Steeling her resolve, she looked him in the eye. "I found the entry."

"Then you know that you have voyaged through my valley before." Abaddon touched the ovulum on the central mount with the tip of his wing. "I set your soul in this very spot and sent you back to those who love you. From the depths of her heart, the healer Ashley called you from this place and restored you."

"So, is that the key to resurrection? Someone calls you?"

"When the Lord called for Lazarus, and a girl called for Goliath using his human name, and tiny companions in crystalline eggs called for their charges using names of wisdom, they rose in answer to the heavenly empowered calls."

Bonnie tilted her head. "Goliath's human name? I don't understand."

"His abode was in the abyss, a most unpleasant place in this realm, reserved for those of evil intent. When the slayer killed him, he came to me in dragon form, a foul creature, and I cast out the Nephilim nesting within him and sealed their spirits in the abyss. He transformed into a human spirit and was sent to Second Eden, the place of new birth. There he lived for over a hundred years as a man of manners, becoming a fine father and holy husband, and, as is true with most who pass through this valley, he maintained no memory of his visit.

"When he died in that life, he came to me again, still as a human spirit. Michael the archangel told me that Goliath, or Dragon as he had been renamed, must have another opportunity to withstand the workings of the evil Nephilim. He had failed the first time, but perhaps his experiences as a man of nobility had regenerated his resolve.

"This test of character was crucial, and it would likely be his last chance to prove himself. So, he was sealed in the abyss with the evil spirits and without a Second Eden companion to help him. Our plan was to keep him there for only a short time, but when I opened the seal, he had already transformed to his dragon self, as malevolent as ever."

Abaddon finished with a long sigh. "In fact, Goliath conspired with Arramos to deceive his former mate in Second Eden. As a result, she took of that world's forbidden fruit, which led to the further fouling of the land."

Bonnie glanced at the hourglass. Even with the extra sand, it was almost empty. This dragon's long story had wasted a lot of time. Still, he seemed to be in no hurry. "How soon till the next resurrection takes place?"

"I have not kept count of any time elements." He extended his neck, bringing his head so close, his hot breath stung her cheeks. "It seems that *someone* has taken my hourglass."

She lifted it to his eye level. "I assumed I could take it."

"You assume a great deal. I merely said that the chamber would be energized when the sand is spent. I said nothing about anyone taking it."

"It's about to run out now, but there's no room to add any more sand."

"It seems that the simplest solutions elude you." Abaddon took the hourglass, flipped it over, and set it on the table. "Now we have plenty of time."

Bonnie's face again flamed. This crazy world was getting crazier by the minute.

"Now, where was I before I told you about Goliath?" Abaddon's snout pointed at the ceiling for a moment. "Oh, yes, your diary. We both know why you never showed it to your father, do we not?"

Again she resisted the urge to look back. Could her father hear everything? Would Abaddon reveal her secrets? Maybe it was better to stay quiet. He probably wouldn't wait very long before continuing.

"Shall I recite for you some of the secrets you shared during your previous visit here?"

Bonnie tried to reply with a formal air, hoping she could convince him. "There is no need for that. If we are both aware of my diary's content, what good would it do to give it voice now?"

"You are a lover of truth, but you seem to have forgotten how powerful words can be. They pierce. They penetrate. They both break and bind. Let us test them once more and see if your incisive lament is the sword of a slayer or the scalpel of a surgeon."

Abaddon shuffled to the opposite side of the table and flipped through the pages of his journal. When he stopped, he touched the surface with his claw.

As before, a three-dimensional image rose from the book, this one depicting a bedroom with pink and purple striped wallpaper. A winged girl lay on the bed, a pen in hand as she wrote in a spiral journal.

Nausea curdled Bonnie's stomach. The scene was all too familiar—her thirteenth birthday, the night the slayers killed her mother. Her father had drawn her blood that day, yet another attempt to further his longevity experiments, though he had promised so many times not to do it again. He had broken his promise only hours earlier and callously filled another tube from her arm.

As the Bonnie in the image picked up the journal and read her entry silently, her voice came through, the tone matching the emotion in her words.

DEAR GOD,

I descended into the shadowlands today. A specter of fear wrapped his cold, cruel fingers around my heart and led me into his chamber of treachery, a sanitary cube of torment that once again enclosed my mind in darkness. Can any instrument of torture deliver cruelty as savage as love betrayed? Does a dungeon's rack stretch a body as sadistically as betrayal stretches trust? Can faith endure a traitor's sinister hand as it turns the wheel, each notch testing conviction until the sword of despair separates peace from its rightful habitat?

He bared my skin. He pierced my flesh. He robbed more than my life's blood; with his brazen face and callous dismissal, he robbed my innocence. He shattered my image of a father's love.

Once upon a time, a tall, strong knight took my little hand and led me to the edge of a cliff. Comforted by his powerful grip, I felt no fear, for this valiant knight would never let me fall. Below lay the jagged rocks, the raging river, and a thousand feet of cold, empty air. As I leaned over the precipice, the joy of beholding danger with unflinching eyes flooded my soul. I have an anchor. I have a sure hold in the land of promise. My father would never let me go.

Yet, he did let me go. Nay, he pushed me over the side. And now I fall, staring up at him as he coldly walks away. The wind chills my heart, and the certainty of eternal torment rushes at me with no savior in sight.

God of wonders, catch me now in your loving hands. Fly down on your stallion and rescue me from this plunge into despair. Let us ride together, buoyed by wings of faith and energized by the love that delivered your only begotten son, for he is the king who catches his falling sparrows. Let us waltz together in this dance of death, for you have called me to suffer with you in willing sacrifice and to burn the image of your crucifixion in my heart. Let us live together in the light of your resurrection, for I cannot survive this walk of faith without the comfort of knowing that you will never let go of my hand.

You are Jehovah-Jireh, my provider in times of trouble. You are Jehovah-Shalom, my peace in the midst of turmoil. And above all, you are Jehovah-Shammah, the God who is always there, a true father who rises to my aid when the specter has taken off his fatherly mask and exposed his treacherous heart.

Ask me for my blood, and I will give it freely. Yea, ask me for my life, for you have already crucified me on Calvary's hill and raised me from the dead, purging the life of sin I left behind. Ask me for my soul, for you have already paid for it with your own precious blood, the holy blood of Jehovah-Yasha, my savior.

And now I see it. I can give you nothing that you have not already given to me. I am purchased, a slave of love. I am your vessel to be used in whatever way you wish. If you make me an urn for ashes, a common earthen jar to bear incinerated bones, leaving me to collect dust in a forgotten tomb, even then, I will be content. For just as you would not leave your son forever in the ground, I know you will raise me up from the land of the dead. You have not ignited this fire in my heart to be wasted in Sheol's pit. Though dead, buried, and forgotten, I will rise again.

No matter what happens, I will never forsake you, for you will never forsake me. You are with me, no matter where I go.

LOVE,
BONNIE CONNER

The projected Bonnie laid the journal down, and the image faded away.

The real Bonnie wept. The words brought back every tortured memory, the pain of every needle that gouged her skin, the scarring of her soul that only savage betrayal can leave behind.

Abaddon looked on quietly, giving no hint of emotion. As Bonnie tried to stifle her sobs, the sound of weeping continued, as if stirred up in an echo behind her. This time, she had to look.

Her father strode out from the shadows, tears streaming. Not bothering to wipe them away, he held up his hands. "I am the traitor," he said, his voice quaking. "I am the one who pushed Bonnie off the cliff."

Abaddon nodded slowly. "Does your posture mean that you are giving yourself up to me?"

"I'll do anything to make up for what I've done. I was supposed to be a doctor, and I gave it up because a little girl died on my watch, but instead I became a torturer, a torturer of my own daughter." He covered his face with his hands, unable to control his sobs. "I am such a fool."

Bonnie ran to him and wrapped her arms around his chest. "I love you, Daddy." She rocked back and forth with him and cried. "Will it help if I say, 'I forgive you' again? I'll say it a thousand times!"

"You *were* such a fool," Abaddon said. "My sources tell me that you finished your life as a hero. You forsook your foolishness and embraced the faith your daughter so valiantly lived in front of you, in spite of your betrayals."

"What good is that?" He kept his gaze low, his head bobbing. "I died! I couldn't make up for all the harm I did. I couldn't stay around and be her daddy."

"Since you have acquiesced to my authority over you, I can now prepare you for a potential resurrection. You will not be able to abide with your daughter yet, but you might have the opportunity to, as you say, make up for all the harm you did."

Bonnie drew back from her father. "A potential resurrection? You mean, he might not go?"

"It depends on the decisions the Second Eden dwellers make. If they do not call for a doctor, the fuel that gives this place the power to send him there will not be set aflame."

Bonnie checked the hourglass again. With most of the sand now in the top half, she had plenty of time to figure out her next step. Fortunately, Sapphira had stayed put. She was smart enough to figure out that Abaddon might not be aware of her presence. If he had decided that Bonnie was the only intruder, Sapphira was free to roam without suspicion.

"Okay," her father said, spreading out his arms. "I'm yours, Abaddon. What do you want me to do?"

The dragon's eyes flashed blue. "For months now you have avoided becoming a statue, because you had no idea how important that initiation was in your preparation for resurrection."

"How could I know? You never told me."

"You refused to listen and learn." Abaddon pointed a claw at him. "You ran and hid."

"I was turning into a statue, and when I ran, my feet started catching on fire. Wouldn't you run from whatever was causing that?"

Bonnie looked down at her father's shoes. Thin smoke rose from the toes and heels, and they seemed to glow.

"We were discussing truth," Abaddon continued. "One must never run from such revelations."

"Even if I'm about to burn? I would suffer excruciating pain and then become a pile of ashes."

"Or so you say, yet you have seen a fiery resident of this place. She neither cries in pain nor burns up, and every statue holds another flaming soul who lives on without suffering. So it is your false perception you fear. If we were to strip the solid shells, to outsiders, the inhabitants of this land would appear to be unapproachable apparitions, sources of discomfort, fit only for viewing from afar or perhaps in videos viewed in museums that display such oddities for parents and children to ponder with head-shaking disapproval. Yet, the one who sees from within the fiery body observes others with new eyes. He sees beyond the blinders that most men wear, some willingly and some in ignorance. The inferno's eyes foil façades and unmask the heart, stripping away lies, pretense, and cultural correctness that cause men to live the lie, though they really do not believe the lie at all. Those who fear this flame value acceptance and approval above truth."

Bonnie glanced down again. Now her father's shoes had sprouted flames, and they crawled up his pant legs.

"That would mean that seeking and believing truth is penalized," her father said. "You have to give up freedom to interact with others."

Abaddon gave him a grim nod. "In the fallen world, yes, this is true. Every man and woman who ever plied truth's trade learned this awful fact. Once he or she strips off the outer shell to try to interact with others, the inner fire becomes clear. From Jeremiah to Joan of Arc, one who treasures truth beyond all things becomes a pariah or a paragon, either of which makes him or her hated with passion or admired from afar, and therefore friendless until the day of martyrdom."

Bonnie's father looked down. Now he knew that flames had enshrouded his legs, but he didn't seem to care. "So what's the purpose of doing this here, I mean, in this valley of souls?"

"To train *your* soul. When you resurrect, you will remember your time here for only a short few moments, but your mind will be prepared for the heartache that accompanies the martyr's path, for no one who resurrects from the dead can ever return to a normal life. To others, you will be considered a prophet or a demon. There is no middle ground."

"So be it." As the flames reached his waist, he lifted his arms, grimacing at the heat. "I am ready. Send me wherever you wish me to go."

"It is not I who sends. It is the one who calls. Both you and another will be ready to go, and either one of you will be able to help in the perils the people face, but I do not know which of you they will choose. Yet, I will prepare you, both by the fire that now envelops you and by these words, which you will remember only while your feet are firmly planted in the garden."

As the flames rose to his chin, Bonnie's father tilted his head upward, like a drowning man reaching for air. Agony strained his voice. "Speak, Abaddon. I am ready."

"Heed my words, Matthew Conner. The death of a little girl and the blame you heaped upon yourself have seared your heart, creating scars that enabled you to cruelly punish your wife and another girl. By this fire, I burn those scars and peel away their remains."

The flames covered his face. His fiery head still tilting upward, he screamed loud and long.

"Your heart will be raw, vulnerable, bleeding. If the Second Eden dwellers call you to resurrection, they will ask you to do something that you will not believe you are able to accomplish. Fear will grip your newly wounded heart, causing pain beyond words, and you will be sorely tempted to deny their request. Yet, you must accept immediately. If you delay, you will soon forget my warning, and all will be lost."

His fire-wrapped body now heaving, he nodded. "I will . . . try."

Abaddon opened the bottle he had used earlier, tipped a drop out onto his hand, and touched the flaming head. As before, a shroud of fog enveloped the fiery body, and when it disappeared, a large egg sat in Abaddon's grasp. "Now you will await word from above."

Inside, Bonnie's father cried out so loud his words penetrated the glass. "Call to me, and I will answer you."

His glass shell radiating orange, he lowered himself to a sitting position. The words repeated again and again, fading each time. His fingers stood out clearly as they pressed against the inside wall.

Abaddon set the egg on one of the table's mounts. "His suffering is great, but it is only temporary."

"Temporary?" Bonnie raised a hand to her mouth and bit her finger. It was terrible! Her father was suffering so much! And there was nothing she could do about it. Nothing.

She looked at the hourglass. About half of the sand had passed through to the bottom. What did that mean? Fifteen minutes? Twenty? However many, with Daddy in so much pain, it would seem like hours.

And what of Makaidos? Surely his pain was just as great. When would one of them be able to go to Second Eden?

Abaddon set a wing tip on Bonnie's shoulder. "It is time for you to go. When the call comes, the room will be swept with fire, and only those already in flames will survive."

CHAPTER 14

PIERCING A GEM

With the coil of rope in hand, Billy reached the top of the ladder and emerged back in Second Eden. He pulled the hood over his head and jumped through the wall of fire. Working quickly, he tied the end of the rope to the iron stake, reeled it out, and tossed the other end into the volcano's throat, making sure the mesh still protected the rope.

Listener climbed to the top of the ladder and leaped through the fire, grinning. "I feel like Superman."

"You've been listening to Walter's stories, haven't you?"

"Superman, Batman, and Spiderman." Squinting, she looked up at him. "Are there any women superheroes?"

As Acacia's snowy head appeared, Billy nodded toward her. "You'd better believe it."

Acacia stood and waved her arms inside the fire ring, keeping the cyclone going. When Dallas and Rebekah climbed to the top of the ladder, Acacia looked at Billy. "It's time to close this door."

He checked the knot at the stake. "It's secure. Let's do it."

While Dallas and Rebekah stood inside the fire circle and looked on, Acacia stepped down a few rungs and, hanging on tightly to the rope, kicked the ladder until it slid away. She climbed back up, grunting and slipping. Rebekah reached down, grabbed Acacia's tunic, and hoisted her the rest of the way.

The fiery vortex slowed. As soon as the flames cleared, a plume of gray vapor rose from the volcano. Mount Elijah was once again open.

Billy helped Acacia reel the rope back into a coil. "I saw you write something on a scroll down there," she said. "What was it?"

"Just a note telling what we did and who we took with us." He shrugged. "I don't know if it'll do any good, but maybe someone will find it."

Dallas wrapped her arms around herself. "This place is freezing," she said, her teeth chattering.

Billy stripped off his cloak and tossed it to her. "That should help for now. We'll call Thigocia and get you a Sahara treatment right away. We brought some extra clothes, but we'll have to wait until we find our passenger dragons before we can get them."

Looking up, Billy shouted into the sky. "Thigocia, are you up there?"

Twin lasers cut through the clouds. Seconds later, the tawny dragon dropped into sight. Since five people now stood on the volcano's top, she had to perch on part of the demolished wall that once covered the cone while slowly beating her wings to keep her balance. "I see that we have new arrivals."

"Mother!" Dallas leaped forward and clutched Thigocia's foreleg. "It's so good to see you. We hardly had a minute to speak after our resurrection."

Thigocia sniffed Dallas's hair. "Ah! Firedda! My gentle one!" As she rubbed Dallas's back with her clawed hand, she looked at Rebekah. "And is this my granddaughter, Legossi?"

With a frigid wind whipping her blonde locks, Rebekah bowed her head. "It's a joy to see you again, Thigocia, yet I notice you did not call me a gentle one."

Thigocia gave her a toothy smile. "Warriors like you and myself are rarely called gentle, my dear."

"Thigocia," Billy said, "can you give us all a Sahara treatment and take these two to Grackle and get them the clothes we brought? The rest of us will hoof it back."

"Very well. They can mount here, and we will meet you at the rendezvous point, though I will watch over you along the way. The Vacants are on the move, but I cannot tell if they will take a path toward us or to the river."

As Dallas rejoined the others in a huddle, Thigocia took in a deep breath and poured out a jet of hot dry air through her mouth and nostrils. All five humans spread out their arms and basked in the flow. After four repetitions, everyone was dry and toasty.

With freezing drizzle still falling, Billy nodded at Dallas. "Keep the cloak. I'm getting used to this place, and Grackle can heat up his scales for me."

Dallas hugged the cloak close to her body. "I am grateful for your chivalry."

Rebekah nodded toward the volcano's throat. "Are you going back to the mines with explosives to blow a hole in the escape tunnel?"

"Probably in the morning," Billy said. "When we resurrect Makaidos at the ceremony, we'll tell him everything that's going on. Maybe he'll have other ideas."

After Rebekah and Dallas mounted and flew away on Thigocia, Billy, Acacia, and Listener retraced their steps down Mount Elijah's switchback trail. With every footfall, an unsettling feeling in his stomach grew stronger, a stewing swill that raised foul odors in his throat and into his nostrils.

When they reached the lava field, Billy grasped Excalibur's hilt at his hip and scanned the ridges on each side, both partially veiled by fog. "I sense danger."

Listener looked into the clouds with her spyglass. "I don't see Thigocia anywhere."

"If I sense it, then she probably does, too." Billy withdrew his sword. "Come on. Let's get to the dragons."

Now jogging with Acacia on one side and Listener on the other, Billy searched through the mist, watching for Vacants as well as for any sign of the Second Eden dragons. Did they fly away, perhaps trying to escape from the enemy? Might they be circling somewhere overhead?

Listener stopped and pointed at the ground. "Here is where we left them."

Billy joined her and studied the rippled rock. "How do you know?"

"White-spotted scat." She nudged a pile with the toe of her boot. "Normally Albatross goes in the woods. He must have been scared."

Billy nodded. "I get the picture."

While Listener again peered through her spyglass, Billy turned in place, scanning the skies again. "We're sitting ducks out here. If we don't see a friendly dragon soon, we should head for the woods ourselves."

"They likely fear you and your sword," Acacia said. "The Vacant who escaped surely told them of your skill."

"Maybe. But I'll bet they're afraid of an Oracle of Fire. They see a powerful warrior at my side."

"I will do what I can." A ball of flames appeared in each of her palms, sizzling in the mix of snow and drizzling rain. "At least we can try to keep them hiding in their holes."

"A dragon just dove out of the clouds!" Listener called.

Billy swung toward her. "Where?"

She pointed at the ridge to the north. "Behind that hill."

A loud growl erupted from that direction. Orange firelight painted the clouds, like flashes of lightning within the mist.

Billy spread out his arms, his sword in one hand. "Get ready. Thigocia's attack might flush them out."

"Should we flee to the woods?" Acacia asked.

"They might already be there by now. We could get ambushed." Billy grasped the hilt with both hands. "I'd rather see what I'm fighting."

Listener put her spyglass back in its holster and withdrew a six-inch dagger from her belt. "Candle taught me how to fight, too."

Suppressing a laugh, Billy gave her a wink. "We'll need all the help we can get."

Listener pointed at a pass in the hillside. "Here they come!"

A line of soldiers poured through the gap, running with swords drawn and spears raised. Fog obscured the landscape. Billy couldn't tell who they were, but his danger sensors sounded a loud alarm.

At least twenty soldiers ran straight toward them. Soon their identity became clear. With small fish-like mouths and big dark eyes, there was no doubt about it.

"Vacants," Billy said. "A bunch of them."

As another dozen Vacants stormed through the pass, Thigocia followed, two riders on her back and her wings beating as she flooded their rear flank with a streaming firestorm. Two Vacants at the back erupted in flames, and a third fell on his face in the lava field. A purple dragon trailed Thigocia, spewing ice on the field, and a white dragon followed, adding another coat of frost.

Acacia stepped out in front of Billy and Listener. She wrapped her arms around herself, then thrust them out to her side and shouted, "Ignite!" White flames shot from her hair and hands, and waves of bright blue sparks coated her body from head to toe. As her fire blazed, her entire body shook, and her face twisted into a pain-streaked grimace.

The leading line of soldiers slowed, their black eyes wide. One charged ahead, screaming a strange word as he raised a curved sword.

Billy jumped in front of Acacia. Excalibur met the monster's sword with a loud clank and broke it in two. He ducked under the Vacant's arm and, with a deft spin, swung his sword into its waist, cutting deeply.

As the Vacant collapsed, Thigocia flew over. "One more pass ought to do it!" she called.

While she made a tight turn, somewhat slowed because of her riders, Billy looked back at the army. More than half were either in flames or blackened and lying on the ground. At least ten retreated toward the hills, but while they slipped on the now frozen ground, the other two dragons coated them with sprays of ice.

Five remaining Vacants charged. Acacia threw flaming balls at two and set their clothes on fire. Billy leaped ahead and cut through the leader's spear at its grip, then with a backswing lopped off his hand. Lowering his shoulder, he rammed into the Vacant and sent him flying backwards.

Thigocia flew over and scorched the fourth with twin jets, but the fifth ducked underneath her fire and dashed by Billy.

With a quick leg thrust, Billy tripped him. The Vacant staggered a few steps before falling to all fours in front of Acacia. Grunting, he raised up, thrust his spear into her leg, and yanked it back out.

Acacia fell backwards. Her flames vanished. Listener dropped to her knees at Acacia's side, while Billy ran toward them.

Still on his knees, the Vacant thrust his spear again, this time through Listener's arm and into her ribcage.

"No!" Billy screamed. Fire spewed from his mouth and splashed over the Vacant's body. Then, he swung Excalibur with all his might and sliced off the Vacant's flaming head.

As Listener toppled backwards, Billy caught her in his arms. "Oh, dear God!" he cried. "Not Listener!"

Her chest heaving, Listener looked up at Billy with glazed eyes. "I . . . I'm hurt."

He kissed her forehead. Tears dripped from his cheek to hers as he gasped, "Yes . . . but you'll be okay. You'll be . . ." He couldn't finish. As blood leaked from her arm, cruelly pinned against her side, he wept.

"Do not remove the spear!" Thigocia shouted as she landed. "Her only hope is to leave it intact until we get her to a surgeon."

Rebekah leaped to the ground and helped Acacia to a sitting position. Dallas followed and dragged the Vacant's burning body away.

Blinking away tears, Acacia reached for Listener's hand and caressed it. "Fear not, precious one," she said, her voice quaking. "We'll get you to Ashley."

"I . . ." Listener swallowed. "I'm not afraid. I thought I was going to die by Timothy's hand, and I wasn't afraid then."

Billy looked up at the weeping sky. "God! Please help us! Don't let this little girl die!"

Albatross landed next to Thigocia. Ice crystals dripped from his eyes as he looked at Listener, whimpering.

"Albatross," Thigocia said in a commanding voice. "Take Rebekah to the village and find Ashley. We will need something to cut the spear's handle."

"And we will bring a stretcher." Rebekah grabbed Albatross's strap and vaulted to the pilot's chair. "Let's fly!"

Letting out a loud trumpet call, Albatross leaped into the air and flew toward the village.

Thigocia looked up at the purple dragon circling low overhead, apparently watching for more Vacants. "Grackle!" she called. "Follow Albatross. We might need another transport. I will stay here and keep everyone warm."

Grackle beat his wings hard and charged after the white dragon. Soon, both disappeared in the fog.

Thigocia covered Listener with a wing and breathed a warm wind over her shivering body. "Try to calm yourself, little one. The more you shake, the more damage you might do."

Acacia scooted under the wing and pushed her fingers through Listener's hair. "Do you remember what you told me this morning?" Acacia asked. "The story about finding the spyglass?"

Listener nodded.

"And the song you and Candle made up about it?"

She nodded again, this time wincing.

"May I sing it for you?"

As her eyelids fluttered, she offered another weak nod. "I would like that," she whispered.

Acacia looked at Billy, then at Dallas. "When you figure it out, please join in."

After clearing her throat, Acacia gazed into Listener's eyes and sang.

My prayers go up;
Your love comes down;
You make me smile
On days I frown.
Our Father above
Sends us baskets of love,
The blessings from his heart.

As Acacia repeated the song, Billy joined in, barely able to whisper the words. But when he saw Listener's lips bend into a weak smile, he reached for more strength and gave it all he had. Soon, Dallas and even Thigocia joined them, the pattering of rain acting as a rhythmic beat.

More snow mixed in. A bitter wind blew. Billy shivered. He looked at Excalibur's blade, still wet with the Vacant's dark blood. It wasn't enough—the sword, his skills, his wisdom in planning for battle. Nothing in his power could have kept this sweet little girl from such an awful fate. And nothing he could do would restore her ravaged body. Saving her now would take a miracle.

When the song ended, he looked up at the cascading flakes of white and whispered, "My prayers are going up, Father. Please make this precious one smile again."

* * *

Marilyn sat on the tunnel's cold stone floor and leaned against the rocky wall. It wasn't the most comfortable seat in the world, but with her arms and legs aching, it was a lot better than nothing.

Gabriel stooped beside her and set a box searchlight on the ground, pointing it down the long tunnel. The high-powered beam illuminated Yereq and two former dragons as they rested nearby.

"Any other ideas?" Gabriel asked. "Think they found a portal or another way out?"

She shook her head. "No ideas. Let's wait for the diver to come back. If he comes up empty-handed, I'll try to think again. My brain's just too tired right now."

"Well, you already know what I think about his chances."

Marilyn bit her lip. Gabriel was probably right. If they had drowned, their bodies would probably be under several layers of hardened magma by now. And with water rising to within a few feet of the top level, every access would be cut off soon.

"I have some great news, though." He unwound a scroll a few inches and showed her the parchment. The leading edge was charred, but the hand printed text, written in dark pencil, was bold and easy to read. "Check this out."

Marilyn leaned closer and read the carefully printed words.

This is Billy Bannister. Acacia and I took Rebekah and Dallas to Second Eden. We couldn't find anyone else. We'll try to come back tomorrow.

Underneath the text, Billy had drawn a sketch of himself and a dragon, both spewing fire.

She took the scroll and hugged it to her chest. Billy was alive! And so were Acacia and two of the former dragons. As tears welled in her eyes, she whispered, "Thank God."

"I heard water running while I was in the museum chamber," Gabriel said. "It's dry in there, at least for now, and a tree's on fire, but it's off by itself so it's not hurting anything. A ladder had been pulled down from the shelves. I guess they used it to climb through the portal."

She clenched her fingers around the scroll. "And we missed them!"

"Yeah, I guess they were here while we were buzzing around in the helicopter."

Marilyn nodded. She was about to ask why Yereq hadn't seen them, but then remembered the huge new hole in the escape tunnel's rubble. Obviously, Yereq had spent most of the time working on the opposite side of the rubble heap. If Billy and Acacia had ventured that way, they wouldn't have seen him from inside the mines.

She read the scroll again. It seemed so wondrous and filled with life, and it communicated so much more than what the simple words said. The drawing meant that Jared was alive, too, or else Billy would have mentioned losing him.

"So," Gabriel said, "assuming the diver doesn't find them, what's the next step?"

"Keep working on Apollo, I guess. We don't have another portal opener."

"Right. That should work great for getting into Second Eden." The muscles in Gabriel's forearms tensed. "But we have three missing in action. What about them?"

Marilyn looked into his fiery eyes. He wasn't ready to give up any of the girls for lost. But how could anyone guess where they were now? Shiloh was in the hands of dragon slayers, who apparently sent their goons back to get the former dragons, and it seemed that Bonnie and Sapphira had simply vanished.

She reached out and took Gabriel's hand. "I don't know what to do. Do you have a suggestion?"

"We have their chopper and some partial names. I'll bet we can find enough clues to get a good start."

"We'll need Larry for that," Marilyn said, "so we should get home and feed him the information."

"Only after we scour the helicopter for data, and maybe by then Mr. Foley will be well enough to travel. But we can't wait around too long. Whoever sent the chopper might come looking for it."

"I'll call Edmund and see what he can do about keeping Carly at my house for a while. If they can make progress on Apollo without us there, staying here for a couple more days should be fine. No matter what happens, if Billy's coming back tomorrow, we have to wait for him."

Gabriel pointed at the floor. "And Yereq will stay longer and keep searching. He can't fit in the airplane anyway."

"And I'll camp out in the museum room. I don't want to miss Billy."

"If it's not flooded."

"Right. That could be a problem." Marilyn touched Gabriel's cheek and changed her tone, hoping to communicate confidence. "We'll find them. You know that, don't you?"

He firmed his lips and nodded. "I know."

"But something else is bothering you."

"Well . . . nothing important. At least nothing that anyone can do anything about."

"Tell me anyway," she said, pulling on his sleeve. "Just getting it off your chest will help."

He rocked from his crouch to a fully seated position. "I'm working like crazy trying to save everyone and get the world back to normal."

"Yes, I know. You've been wonderful."

"But do you know what will happen if we succeed?"

"I'm not sure what you mean. Some kind of trouble?"

Gabriel set his fingers together and let them spring apart. "Poof! If we separate Earth and Hades, I lose my physical body and become nothing but light energy."

Marilyn covered her mouth. "I forgot about that!"

"I can't say I blame you. This world merging thing is pretty crazy. And the only place I can have a real body will be in Hades. I don't know about you, but that's not even a nice place to visit, and no one would want to live there."

"We'll find an answer. Between Sapphira and Acacia and Enoch, someone has to know how to make you permanently whole."

"Maybe." He stayed quiet for a moment. Then, his voice spiking in anguish, he said, "And what if they do solve it? Will I have to live life as a freak? How could anyone ever love a teenaged senior citizen with dragon wings?"

Marilyn took his hand. Intertwining his fingers with hers, she kissed his thumb. "Oh, Gabriel. I know who brightens your eyes. I know who makes your heart flutter. Everyone does. And she's also a teenaged senior citizen."

Redness colored his cheeks. "I guess I haven't hidden it very well."

"There's no need to hide it. Who would ever say you're too young for romance? Shiloh has to know that you'd make a wonderful husband."

"I'm glad you think so." He pulled a wing tip in front of his eyes and rubbed the leathery canopy. "But would she want to marry a freak?"

"If you insist on using that term, then I'll oblige." She pointed at herself. "I'm a freak, too. I married a former dragon. And of course, my husband's a freak, and so is my son." She began counting on her fingers. "Bonnie's a freak for obvious reasons, as is Sapphira, Acacia, and even Shiloh. Who ever heard of a girl surviving for forty years eating only a poisonous plant? And she didn't age a day!"

Gabriel let a thin smile break through. "Okay. You got me. But there's still the light energy issue to deal with."

Marilyn climbed to her feet and reached down a hand for Gabriel. When they locked wrists, she hauled him up with a strong pull. "You feel solid to me, and if we have to move Heaven and Earth to keep you that way, we'll do it."

CHAPTER 15

IS THERE NO BALM IN GILEAD?

Billy pushed a finger through Listener's hair, no longer braided in her usual pigtails. Someone had brushed it out and splayed it on the soft pillow beneath her head. Lying on an elevated cot, her face pale, her skin soft and smooth, she looked like a sleeping angel. Yet, every few seconds, her lips puckered, and lines dug into her forehead, signs that pain tortured her unconscious brain. This angel was being tormented.

Standing next to Billy, Sir Patrick read the pressure meter. "Eighty over forty, William. The rate of decrease is slow, but it is dangerously steady. Her internal bleeding must be significant."

Billy looked down at Elam as he sat on a nearby cot. "Did you hear that?" Billy asked.

Elam nodded, his face as pale as Listener's. "How much longer does she have?"

"At this rate of blood loss?" Patrick looked up at the ceiling for a moment as if calculating. "Perhaps two hours. It is difficult to be certain."

As tears welled in his eyes, Billy moved his hand to Listener's arm, now bandaged and resting under a three-inch wooden stub, the new end of the spear. Earlier, Rebekah sawed it off and Steadfast withdrew the severed end from Listener's arm. Steadfast was able to patch up the wound in the fleshy part of her bicep, but the more dangerous puncture through her ribcage still lay untouched.

Covering Listener's bare chest up to her collarbone, a white sheet was turned up at the side to expose the wound. Listener's companion floated just above her hand as it rested on her stomach. Emanating a pale blue light, the companion blinked at a tube that protruded from her skin, leading to a bag of blood hanging from a hook attached to an upright wooden pole. Valiant, after learning that his blood matched Listener's, had donated as much as Ashley would allow. And since five other villagers also matched, they still had donors eager to help, yet, at the rate Listener was fading, it seemed hopeless.

As blood oozed from her side down to the lower sheet, Billy glared at the sawed butt of the spear. He had been too slow, too confident, too stupid. Why had he allowed her to go with them? Why hadn't he taken her to the forest when the Vacants came into view? Sure, an ambush was possible, but he could have hidden her somewhere and fought those beasts alongside Acacia. Risking a child was stupid. It was criminal.

Raising a clenched fist, he muttered under his breath. "I should have taken that spear and—"

"William?" Patrick grasped Billy's wrist. "Are you punishing yourself?"

Letting out a long breath, Billy slowly loosened his fingers. "I guess so."

"May I suggest that we concentrate on what we must do now rather than what we have done? A very important decision must be made without delay."

Billy shifted his gaze to Listener and kept his voice low. "You mean, surgery?"

"If we fail to make the attempt, she will die."

"But who could do it without killing her even faster?"

"Our best chance is Ashley. Steadfast told me he can brew an elixir that will give her a burst of energy. It won't last long, and it will make her recovery take longer, but she might have enough strength to give surgery a try."

Billy looked at Ashley lying on a cot next to Walter's. She had stripped down to shorts and a T-shirt, and no blanket covered her flushed body. Pearl knelt on the floor and mopped Ashley's bare arms with a sponge. If Ashley hadn't attempted a healing, Listener would have died hours ago. At least they had bought some time.

"But Ashley's never done anything like this before," Billy said. "Not even close."

"I suggest consulting with Elam and Valiant. They must make the decision soon."

"I guess you're right." Billy shuffled over and sat next to Elam on the cot.

Elam buried his face in his hands. "Now what are we going to do? If I wasn't so stupid . . ." His voice faded away.

Billy laid an arm over Elam's shoulders. "Don't kick yourself." He glanced at Sir Patrick. He was listening, his knowing smile indicating his pleasure at hearing Billy pass along his words of wisdom. "We should concentrate on what we have to do now," Billy continued. "You made the right decision."

"The right decision?" Elam jumped to his feet and spun back toward Billy. He waved a hand toward the other cots in the triage hut. "Ashley's fever is a hundred and five. Acacia's hurt, her flames are spent, and she's supposed to energize the bones in less than an hour."

Billy said nothing. It was probably better to let Elam give himself a swift kick in the pants, in spite of what Sir Patrick had said.

Running a hand through his mussed mop of hair, Elam lowered his voice to a whisper. "She'll probably die anyway, and now we can't call for Makaidos. Everything's messed up."

Billy lowered his voice as well. "Sir Patrick said we have to make a decision. Do we give Ashley an artificial energy boost so she can try surgery, or do we just let Listener die, probably in the next two hours?"

Elam stayed quiet for a moment before answering in a whisper. "I didn't know about the energy boost. We should give it a try."

"But there's another option I haven't told anyone yet." Billy licked his dry lips, unsure of how to explain his idea. It sounded crazy even to him. "When we go to the garden tonight, maybe instead of calling for Makaidos, we should call for a doctor."

"A doctor?" Elam gave Billy a puzzled stare. "What are you talking about?"

"Just play along with me here. Suppose I said there might be a way to use the garden to call for a doctor instead of for Makaidos. What would you do?"

"I guess it won't hurt to speculate." Elam sat next to Billy again. "We're preparing for war, and sometimes innocent little girls die in wars. We need more warriors. You've seen the people here. They're loving and kind, but only a few are real soldiers."

"But if the garden works, we'll have Legossi and Firedda. I have seen Legossi fight with Sir Barlow riding her. If she's at full strength, watch out."

Elam stroked his chin. "With the wall of fire still intact, we'll probably have enough warriors for a while."

"Exactly what I was thinking."

Letting out a quiet laugh, Elam shook his head. "Wishing for a doctor isn't going to get us one."

"But maybe calling for one will."

Elam propped an elbow on his knee. "Okay. Give it to me straight. What's your idea?"

"Just something I saw in the mines. It reminded me of a story Walter told me." Billy touched Bonnie's string of beads, still draped around his neck. "Back when all this started, Devin's cronies were trying to find Bonnie in her house, so she hid in her attic. Walter and his dad were in her bedroom looking for her, and they saw a poster of a girl praying, and a Bible verse on it said, 'Trust in the Lord with all thine heart; and lean not unto thine own understanding.' But I don't remember the rest of it."

"In all thy ways acknowledge him," Elam said, "and he shall direct thy paths."

Billy flushed. He should have known that a guy who's been around for thousands of years would know the Bible so well. "Right. Anyway, another poster said, 'Call to me, and I will answer you, and I will tell you great and mighty things, which you do not know.' The words 'Call to me' were underlined in red. So Walter decided just to call Bonnie's name."

"And it worked?"

Billy nodded. "Bonnie came down from the attic. She was kind of beat up, but she made it through."

Elam mimicked Billy's nod. "Just like the other verse said, 'Trust in the Lord with all your heart.'"

"Exactly. And Bonnie always trusted. She never doubted." Billy studied Elam's face. Although he had listened attentively, a look of doubt shaded his expression.

"Okay," Elam said. "I think I see where you're going. When Paili switched the words in her song to "the dragon," Goliath came out instead of Makaidos."

"And he was once a human named Dragon," Billy added. "Maybe if we call for a doctor, we'll get one."

"But how do you know a doctor is available? I mean, is someone from every profession lying around under our garden waiting to be called up? I'm not trying to be funny or cruel, but if we called for a plumber, do you think we would get one?"

Billy grinned. "Maybe he could get running water to our bathhouses."

"I know what you mean. But do you get my point?"

"Sure, but that's where what I saw in the mines comes in. When Listener and I were moving a ladder from the museum room shelves, a scroll fell off and rolled to the Tree of Life. It caught on fire, so I grabbed it and snuffed it out. When I unrolled it there wasn't much left besides this sentence." Billy pulled the strip of parchment from his pocket and showed it to Elam. "Do you know Hebrew?"

Elam murmured his translation. "Is there no balm in Gilead? Is there no doctor there? Why then is the health of the daughter of my people not restored?"

Billy touched one of the strange characters. "That's pretty much how Acacia translated it."

"It's from Jeremiah," Elam said. "That wasn't even written when the museum was built."

"Acacia said she or Sapphira picked it up during one of their scavenging hunts." He gave the parchment to Elam. "Since it kind of fell in my lap, and since it glowed white, I thought it might be something we should pay attention to."

"It glowed white?"

"Kind of like a phosphorescent powder. I think the scroll picked it up at the Tree of Life. The dirt in the tree's planter is covered with the stuff."

"I see." Elam rolled the parchment into a miniature scroll and then back out again. "So you believe this is some kind of sign from God that we should call for a doctor instead of Makaidos."

"I'm not sure what I believe, but I was thinking—"

A new voice broke in. "Billy doesn't have much experience with calling people back from the dead in resurrection gardens."

Billy turned toward the sound. "Walter?"

Sitting up on the cot and holding a hand against a bandage that wrapped around his bare chest, Walter nodded. "You guys sound like there are only two choices."

"Is there another?" Elam asked.

"I've been around Ashley the logic queen long enough to recognize a false dilemma. Why should you have to choose between Makaidos and a doctor? Why not call both?"

Elam stared at him. "Call both?"

"Sure. That garden changed a girl into a woman, and it's been sprouting dragons right and left. It's already proved it can handle multitasking."

Billy looked at Ashley, still asleep. If she knew Walter was sitting up, she would have a heart attack. He was supposed to stay in bed until morning.

"Okay," Elam said slowly. "We can try both, but if the theory is wrong and the ceremony is good for only one resurrection, which should we call first?"

Setting a hand against his forehead, Walter lay back down in his cot. "Sorry. I'm overloaded now. My brain is choking."

Billy interlaced his fingers into a double fist. "I say the doctor."

"And you?" Elam said, looking up at Sir Patrick.

Patrick eyed the blood pressure meter. "My heart cries out for a doctor for this precious girl, but my head says this might be our last opportunity to call the king of the dragons." With a sigh, he added, "I usually listen to my head, but my heart is holding sway. I think surgery is demanded, so to give this little fighter the best chance, we should ask God for the best surgeon."

"Well stated," Elam said, "but what about Enoch's commands? We didn't call for Makaidos the first time, and our choice ended in a disaster. Are we going to fail again to—"

The door swung open, ushering in a snowy breeze. Acacia and Ruth entered, dressed in heavy cloaks, their shoulders and hoods coated with snow. Acacia limped, but not badly. Apparently her leg wound wasn't severe.

Billy and Elam rose to their feet. "Greetings, ladies," Elam said with a bow.

As Ruth closed the door, Walter waved from his cot. "I'd be chivalrous and stand, too, but I might drop a lung on the floor."

Smiling in spite of her pale and haggard face, Acacia brushed snow from her shoulders. "The time has come," she said softly.

"Will Ruth recite the same poem?" Elam asked.

"We see no reason why she shouldn't."

Elam showed Acacia the strip of parchment. "I assume you and Billy talked about this."

She nodded. "If you wish to change the word 'Makaidos' to 'a doctor,' we will do as you ask. We are the couriers of the call, not the composers."

"You know what happened the last time I authorized a change."

Acacia looked at Listener, motionless and quiet on the elevated cot, save for her rapid, shallow breaths. "You are the warrior chief," Acacia said, her eyes sparkling with tears. "We will trust and abide by your decision."

"Warrior chief?" Elam shook his head and sighed. "I'm just a rookie general from another world. This isn't a war decision. This is ethics. This is spiritual. And it's about the life of a girl from a world I barely know. I'm just not qualified."

"So who is?" Billy asked.

"Abraham appointed Valiant to take his place. We'll have to get him up to speed fast. The ceremony is in about half an hour."

"Where is he?" Billy asked.

"Praying at the garden, most likely."

"In the snow?"

Elam nodded. "Ever since he became Second Eden's new prophet, he's spent as much time praying as he has training the troops. Since there's a portal at the garden, he likes to pray there. It gives him a peaceful feeling."

Ruth bowed her head. "I will go to him now and explain the situation."

"Good idea," Elam said. "I'm sure Ember will give you a ride. She is likely staying warm in Emerald's hut."

"I will find her."

As Ruth hurried out the door, Billy nodded toward the garden. "My father's taking his turn patrolling out there. I told Dad about the doctor, so maybe he gave the message to Valiant already."

"Good. He'll have some time to think about it." Elam picked up a cloak from the cot. "Acacia, I don't mean to offend you, but you look spent. I have never seen you like this."

She laid a palm on her cheek. "I have felt ill all day, and the healing exhausted me."

"You should ride, too. Dikaios is in my hut. He'll be happy to carry you."

Acacia lowered her head. "I would like that."

"Sir Patrick," Elam continued, "please give Ashley the elixir that will give her more energy, and the two of you can prepare Listener for surgery. I'm hoping we'll come back with a doctor, but even if we don't, we'll have to try to save her without one. "

"Very well," Patrick said. "We will be ready."

Elam turned to Billy. "You should go. Make sure Valiant knows the whole story. I'll gather the villagers and meet everyone at the garden."

"I saw no villagers on my way over here," Acacia said. "Maybe the weather has kept them inside."

Elam furrowed his brow. "No villagers? Not even the children?"

"Only Cliffside preparing the lanterns for the night. I thought it odd, as well. The snow would be quite a draw for people who have never seen it before, especially the younger ones."

"I'd better get moving," Billy said. As he turned to go, he glanced at Listener again. She was so weak, so close to death. Should he keep trying to persuade them to choose a doctor? Was what happened on Second Eden really his business? Was Elam right about innocent little girls dying during times of war?

He picked up his own cloak and hurried out of the triage hut. He thrust his arms through the sleeves and balled his fists. They had to ask for a doctor! They just had to! Warrior or no warrior, it didn't make sense to watch Listener die without trying to do something, anything, even following a wild hunch, a crazy guess that fell from the sky in the guise of a burning parchment in an ancient scroll.

Jogging through gently falling snow, he approached Cliffside, who was lighting a hanging lantern at the end of the street. "Good evening," Billy said.

Cliffside nodded. "It is evening, to be sure, but it is not a good one."

Billy stopped, puffing white vapor. "You're right. It's a greeting we have in my world. We don't always mean that it's good."

"I have used the greeting many times, Sir Billy, but with that precious girl bleeding to death, and a season of more death upon us, I see no reason to call it good."

Billy dragged his shoe through the snow. Cliffside was right. Listener was a favorite among the villagers because of her willingness to sacrifice herself. With her suffering so much, a heavy gloom seemed to blanket everything. "Well spoken," was all Billy could muster as he resumed a steady jogging pace.

As he entered the forest, he looked down at the path. With snow and rain moistening the ground, mud had formed, revealing recent footprints, dozens of them from child-sized to adult.

Kicking into a higher gear, he rushed out into the field. At the edge of the garden, a sea of lanterns lit the area, highlighting hundreds of people kneeling in the midst of thousands of swirling snowflakes.

Billy slowed his pace. The weight of gloom had lifted, and now a feeling of holiness took over. This place of prayer was a sanctuary that pleaded for silence or quiet singing.

As he neared, he found Valiant kneeling in the middle of a circle of villagers. Quite a number of the younger girls wore pigtails, perhaps in honor of Listener's style. Or perhaps they were from Peace Village, Listener's home, and the girls there often wore their hair that way.

Billy's father sat on one side of the crowd, extending his neck to breathe warm air across as many as he could, while Hartanna and Thigocia sat on the other side doing the same. Ruth knelt next to Valiant, apparently whispering into his ear while Ember, the sorrel mare, stood nearby.

Stopping at the outer edge of the circle, Billy crossed his arms over his chest and took in a deep breath. The scene spoke volumes. Valiant the warrior had called his people to battle.

Hoofbeats sounded. With the lantern light making her eyes gleam, Acacia rode Dikaios across the field. When the great horse stopped, Billy took Acacia's hand and helped her dismount. Her skin felt cold, her hand thin and frail. Her woolen tunic and trousers hung loosely on her as if on an emaciated waif. Again, Acacia's call to sacrifice had drained her vitality. How could she once again summon the fires of heaven to ignite the garden of resurrection?

"Are you all right?" Billy asked.

She nodded firmly. "God will provide. He always does."

Billy gave her an affirming smile. Although her fragile voice didn't match the fire in her eyes, there was no doubt about the passion in her heart. She could do this.

As Billy released her hand, allowing her to walk toward the waiting people, Dikaios whispered in his ear. "I fear for her. She is wasting away. Although she has taken from the Tree of Life, she should eat more to gain strength. A morsel of berry bread for each meal will not sustain her."

"When this is over, I'll talk to her. Maybe I can—"

"Look!" Dikaios bobbed his head toward the crowd.

As Acacia walked toward Valiant, the people stood as she passed, every man, woman, and child pressing their hands together and bowing their heads. Acacia herself glowed from head to toe. A bluish white aura dressed her in sparkling brilliance as she seemed to float across the snow-covered grass.

Valiant stood as well. With a sweep of his arm and a low bow, he said, "Welcome, great Oracle. The garden awaits."

CHAPTER 16

AN ORACLE OF FIRE

"I want to stay," Bonnie said to Abaddon. "I figured out what it means to become ablaze with fire."

"You have, have you?" In the dimness of the resurrection chamber, the dragon's head seemed to hover in midair. "You do not fear pain?"

His hot breath stung her skin, raising a shudder. "I fear it. I never enjoy pain. But if that's what I'm called to do, I'll just endure it. I'm strong enough."

Abaddon's eyes sparkled. "How refreshing, a human who is willing to reveal both weaknesses and strengths. Most of your race would interpret self-deprecation as the only honesty, but such expression is usually nothing more than false humility." He shook his head sadly. "Masks. Nothing more than masks. When in the company of cats and clowns, mice and cowards paint on frowns."

"So do you think I'm wearing a mask?"

"Do *you* think you are?"

"No. I was wondering if you thought I was."

Abaddon looked her in the eye. "You have confidence, but even that can be a disguise. Pride is the most sinister of masks, for it blinds the wearer. The parading peacock does not recognize how ridiculous he looks. He fans his tail, and no one is impressed, save for the foolish fowl himself."

Bonnie spread out her hands. "I have confidence because of who gives me strength. Without God, I'm nobody. But with God, I believe I can do anything."

"Is that so?" His gaze ran up and down her face. "Are you also confident that your motivations are pure?"

She nodded. "I am. I have confidence in the one who has made me pure."

"Then tell me, dragon girl, are you ready to be set aflame in order to go to Second Eden and give yourself up for those who need your help? Or do you really want to go there to see a young man to whom you *think* you are prophetically promised?"

"*Think*?" She half closed one eye. "What are you trying to say?"

"You believe you have trusted in prophecy, yet you have merely trusted in your interpretation. Surely you cannot fail, you say to yourself, because the prophecy guarantees your future betrothed bliss. Shall I quote the verse that has emboldened you to risk your life in the past, the one upon which you rely, thereby making you think of yourself as indestructible?"

Bonnie stared at him. Should she answer, or was this rhetorical? She didn't have to wait long to find out. The dragon spoke the words in a low sing-song voice.

The child of doubt will find his rest
And meet his virgin bride
A dragon shorn will live again
Rejecting Eden's pride

His head shot toward her, stopping just before his snout touched her nose. "There are other children of doubt. There are other virgin brides.

Elam and Sapphira fit this prophecy as well as Billy and you do, and when Makaidos rises, the dragon shorn will live again. He was the dragon king who tried to hold his family together in spite of the rebellion of his own children. Surely that qualifies him as one who has rejected Eden's pride, does it not?"

Closing her eyes, Bonnie lowered her head. "I see what you mean."

"Now you know that this prophecy promises you nothing. If you go to Second Eden, you could die, and you would lose the life you have dreamed about for these many months."

Smelling something burning, Bonnie opened her eyes. Her shoes smoldered, and her laces were on fire. The heat stung, but it wasn't too bad yet. "I still want to go. My purposes don't conflict. I mean, I can see Billy and give myself up for people at the same time."

"Your point is valid, but if a situation arises in which you must choose death to save someone, will you do so, knowing that you will certainly lose your future with the young man?"

Bonnie closed her eyes again, this time tightly. She had faced danger so many times, but had she been willing to die for someone else? Did it occur to her during each instance of danger that the prophecy protected her, or did she just act sacrificially without thinking about herself at all?

As if answering her question, a memory rose from the depths of her mind, the image she had recently seen played out above Abaddon's book. In the vision, she pushed a board into an electrified doorway in order to let Shiloh out of the sixth circle of Hades. When it sprang back and flew out of her grip, she replaced it with her wing, blocking the deadly field. Shiloh escaped, and Bonnie was thrown out into the street. A few moments later, she died.

She opened her eyes and looked straight into the dragon's. "I would choose death."

"Would you really? Have you enough courage to face the flames? Would you refuse to recant your testimony or recoil at the agony of rejection and repudiation? When the fires of persecution scald your skin, and the daggers of those who were once your friends cut out your heart, will you give praise to the Maker that you were found worthy to travail through these torments?"

With heat now burning her ankles, she grimaced but nodded firmly. "I would never recant or recoil, and I will always give praise to Jehovah Yasha, and my savior, Jesus Christ."

Abaddon's nostrils flared. "We will see about that."

Flames shot up to Bonnie's knees, and pain ripped through her body. Screaming filled her ears. Was the screaming her own? Darkness trickled across her vision. The agony was unbearable. How long would it last?

Bonnie let out a long wail. "Oh, God! Oh, God, help me! It burns!"

She glanced at the ovula on the table mounts. Makaidos and her father stared at her, obviously sharing her pain, but they could do nothing to help.

Seemingly unaffected by her anguish, the dragon continued. "Now for another question." As the sizzle and stench of her burning flesh permeated the room, he turned on his lasers and focused the beams on her eyes. "You say that you now know why you must be set aflame." He paused for a moment as if to let his words add to her suffering. "Why?"

"I . . . I . . ." She couldn't speak. The flames climbed to her waist and slowly crawled up her back, onto her wings, and up to her chest. Heaving, gasping, panting, she tried to force out an answer, but the words wouldn't come. Were they even in her mind? Did she really not know after all?

"Bonnie Silver!" Abaddon shouted. His call echoed throughout the chamber, repeating again and again. "Why must you be set aflame?"

Even as he finished his question, her name continued to echo. *Bonnie Silver . . . Bonnie Silver.*

She spat out her words, each one a torture. "My . . . my name . . . is Silver. All dross . . . is purged . . . and my body . . . is a living . . . illustration."

"But you must have some dross remaining. Hidden lies in secret places?" His eyebeams brightened. "Envy? Lust? Or do you seriously want me to believe this notion that the dross is already gone? Is your mask one of pride after all?"

"No!" she screamed. "Not a mask. . . . God purged . . . my dross . . . long ago."

The flames shot out across her arms and up to her neck, forcing her to lift her chin. Gasping, she screamed again, this time a wordless, gut-wrenching cry.

The book on the table flipped open on its own, and a feather-tipped pen flew into Abaddon's clawed hand. An image rose from the pages, taking shape as it expanded. It looked like a three-dimensional Christmas card, dozens of people gathered in a circle in the midst of a heavy snowfall.

Abaddon pointed the pen at her. "You, dragon girl, hid your wings in a backpack from the time you were six years old. Were you protecting your mother from a slayer, or were you just afraid of being called a freak? When you had the opportunity to give up your wings, what went through your mind? Were they a gift from God, or were they a curse?" He snorted twin jets of fire from his nostrils. "Oh, I know you display them now, but you have cleverly concealed your earlier decision from all except your mother. Such is the character of hidden dross."

With light fading in and out, Bonnie shook her head hard. She had to stay conscious, no matter the pain. Still, she couldn't answer. Agony clamped her throat shut.

Abaddon transferred the pen to his tail and reached it toward the book. He poised it over the page as if ready to write. "What did you decide? If you kept your wings, was it to parade like the proverbial peacock because of the power they gave you?" He let out a low laugh. "Yes, that would be it. Power. A greedy lust for power is surely your hidden dross."

Summoning all her strength, Bonnie cried out. "My dross . . . is gone! . . . Leave me alone!"

"But you have not answered. Did you give up your wings?" As Abaddon scratched something down with the pen, smoke rose from the page. "Perhaps that is it. You considered a gift from God something to be spurned. You lacked contentment with how he created you."

Bonnie pressed her lips together. The torture was awful . . . worse than awful.

He set his head directly in front of her face and shouted, "Answer me!"

"No!" The fire leaped over her nose and roared across her eyes. Heaving scalding breaths, she coughed out each word. "I . . . will . . . not . . . answer!"

Suddenly, the pain vanished. The broiling heat eased to gentle warmth. Bonnie looked at her hands, still on fire. Flames crackled on her arms and legs, yet there was no pain, not even a hint of discomfort. She looked up at the dragon. "What happened?"

With a flick of his tail, Abaddon dropped his pen and smiled. "You have withstood the test, precious child. Your confidence in God's purging power is exceedingly rare, and your steadfastness has proven the purity of your silver." He let out a long sigh. "It is such a shame that others choose chastisement. Those who hide God's purifying handiwork will never learn to stop suffering. They will wear the masks of fear, false humility, and fetters until they discover freedom."

She turned her hands over and back and watched the flames curl with her motions. "So will I stay on fire now?"

"Physically? Yes, for a time. When you are called from the place of resurrection, you will rise without perceptible fire, but those who love you will know that you still burn. They will enjoy its warmth and rally with its unquenchable passion. Those who despise truth, however, will flee from your fire. You will be a flaming sword that cuts deeply to the heart, exposing the lies they tell themselves. They will not understand that you strike with love, for your words will feel like flaming arrows."

Bonnie gazed at her fiery torso. It felt wonderful, like floating in sunshine. Her vision had magnified. Every scale in the dragon's hide seemed divided by deep crevices, and the capillaries in his eyes looked like pulsing rivers of red.

The scene floating over the book also clarified. A small group of people huddled at the center of the circle, apparently talking about something, concern bending their expressions. Their emotions seeped into her mind—turmoil, lack of trust, indecisiveness. And a familiar face turned toward her. Was it Billy? Yes, it was! Maybe this was a picture of Second Eden, and they were getting ready to call someone to resurrection. Soon either her father or Makaidos would be swept into that world, and their suffering would be over.

Still, something was wrong. A strange sense of melancholy weighed down her mind—troubled thoughts, sadness, heaviness of heart.

"I . . . I feel strange."

"You do?" the dragon asked. "Describe your feelings, please."

She laid a hand against her chest. "Heartache and loneliness, the despair of souls wandering lost."

"Your eloquence is exquisite, and your emotions are inexpedient, to be sure. Now that you have become what you are, this will be your burden forevermore."

"What am I?"

"There is someone else here who could tell you." Abaddon's eyebeams lifted over Bonnie's body and settled over a shadow on a wall behind her. "You may come out, Sapphira. I know where you have hidden yourself."

Bonnie turned that way. With all the pain, she had forgotten about Sapphira.

A white-topped head poked out from the shadow. "I am here."

"Bonnie Silver has questions that you are able to address, but first, I will ask *you* one."

Folding her hands at her waist, Sapphira stepped fully into the light. "I will try to answer."

"Why did you stay hidden while your friend suffered?"

"Because I figured out what you were doing," Sapphira said. "It was not my place to interfere or distract from your purpose. During this initial suffering event, Bonnie had to be alone."

"Your years of experience have produced a great deal of wisdom, Oracle of Fire. Now you may address Bonnie's questions."

"What questions?" Bonnie asked.

"You asked what you are," Sapphira replied, "and you wondered about your feelings of heartache." She raised a hand. Her fingers caught fire and caressed Bonnie's flaming cheek. "To become what you are now, you had to suffer, and you had to suffer alone. You can now see what others cannot, and you feel the pain of those who lack your perception. They toil in misery and heartache. Because of their bondage to the things they see with their physical eyes, they cannot see the light of freedom and the key that will unlock the chains of slavery."

Sapphira's flames crawled down her arm and spread slowly across her body. "And even as you offer them the key, they will flee from you, because your light is too bright, and your fire is too hot. They are so accustomed to slavery, they cannot comprehend the freedom that comes from walking in the fire of God. They fear the pain of purging. They disbelieve the results. They cannot conceive of pure silver, unsullied by even a pinch of dross. You are an illustration, as you put it, a portrait that ignites their fears and raises their retaliating fists, yet instead of fighting back, you reach out again and again, because you feel their pain in your heart, their lostness, their despair."

Now fully engulfed in flames, Sapphira took Bonnie's fiery hand in hers. "You sense the pain because you are now an Oracle of Fire."

* * *

Holding his sword in place at his hip, Elam ran across the field toward the birthing garden. Ahead, a gathering of villagers had split into two groups, allowing Acacia and Billy to pass between them as they walked toward Valiant, who had bowed low when Acacia drew near.

When he caught up with Billy, he slowed his pace and walked at his side. "Cliffside is guarding the triage hut," Elam said.

Billy whispered, "Why didn't anyone tell you about the villagers gathering out here? Aren't they keeping you informed?"

"I'm not sure." Elam patted Billy on the back. "Let's talk about it later. The moon's about to rise. When the light strikes the garden, it'll be too late to do this."

As Elam and Billy approached, Valiant bowed, though not quite so low as he had for Acacia.

"Valiant," Elam said, returning a quick bow, "we have only a few minutes before we must begin. Have you considered our dilemma?"

The cold breeze tossed snow from Valiant's black curls, but he seemed warm enough in his thick, fur-lined cloak, though the front was partially open, revealing his battle uniform. "I agree that the matter raises serious questions. Another from your world has provided more information than perhaps even you know." He nodded at Rebekah, who sat with Dallas at the inner part of the circle. "It seems that a surgeon, a former dragon named Kaylee Saunders, wants to come here to aid our cause. If we call for a doctor, perhaps she will be able to pass through the portal."

Elam crossed his arms and shivered. "*Perhaps* is a crucial word. I already erred in changing Enoch's words once, and it brought an evil force to this world that waits for an opportunity to attack. Do you think it's wise to alter the prophecy again? Are these events a sign from God, or nothing more than a coincidence?"

"A little girl lies drowning in her own blood, and there is no one here who can save her life." Valiant touched his chest, his thumb lingering on a dragon insignia. "I am a warrior. Whether I fight with weapons of steel driven into the dark hearts of our enemies, or weapons of song lifted to the Father of Lights, I do so for one purpose, to protect the little ones. It is true that casualties of war are inevitable, and losing one or two might not seem much of a sacrifice when compared to gaining a warrior of Timothy's caliber, but if we gain his help at the cost of Listener's life . . ."

His voice faltered. Gripping the hilt of a dagger attached to his belt, he swallowed before continuing. "I have been in many battles, and it is always for the little ones that I take my blade into the midst of bloody conflicts with no thought for my own life. Without the Listeners of this world, there would be nothing to fight for. If we do not do all we can to save her from perishing . . ." He withdrew his dagger and dropped it to the ground. "I will not fight, for I will then be a traitor to the very cause for which we have shed our blood."

Elam looked at the dagger lying on the ground. As it reflected the light of Pegasus, which peeked over the horizon, he could only stare at the blade in silence.

Valiant picked it up and shoved it back into its sheath. "Timothy himself refused to sacrifice that precious girl, even at the cost of his own life. He had no assurances that his sacrifice would bring about the salvation of his daughters, just as we do not know if our call for a surgeon will raise one from this garden. But do you believe that he would fight for traitors, the betrayers we would be if we sacrificed this child now? I say no. And I would join him in his refusal. I say we trust the Father of Lights to honor our faith in him, whether we are foolishly believing in scrolls falling from a museum shelf or a spyglass falling from the sky."

Without a second's hesitation, Elam nodded at Acacia. "Let it be so."

Acacia reached for Ruth's hand and helped her stand up. With the people again rising and bowing, she and Ruth walked hand in hand and stopped at the edge of the garden. As she faced the rows of plants, Ruth lifted her hands and called out, "Let every lantern darken, and I will begin when the last light fades."

As the flickering lights died away, Elam whispered to Billy. "She's repeating the ceremony."

"I guessed that. I was standing at the side last time, so I couldn't hear much." Billy watched Ruth, a woman he had only recently learned much more about. Although she seemed normal, she was once Paili, a plant hybrid much like Acacia, and she blossomed into a lovely woman who eventually became Patrick's wife.

With the rising moon breaking through the thinning snow clouds, Acacia raised her hands. Two balls of blue fire appeared in her palms, though not as bright and sparkling as they were during the previous ceremony. They had been effervescent and alive. Now they seemed dull by comparison.

Ruth hummed as she and Acacia walked single file along one of the garden rows, stepping carefully to avoid the scattered bones of Makaidos. The blue glow spread out from Acacia's hands and enveloped them both. When it reached their feet, the radiance crawled along the ground, instantly devouring the snow. As it touched the bones, each one burst with a glow of its own, whiter, like luminous frost. Soon, the entire garden, the soil, the plants, and the two women, pulsed with an eerie light.

Acacia waved her arms in a circle, though not as fast as usual. The balls of fire narrowed into spinning cylinders of blue flames. With a grunt, she threw them farther into the garden. They splattered into hundreds of dots of blue light that sat on the soil like glowing marbles.

Unlike last time, the flames crawling along the ground didn't rise up into a dome over the plants. The glowing bones sizzled and popped as before, and the fire ate away their white coats, but the entire scene was dimmer than last month's spectacle, less vibrant.

Her brow furrowing, Acacia turned and left the garden, leaving Ruth alone as she stood in the midst of the sparkling dots of blue. Ruth raised her hands again and sang, her voice resonant as it passed like a wave across the hushed crowd.

When phantoms knock on doors of light
To open paths to worlds beyond,
A friend replies, "Insert the key
To leave the dark and greet the dawn.

"The key is light, the words of truth;
No lie can break the chains of death.
A whispered word of love avails
To bring new life, the spirit's breath."

So now I sing a key for you,
The phantom waiting at the door;
We call for you, a doctor who
Will join us now in holy war.

As she lowered her hands, she kept her gaze on the garden, quiet and still. Like glittering gems, the blue lights continued to twinkle, but nothing else happened, certainly nothing similar to last month's events, no earth-shaking rise of a shadow in the midst of the plants.

A low murmur ran through the onlookers. Elam looked for the reason and found Hunter and Semiramis standing at the garden's edge, Semiramis holding something in her closed hand.

Elam stormed toward her. "What are you doing?"

Still cupping her hand, she turned his way, trembling. "I most humbly beg your pardon, Elam. The people are whispering that the Oracle's fire is lacking power. We all want the doctor to come and rescue Listener, so I offer my services to bring increase to her energy."

Elam looked up at Pegasus. In a few minutes it would rise above the line of trees that shaded the garden. As he looked into Semiramis's eyes, a hundred thoughts blazed through his mind. Acacia lacked energy because he had authorized her attempt to heal Listener, but without that try, Listener would probably be dead already. Had he made the wrong decision? Had God wanted him to let Listener die and call for Makaidos after all? But how could that be? And now with only moments remaining, he had to make another decision that might save or destroy the entire population. Would it hurt just to listen to this woman's idea, the same woman who insisted that he couldn't cross the bridge that provided the key to Heaven's Gate?

Glancing at Pegasus again, he gave her a quick nod. "Let's hear it, and make it fast."

She opened her hand, revealing a small rectangular box, tied with twine and sealed with wax. "This morning, while I was out walking in the launching field, the dragon I told you about came to me and offered me this box. At first I refused to take it, knowing him to be a crafty deceiver, but he said that it would help energize the garden during the ceremony, that I need not open it unless the power to resurrect runs dry. If it is opened and the gem is placed in the garden, the energy will increase tenfold."

"The gem?" Elam took the box and looked it over. The wax bore an insignia that looked like a dragon. Apparently Semiramis hadn't opened it, or so she would have him believe.

He untied the twine, broke the seal, and lifted the lid. Inside, a severed finger rested in a bed of bloody cotton, a gold ring with a red gem still in place around it.

Elam's stomach knotted. Heat flashed across his skin. Backpedaling, he nearly fell, but Billy caught him just in time.

"What is it?" Billy asked.

When Elam showed it to him, Billy's mouth dropped open. "That's . . . that's evil!"

Rebekah, sitting on a blanket, pulled Billy's sleeve. As they whispered to each other, Elam thrust the box toward Semiramis. "Did the dragon say who owned this finger?"

Semiramis looked inside. Her face turned pale as she backed away, holding a hand against her chest. "My lord! I hope you do not think that I did this thing!"

Barely able to keep from gagging, Elam put the lid back in place and shouted, "I repeat! Did the dragon say who owned this finger?"

Her eyes darting back and forth between Elam and the box, Semiramis spoke as one begging for forgiveness. "His words were cryptic, my lord. He said that the energizing gem would be familiar to the dragon boy, the son of Clefspeare."

"Is that all? Nothing more?"

Heaving fast breaths, Semiramis's eyes grew wider. "Now that I perceive his malice, I hesitate to repeat his foul words."

Elam gripped the hilt of his sword. "Tell me! You must!"

She gulped before continuing. "He said that if the dragons and their offspring continued to ally themselves with the residents of Second Eden, this gift would be accompanied by more of the precious puzzle at a later time."

"Precious puzzle!" Elam gritted his teeth. "How dare you bring this serpent's poisonous words here!"

Semiramis trembled. "His words sounded gracious, an act of surrender to our noble cause. I had no idea that the gift was a cruel gesture designed to mock my lord and his valiant army. I see now that the dragon desires to weaken your spines through an instrument of terror." Steeling her body, she clenched her fist. "But I assume you will fight back. This mad dragon cannot be allowed to use fear to make you cower in submission."

"On that, we can agree." Taking the lid off again, Elam turned toward Billy. "Do you recognize the gem?"

His face twisting in pain, Billy nodded. "It looks just like Bonnie's ring."

"That's what I was afraid of." Elam studied the contents again. Something besides cotton lay under the finger. Was it hair? Careful not to touch the finger, he pulled out a two-inch lock of light brown hair. "Do you recognize this?" he asked.

Billy stared at it. As he tightened his jaw, he nodded again but said nothing.

Rebekah jumped up. "The finger is probably not Bonnie's."

"What makes you think that?" Billy asked.

"When some people came to kidnap Bonnie, they mistakenly took Shiloh instead. She pretended to be Bonnie."

"But Bonnie was gone when I got there. How do you know they didn't get her, too?"

Lowering her chin, Rebekah shook her head. "I don't."

"And does it really matter?" Elam asked. "Whether the finger was Bonnie's or Shiloh's, will it cause us to alter our course? Will we submit to this wicked beast who taunts us, who believes that we can be shaken by threats? We cannot allow ourselves to be diverted from the path God has set before us."

Hunter stepped up and pointed at his face, still oozing from the dragon's blast. As his companion floated near his chin, flashing red, he spoke with a firm tone. "Do not doubt that Arramos will chop that girl to pieces, and he will do so in a way that will prolong her suffering one body part at a time."

"Are you saying that we should appease this devil?" Elam asked. "That we should allow his minions to rule Second Eden by the edge of a sword?"

"I say that when this girl's body parts arrive one piece at a time, the sympathetic hearts of these people will melt. When the wall of fire dies away, they will be unable to fight the onslaught of Nephilim, Vacants, and shadow people that will swarm into the village by night and slaughter them without mercy or pity."

"Hunter!" Semiramis snapped. "Do not speak from faithlessness! Such cowardice is not becoming of a son of mine." She clasped her hands together. "My lord, if I see the dragon again, allow me to spy out his secrets. Since I have stupidly followed his will in the past, it will be easy to feign allegiance to him and learn where he holds the girl captive, whoever she may be."

Elam looked at Valiant. He stood with his arms crossed over his muscular chest. As if summoned by his glance, Valiant stepped closer to Elam and whispered, "If she is a spy for the evil dragon, her pretense is against us, not him. I say that it will do no harm to send her to him, but we should keep our counsel away from her ears."

Elam nodded. "Agreed. But what of energizing the field?"

"Perhaps this so-called gift would help," Valiant said. "If she is a deceiver and the gem fails or causes a disaster, she would not want to stay in our presence. Give her leave to go to the dragon, but only after the gem has proven its value. If it causes us pain, then she will suffer as well. Yet, you know her better than I, so I leave the decision in the warrior chief's capable hands."

Elam glared at the box. This was just too much. He couldn't afford to make another mistake and thereby erode the villagers' trust in him further.

He looked at the people, each one staring at him as they waited for something to happen. The moon's light spread across the snow, sparkling as it crawled toward the garden. When it illuminated Semiramis's face, his mind flashed back to the time she stood at the foot of the bridge as he dangled from its ropes.

"Oh, the folly!" she had shouted. "The folly of those who think themselves holier and wiser than the sages who went before them!"

Elam winced as the words echoed in his mind. Was she right? How could he make such important decisions for these people he barely knew? Should he risk everyone's safety for the sake of a dying little girl? Yet, two truths kept echoing in his brain. One—he wasn't ready to trust Semiramis, and two—Valiant's idea was sound.

Finally, he reached into the box and carefully slid the ring off the withered finger. "If this gem energizes the resurrection garden and all is well, then you may go and spy out Arramos's secrets. But you will remain with us for tonight and tomorrow so we can make sure nothing evil befalls us because of this choice. If it becomes clear that this is an instrument designed to bring us harm, then you will suffer the same fate as the owner of this finger."

She bowed her head. "You are wise not to trust me, for I have doubted you and tried to dissuade you from crossing the bridge. Arramos sent me here to plant seeds of evil, but when he burned my son's face, I rebelled against him, and I am now in your service. God has provided the power to energize this garden, and I hope you will trust in it though it was delivered by a hand you are not willing to trust. Surely you know that the ring and the finger that wore it are holy." She fell to her knees and pressed her wrists together. "Lock me in chains until my worth is proven. I trust you to make the right decision."

Now shaking, Elam glanced at Ruth, still waiting patiently in the midst of the garden's blue gems. He then checked the moon's encroaching light, only inches from the garden. Clenching his fist around the ring, he nodded at Valiant. "Have your men take her to the triage hut and bind her hand and foot. It's warm there, and Sir Patrick and Cliffside will keep an eye on her."

"Very well." Valiant gestured for a trio of men to follow Elam's instructions. As they led Semiramis away, Elam grabbed Hunter's wrist and pushed the ring into his hand. "You will take the gem out to Ruth. If there is harm in this, you and your mother will suffer the consequences."

Hunter bowed his head. "I trust that your faith in us will soon be restored." He marched into the garden and handed the gem to Ruth. Stooping, she placed it on the ground next to one of the bones.

When Hunter spun back toward the field, he lost his balance and toppled over. As the garden's radiance crawled over his body, he pawed at the soil with one hand and reached out with the other. "Help me!" he called.

Elam ran into the garden, still arguing with himself. Of course this "accident" might be a ruse, but he didn't have any choice. He couldn't let a wounded man flounder in the mud.

As he followed one of the furrows, new sparks erupted around Ruth and spread out, like fire on oily water. Feeling a stinging sensation through his trousers, Elam broke into a trot. When he arrived, he grabbed Hunter's hand and pulled him to his feet. "Are you all right?"

"Yes," Hunter said as he brushed off his clothes. "I think so."

Billy pointed from the edge of the garden. "Elam! Look!"

Elam turned toward Ruth. As the newly energized light dressed the garden in a dawnlike aura, a human-shaped shadow rose from the ground just a few feet beyond her.

"Can you tell what it is?" Elam waded toward her through the rising flood of radiance.

"A man," Ruth said. "At least, I think it's a man."

Elam stood at her side. Rebekah had said that the doctor was one of the former dragons. Shouldn't a woman appear?

As the shadow took on a distinct masculine shape, Elam set his hand on the hilt of his sword again and shouted. "Who are you?"

The man, still more ghost than human, laid a hand on his forehead. "I am . . ."

Suddenly, he solidified and collapsed. Elam charged ahead and helped him up, taking an arm and hoisting him to his feet. Since the newcomer's legs remained unsteady, Elam had to keep a shoulder under his arm. "What's your name?"

Wearing a long-sleeved dress shirt and khaki pants, the man shivered in the snowy breeze. "Conner. Matthew Conner."

Elam pulled off his cloak and helped the man put it on. "Are you a doctor?"

"Yes. . . . Well, I was one." Dr. Conner looked at Elam curiously. "How did you know?"

"We called for a doctor, so we were expecting you. . . . Well, not exactly you, but . . ."

"Oh, yes. I remember now." He firmed his stance and looked around. "Who needs me?"

"A little girl."

Dr. Conner's eyebrows shot upward. "He was right!"

"Who was right?"

As if dizzied by the sparkling lights, Dr. Conner's eyes darted all around before settling. "Never mind. I think I was dreaming."

Elam took him by the arm. "Come on. You'll need to do surgery right away."

"Surgery?" He followed along, though staggering somewhat through the fading radiance.

Ruth trailed them by a few steps. "Shall we try it again and call for Makaidos?"

"The moonlight is already touching the garden," Elam said, "so we'll have to wait for the next eclipse. Just pray that we have enough warriors and that Acacia is healthy by then."

CHAPTER 17

THE PHYSICIAN

Bonnie and Sapphira approached the hologram that floated over the book. Keeping her flaming hands away from the wooden table, Bonnie bent over to get as close as she could. With her vision so sharp, every detail was clear, and since they were inside a portal, Sapphira likely could see just as well.

In the image, two females walked into a garden, the shorter one a white-haired teenager.

"Acacia," Sapphira whispered.

"I guessed that. She looks just like you."

Acacia created a ball of fire in each hand, and the radiance spilled to the soil and spread out. Something sparkled near her feet, something white and luminescent. She threw the balls into the garden. The flames crawled along the ground and spread a shimmering radiance. Acacia then walked away, leaving the other female alone.

"That's Ruth," Sapphira said, pointing. "She was once Paili, an underborn."

A rushing wind blew through the resurrection chamber. Like a wave catching a sandcastle, the gust picked up the hologram and spread it around the room, repainting it as if everyone in the image had grown to life size.

The air seemed charged with electricity. The garden radiance danced at their flaming feet. Soon fire swirled in the air until it created a cylinder that spun slowly in place.

"The portal is opening," Sapphira said. "But it looks kind of weak."

Bonnie walked close to the image of Billy and looked into his eyes. She felt his emotions streaming into her mind—confusion, distrust, fear. Yet, something wonderful colored every feeling. What was it? Love?

She passed her hand, orange and flickering, across his eyes, then tried to hold his hand. Yes, that was it. Love. That was the truth that kept him from despair.

"Keep trusting, Billy," she whispered. Now her own emotions blazed, almost overwhelming her. "I hope to be there soon."

With her hands raised and her head tilted upward, Ruth seemed to be singing. As with most of this vision, they couldn't hear the words, but after a few seconds, a woman's lovely voice broke through, as if spoken from a loudspeaker above.

"We call for you, a doctor who will join us now in holy war."

The ovulum holding Bonnie's father floated upward and hovered about six feet from the floor. Inside, still glowing orange, he pressed his palms against the glass, obviously confused.

When Ruth finished, she stood in the midst of the radiance, as if in a trance, and no further sounds broke through the portal barrier.

The people in the middle of the circle seemed agitated. A young man marched to the edge of the garden and confronted a man and a woman Bonnie hadn't noticed before.

"Elam!" Sapphira said, this time louder than a whisper.

Bonnie pointed a fiery finger. "The one with the strong chin and dark hair?"

"Yes." Sapphira guided her body in front of Elam. Raising her hand, she wiggled her fingers in front of his face. Although she said nothing, her emotions came through loud and clear. She was homesick, homesick for Elam.

Soon, Billy and a few others joined Elam, and they argued with the man and woman while looking at something inside a small box.

"Can you tell what's in there?" Bonnie asked.

Sapphira eased closer. "It's a finger. Is it from a human?"

The woman Elam confronted dropped to her knees. While some men led her away, another man walked into the garden. His face was swollen and marred, as if recently burned.

Sapphira gasped. "It's Mardon!"

"It is? I didn't know he had burns on his face."

"He didn't. But I worked with him closely for a long time. I would recognize him anywhere. Even the way he walks gives him away."

The man fell and clawed at the soil. Elam chased after him. The radiance covering the soil suddenly blossomed. The swirling cylinder strengthened and spun faster. The ovulum holding Bonnie's father lifted higher and faded as it neared the ceiling. Seconds later, it was gone.

The fiery cylinder slowed and quickly fizzled out. From the spot where the ovulum once sat, something broke through the ground in the hologram projection. As it rose, it took on a human-like shape and cast a shadow over Ruth. After a few seconds, it became a man and fell limply to the ground.

Bonnie ran to him and instinctively reached down to help. Elam did the same, but only Elam's hands could provide support. As he lifted the new arrival, Bonnie backed away. "It's my Daddy!" she cried. "He made it!"

Suddenly, the wind gusted again. The book blew shut with a thud. The projected scene broke apart, and the pieces scattered into nothingness.

As the breeze died away, Abaddon shuffled to the table and set his pen on top of the book. "This entry has ended."

Bonnie stepped closer to Makaidos's ovulum. "Will they ever call for him?"

"Second Eden has the opportunity with every eclipse, but during this resurrection, I sensed a foul wind blowing in that realm—snow in a world that never knew it before, sweetness in the lips of liars, evil intentions disguised in deceptive words. These were never part of Second Eden before. They portend terrible trouble."

"So what do we do?" Sapphira asked. "When do we leave?"

Abaddon lifted the ovulum from the mount and looked at the miniature dragon within. "Did not Enoch tell you that you would wait for a long time?"

"Yes, but I thought he meant in the mines."

"I am sure he did. Yet, the only word he received was that the two of you would have to wait in a lower level, and that you would need each other. The precise place was merely his interpretation." Abaddon looked at Bonnie. "And you have learned that an interpretation of an obscure oracle is not the same as certainty."

Bonnie let out a sigh. The feelings of heartache and loneliness returned, heavier than ever. "Yes, I remember."

"So now you will wait." Abaddon waved a foreleg toward the exit hallway. "There is a room that holds a treasure trove of wisdom, books similar to my journal that will show you story after story in the same lifelike way. Listen. Learn. Live. If the people of Second Eden call you to their realm, you may well need every precious poem you find in those treasures."

Bonnie looked at her fingers as she pressed them together. Although vague within the flames, she could distinguish their outlines. "What about our bodies? Will we have to eat? Will we age?"

"Your food will be knowledge and wisdom, and these will cause you to age at the same rate as those you love in Second Eden." Abaddon chuckled. "I am not a heartless fiend. I know that you both long to be with your young men. If God so deems that you unite, your apparent ages will be acceptable to all."

Bonnie took Sapphira's hand. As their fingers intertwined, Sapphira's thoughts streamed into Bonnie's mind, though she said nothing. *We can do this, Bonnie. I'll show you how to endure.*

Bonnie smiled. This felt like the way she communicated with others in the candlestone. Concentrating on the connection between them, she sent back a stream of thoughts. *I believe you. Let's use the time to make ourselves ready to fight alongside our men. From one Oracle of Fire to another, they might need some woman power to back them up.*

* * *

When Elam and Dr. Conner returned to the field at the garden's edge, they stopped and looked around. With snow still falling lightly, the people studied the new arrival, some with curious smiles and others with skeptical frowns.

Billy stepped forward. "Dr. Conner?"

"Yes?" Dr. Conner looked at Billy, his eyes narrowing. "Billy Bannister?"

Billy clapped him on the shoulder and shouted to the crowd. "It's all right, everyone. I know him. He's Bonnie Silver's father. He's a doctor."

A buzz spread across the field, then cheers. Dr. Conner wrapped Elam's cloak around himself and shivered. "The last thing I remember is being in my laboratory. The mountain had collapsed, and Devin was shooting bolts of electricity at us. I think I was hit."

"You were." Billy waved for Clefspeare to come closer. "Dad, can you and the dragons warm him up?"

"With pleasure." Clefspeare, Hartanna, and Thigocia aimed their jets at Dr. Conner. Within seconds, he loosened his grip on the cloak and blew out a long breath.

"Thank you," he said as he marched in place. "I think every joint is in working order."

Billy looked at Hartanna. The gleam in her eyes spoke volumes. Her husband was now alive, but for some reason, she stayed silent, apparently waiting to see how this new miracle would play out. There was no need to distract him now.

"I'll get him started right away," Billy said, nodding at Elam.

"Good. I want to talk to Valiant for a minute. I'll be there soon."

Billy pulled Dr. Conner's arm. "Come on. It's warm in the triage hut. That's where we need you to do surgery."

As they walked briskly toward the forest boundary, Dr. Conner spoke through his chattering teeth. "I have done only simple surgery, removing warts, excising hemorrhoids, and one appendectomy, that sort of thing."

"Okay." Billy grimaced. What should he say? Should he warn him what to expect? A spear embedded in a girl's side that might have punctured her lung was a lot worse than an inflamed appendix. As they hurried through the forest, guided by the lantern lights in the street ahead, he sighed. "Then this is going to be a challenge."

"What kind of surgery is it?"

"You'll see." Billy opened the door to the triage hut and guided Dr. Conner inside. As they shook snow from their clothes and shoes, Billy looked around the room.

As before, Walter lay on his cot, apparently asleep. Ashley stood next to Sir Patrick, both watching Listener as she lay on the elevated cot. Ashley, still in a T-shirt and shorts and her hair now tied up in a bun, swabbed Listener's side with a wet cotton ball. "I think we'll have to make an incision here," she said, pointing. "And another right here."

Billy whispered to Dr. Conner. "She's too absorbed to notice, as usual."

"She looks familiar." Dr. Conner took a step closer and squinted. "Ashley?"

Ashley looked up. For a moment she just stared, as if caught in a trance. Her lips formed a word, then repeated it, this time adding in a quavering voice. "Doc?"

Dr. Conner echoed his own call. "Ashley!"

She rushed around the cot, slipping for a moment before running into his arms. "Doc!" As they hugged, Ashley chattered at her usual breakneck pace. "I heard about the resurrection garden, and I hoped that maybe you might be the doctor who would come, but I didn't really believe it, because you haven't practiced medicine in years. I mean, Listener needs a thoracic surgeon, and you're not really a—" She pulled away, her cheeks flushed. "I'm sorry. I didn't mean to—"

Dr. Conner set a finger over Ashley's lips. "Never mind that." He looked at Listener as she lay motionless on the cot. "Is this our patient?"

Ashley nodded and pulled him closer to Listener. "A spear penetrated her ribcage here," she said, pointing. "I can't tell how far it went in, but it might have pierced her right lung. I can't tell if the point went into her heart, but her loss of blood would indicate that the damage is significant. We're guessing that the spear itself is plugging the holes and keeping her lung from collapsing and hemorrhaging even worse, so obviously we couldn't pull it out."

Dr. Conner's face turned ashen. As he stared at Listener, his mouth dropped open. "I . . . I can't possibly do surgery like this. I removed ingrown toenails. I stitched up playground cuts. I mended a few monkeys."

"Don't talk like that!" Ashley grabbed his arm. "Remember back in Missoula what you did for Stacey in the alley? That man had a dagger against her throat, and when you kicked him in the head, he sliced her jugular." She shook him hard. "Don't you remember? You stitched her up with a sewing kit! You saved her life! And when you heard Karen had a compound leg fracture, you grabbed a first-aid kit and ran into a dark tunnel ready to do whatever you could to rescue her."

"But this is . . . this is different. Far worse."

"I *know* it's worse!" Ashley lifted her hands and splayed her fingers. "Look at these. Together you and I built the most advanced mechanical photosynthetic lab in the world, and now these are healing hands. You cut and I'll cauterize." Shaking him again, she yelled, "We have to save this little girl's life!"

He stared at her, as if in a daze. After a few seconds, he laid a hand on her shoulder and nodded. "Show me the tools we have. I'll do the best I can."

Ashley clenched her fist. "Yes! That's the Doc I remember!"

While Ashley showed Dr. Conner the instruments on a nearby table, Walter rose to a sitting position and waved toward Billy. "Come here a second."

Billy hurried over and sat next to him. "What's up?"

Walter nodded toward a corner of the room, whispering. "Check it out."

Turning, Billy found Semiramis sitting on the floor, bound hand and foot and leaning against a wall. She stared back at him, her face melancholy.

"I heard the deal Elam made. Since a doctor showed up, are you going to let her go?"

"I suppose we'll have to. Why?"

Walter lowered his voice further. "Don't trust her, not for a second. I saw her at the bridge. She's as smooth as silk. She could take your wallet, your shoes, and your belt, and you wouldn't even notice."

"I don't think Elam trusts her, but a deal's a deal. Did they tell you about the finger?"

Walter shivered. "Yeah. That's twisted."

"It's probably Shiloh's." Billy felt the blood drain from his head, making him dizzy. "It has to be."

"Yeah. That makes sense. But just because it's not Bonnie's finger, it doesn't make any difference."

"No." Billy shook his head hard. "No, of course not. I was just saying . . ." He let his voice drift away. He wasn't sure what he meant.

"Don't worry about it." Walter patted him on the back. "I get the picture."

"Billy!" Ashley called. "Wash up in case we need more hands." Turning toward Walter, she frowned. "Lie back down. I don't want to stitch you up again."

As Billy rose to his feet, he grabbed a blanket and tossed it in Walter's lap. "Don't get used to the easy life. I'll have you back out in the sparring circle by the end of the week."

"Against you?" Walter waved a hand. "Piece of cake. I expected a real challenge."

Billy kicked the cot's leg. "Not me. Listener. She'll need an easy opponent if she's going to get her confidence back."

"That's cool." Walter's smile slowly diminished. After a few seconds, a grim expression took over, and he lay back on his cot. "Give me a blow-by-blow from the surgery table. I'll be praying for that little warrior."

* * *

Abraham's hut had become the operating room. With the exception of Walter, who lay on his cot in obedience to Dr. Ashley's orders, no other patients remained for recovery. Still, the interior was crowded, helping raise the temperature, a benefit on this snowy night. Besides Ashley, Dr. Conner, Sir Patrick, Billy, and Semiramis; Listener's family—Candle, her brother; Mantika, her adoptive mother; and Windor, her new brother—stood in the close confines, huddled near the door as they watched in silence.

And many who hoped to join them waited outside in the frigid weather, praying for Listener on the coldest night the villagers could remember, the beginning of the season of death, as they had called it.

Billy had listened to some of their prayers, so warm, so thoughtful, and so filled with passion. Valiant had reconstructed the circle of people and lanterns in the middle of the street just outside the hut, and every once in a while his deep voice would drift in, reminding everyone inside that heartfelt appeals were constantly rising to the Father of Lights. With tight lines on every face in the triage hut, and more than a few trembling hands, prayers riding upward on brisk winds outside created a comforting thought indeed.

Billy stood next to Ashley, trying to keep his eyes on her and away from Listener. Seeing all the blood and her exposed beating heart would be too much . . . way too much.

Fortunately, the lung machine kept her lung from deflating, though it added a network of homemade tubes going into and out of her body, making her look even more pitiful than she had before. Running on a combination of springs and a solar cell, the machine let out a low hum, not unpleasant, but a constant reminder of the life-and-death tightrope Listener was walking.

Her companion floated lazily back and forth in front of her closed eyes. Much dimmer than usual, it seemed sluggish. Every few seconds, it would flash blue light from its core, but it quickly died away. Candle had explained that the companions often reflected the health or vigor of their charges. A brighter light and more active companion signaled a well-rested person, and a dimmer glow and lethargic companion usually reflected exhaustion.

Billy shifted his gaze to the IV stand. A bag of blood hung there, dripping rapidly into a tube. Three more bags lay on a table near Listener's head, recent donations from villagers. If this kept up, they would run out in a hurry, but they had found six more matches, and the donors were told to be ready at a moment's notice.

Sir Patrick stood next to the table, leaning toward the cot, his body arched over Listener's face. With Ashley's stethoscope draped around his neck and a suction tube in his hand, he extended the tube toward the wound every time Ashley nodded in his direction. It took only a few minutes for him to learn where to whisk blood away and how long to keep the tube in place. The blood pressure gauge lay in his other hand, ready to be pumped and checked, which he did precisely every thirty seconds. From the start of surgery until now, Listener's pressure had stayed low but fairly steady, a miracle really, considering how much blood she was losing.

Near the door, Mantika, Candle, and Windor fidgeted. Candle held the spyglass and Windor fingered the hilt of his sheathed knife. Candle's companion perched on top of his head, its blue light strobing. It was his job to watch the lung machine and wind up the springs if the solar cell ran low. So far, that hadn't been necessary, but Candle kept his ear close to the machine, just in case.

Dangling from ropes, several lanterns hung directly over Listener's cot. They cast several competing rays over her body, some brighter than others, but all steady enough to keep the surgical area bright. With a barricade of empty cots in front of the door, no one would come or go and stir up the air, which would surely disturb the burning wicks.

Ashley, her hair tied back and covered with a tight bandana, stood next to the cot, her elbows up and her fingers inside the cavity. Her eyes darted back and forth, riveted for a second at one spot, then at another. "I got this vessel, Doc. Sealing it off."

Dr. Conner, his sleeves rolled up to his tense biceps, lifted a piece of the spear's shaft out of the hole and showed it to her. "That's the last big piece of wood. I'm going after the point."

"Perfect. Good work."

He pushed his fingers back in. "The point's just barely touching the heart, so we're good there. I'm taking it out."

"There's a splintered piece attached," Ashley said. "Be careful."

"I see it. If I pull straight out, the barb will get caught on lung tissue on your left."

"I can't push the tissue back, Doc. My hands are full." She looked at Billy. "I need a finger."

Billy raised one. "Show me what to do."

She gestured with her eyes. "See where the spear point's barb touches the lung?"

Billy licked his lips. "Yeah."

"Push down on the tissue until it's clear."

He eased his finger into the cavity. "This pink stuff?"

"That's it. . . . Good. Perfect." Ashley looked up at Dr. Conner. "I think we're clear, Doc. Take it real easy."

"Don't worry." Using both hands, he eased the point toward himself, then lifted it out of the cavity. "Got it."

Billy looked at Ashley. "Can I pull out now?"

"Yes. Slowly."

As Billy eased his hand away, Ashley's brow knitted tightly. "I've got bleeding, Doc! Big time!" She looked at Patrick. "Suction! Now!"

Patrick reached the tube toward her, but Dr. Conner grabbed it. "It's the heart. Have to be delicate."

Listener's companion landed on her forehead and dimmed further. Billy looked at Sir Patrick. Their gazes met. As the old former dragon pressed his hands together, Billy nodded. The prayer posture. Doctor or no doctor, Listener's only real hope lay in the hands of a higher power.

"I don't know what's wrong," Ashley said. "My hands aren't sealing the leaks like they were before."

"What's going on?" Walter asked, still lying on his cot.

His throat tightening, Billy could barely talk. "Bleeding," was all he could manage.

"Patrick!" Ashley barked. "Hang another bag!"

While Patrick hurried through the procedure, Billy let his gaze wander over to Semiramis. She stared back at him, still sad, still as innocent looking as a lamb.

"May I speak?" she called in a quiet voice.

Billy nodded. "I guess that won't hurt."

"My words were proven true. The garden energized, and you have a doctor."

"We don't know why that happened," Billy said. "Maybe it was the ring. Maybe not."

"In any case, please allow me to offer my assistance. I am skilled in many arts."

"What kind of assistance?"

"When Steadfast worked on my son, I noticed that the doctor who was once here was a mistress of exotic potions, and I am familiar with her craft."

Billy turned to Ashley. "Did you hear that?"

The sweat-dampened bandana over her brow slid higher as she nodded. "We're already using Angel's clotting factor."

"I assumed so," Semiramis said. "I saw it on the table earlier. There is another potion I thought she might have, but I did not see it."

"What does it do?" Billy asked.

"It will slow Listener's functions, including her heart, until she will be near death, though still safely in the grip of life. While her bleeding is slower, you can repair her body."

Dr. Conner looked up at Ashley. "A chemically induced coma?"

"Sounds like it." Now breathing rapidly, Ashley shot Semiramis a suspicious stare. "What's in it? Tell me quick!"

"Ingredients with which you would not be familiar."

Sir Patrick's voice pierced the tense air. "Blood pressure has dropped. Seventy over thirty-five."

"I can't seal it!" Ashley cried. "My touch isn't doing anything!"

Dr. Conner lurched toward the table. "Sutures!"

While they scrambled, Semiramis pushed against the wall and struggled to her feet. "Untie me!" she shouted, extending her bound hands. "I can help you!"

His sword hand covered with blood, Billy set his fingers just above Excalibur's hilt. Should he release her? Would she really help, or would she brew poison?

The sound of metal sliding on metal made Billy twist toward his scabbard. Walter stood next to him, holding Excalibur in both hands. "There really isn't any choice, is there?" Walter stalked toward Semiramis. Although he staggered a bit, his path was straight and true. With a deft swipe, he cut through the rope, and the pieces fell to the floor.

While Ashley and Dr. Conner continued working frantically, volleying sharp commands back and forth, Semiramis massaged her wrists and turned to Mantika and her sons. "Dwellers of Second Eden. I will need narla root, sempian bark, and one drop of venom from a cave spider. The other ingredients are already here."

Candle pointed at himself. "I know a burrow where two cave spiders live."

Windor nodded. "I get root and bark."

Tossing aside the pile of cots in front of the door, Candle and Windor dashed outside. As a snow-filled draft rushed through, Mantika quickly shut the door.

The hanging lanterns stirred, troubling the light over Listener and her surgeons. Ashley looked up at the swinging ropes. "Somebody stop those things! I can't see!"

"Sixty-five over thirty-five," Patrick announced.

Billy grabbed Excalibur from Walter. He slid a cot close to the surgery table, stood on it, and reached the sword toward the ceiling. As he touched the ropes one at a time, he looked down at the steadying light. From this perspective, Listener's pale body seemed small and faraway, yet the hole in her chest seemed cavernous as blood flowed over the four frantic hands. Her companion wobbled as if ready to fall.

Semiramis marched to the potions table, slid a wide-mouthed jar to the front, and, one by one, picked up small glass bottles filled with crushed red, green, or brown leaves. "Yes, the other ingredients are here." She looked up at Billy. "This potion must be heated. Where can I find a fire?"

He jumped down from the cot and slid it out of the way. "I've got that covered. Just say the word."

Windor burst in. In one hand he carried two thick wet roots, still covered with dirt. In the other, he clutched a hunk of green bark and a serrated knife. "Covered with snow," he said. "But Windor find."

Mantika immediately closed the door. The lanterns swayed, but only a little. Her dark face taut and her eyes wide, she pointed at the ingredients table. "Roots need skin peeled."

"Yes, yes, I know," Semiramis said. "Bring them here."

As Windor dropped the ingredients on the table, Candle hurried in, his dreadlocks flying. He lifted a gray spider between his thumb and forefinger. Its wiggling legs spread out as wide as his hand. "I got him!"

"Hurry it over here before it bites you!" Semiramis reached for Windor's knife. "I have to draw out the spider's poison."

Windor pulled it away and looked at Billy, his brow arching. "Windor give?"

"Sixty-five over thirty!" Patrick announced.

Ashley called from the surgical cot. "Get that potion! We're losing her!" Her voice seemed strained, weaker. Listener's companion toppled from her forehead and fell to the cot.

Raising Excalibur, Billy nodded. "Go ahead."

Semiramis glared at him. "Your faith in me is so inspiring."

"Just get the potion done. If it works, I'll be the first to apologize."

CHAPTER 18

A POTION FROM POISON

Windor extended the knife. Still glowering at Billy, Semiramis snatched it and drove the blade through the spider's head, pinning it to the table. Dark blood oozed from underneath and inched along the wood grain. A blue stream, bright and sparkling, added to the flow, but the two colors stayed unmixed. She freed the knife and, using the tip of the blade, picked up a drop of the blue liquid and let it fall into a jar.

Her hands zipping from the ingredients to a mortar and pestle to a bottle of water, Semiramis seemed to be a woman possessed. As her hair fell in front of her eyes, she just blew it back and kept working. In less than a minute, she presented Billy with a glass jar containing about half an inch of brown liquid at the bottom. "Heat it until it turns green."

Billy pulled a glove from his pocket and put it on. Holding the jar by its top, he blew a stream of fire just under the glass base. For a few seconds, nothing happened. Then tiny bubbles formed on the surface and began popping, releasing a brown gas that rose over the brim and dribbled to the floor.

"Give me an update!" Ashley wiped her sleeve across her brow. "I think the invigorating potion is losing steam. I'm not going to last much longer."

"I see green!" Billy shouted. "It won't be long."

Semiramis grabbed the jar. "It's enough!"

"Wait. That jar has to be as hot as—"

"I know!" Stirring the concoction with a tongue depressor, Semiramis rushed to Ashley's side. "Drinking it is too dangerous and slow. You must rub it directly into her heart."

Ashley looked at Dr. Conner, alarm blazing on her face. "Doc?"

"Just do it. She's a goner if we don't try something."

Turning away from Listener, Ashley extended a bloody palm. "Pour some on."

"It will sting like no wasp you have ever felt." Semiramis held Ashley's wrist and tipped the jar just enough to let a trickle of greenish sludge fall.

When it touched her skin, Ashley cringed but made no sound. Coffee-colored fumes rose from her hands, and tears streamed down her cheeks. She gasped for breath. Sweat poured. "I'm . . . I'm all right. It's not really that hot. It's just having a weird effect on me."

"It's slowing your metabolism," Semiramis said. When a small pool had formed in Ashley's palm, Semiramis pulled the jar upright. "Now, massage it in. Hurry."

Ashley turned back to Listener, let the potion drip onto the exposed heart, and massaged it in with her other hand. After a few seconds, she looked up at Dr. Conner. "It's slowing down."

"I see that. So is the bleeding."

"That's enough." Semiramis pulled Ashley's hand back. "Too much will kill her."

Ashley staggered backwards, but Patrick caught her before she fell. "I'm so dizzy."

Walter jumped up. "Ashley!"

"She is not in danger," Semiramis said, "but she must rest."

Ashley stared at her, her eyes wide and glazed. "Your mind is unguarded. I sense . . . I sense . . . murder." Her head lolled to one side, and her eyes closed.

"Take her, Walter," Patrick said. "I must return to my suction duties."

As Walter eased Ashley to the floor, Billy pressed Excalibur's tip close to Semiramis's throat. "What did you do to her?"

Her eyes riveted on the blade, she swallowed. "I assure you, gracious knight. This is a natural result of the potion in concert with her exhausted condition. The invigorating elixir is wearing off, and she absorbed some of my potion. She has merely passed into a swoon."

He set the point against her skin and growled. "She said she sensed murder."

"Please forgive my indiscretion and the weakness of a mother's protective instincts. I sorely wish to kill Arramos to avenge what he did to my son. Surely this is what Ashley detected."

"Her heart is down to ten beats per minute," Dr. Conner said, "but the bleeding's almost stopped. I can sew up the worst hole now."

"As you can see," Semiramis continued, "my potion is working. I have no intent to hurt anyone in this village, especially an innocent little girl."

Billy pulled the sword away and nodded at Candle. "You and Windor tie her up again. I'll go out and speak to Valiant and Elam."

"I willingly submit to your authority." Semiramis pressed her wrists together. "I am trustworthy. You will see."

As Candle led her to the corner, Billy shoved Excalibur back in place. "How's she doing, Doc?"

"Whatever that potion was, it has done much more than simply slow Listener's bodily functions. If I may venture a guess, that potion absorbed some of Ashley's healing characteristics, her photoreceptors, and her heart is pumping them throughout her body. It's as if the wounds are sealing themselves."

"Her diastolic pressure has stabilized," Patrick said. "With the slow heart rate, her systolic is difficult to measure, but I believe it, too, has stabilized."

Walter piped up from the floor where he cradled Ashley. "Her palm's bleeding. I'll bet her blood mixed in with that potion."

"Is she all right?" Billy asked.

"I think so. She's breathing okay. Knocked out cold, though."

Candle tapped on Billy's shoulder. "We tied up Semiramis. Windor showed me a new knot. She'll never get loose."

"Thank you." Billy unhooked his scabbard and gave it to Candle. "Keep an eye on her. I'm going out to talk to Elam."

As he reached for the door, Semiramis called from the corner. "Son of Clefspeare!"

He turned toward her. "Yes?"

With her eyes reflecting the lantern light and her voice calm and soothing, she seemed more like a storybook muse than a woman. "I have saved the little girl's life. If she and Ashley arise from their slumbers, I will await the apology you promised."

Billy looked at her for a long moment. Turmoil swam through his mind. There were just too many conflicting signs, too many hard decisions to make. Figuring out if this strange woman was truthful seemed impossible. First she seemed in league with the Nephilim, and now she breathed murderous threats against Arramos right after working so hard to save the life of someone who couldn't help her in the slightest.

He looked back at Listener. Her companion again perched on her forehead, but it was still dim.

Finally, Billy nodded. "We'll see very soon, won't we?" He opened the door, stepped outside, and shut it behind him. After taking two steps to the edge of the wooden walkway, he stopped and scanned the area.

Illuminated by lanterns at each side of the street, Valiant stood at the center of a throng of seated villagers, his hands uplifted as he paced back and forth in the midst of falling snow. Wearing a fur cap that covered his ears but not the dark curly hair that protruded from underneath, and a thick forest green cloak that fell to his knees and fanned out as he walked, he looked like a warlord exhorting the troops. Yet, his words said otherwise. Though his voice resonated in a rich baritone that demanded attention, and his companion's light flashed in cadence with his rhythm, each syllable carried the flavor of entreaty rather than the bark of command.

"Father of Lights, now that each man, woman, and child has lifted up cries for a miracle, songs begging for deliverance, and lamentations for this precious girl, this selfless little lamb, I add my final appeal."

He paused for a moment and swung back to pace the other way. As murmurs of "Hear him" mixed in with the whistling breeze, he continued. "Listener is a precious flower. Though she sprouted from our garden soil weak and fragile, mute and masked in scaly skin, we loved her. For no child in this world is ever considered of lesser value than any other. We have heard from our visitors that people in the world she came from cast away unwanted children, even butchering them more savagely than they would a murderer or a dog. So you sent her to us, and we have cared for her, this daisy, this rose of suffering, and she carried within her frail shell a heart of fire, proven by her willingness to suffer and die for the deliverance of others."

Again he paused and turned. Billy wanted to shout out, "Listener's recovering!" but the news was premature. It was still touch and go, and besides, interrupting a prayer like this seemed irreverent.

He spotted Elam across the street walking his way around the perimeter of the circle. With snow capping his black hood and a slight bend in his slow gait, he looked like a gray-haired old man trying to cross a slippery street.

Valiant glanced at Billy. Heaving a sigh that blew out in a stream of bright white, he continued. "Perhaps even now the struggle in that hut is over. Perhaps you have touched her with your healing power or provided the skills necessary to heal our little flower. Or perhaps you have decided to take her to your heavenly home and leave us bereft of the beauty and joy she has brought to our world. Whatever your decision, we will never forsake the love that you have called us to give to you and to our neighbors. For it is love that courses through our souls as blood courses through our veins, and by that love we will survive and carry on your work in this land." He clasped his hands together and shouted, "Father of Lights, hear our prayer!"

Young and old, the crowd echoed his call. "Father of Lights, hear our prayer!" Companions flashed all around, like twinkling blue lights in a Christmas display.

Valiant turned and walked slowly toward Billy, weaving past the villagers who were now rising. Elam arrived at the sidewalk first and, hugging his dampened cloak close to his body, whispered, "Any word?"

Billy clutched Elam's arm and moved him under the protection of the roof's overhang. "Let's wait for Valiant." Rising to tiptoes, he scanned the heads in the crowd for Rebekah's blonde locks. "Are Rebekah and Dallas here?"

Elam shook his head. "We decided to let them transform while there was still some energy in the bones of Makaidos. They are now Legossi and Firedda, and they are at the garden with the other dragons."

"Excellent. Where is Acacia?"

"At her hut. Asleep, probably."

"All for the best." Billy imagined the dragons huddling in the snowy garden. How would they stay warm? Could the villagers build shelters for them?

Valiant jumped up to the walk. "How is our little flower?"

"Still alive," Billy said, "but barely. Semiramis concocted a potion that—"

"Semiramis!" Elam's voice spiked. "You let her loose? You let her brew a potion?"

"Calm down. It looks like it worked. Listener was about to die, and Semiramis said she could help. What was I supposed to do?"

Valiant clapped Billy on the shoulder. "A wise decision. Choosing a potential danger over certain death was your only option."

Elam gave a nod of surrender. "Okay. If she's decided to help us, I guess we can accept it, but I won't believe it's not for her own benefit until proven otherwise."

"Same here," Billy said. "Apparently handling the potion knocked

Ashley out, or at least aggravated her exhaustion, so that's more than suspicious. And another strange thing. Just before Ashley conked out, she got an impression from Semiramis's mind, something about murder. Semiramis claimed that she wanted to kill Arramos because of what he did to Hunter, but I'm not sure I'm buying that story yet."

"A reasonable concern," Valiant said. "For we now also suspect Hunter is not genuine. He no longer has a companion, and no Second Edener can be separated from his companion without immediate sickness and eventual death."

"And he shows no signs?" Elam asked.

"He seemed healthy for a while, but after one of our little boys mentioned that he should be ill, Hunter began complaining of nausea and dizziness."

Billy rolled his eyes. "How convenient."

"Indeed. We would not let him go into the medical hut to see his mother. He is now at Cliffside's hut with Cliffside guarding him."

"What about the companion?" Billy asked. "Any sign of it?"

Valiant shook his head. "We searched the garden, but with snow and darkness covering the field, any further attempts by humans seemed impossible. The dragons, however, will begin melting the snow and searching the grass with their laser eyes. If the companion is out there, they should be able to find it."

"Companion or no companion," Elam said, "we can't take any chances. Given Hunter's charade and Ashley's report about Semiramis's murderous intent, I say we send them away."

"Banishment to the northern lands?" Valiant asked. "During the season of death?"

Elam rolled his fingers into a fist. "If we're going to stay strong, we have to make sure all corrupting agents are gone."

"I'm not sure of that," Billy said. "If she's really an enemy, I'd rather have her close where I can keep an eye on her."

Valiant smiled. "A keen observation. Yet, if your enemy desires to be close to you, then you can be sure that her intent is to watch and wait for the moment when your back is turned."

Elam gazed at the door to the triage hut. He seemed pensive, worried. "We will discuss it in the morning. By then we'll know if Listener and Ashley are going to recover."

"And if Hunter is a true resident of Second Eden," Valiant added. "If he is, he will be dead by dawn."

The door opened behind Billy, and Walter shuffled out with a blanket draped over his shoulders. "Brrr! It's colder than Morgan's heart out here."

"How's Listener?" Billy asked.

"That's why I came out. The bleeding stayed under control, and her pressure went up. Just a little, but it's positive. Not only that, her companion's buzzing around again, happy as a lark."

Valiant spun toward the street and clapped his hands. The villagers, some milling around and others dispersing toward their homes, stopped in their tracks. "Praise the Father of Lights!" he shouted. "Our little flower is recovering!"

Some of the villagers jumped in place, repeating, "Praise the Father of Lights!" while others joined hands and danced, sliding on the snow-covered street and laughing gaily while their companions flashed and zoomed in tight orbits around their heads.

Billy laughed with them. Seeing such an outburst of happiness after so much tension felt fantastic.

Walter nudged Billy's side. "And Doc says Ashley's okay, too. Her vitals are stable, and she's sleeping like a baby."

Billy clasped Walter's shoulder. "That's cool, Walter. That's really cool."

"Not to put a damper on the celebration . . ." He flicked his head toward the triage hut. "What're we going to do with spooky Semiramis and her suddenly companionless son?"

"You heard about that?"

"Yeah. You guys are loud."

Billy pushed a hand into his pocket. "First I'm going to have to apologize to her."

"And then banish her?" Walter smirked. "Not exactly a believable apology."

"That part's not my decision." Billy reached for the door. "Come on. I might as well get it over with."

Once inside, Billy scanned the room. Walter walked straight to Ashley's cot, while Mantika sidled up to Billy and took his hand. "Listener lives," she said, smiling at him.

Billy patted her hand. As he looked at her dark, gleeful face, tears welled in his eyes. "I heard, Mantika. It's a miracle."

"Miracle. Yes. It is miracle." Mantika compressed Billy's hand. "Praise the Father of Lights." She pulled away, joined Candle and Windor near Listener's side, and kissed both boys on the cheek.

Billy took a few steps closer to the surgery cot and peeked at Listener. Still unconscious and pale, she seemed barely alive, but with her chest now sewn back together with thick dark sutures and her skin free of blood, at least she didn't look like the victim of a bomb attack.

Dr. Conner sat on a nearby cot, his elbows resting on his knees as he looked up at Billy. "Pressure's eighty over forty. Her heart's strong. Her lung inflated. If infection doesn't set in, I think she'll make it."

"Way to go, Doc." Billy tightened his trembling fingers into a fist. "You were amazing."

Dr. Conner nodded toward the opposite corner. "If not for our prisoner, we would be telling a different story."

Billy looked at Semiramis as she sat with her back to the corner. Once again she had taken on the aspect of a mythical siren, her eyes wide, her gaze entrancing, her lips quivering in a mournful pose. With her bound wrists resting on her knees and her hands clasped, she looked more like a supplicant begging for mercy than an imprisoned witch.

With a shrug of resignation, he walked toward her, trying to avert his gaze, but something about her deep pleading eyes kept him entranced.

He pushed his hands into his pockets again and stopped in front of her, shifting back and forth. "I . . . uh . . . I guess I owe you an apology."

"You owe me nothing, son of nobility. If you wish, however, to offer a gift of gracious words, then I am ready to receive it."

Billy cleared his throat. "I'm sorry for what I said. Your potion made all the difference in the world."

"My potion, as you call it, is nothing more than a mixture of natural elements." She lifted her eyebrows. "Do you understand my meaning?"

"I think so. You're trying to tell me that you're not a witch or a sorceress. You didn't conjure the stuff up through some magical power."

"Yes, Billy. It is your trust I crave, not your willingness to praise a jar of green liquid. I am merely a mother who lost her way. I trusted a vile dragon and obeyed his command to guard a dangerous bridge. I had no idea that he wished to use the chasm to bring these people to destruction. Now that I have rebelled against him, I am a woman without a country, without a home, for I have deduced that the people of this village will send my son and me away."

"Probably. Hunter lost his companion, and since he doesn't seem to be suffering, they think you lied about him being a Second Edener, especially since he started putting on an act. Elam and Valiant said they would decide your case in the morning."

"Ah, how I pity these villagers! Their lack of knowledge begets such naïveté. Hunter comes from a village in the northern lands, a place these people have never visited because of their tradition that these two villages hold God's only chosen people. They assume that all true Second Edeners are like themselves. If there is the slightest difference, prejudice is born, and they assume the peculiar man or woman is one of the altered tribes. And now Hunter is trying to be something he is not. He is frightened and wishes to preserve his life and mine. You see, his companion will return to him. Have no fear of that. While he waits for it, imprisoned by a people who mistrust him, Hunter is doing what he can to survive."

"So what do you want me to do? Try to convince them?"

"No, Billy. It has become clear that we cannot live in harmony here, at least not until the people learn to tolerate those who are different." She lifted her wrists. "Cut my bonds. Allow us to go in peace. If we wait until morning, the pass through the mountains might well be blocked with snow."

He shook his head. "I don't have the authority to do that. I'm just a soldier. Elam and Valiant make all the decisions."

"Then make an appeal for my release now. If your apology is sincere, if your words of trust are more than mere sounds from your lips, then do whatever you must to let us leave this place with our lives and a scrap of dignity intact."

"I guess I can do that." He dragged his toe across the floor. The tension felt thick, heavy. The struggle between loyalty to Elam and trying to get justice for this woman was too intense for words.

Curling a finger, she whispered, "Come closer. There is something else that must remain a secret between us, at least for now."

Billy closed the gap and stooped. "I'm not promising to keep anything secret."

"Very well. But choose wisely whom you will trust and when you reveal it." She scooted so close, her breath warmed his ear. "The finger in the box haunts you, does it not?"

He nodded. "Yeah. It shook me up."

"Although I am not a sorceress, I am familiar with the arts of the evil dragon who devised that cruel plan. He knew you would need an energizing device, so he provided it, also knowing that your use of it would create an advantage for him."

"What advantage?"

"The garden will now generate a plant that will look unlike the others. It will be ugly in comparison, and some might be tempted to uproot it as a weed. But they must not. The life of that plant will be tied to the life of the girl who wore the ring. If it dies, she will die."

Billy tried to draw back an inch, but the woman's tractive draw seemed stronger than ever. "How will the plant help Arramos?"

"By causing the people to do someone harm. As you have heard, when the people of Second Eden do any sort of evil, it allows greater evil to enter the world, as happened with Angel's lie and the coming of the Nephilim. With the new dragons you have in your army, Arramos knows that he has to fortify his own army. He cannot do this without help from someone willing to do evil."

"But if they don't know it's wrong to uproot the plant, it won't be evil to do it. I mean, not a real evil. Just an innocent mistake."

Her whisper lowered even further. "You are correct, and that is why our enemy's plan is so diabolical. Since I know the secret tie between the plant and Bonnie, I am bound by goodness to warn you, and since your love for her obligates you to protect her, you are bound by goodness to warn the others, and since they are bound by goodness to heed your warning to protect Bonnie and prevent a new assault of evil, they will allow the plant to grow unhindered."

"Will the plant spawn anything? I mean, will it carry a life inside like the others?"

"That I do not know. I can only guess that it will spawn a life, something that will be in league with Arramos, perhaps even worse than the evil that would come as a result of uprooting the plant."

"Then we'll watch it night and day," Billy said, touching the hilt of his sword, "and if it delivers, we'll destroy the fruit, whatever it is."

"Destroy it?" Semiramis grasped his hand. "Billy, you cannot kill something that has not proven itself evil. As I told you, I do not know anything about what might be spawned. That is part of the dragon's plan that extends beyond my knowledge. As the bridge's guardian, I had the opportunity to learn about some of his ways, because he would often pass to and fro in that land. But it is clear to me now that he always kept his darkest counsel to himself. All I know with certainty is that the plant's life will be tied to Bonnie's."

"You keep saying Bonnie. How do you know the finger didn't belong to . . . to someone else?" Billy was tempted to mention Shiloh, but giving Semiramis more information than she needed probably wasn't a good idea.

"There is no need to hide your thoughts. I heard your theory about Shiloh. It holds merit, but neither of us has any way of knowing. Since Bonnie is missing, I think it is wise to assume that our enemies have her in their grasp."

"What about Arramos's threat? Will he send more body parts?"

"I am not sure." Semiramis gazed at one of her long, narrow fingers. "Perhaps he will send more fingers and maybe some toes until the plant is well established. Once he is sure that it will be protected, he would be a fool to slice her further. At that point, we would hold the plant hostage in the same way he is holding her hostage. We each will be demanding a ransom of protection."

As he tried to untangle the web of possibilities, the message Semiramis delivered repeated in his mind. *"If the dragons and their offspring continued to ally themselves with the residents of Second Eden, this gift would be accompanied by more of the precious puzzle at a later time."*

"He's got us in a bind. If we don't want any more body parts delivered here, the dragons have to vow not to fight with us, and he's free to keep slicing her up until the plant sprouts."

Looking away, Semiramis nodded. "Yes, it is ingenious, I must admit. Yet there is a way to stop him."

"What's that?"

"To rescue Bonnie . . . or Shiloh, whoever he is holding hostage."

"How? Do you know where he might be keeping her?"

"I do. That is one of my purposes for leaving. I must try to get to his lair and attempt a rescue."

Billy grasped Excalibur. "Let me come with you. I think Arramos is the dragon I faced in the abyss below the seventh circle."

"Then who will protect the plant? Is there anyone here besides you who will believe my words? Will Elam believe me?"

As he stared at Semiramis's gleaming eyes, Elam's words rushed back into Billy's mind. *"I won't believe it's not for her own benefit until proven otherwise."*

"You know that he wouldn't," Semiramis continued. "And Valiant would heed his counsel. It would be up to you to protect the plant, and if you are not there . . ."

Billy pointed at himself. "But how do *I* know you're telling the truth about the tie between Bonnie and the plant? Maybe I would be an idiot to believe something like that without proof."

"If Arramos is using the binding tie that I believe he would use, then a simple test would prove the connection." She looked toward the hut's door. "You preserved the finger, did you not?"

"Elam put it on ice. The ring's gone, but, yeah, we still have the finger."

"When you see the first tender leaves of a new plant sprout, which should be very soon, check for orange and black tips. Those are the colors of Arramos, which will be the sign that you have the correct plant. Retrieve the finger and let a drop of blood touch a leaf. If the leaf withers, it is because of the connection between it and the prisoner of Arramos. The spillage of blood is reflected in the plant, just as harm to the plant would be reflected in Bonnie. Then quickly pinch off the withering portion so that death does not spread to the rest of the plant."

Billy imagined a voodoo doll with Bonnie's face on it. If not for Semiramis's serious expression and tone, he would have dismissed her story as ridiculous superstition. It just didn't make sense.

"I sense disbelief in you," she continued, "so you would be wise to wait for this proof before you commit to anything. Still, while you await the first leaves, you run the risk of receiving another body part from Arramos. The only other options would be either to get the dragons to vow to refrain from battle or else to rescue Bonnie quickly. My hope, however, is that the plant will show itself immediately; then the risk will be low."

Billy imagined once again the severed finger lying in blood-stained cotton. His thoughts then wandered to a dark room where Bonnie sat crying in a corner, her hand covered with a bandage, red where her finger used to be. The thought churned his stomach. And even if the hostage was Shiloh instead of Bonnie, the image stayed the same. It was tragic.

Billy shook his head. "You're right. No one else would be willing to do all that. I'll stay here."

"Then appeal for my release. When I find Bonnie, and you have had time to prove to the others that the connection is real, I will send for you. Then together we will rescue her before she loses another finger . . . or worse."

CHAPTER 19

RETURN TO PERDITION

Marilyn let her head droop until it tapped against the desk. A pencil fell from its perch atop her ear and rolled. Looking at it from the corner of her eye, she watched it fall to the computer room carpet. No matter. She was too tired to use it anyway.

With only a lamp and Larry's panel monitor illuminating her work area, the surrounding dimness eased her eyelids downward. Tomorrow. She would do more research tomorrow. Gabriel was already following up on the best leads—the helicopter registration, the pilot's license, and a flight log. Apparently the soldiers didn't cover their tracks very well, likely not thinking their chopper would be commandeered by their prey. Still, that didn't mean they were sloppy enough to leave a link between the pilot and whoever held Shiloh, so making that connection might be impossible, but it was worth a try.

A feminine voice reached her ear. "Mrs. Bannister?"

She lifted her head. Carly stood at the doorway to the hall, wearing the flannel pajamas she had borrowed from Shelly. "Yes, Carly?"

"Still no word from Bonnie?"

"No, dear." She touched the telephone on the desk. "Yereq called an hour ago. The water finally stopped rising, but the museum chamber and all the tunnels are flooded, so no one could be there."

"And the other divers?"

"Neither one found anything. I think Bonnie and Sapphira must have escaped through a portal. That's Sapphira's way."

"I hope so." With her hands behind her back, and her head low, she walked in, half sliding in a pair of oversized slippers. "I'm sorry we didn't get Apollo working."

Marilyn waved her hand. "Don't worry about it. It's not your fault. It took Ashley longer than you and Adam have had to work on it."

"Ashley worked from scratch. We had all the schematics and software."

"Don't beat yourself up. Ashley's a super genius." She tapped a finger on Larry's main keyboard. "He's a genius, too, but he doesn't have hands and eyes to help you with."

"Marilyn," Larry said. **"May I be so bold as to offer my insight without being asked?"**

"Certainly."

"Some of our failures are due to lack of supply of the newest generation parts. The panic that has arisen because of strange creatures lurking in the streets and long-dead people surprising the populace has put quite a pinch on commerce."

"Especially the appearance of long-dead dictators, mass murderers, and gangsters."

"Precisely. I suggest using these phenomena to our advantage."

"How would we do that?"

"You need a human genius. My guess is that there are a few geniuses residing in Hades who are unable to fit back into society, perhaps due to fear or a desire to be alone. Find one of them and request his or her help. I think he or she will be happy to be of use in a concrete way."

"But one of our goals is to separate Earth and Hades," Marilyn said. "The genius will be helping us condemn himself."

"Questions of ethics are beyond the scope of my programming, but my commonsense engine suggests that you tell the genius everything so that your conscience will be clear. He or she will likely dismiss your concerns because of eagerness to work on the project."

"So how do we find one?"

"I am already searching news stories for appearances of the dead. I will filter them using a list of physicists who would have enough brainpower to help us."

Marilyn looked at Carly and winked. "They would have to be physicists who didn't go to Heaven. Good luck with that."

"Their eternal destination is not in my database. I will check all on the list."

"Okay, Mr. Data Sleuth. You and Carly come up with the best option. I'll help her contact our condemned physicist in the morning."

* * *

Shiloh sat on the familiar bench in front of the abandoned dry goods store. Sniffing back tears, she rubbed her index finger along the marks she had etched into the backrest, one for each of the forty years she had spent in the sixth circle of Hades. Her release had been the most wonderful day imaginable, and when she leaped into her father's arms and felt his warm embrace, she knew, she just knew without a doubt, that all the suffering, all the fear, all the anguish had finally ended.

She stared at the stub on her hand, bandaged and still damp with blood. She was wrong. The suffering had begun all over again, worse than ever, and she was back in the clutches of her never-ending nightmare. And who could rescue her this time?

When Morgan kidnapped her, at least her father knew where she had gone, but now no one knew. With Daddy, Billy, Walter, Acacia, and so many others in Second Eden, who on Earth would guess that she had been taken to this God-forsaken place? Sapphira and Bonnie? Maybe. But they were being chased, too. How could they come out of hiding to rescue her? And even if they did try, could they get into this part of Hades at all? Even with Hades and Earth combining, would they figure out the path?

A loud rumble sounded from her abdomen. She pressed the heel of her hand against her stomach. Four days without food. The first three weren't so bad. Pressure made the pain go away. But not this time. Now she would have to face the part of the nightmare she had avoided since coming here. The watering trough near the stables had kept her from getting thirsty, but the only source of food lay in the direction she hadn't yet dared go.

She got up and shuffled to the street. With her hands folded behind her, she strolled toward the central circle, kicking any pebble that happened to be in her path. There were no wandering spirits, no Frankie, no Bat Masterson, no humanlike entities to alter the stark deadness that settled around her. With her hand throbbing and the threats of more disfigurement looming, what could be worse? Could anyone survive the misery of being slowly butchered in a strange world?

Yet this wasn't really a strange world. She knew exactly what to expect—the same routine she suffered through for forty years.

When she reached the town's circle, she found the pitcher pump, exactly where it had always been, anchored in the raised garden area with the spout extending over the dirt at the side of the street. Shading the pump from the morning sun, a twenty-foot-tall statue stood in its usual spot, Captain Autarkeia riding a rearing horse.

Shiloh pumped the handle. Water poured out and made a swirling puddle in the mud. Yes, it was all the same. Soon, the plant would grow, she would eat its fruit and get violently sick, and once she felt better, she would wander around until nightfall until she made a bed among the broken crates in an alley.

She sat on the raised curb and waited. Nights were the worst. Sleeping inside the abandoned buildings always produced the most horrible nightmares, and strange noises seemed to stalk the streets. Maybe it was always the wind rattling broken window shutters and rusty chains, but the sounds were enough to keep her in hiding behind the alley crates. Besides, they provided shelter from the wind's chill.

Soon, the plant sprouted, and its green stalk grew at its usual fast rate. When the five-leafed bulb appeared, she plucked it, peeled away the stubborn leathery leaves, and tossed them to the side. With a sigh, she stared at the fibrous white fruit. Just looking at it brought stabs of pain to her stomach. But it had been four days since her last meal, and it hadn't killed her the previous ten thousand times she had eaten it, so it didn't make sense to fret about it now.

Just as she opened her mouth, someone called from the other side of the circle. "Greetings!"

Shiloh turned toward the voice. A woman dressed in red from head to toe walked out from behind the statue.

"Who are you?" Shiloh asked, remembering to continue faking an American accent.

Smiling, the woman lowered her hood and sat next to her on the curb. "I was going to ask you the same question."

Shiloh half closed one eye. "I asked you first."

She laughed and touched herself on the chest. "I am Semiramis. I have come to find a way to rescue you from this place."

Shiloh leaped to her feet. "You have? Who sent you?"

"Why, your friends in Second Eden, of course. Billy hasn't so soon forgotten you."

"Billy?" Shiloh's face flushed hot. Obviously Semiramis thought she was Bonnie. Had she already blown her cover? And if Semiramis was a friend, would it be okay to let her know the truth? Probably not yet. Better to feel her out and get more information.

Shiloh sat down again and calmed her voice. "Yes, of course. I know Billy would send for me if he were able, but how did he find out I was kidnapped?"

"Your captors sent us your finger, a hideously cruel act designed to instill fear in our hearts. Not only did the finger have your rubellite ring still on it, the box included a lock of your hair, and Billy recognized your blonde highlights. Also, two former dragons, Rebekah and Dallas, have come to Second Eden, and they told us that Shiloh had been taken and Bonnie went missing later. We wondered if the finger might have been Shiloh's, but since the kidnappers did not deliver it until after Bonnie's disappearance, we decided that they had waited until they had her, the real former dragon girl, in their clutches."

Semiramis pulled a wad of gauze from her pocket along with a small bottle. "Here is material for a clean bandage and an infection-fighting potion. When I heard about your finger, I assumed you would need these. There is an adhesive strip in there as well."

"Thank you." Shiloh peeled off her old bandage, red and sticky from the still-oozing blood.

"Here," Semiramis said. "I will dispose of that for you."

Shiloh gave her the old bandage and took the gauze and bottle. As she applied the potion, she said, "Where did they take Shiloh?"

"I do not know. I suspect that, once they discovered that she was not who they thought she was, they simply did away with her. There would be no need to hold her captive."

Shiloh drooped her head. "I see."

"It is tragic, I know, but we must put that aside and concentrate on how to get you out of here. As you likely have discovered, the path to freedom is not easy to find."

"I know." Shiloh finished constructing the new bandage and looked up at Semiramis. "On the way here, they blindfolded me, so I couldn't tell how I got here. I felt a lot of wind, like I was flying on something with wings, but I don't know for sure. And now whichever way I go, I run into a transparent shield. I can see a land covered with snow beyond it, but I can't get through. What's even stranger is that it doesn't snow here like it does out there. It's like I'm in a big bubble of some kind."

"Yes, and that is just the first obstacle. Even if you were able to get beyond the shield, you would find a long journey through snow and ice that you are ill prepared to take."

"Then how did you get here?" Shiloh asked.

"If I told you, you would likely not believe me. You see, I was once in league with Arramos, the mastermind of this sinister plot to destroy Second Eden and overthrow Heaven itself, so I have abilities you would not understand. I am able to travel here with relative ease."

"But where is here? I mean, where physically? If you came from Second Eden, and Hades and Earth merged, how did you get here?"

"An excellent question. When Earth and Hades joined, the seven circles had to reside somewhere physically, so most took up space in their earthly counterparts, and some moved elsewhere. The physical attributes of one land gave way to another, so that both reside together, though one set of attributes necessarily became invisible to the eyes of the inhabitants.

"For example, Morgan's former home in the third circle is now at the Glastonbury Tor, and the grass fields of the second circle are in the plains of the United States while the bordering forest land where the Caitiff once lived is now in the eastern U.S."

Semiramis spread out her hands. "This village was unique. It already had a close tie with Dragons' Rest, which you know much about. When Dragons' Rest was destroyed, God granted Arramos's request to move this village to the northern lands of Second Eden, and since I dwell in Second Eden, I was able to come to you."

"How?" Shiloh asked. "Do you just walk through the shield? Is it passable going one way and not the other?"

"It is passable only to those who are dead." She lowered her gaze. "This is the truth that I dared not tell you earlier, but now I think you need to know. You see, I, in fact, am dead."

Shiloh drew her head back. "You're dead?"

"Ah, yes," Semiramis said, looking at Shiloh again. "It is true. I died to Earth's realm millennia ago. Being dead is a great disadvantage most of the time, but it allows me to come and go from this village as I please. And the presence of the sixth circle created a gateway for me to come from the Bridgelands where I once worked for Arramos as the guardian for Zeno's Chasm.

"When Arramos learned that I had lost faith in him, he decided to put me away for a while, until I, as he put it, came to my senses. I was far too valuable to destroy. So he snatched me up in his claws, flew down here, and deposited me in this very spot. That is why you felt the sensation of flying. You likely rode on his back to get here." She looked up into the clear blue sky. "It is impossible to get back up without help from another flying creature, perhaps a helpful dragon."

"So how did you know to find me here?"

"A guess, really. I had to come to this region, anyway, so it made sense to look here. You see, I had to leave the village where Billy is, because, although I saved the life of one of their children, they did not trust me. I felt, however, that Billy trusted me, at least a little, so now that I have found you, I will send for him. It took me more than a day to get here, and with the mounting snow, it will likely take more than that to get word to him, then another day for him to come. Perhaps he can fly on a dragon and get here more quickly. We will have to see."

Shiloh stood again and, sliding her hands into her jeans pockets, walked a few paces away. "That would be great, but . . ." Heaving a sigh, she looked at the doorway to the Feed Store, the place where Bonnie had given her life to save her own. She had been so sacrificial, so willing to do what was right no matter the cost to herself.

Raising her hand, she looked at her bloody bandage. Sure, being Bonnie was costing her body parts, but if word got out that she was Shiloh, the kidnappers would likely kill her. But did that matter? Shouldn't she be willing to risk death, just like Bonnie did? Yet, if she revealed who she really was to this woman, could she be trusted? The whole point of her masquerade was to protect Bonnie, and any hint that Bonnie was still free would put her in danger. Still, it wouldn't be right to ask Billy to put his life on the line to rescue her without letting him know who she was. Yes, he would do it no matter what, but giving him the opportunity to make the decision based on truth would be the honorable thing to do.

Semiramis rose from the curb and touched Shiloh's arm. "What is it, Bonnie? Speak your dilemma, and I will try to solve it."

She spun back to Semiramis. "Don't tell Billy I'm here."

"What? Why not? Don't you want to escape?"

"Of course. It's just that . . ." Shiloh looked away

"You are not willing to draw Billy here on pretense."

"That's right. I wouldn't want to—" Shiloh swung back toward Semiramis. "What did you say?"

Semiramis laughed gently. "Do not fret or fear, Shiloh. It was not difficult for me to discern who you are."

Shiloh reverted to her British accent. "How did you figure it out?"

"When I mentioned that Billy might be coming, you were seized by a dilemma. If you were really Bonnie, there would be no hesitation."

Shiloh crossed her arms and scowled. "I'm such an idiot."

"It is an unfortunate truth that those who hold to high morals have a very hard time deceiving others. Withholding truth creates dilemmas that do not occur to the unscrupulous, and even if they did, they would not be bothered by violating codes of honor."

Shiloh looked at Semiramis again and spoke in a pleading tone. "So what are you going to do?"

"Send for Billy, of course. Since he is honorable, he will not view you as any less valuable than Bonnie."

Shiloh tightened her chin and nodded. "Okay. Thank you."

"Come with me," Semiramis said, taking her hand. "I want to show you something."

Flinching at Semiramis's touch, Shiloh went along, pondering the strange woman. Maybe this is what dead people felt like, cold and tingly. It stood to reason that she would be different, even in speech and mannerisms, but why was she so willing to help? What was in it for her?

Semiramis led her past the final building in town and into a field of bare ground, decorated only by prickly pears and acorn-sized stones. Of course, Shiloh had walked through this field many times in search of a way out, so she knew the invisible shield lay only twenty or so paces away. Yet, even if she didn't know, the boundary was obvious enough, an abrupt line that separated the dry, desert-like landscape from a sea of snow.

From her vantage point at the top of a high hill, she could see tens of thousands of acres of valley lands. Only the tops of evergreen trees and a few boulders protruded, creating splotches of green and gray that dotted the white expanse.

"As you can see," Semiramis said as she gestured toward the scene with her hand, "the snow has already mounted beyond what can be easily traversed, and it is still falling. I will do what I can to fetch Billy, but if the snow persists, I might have to wait a few days. Keep watching through this wall, and when the thaw comes, know that your deliverance is at hand."

Shiloh nodded. "I will watch. I was here for forty years. I can handle a few extra days."

Semiramis kissed her on the cheek, a frigid kiss that made Shiloh shiver. "Whatever you do," Semiramis said, "do not trust Arramos. He is treacherous."

"Don't worry. I won't."

Semiramis raised a finger. "And one more thing. I will need a token of some kind that will prove that I found you. Elam and Ashley do not trust me. In order to mount a rescue, Billy might need their support, and—"

"You don't have to explain. I understand." Shiloh pulled her sweatshirt over her head, then the long-sleeved shirt underneath, leaving only a thin undershirt. After putting the sweatshirt back on, she handed the shirt to Semiramis, letting her hand linger over the imprint, a sketch of a majestic lion.

Semiramis lifted the shirt and read the lettering. "What does, 'He's not a tame lion' mean?"

"It's hard to explain. Just give the shirt to Billy. He'll know it belongs to me and what it means. And if anything happens to me or Bonnie, and he discovers that you're part of the reason, you'll find out what it means, too." She tried to bend her brow just enough to show a fighting spirit. "You'll find out the hard way."

A nervous smile quivered on Semiramis's face as she folded the shirt. "Well, we won't have to worry about that, will we?"

Shiloh smoothed out her sweatshirt and drilled her stare at Semiramis. "I hope not."

"Well, then, I will be going now." Semiramis stepped through the shield and out into the waist-high snow. A man walked out from behind a boulder and tromped toward her on snowshoes. With severe burns marring his face and a limp in his gait, he seemed to be in pain, but when he reached Semiramis and gave her a pair of snowshoes, a strange smile appeared. They spoke for a moment, both laughing afterward, but Shiloh couldn't hear their words or their laughter.

She pressed a palm against the shield. Apparently soundproof, it felt like glass, but her hand left no mark. Backing away, she sighed. Even if Billy showed up, how could he rescue her? Thinking about a knight in shining armor charging in on a noble white steed sounded like the most wonderful sight in the world, but if he could only stand outside and knock, what good would it do? She had already tried to break the barrier with a hundred different objects—stones as big as her head, an old sledgehammer, and even a rusty drill. Nothing worked.

Closing her eyes, she turned away and took a deep breath. She could do this. She could endure another few days, even a week or two. At least someone knew where she was and how to get to her. After forty years of dreadful misery without hope of rescue, these days would pass quickly, wouldn't they?

She lifted the plant's fruit to her mouth, bit off a large hunk, and marched toward the town's circle. As she chewed, the familiar sweet taste coated her tongue, and the gentle scent of honey filtered into her nostrils. The flavor was even better than she remembered, probably because she was so hungry and hadn't tasted it in such a long time.

When she reached the circle, she squinted at the statue. The descending sun was just touching Captain Autarkeia's head, and as it continued its downward journey, his shadow fell over her eyes.

Pain stabbed her insides, like ten spears being driven into her belly. Clutching her stomach, she dropped to her knees and then to her side, now lying fully within the lengthening shadow. As the agony increased, she looked up at the man's face. He seemed so kind, so caring, as if he would reach down from his mount, scoop her up, and ride off to safety, far away from this hellhole. Yet, he just sat there and looked. He wasn't Timothy Autarkeia or the great Makaidos. He was nothing more than a hunk of carved stone.

"Augh!" More stabs. More ripping pain. She panted, wheezed, groaned. As the roaring spasms climaxed, she cried out, "Jesus, help me!"

Within seconds, the spasms eased. Still breathing heavily, she closed her eyes and let her hands fall away from her stomach. It was almost over . . . almost over.

As she lay on the cold ground, she let her mind wander to images of apple pies and ice cream sundaes. Maybe this place was all a dream. Maybe she had eaten too many goodies and her stomach ached from the overindulgence. Soon she would wake up from this nightmare and find herself in bed snuggling one of her stuffed animals, probably Winnie, her longtime favorite. Oh, when would that alarm clock go off? When would her father come in with a cheery greeting? "It's time to get up, Shiloh!"

She blinked her eyes open. No bed, no alarm clock, no Winnie, just the town's central garden with the dead eyes of the high-riding man still staring at her.

She climbed to her feet, brushed the dirt from her clothes, and strode to her alley hideaway. She pulled crates to the side and arranged the straw and horse blanket she had found at the stables the day before. Then, after pulling the crates again to hide her from any peering eyes, she nestled into her bedding.

It would be all right. Billy would come. And a dragon, too. And maybe even the noble steed. No matter how long it took, she would wait patiently. If God could help her endure this place for forty years, surely he could do the same for a few days. Just a few more days.

As evening fell, darkness arrived with it. It felt heavy, oppressive, and lonely . . . very lonely. Shiloh pulled her knees close to her chest and wept.

CHAPTER 20

THE PROTECTED WEED

Billy knelt next to the tiny plant. With only two circular leaves, each the size of a quarter, and a thin green stalk supporting them, the plant seemed fragile. The leaves weren't even green. They were black on one side and orange on the other, more like a fungus than a harvestable plant.

He looked up at the field. Elam struggled toward the garden, his head down as if in deep thought as he pushed through the waist-deep snow. His dark cloak fanned in the cold breeze and floated above the drifts.

When Elam reached the garden, he picked up his pace, now walking on mud between two rows. Although the dragons had done a great job keeping the snow from freezing the plants, the huge green leaves still seemed cold as they trembled in the breeze, as if the babies inside were shivering.

After sidestepping a bone and hopping over another, apparently honoring the man who once owned them, Elam arrived, shivering as he set his hands on his hips. "So this is it?" he asked. "It's not even in the right place. It's in between the rows."

Billy touched one of the sickly leaves. "I'm not sure if it's the right one. That's why I called you out here to witness the test."

Elam stooped beside him. "Have you heard from Semiramis yet?"

"Not a word. With all the snow, we might not hear for a while." Billy pulled a small glass vial from his pocket and removed its cork stopper. He stared at the red liquid inside and gave it a swirl. "I have to hurry, or it'll clot."

Snow flurries began to dance around their faces. "No argument from me. The clouds look pretty ominous."

"I noticed. That's why we canceled Mount Elijah again. Dad did a flyover. The flat part on top has a mound of snow and ice. He tried to melt it, but with no place to land, he couldn't do much, and the path up the side is impassable." Billy tilted the vial and let a drop of blood fall on the tip of one of the leaves. Instantly, it curled and rotted. As if burning, the rot spread toward the stalk.

Billy pinched off the tip and dropped it to the soil. The leaf, now only three-quarters its original size, no longer shriveled.

He put the stopper back in the vial. "Exactly the way she said it would happen."

Elam picked up a clump of dirt and crushed it. "Witchcraft!"

"Witchcraft?" Billy straightened to his full height, adrenaline pumping his muscles into tight knots. Of course, Elam had good reason to doubt Semiramis, but how far would he take his lack of trust? "So do you think she's a witch?"

"Whether she's a witch or not, it doesn't really matter. The connection might be real, even if her black magic caused it. So now we have to protect something that Arramos put here." Elam shook his head. "It's like giving a burglar a gun and the keys to your house."

"What choice do we have? We can't uproot it."

"Of course not. I'm just venting." Elam gestured with his head. "Let me show you something."

Billy followed him to the rear part of the garden. They reached a circular area that contained no growth except for a single plant near the middle, smaller than the one they had just tested. This one, however, was green and lively.

Elam crouched and touched one of the twin leaves. Like the others in the garden, the leaves resembled praying hands, though these weren't yet touching each other.

"Cliffside told me that when the leaves come together, the baby usually shows up in between within the next week, though sometimes it takes a month. He enjoys shining a light through the leaves to see its early development stages, and he has a journal filled with drawings that show the typical growth pattern of the plants and the expected shape and size of the baby inside."

Billy nodded. "That's very cool. He must really love babies."

"He does. He wants one of his own, but he has never married, so he can't be part of the parent lottery."

"Any candidates?" Billy gave Elam a wink. "I mean, is he looking?"

"I heard just today that he and Emerald are betrothed. You should have seen Cliffside. He was like a young buck, picking snowball fights with the other unmarried males, and he even went door to door and left candy boxes for the kids."

"Nothing like requited love to perk a man's spirits."

"Trust me," Elam said. "I know what you mean."

"Sapphira?"

Elam's smile provided the answer.

"I heard the story from Acacia," Billy said. "Why didn't you ever tell me?"

"It hurts too much. I have loved that girl for thousands of years. Ever since she risked her life to feed me stew on her fingers, I knew there would never be another one for me. When I worked in the shipyards in Glasgow, lots of girls tried to charm me. A few even proposed marriage. Some were very attractive, both in appearance and in depth of spirit, but I couldn't entertain any notions like that. They were nice, but they just weren't Sapphira."

"Does she feel the same way about you?"

"Well, I saw her briefly a few weeks ago. I was standing near Heaven's Gate, and she was on Earth. I guess that's about as far away as you can be from someone and still see her. She wiggled her fingers at me, so I have hope."

Billy cocked his head. "Wiggled her fingers?"

"That's our love sign." His voice pitched a notch higher. "It reminds us of when she fed me."

Billy grasped Elam's wrist. "Then there's no doubt about it. She's as tied to you as you are to her."

"How about you?" Elam asked. "Do you miss Bonnie?"

"Well . . . sure. I mean, it's not like I've loved her for thousands of years or anything, so I can't compare with what you're going through, but . . ."

"Come on. I spilled my guts. It's your turn. No one's listening but me and the birthing plants."

Billy looked into Elam's eyes—piercing, wise, gentle. He would guard any secret. "I love Bonnie. She's the most amazing girl I've ever met. It's like she's so perfect, it's unbelievable. I mean, if you described her to someone—her kindness, her faith, her self-sacrifice—most people either wouldn't believe it was true or they would hate her for being so good. Do you know what I mean?"

"Jealousy, I think. The spitefulness of inferiority that tries to defame their betters in order to drag them down to their pitiful level."

"Something like that, but Bonnie would love them anyway, no matter what they thought of her." Billy rubbed his finger gently across the top of the plant. "She's a gem, a lump of coal that God made into a perfect diamond."

Elam stroked the side of the plant as if caressing a girl's hand. "It's amazing what suffering can turn someone into. Some become bitter and hateful, and others reach out with love."

"Right. So, yeah. I miss Bonnie. I miss her a lot."

"Anyway," Elam continued, "there's something special about this plant, too. This is the place where Abigail landed. A plant sprang up here much faster than the others, and Roxil came out of it. When I looked at the remains of the plant, I found a seed-like thing, kind of egg-shaped in the roots. I decided to plant it to see if it would grow."

"And this is the result?"

Elam nodded. "It grows slower than anything Cliffside has ever seen, maybe a fourth of the normal rate."

"Any idea what it means?"

"Not really. I've had dreams that a dragon came out of this one, like Roxil did. But it was probably because of the swamp peppers on my sandwich. Fire breath, you know."

Billy laughed. "Trust me. I know."

"Yes, you would." Elam rose to his full height and scanned the skies. The snow had thickened across the darkening canopy. "If we get another storm like the last three nights, the dragons will have to clear the garden again. They've been working much too hard. They haven't even had a chance to build good regeneracy domes."

"I know what you mean," Billy said. "I asked Legossi and Firedda to get some rest. I'm hoping they'll take Acacia and me back to Mount Elijah tomorrow. By air is the only way now, but if we don't get more sunshine, no Earth dragon will be able to take us. Valiant said he would help us get there on Grackle and Albatross, if we can find them."

Elam tilted his head upward and let the tiny flakes collect on his forehead. "No one's seen them. Candle even tried to use Listener's spyglass from the top of the ridge, but no luck."

"How is she?" Billy asked. "I haven't seen her since this morning."

"Still on the heart machine, but Dr. Conner thinks she'll be off it in a few days."

"Speaking of Dr. Conner, did he and Hartanna reunite? I remember when my mother and father got back together after he became a dragon again. It was pretty clumsy for a woman and a dragon to show affection."

"They spoke," Elam said. "They were friendly, but, like you said, there's a barrier they really can't cross. And since he was part of the reason she died . . . yes, *clumsy* is a good word. But I think they'll warm up to each other."

"Look." Billy nodded toward the field. "Here comes the dynamic duo."

Walter and Ashley plowed through the snow side by side. Soon, their chatter reached Billy's ears.

"If you had worn boots," Ashley said, "your socks wouldn't be wet. Didn't your mother ever teach you how to dress for the snow?"

"Of course she did, but my boots are in my closet back home. If you know how to get Federal Express to deliver something across dimensional barriers, I'll use your new radio to give them a call. I'm sure they'll rush my boots here by overnight delivery."

Billy grinned. "Will they ever stop?"

Elam shook his head. "They enjoy it. Look how they're smiling."

"I'll give you a Federal Express package!" Ashley scooped up a handful of snow and threw it at Walter, smacking him in the chest.

Walter covered his heart with his gloved hands. "Oh, no! You opened the wound! I can feel blood in my lungs."

"Really?" A look of concern flashed across Ashley's face. "Let me see."

When Walter leaned close, Ashley pulled his collar, grabbed another handful of snow, and stuffed it down the front of his shirt. "That ought to seal the wound!" Laughing, she ran toward the garden. Walter followed, but at a much slower pace. As he shook out his shirt, his grin stretched from ear to ear.

Billy held up his hand. "Stop! Wait!"

Ashley halted. "What?"

Quick-marching through the mud between the rows, he pointed at the weedlike plant just a few feet in front of Ashley. "Don't step on that."

She edged closer and stooped. "What is it?"

When Billy arrived, followed by Elam and Walter, Billy retold the story. Of course, Walter and Ashley asked so many questions, it took longer to tell it this time than the first. By the time he finished with Semiramis's claim that Bonnie or Shiloh was imprisoned in the northern lands, the snow had thickened in the air, and a thin coat of white dressed the soil.

Walter grasped Billy's arm. "Let's hit the northward trail right away. Ever since I saw those fountains from the top of Mount Elijah, I wanted to see what was out there."

"If Semiramis is telling the truth about where Bonnie or Shiloh is," Ashley said.

"What's the consensus?" Billy asked. "Is Semiramis on our side or Arramos's?"

Elam raised his hand. "Arramos's. I don't buy her story."

"I agree," Ashley said, lifting her hand. "The murder I sensed in her heart didn't feel like righteous indignation to me."

Billy lifted his eyebrows at Walter. "And you?"

"I think Semiramis is working for Semiramis. She's playing both sides. You can't argue with real burns. They were recent, and her care for Hunter wasn't fake. She doesn't like Arramos, but she's no friend of ours, either." He gripped Billy's arm again. "But it doesn't matter. If she comes back and says she found Bonnie or Shiloh in the northern lands, and you want to head that way, then I'm at your side, no matter what."

Ashley poked Walter's stomach. "Not until you're completely healed. You can't even swing a sword yet."

"Is that so?" Walter rotated his shoulder. "With all the tender loving care I'm getting, I think—"

"Uh-oh," Elam said, pointing toward the field. "Speak of the devil."

Billy and the others turned. A tall slender woman trudged through the snow. Dressed in a thick hooded cloak, red from head to toe, she broke through the final drift and walked into the garden. As she approached, she lowered her hood, revealing her familiar auburn locks.

"Semiramis," Billy whispered. "Her timing is—"

"Suspicious," Ashley interrupted. "I still didn't sense her presence."

When Semiramis came within ten feet, she dipped low, her head bowed, apparently unconcerned that snow and mud seeped into her cloak as her knee pressed down. "I have come, just as I said I would."

Billy set a hand under her elbow and helped her rise. "Did you find her?"

As she straightened, she trained her eyes on Billy. "I have." She reached under her cloak and withdrew a folded shirt. "Shiloh said you would recognize this."

"Shiloh?"

"Yes. For a while, she concealed her identity, trying to protect Bonnie, I am sure, but I discerned the truth soon enough."

Billy took it by the collar and let it fall open. "It says, 'He's not a tame lion.'"

"Aslan," Walter said. "The Narnia shirt Bonnie gave her."

Billy nodded. "I remember."

Elam crossed his arms over his chest. "So why didn't you bring her with you?"

"It is a complex situation, Elam. She is once again in the sixth circle of Hades, but it has been moved to the northlands of Second Eden. It is now behind a shield that is impenetrable to the living."

"To the living?" Walter pointed at her. "Then are you . . ."

"Dead?" Semiramis gave him a sad nod. "Yes, Walter. I died millennia ago. Arramos received permission to use me in the Bridgelands for his purposes, and now, before I am cast into the Lake of Fire, I want to make amends for my many misdeeds. Perhaps by the grace of Elohim, I will be allowed to wander in the lands of the dead and delay my suffering."

"Then how are we supposed to get her out?" Billy asked.

"You must break the shield. I know of no way to do this deed, but perhaps between your brilliant scientist and the many dragons at your disposal, you will be able to penetrate it."

Ashley furrowed her brow but said nothing. Billy looked at Ashley's narrowed eyes. It was easy to read her mind this time. She didn't trust Semiramis, not in the slightest. This dead woman who seemed impenetrable to Ashley's powerful mind was hiding something, something sinister, something deadly.

"We'll discuss it," Elam said, nodding toward the field. "Alone."

"I understand." As Semiramis bowed her head again, her eyes

suddenly widened. "The plant!" She stooped and touched the torn leaf, then looked up at Billy. "You tested it."

"Yeah. It worked, just like you said."

"Then can there be any doubt about my allegiance?" She straightened and looked around, her gaze pausing at each person. "I have told you everything, Arramos's plans regarding this plant, how it is tied to his prisoner, and the location of his prison. I have kept nothing from you."

"Like I said . . ." Elam's tone grew stern. "We will discuss it alone."

For a moment, Semiramis just stared at him. Then, her lips trembling, she bowed her head again. "Very well." She raised her hood, turned, and walked toward the field. "I will wait for word at the center of the village."

Billy and the others watched her in silence. She retraced her steps through the furrow, and when she reached the forest bordering the village, Elam spoke up.

"She plays this game well."

"Maybe." Billy let the shirt flap in the snowy breeze. "But we can't ignore this."

"So what's the verdict?" Walter asked. "Round up the dragons and assault the northern lands?"

Elam shook his head. "That's exactly what she wants us to do. If we send our dragons up there, we're vulnerable. There's no way I can allow that, not with the Vacants lurking."

Billy wadded up the shirt and held it close to his chest. If Bonnie were imprisoned, he would stop at nothing to rescue her. It wasn't right to do anything less for Shiloh. "Then I'll take my father, and the two of us will check it out. With Legossi and Firedda here, you should have plenty of firepower."

"Fair enough." Elam gazed toward the north through the snowy air. "If Clefspeare can't break through, no one can."

Walter pointed at himself with his thumb. "And I'm going with Billy."

"Over my dead body," Ashley said. "You won't be ready for dragon riding for at least a month."

"But if Billy gets in trouble—"

"Don't worry about me, Walter. My dad will—"

"Wait just a minute!" Elam waved for everyone to settle down. "Let's plan this calmly. If we can agree on a course of action, and Valiant adds his vote, we can move ahead as a team. It's important to be unified. That way, no one can say, 'I told you so.' We're in this together."

Billy nodded. The warrior chief was right, and he was showing his talent as a leader.

"You," Elam said, pointing at Billy, "will try to find Shiloh. Get directions from Semiramis, and we'll hold her in custody until you get back with a report." He shifted his finger to Walter while looking at Ashley. "Is he well enough to oversee construction of shelters for the dragons so they can build regeneracy domes?"

Pressing her lips together, Ashley nodded. "I don't see why not. As long as he uses his brain and not his brawn, I'm fine with that."

Again Elam moved his finger, this time pointing at himself. "I'll alert Cliffside and the dragons regarding the new plant. We'll rotate armed guards to make sure it stays safe, and we'll capture anything that comes out of it."

"What about me?" Ashley set her hands on her hips. "With Dr. Conner here, I'll be freed up to help. Everything's in deep freeze mode, so we're not likely to get attacked anytime soon."

"Three projects," Elam said, holding up a trio of fingers. "Keep working on the radio. We need to get in touch with Earth to get the other dragons here. And the second is to come up with a way to get back to Mount Elijah. That's our only portal. Number three is to figure out how to survive in the cold. We'll need greenhouses, more solar power cells, and a way to tap geothermal energy."

"Sounds doable." Ashley raised two fingers of her own. "And a couple more projects. I want to build a microscope for medical use. I learned a lot about glass grinding when I had to reconstruct my regeneration light at the visitor center back in Maryland. I'm also going to research my fireproof coating for the cloaks and make it stronger. If we can get someone into enemy territory, we can spy on what they're doing and maybe figure out how to use the tunnel portal in the Shadow Lands."

Walter let out a whistle. "You go, girl!"

Ashley drew her head back. "*I'm* not going to be a spy. I'm just cooking up the protectant." She sidled up to him and rubbed his upper arm. "We need a strong, brave, chivalrous knight who would surely be healed by the time the cloak is ready."

Walter scratched his head. "Can't imagine who that would be."

She gave him a hefty shove. "Oh, just knock it off!"

He faked a backwards stumble, then quickly regained his balance. "Well," he said, holding out his arm for Ashley. "Shall we go back to the village and rustle up something hot to drink?"

"Sounds good." Ashley hooked her arm around his and looked at Elam and Billy. "You two coming?"

Billy waved a hand. "In a minute."

As Walter and Ashley exited the garden and high-stepped through the snow, Billy laid an arm over Elam's shoulders and spoke in a low tone. "Whoever goes to Mount Elijah or the Shadow Lands in search of a portal will need Acacia to open it."

"Sure." Elam matched Billy's tone, his face expressing mild curiosity. "Then we would need two protected cloaks."

"That's not my point. I'm worried about her. She seems to be getting weaker. Her fire-making power isn't what it used to be. And her mindset is . . . well . . ."

"Just say it, Billy. No use holding back."

"She's kind of down. Not really depressed. Just sort of . . . I don't know how to describe it."

"Wishing it were all over?" Elam offered.

"Yeah. Maybe that's it."

Elam patted Billy on the back, and the two walked slowly out of the garden. "I know the feeling. She and Sapphira and I are thousands of years old, and living in a corrupt world gets kind of old after a while. Sometimes I just want to quit fighting and go to Heaven."

When they reached the snow, they shifted to walking single file, Billy in front. "I think I understand," Billy said. "I can't relate, of course, but it makes sense."

Elam heaved a sigh. "Acacia just wants to go home. With her firepower decreasing, she probably feels kind of useless."

"Then maybe a new mission to the Shadow Lands will recharge her spirit. I get stoked just thinking about opening the tunnel portal. I'm going to ask Ashley to get three cloaks, so I can go, too."

Elam laughed. "We'll see about that."

Billy stopped and turned around. "Let me take Acacia to find Shiloh. Maybe her fire would do something to the shield that my father's wouldn't. If not, just keeping her busy might help."

"Sure," Elam said, shrugging. "I don't see why not."

"Super! I'll get Semiramis to give us good directions."

"And while you're flying around, could you check on the guards at the wall of fire? With all the snow, we haven't been able to see if they need more supplies, and I'd like a report on how the wall is faring, especially at the river entry and exit."

"You bet. We'll pack some extra food and supplies for them and leave first thing in the morning."

* * *

With a hint of dawn lighting the horizon, Semiramis stood at the entrance to the alley in the sixth circle's rundown village. It had taken all night to make the journey, but time was of the essence. Now that Billy knew where to go, he would likely arrive soon, so she had to prepare the bait.

Since Mardon was free, escaping from Elam's guards had been easy enough. A little sleeping powder worked wonders. Of course, it would be impossible to convince Elam that her escape was for a noble cause. She would have to stay away from him and Billy, at least for now, and Mardon would never be able to go back to the village, since "Hunter's" companion didn't return. For now, she would stay scarce until the next step in her plan was complete.

She searched the sky. Arramos would be there soon, flying down from the Bridgelands and demanding a report. So many times she had been tempted to laugh, point at the barrier to Second Eden, and say, "If you are so powerful, then get your own report. Of course, you would have to die to penetrate the shield, so be my guest."

Yet, Satan dwelling in a dragon's skin would not be pleased with her lack of outward obeisance. Since all her plans danced on such a thin thread, now was not a good time to show him her true feelings.

With light now filtering into the alley, a haphazard collection of crates became clear, including Shiloh's legs protruding from the pile. She had slept fitfully for the past half hour, but the powder Semiramis had sprinkled in the air would keep her asleep long enough.

Soon, Arramos flew down and alighted next to her. With a shudder of wings, he settled and growled his question. "Shall I assume our plans are on course?"

She crossed her arms over her chest. "Have I ever failed you?"

"You answer a question with a question. This is the pattern of a deceiver."

"As well you should know."

Arramos let out a throaty laugh. "This I cannot deny. Nor can you. Your deception prowess far exceeds Morgan's. She was clever, but she was too straightforward. Her inability to avoid direct confrontation proved to be her downfall." He set his eyes near hers. "That is why I must always watch you closely."

For a moment, she froze, but she couldn't let this foul dragon intimidate her. She drilled her stare directly into his and spoke with a confident air. "To answer your question, our plans are coming along better than I ever thought possible."

"How so?"

"Mardon's reprogramming is working, and Acacia is weakening. If she dies, we will be able to safely collect her blood and perhaps her ova.

Also, I kept Shiloh's bandage, and Mardon analyzed her blood. Her exposure to the plant she eats created a high amount of antitoxins, making her immune to Morgan's poison. We believe the blood Billy poured on the plant will surely transmit a similar yet even more substantial invulnerability to the fruit."

"Of course," he growled. "I planned this long ago."

Semiramis forced herself to keep her face calm, but deceiving a deceiver wouldn't be easy. "As I suspected. You would not be fooled by Shiloh's pathetic disguise."

"She was the one I wanted in the first place. What do I care about capturing the winged girl? That is Devin's obsession, not mine. As long as she comes to Second Eden with your rope intact, her purpose will be complete, and our greatest enemy will see to that."

"So, you were already acquainted with Shiloh?"

"Of course. I saw Shiloh's invincibility, so I wanted to harvest it. I knew she would act as Bonnie's substitute. She has fooled Morgan with that act before." His scarlet beams flashed into her eyes. "I recognize liars quickly."

"And since I am a liar, it would be foolish to try to hide lies from you."

His growl sharpened. "Do not patronize me. I know you hate me because of what I did to your son, but your loyalty, if you still have any, will be rewarded. We must remain on the alert. During the time we wait for Bonnie Silver to arrive, the boys you have deceived will grow into men. They will not be so easily blinded by your wiles."

"I know. Elam is older and wiser than Billy. He sees through me already, but he suffers from a wound that hinders him. When he forced Angel to tell the lie she had concocted, the results were disastrous, and since the lack of trust among the villagers grows, he will not be quick to pass judgment on me."

"Excellent. All is well. My only concern is the ropes that bind the realms together. When the final piece of our interdimensional puzzle is set in place, the Bridgelands will crumble, and our ropes will be exposed. Anyone who comes upon them will be able to cut them."

"Not without a staurolite blade," Semiramis said.

"The winged boy Gabriel had one. Do you know what became of it?"

She shook her head. "That is a concern, but if we kill them all, even that worry will be eliminated."

"When the army I am assembling is able to enter Second Eden, killing them all will be an easy task."

Arramos lifted into the air and flew straight up. Soon, he disappeared from view.

Semiramis tiptoed into the alley and moved the crates that protected Shiloh's body. Giving her arm a gentle shake, she called out, "Shiloh. I have news for you."

After stretching her arms, Shiloh blinked. "Oh. You're back." She pushed up to her feet, wincing as she laid a hand on her head. "I have a terrible headache."

Semiramis steadied her. "I apologize. You are suffering from a side effect of a sleeping powder I gave you. You seemed so fitful, I wanted you to sleep more deeply, but now that dawn has come, I was sure you would want to hear my news. I told Billy that you're here. He will be coming for you as soon as possible."

She smiled through her grimace. "That's really cool! Thank you!"

"There is another reason I made sure you were asleep." Semiramis looked up again. Arramos was now long gone. "Arramos, the foulest creature in all the cosmos, visited here, and if he thought you were awake, he might have done you harm. He does not want anyone to know his plans. The only reason he keeps you alive is to make sure Billy protects a certain plant, but that would take too long to explain right now. When Billy comes to rescue you, I am sure he will tell you all about it."

Shiloh nodded. "Thank you again. I'll be watching for him."

"Excellent." Semiramis stepped back and pulled her hood up over her head. "For now, it is important that Arramos never know that I am working against his plans. I am a double agent, of sorts, and I hope to destroy him for what he did to my son."

* * *

Enoch stepped out of the anteroom, the small library that welcomed anyone who entered Heaven's Gate. Now walking in the great altar chamber, he listened to the buzz—prayers whispered and shouted from the lips of thousands of petitioners. With high and low voices rising and falling, it sounded like a choir warming up for a performance.

He strode along the side aisle and looked down the rows of praying stations. With each person kneeling on pillows, their hands folded on chest-high, wooden shelves, surely it would be easy to spot the two females. Both were shorter than most, and the distinctive red hair of one of them would be obvious even under a prayer shawl.

As he searched, he took in the sweet aroma. Of course, he had smelled it thousands of times. The prayers of the saints always carried this rich fragrance, but for some reason it seemed especially vibrant today, as if something unusually important stirred the hearts of the white-robed prayer warriors.

He stopped at row forty-one and scanned the heads and faces. The two he was looking for sometimes used this row because of its proximity to the painting of Stephen's stoning at the far end.

Standing on tiptoes, he spied the redhead and her dark-haired counterpart. Each wore sheer lacy veils that draped their heads and fell past their ears.

Sidestepping between the two rows, he hurried toward them. Of course, calling their names was allowed, but there was no use distracting people from their fervent prayers.

As he passed, he eyed each hologram in front of the prayer stations. One scene, floating in front of a male teenager, showed an elderly lady lying in a hospital bed. The boy prayed out loud, asking for healing for this missionary, the lady who had led him to faith only days before he was killed for converting from Islam.

The next scene showed a man, bound and gagged. A hooded man stood next to him with a machine gun barrel pushed against his prisoner's head. A lady knelt at the altar, praying for her son, her only son, a victim of terrorism.

Enoch hurried on. Listening to this lovely chorus of prayers could captivate him for hours, but there was too much work to do, and he would have many more years to bask in this rich flood of love.

When he arrived at the end of the row, he stooped between the two females and whispered. "Karen. Naamah. I must ask you to come with me."

Karen raised a finger. "Can you wait one second?"

"Yes. Yes, of course."

Naamah glanced up and smiled. "And I will be only a moment, as well."

Enoch looked at their holograms. In front of Karen, Ashley sat at a table with a collection of beakers containing liquids of various colors. Holding an eyedropper, she let a few drops of blue syrup fall into one of the beakers.

"Father," Karen whispered. "Please help Ashley find the best formula for protecting the cloaks." Breathing a sigh, she added, "And let her know that I love her."

In the hologram, Ashley looked up, as if listening. She gave the ceiling of her work area a curious glance before smiling and going back to work.

In front of Naamah, Elam and Walter stood next to a different table. With a lantern at one side, Walter pointed at something that looked like plans for constructing a building. The words at the top of the oversized page read, "Dragon Shelter."

Naamah sang her prayer, her voice lilting sweetly.

Grant them wisdom to increase;
Grant them vision to find peace;
Help them build a dragon's lair;
Gracious Father, hear my prayer.

When the song ended, Karen and Naamah stood and followed Enoch to the closer aisle. He marched toward the first row, turned in front of it, and passed a giant altar—a high table covered with a white cloth. As he walked swiftly by, the cloth's purple tassels swayed, so low, they nearly swept the floor.

Upon reaching the anteroom door, Enoch raised his voice above the choir's din. "You may take off your coverings now."

"Yes, sir." Karen pulled off her veil and helped Naamah remove a pin that held hers in place.

Enoch lifted the latch and led them inside. As he closed the door, the song died away.

"It is time to plan," he said, gesturing toward an old table and the benches that sat on either side.

Karen and Naamah sat on one side, while Enoch sat on the other. "I've been wondering when you'd pull the trigger," Karen said. "It's been in the prayer wind for quite a while."

Smiling, Naamah gave Karen a nudge with her elbow. "I think you have been putting most of it in the wind yourself."

"Well, that's true, but Prof was talking about it before he left. I didn't plant the idea in his mind."

Enoch lifted his brow. "Did Charles say when he would return?"

"Not to me." Karen shrugged. "When he got the news, he was like a man on a mission. He almost danced down the aisle."

Enoch laughed. "Well, it's no wonder."

Karen laid her palms on the table. "So, what are we supposed to do? Call the Seraphim and ask them to go to war? They could beat Flint's army in a heartbeat."

"No one in this realm will be allowed to participate directly in the battle, though I have heard that a temporary visit may be allowed later. In any case, God delights in using weaker vessels, so . . ." He forked two fingers at them. "So your request to be in charge of planning has been granted."

Naamah enfolded her hand in Karen's. "We are weak in body, Father Enoch, but we are strong in spirit."

"Yes," he said, laughing again, "I know that quite well. You are the two copper coins, the widow's mites that toppled Mardon's tower. No one will ever doubt your courage."

"This is going to be fun." Karen rubbed her hands together. "I have some cool ideas."

"Excellent, and since Charles is also so interested, you may want to include him in your strategy."

Naamah's lips spread into a lovely smile. "We have already consulted him about the portal situation. We think—"

The latch clicked. As the door opened, the choir of prayers again filled the library. A head poked in, the face wrinkled, the hair wild and white. "Enoch, you sent for me?"

"Professor Hamilton!" Karen jumped up and hugged him around his robed waist. "You look like yourself again!"

He smoothed back his hair and sat down next to Enoch. "Yes, the youthfulness I gained when I entered the heavenly realm was splendid, but, in light of the coming events, I thought it best to revert to this appearance."

Naamah smiled. "You are dashing in either form."

Professor Hamilton bowed his head. "I thank you, fair lady. The beauty of Heaven's grace rests upon you, as well."

"So . . ." Karen set her finger on the table and began an invisible sketch. "I think we should—"

"Dear Karen," Enoch said. "The technology here is not so lacking that we must imagine what you are scribbling there."

"Oh, yes." Professor Hamilton withdrew a pen from a pocket in his robe. "It seems that restoring my old body has also brought back my feeble brain, so I almost forgot about your request for this sky marker."

"Perfect." Karen took the pen and drew in the air. As the tip swept up and down and left and right, a full-color, three-dimensional image took shape, a battle scene with dragons, giants, humans, an airplane, and a white horse. "This is what I was imagining during the last prayer cycle." She pointed at a dragon. "The battle is inevitable, and since Goliath knows how to protect the army from Excalibur's beam, we will have to counteract that protection."

"The beam has not yet been restored," Enoch said. "What good will that do?"

Karen pointed at Charles. "That's where Prof comes in."

"Yes, I have already consulted with the angel who controls the portals. The tunnel portal in the Valley of Shadows has been redirected to the former mobility room, which, of course, is at the bottom of a pit in Montana. Now we must rely on the wisdom and intelligence of Marilyn and company as they learn how to use it."

"I have a prayer song," Naamah said, "for the reconstruction of Apollo and for guiding the rubellite from Earth to Second Eden. It will take a miracle to get it into Billy's hands."

Enoch nodded. "Indeed it will. I have not even imagined how it could happen."

"Our plans depend on it." Karen pointed at her drawing. "Anyway, since we control the weather, here's what we have to do. When Goliath's army brings out their secret weapon, you can bet that the weapon will be looking for the most dramatic way to make his appearance. My guess is that he will wait for the lesser minions to thin our ranks and then ride in on a horse at the rear of the attack forces. When that happens, we will begin our weather changes."

"I see," Charles said. "The ice cap over Mount Elijah will cause the pressure to build until it explodes in an enormous eruption. The chemical composition of the cloud mass should be perfect."

"And the reason for the long season of death in the first place," Karen added. "But the difficult part will be controlling the weather with enough precision to do the job while keeping it from hurting the plants in the birthing garden."

"Quite right," Charles said. "It would be toxic, indeed."

Enoch patted Charles on the back. "Have you selected appropriate attire, my friend?"

"A cloak that matches the one you plan on wearing. The colors will be dazzling."

"I wish our Father would let us go," Karen said. "The clothes Naamah and I are making for the celebrants are going to be amazing, too."

The professor set a hand on her shining red hair. "Keep asking, my dear. The glorious one has not yet denied your request. He has merely said to wait. We must see how events unfold. Nothing involving the will of mankind is set in stone."

"Speaking of that," Enoch said, "Bonnie and Sapphira come to mind. Have you decided how you will guide the new Oracle of Fire?"

Naamah borrowed Karen's pen and drew a sketch of two flaming bodies. "I have also composed a song for Bonnie. She will have to be aware of the Spirit's voice and listen carefully, but I think she has the wisdom to understand where her protection originates."

Enoch rose from the table. "I think the three of you have this well under control. I must go back to my viewing room to see if God has granted me access to the Valley of Souls. Since my contact with Bonnie and Sapphira has been cut off, and since I am not allowed to journey to Second Eden, I have very little else to do."

"Your screen still doesn't work?" Karen asked.

Enoch shook his head. "It has happened before. When God decides to allow his warriors to battle on their own, I must be content to stay out of the action. If they really need my help, God will again open my communication window."

He left the library and closed the door behind him. Again walking along the aisle, he searched for an empty prayer station and found one next to the teenaged male he had seen earlier. His hologram had switched to a primitive playground where one little girl pushed another riding on a tire swing.

As Enoch knelt on the soft pillow, the young man looked at him. "You're still among the disadvantaged, aren't you?"

Enoch smiled. Heaven's euphemism for those who had never left the shackles of physical life would seem odd to the "disadvantaged" ones on Earth, the living souls who had no idea what real life was all about. "For whom are you praying?" Enoch asked.

The young man pointed at the girls. "My sisters, that they won't fear death when the missionary tells them about the Messiah."

Enoch watched the two dark-skinned girls playing on the swing while a middle-aged woman stooped and laughed with them. As he gazed over the sea of prayer holograms, his words came back to him. *Since I am not allowed to journey to Second Eden, I have very little else to do.*

Shaking his head, he waved his hand across his empty hologram area. "Young man, being in my disadvantaged state, I am unable to create a prayer image. Would you please bring up your parents? I would like to pray for them."

A broad grin spread across his face. "Absolutely!"

As the image took shape in front of him, Enoch folded his hands on the altar. There was plenty to do, and for now he would be content to wait for God's next assignment.

CHAPTER 21

BREAKING THE BARRIER

Riding atop Clefspeare's back, Billy pointed to his right. "Is that the lake?"

Acacia, hanging onto his waist from behind, shouted, "Probably. It looks like a flat icy area."

"We shall see," Clefspeare said as he banked that way. They had been flying north with a tailwind, which had made for speedy travel and tolerable breezes, but with the shift into a crosswind, bitter cold returned with a vengeance.

Billy felt Acacia's shivering body, but she offered no complaints. When he had asked her to go, she jumped at the chance, and the sparkle in her brilliant blue eyes returned. Still, her silence through most of the journey and her shaking arms proved that her exhaustion lingered. He would have to keep a close eye on her.

Patrick had also wanted to come on the journey. After all, Shiloh was his beloved daughter. But Clefspeare told him that a third rider would make the burden too great, and bringing another dragon into unexplored territory was unwise. What Clefspeare did not say, but later confirmed to Billy, was his concern for Patrick's age and the bitter cold they expected to encounter. Disappointed, but eager to help, Patrick opted to pack the supplies for the boundary guards and draw an excellent map based on directions Semiramis supplied the night before.

Of course, her escape had set everyone on edge. Elam wondered about a possible ambush and questioned the wisdom of continuing with the search plan, but, in the end, it seemed best to go ahead. Clefspeare would see to their safety.

When they flew over the snow-covered expanse, Billy pulled a scrap of parchment from under his cloak and looked at Patrick's map. The lake, the final landmark before Shiloh's prison, was roughly elliptical with at least five wiggling streams that protruded to the north like gnarled fingers. These, too, were frozen. The season of death, the worst Valiant could remember, had taken its toll here as well.

Billy glanced back and forth between the map and the landscape below. The widest stream bent away on the northeast side. That would lead them to the valley, their final destination. Since they were now heading east, they would have to adjust.

"Head left about forty-five degrees," Billy called. "Follow that river with the cluster of evergreens on each side."

Clefspeare's eyebeams flashed on. After making a slow turn, skimming the bottom of the low cloudbank, he followed the river upstream, but it soon disappeared under a deep blanket of snow. Keeping the same heading, they traveled over a ridge and then a valley on the other side. A few trees and large boulders managed to find daylight above the snow's surface, marring the smooth blanket of white.

"What is that?" Acacia asked.

Billy looked back. She pointed toward something glimmering to the east. With barely any sunshine leaking through the clouds, whatever it was had to be huge to capture the light and reflect it. "It looks like a curtain of glass."

"I sense a portal," Acacia said. "If it's behind that glass, it must be enormous for me to feel it from so far away."

"It is less than a mile," Clefspeare said as he turned toward it. "Get ready. We will be landing in a moment."

With a great beating of his wings, Clefspeare settled to the ground between a high snowdrift and a dragon-sized boulder, about ten paces or so from the glass. Billy jumped down and helped Acacia dismount Clefspeare's neck.

All three hurried to the glass, Billy arriving first. With the surface curving slowly away in each direction, it seemed to be a huge cylinder. It would probably take at least fifteen minutes to walk around it.

Snow had piled in drifts against the glass except at one three-foot-wide section where it seemed that someone had recently cleared it away, allowing Billy to walk right up to the partition and peer through. On the other side, the landscape looked more like a desert than a snow scene. A few scrubby trees dotted the area here and there, and some old buildings stood in the distance. The closest one seemed very familiar. This place definitely looked like the old town in the sixth circle of Hades.

Standing in knee-deep snow, he pressed a finger against the glass, but it left no mark. "This is really weird, Dad. What do you make of it?"

Clefspeare set his snout close to the window and blew twin flames, narrow and orange, and kept them there for several seconds. When he pulled away, Billy touched the spots. "Cold. Cold as ice."

Acacia pushed her body against Billy's side and shivered harder than ever. "I will try my fire, but first we should see if we can call Shiloh. If our voices won't penetrate the glass, maybe she can hear us knocking."

Billy rapped on the window with his knuckles and shouted, "Shiloh! It's Billy! Can you hear me?"

He pressed his ear against the glass. "I don't hear anything, but the wind's in my ears, so that doesn't mean much."

Clefspeare swung his tail and whipped the partition. A loud *thwap* rocked Billy's eardrums. Although the glass shimmered slightly, it showed no sign of cracking.

"It is clear," Clefspeare said, "that Semiramis's story has proven true to this point. Perhaps we should also assume that Shiloh is, indeed, trapped in there, which would give me reason to make a more strenuous attempt."

"A full-speed body slam?" Billy asked.

He focused his eyebeams on the glass. "With white-hot blasts of fire aimed at the collision point immediately before I strike."

Billy touched the scarlet target. "I can help with that. I'll blast it with my fire while you're on your way."

"Look!" Acacia laid a palm on the window and pressed her nose next to it. "I see someone."

A girl peeked around one of the buildings. She seemed hesitant, frightened, and too far away to be recognized.

"It's Shiloh," Acacia said. "My vision is so sharp, I can see her wounded hand."

Billy rapped on the glass again and waved. "Shiloh! It's me, Billy!"

Shiloh crept around the corner, easing one foot in front of the other. Suddenly, she burst into a sprint. With her blonde-streaked hair flying behind her and a beautiful smile decorating her lovely face, she looked exactly like Bonnie.

Swallowing down a lump, Billy shouted again. "Can you hear me?"

Shiloh stopped a few feet away from the glass and mouthed something, but he couldn't read her lips. She pointed at her ear as if to indicate that their voices weren't coming through.

Acacia narrowed her eyes. "I think she said, 'Do you know Mars code?'"

"Probably Morse code," Billy said. "She wants us to tap out our words."

"I learned it long ago." Clefspeare touched the partition with a wing tip. "If a tap vibrates the glass enough to transmit sound, then why do our voices not penetrate?"

"It's a barrier between dimensions," Billy said, "probably not real glass at all. Maybe she'll watch our taps and figure them out, or, then again, maybe it responds somehow to physical touch."

"If that's the case . . ." Acacia stripped off her rabbit-fur cloak and handed it to Billy. Then, spreading out her arms, she flattened her body against the partition. Her white hair streaming in the breeze along with her long woolen skirt, she called, "Ignite!"

Starting at her bare hands, two-inch-high firelets crawled along the sleeves of her leather tunic. Although the flames looked hot enough, they didn't burn her clothes or even raise a puff of smoke. Soon, her body blazed.

Laying her cheek against the glass, she called out, "Shiloh! Can you hear me now?"

Shiloh stepped closer. A smile trembled on her lips. "Yes! Yes, I can!" Her voice seemed far away, like a call from a distant canyon.

Billy stood directly behind Acacia. The warmth from her body thawed his frozen cheeks. "Shiloh, do you know of any spots in this wall that look weak? Clefspeare and I want to try to break through."

Shiloh shook her head. "I walked every foot of this thing and hit it with a big hammer until it wore me out. It's tougher than steel."

"Then we might as well try here," Billy said. "Stand back."

As Shiloh stepped away, Acacia did the same. At the spot where she had pressed her body, the glass seemed darker, as if smoke-stained.

Billy touched it. The surface felt warm, but not hot. "Let's concentrate here, Dad. Acacia might have made the dimensional barrier thinner."

"Then perhaps she should try a portal opening cyclone," Clefspeare said. "We have enough firepower."

Billy looked at Acacia. "Could you?"

Acacia spread out her arms. "It feels like the portal wraps around the entire town she's in. To open it, I would probably have to make a vortex at least as big, but with your father's help, perhaps we could do it."

Billy read her sincere expression. She seemed so weak, yet she wanted to help. But should she? Did it make sense to drain her energy if they didn't have to? Yet, allowing her to use her gifts might be the emotional boost she needed. "Dad," Billy said, "let's try brute force first. If it doesn't work, we'll give Acacia a shot at it."

"Very well." Clefspeare launched into the air and flew in a wide circle, gaining altitude with every second. When he turned back toward the window, Billy pushed Acacia behind him and, taking a deep breath, blew a narrow stream of fire at the target. The flames bounced to each side and spilled to the ground, melting the surrounding snow.

He slid to the side to give Clefspeare room to attack. As he took another breath, a volley of flames rocketed out of the sky and blasted the same spot. Billy added his jet again. With steam rising and water streaming at their feet, he glanced at Shiloh. Bouncing on her toes, she folded her hands at her chest, the bloody bandage obvious over her stub of a finger.

Seconds later, Clefspeare stormed through the fire and, his wings now folded, slammed the side of his body into the partition. With a thunderous *smack*, he bounced to the side and slid through the snow. The wall trembled for a moment but quickly settled down.

Billy ran to where his father lay. With his tail turned one way, his neck turned the other, and his head lying motionless near a spine on his back, he looked dead. "Dad! Are you all right?"

A puff of smoke rose from each nostril. "I think so. I feel no broken bones, but I will likely have a very large bruise."

Billy touched Clefspeare's side. Some of the reddish scales had already turned purple. "Can you get up?"

"I will try. Perhaps you should speak to Shiloh while I gather myself together."

Billy ran back to the wall. Acacia was already standing in front of the impact point, touching the glass with a fiery hand as she spoke. "Shiloh, I am going to try to envelop as much of this area as I can. If it looks like the wall is deteriorating, try to walk through it."

Shiloh nodded and backed away again.

Her facial features sagging, Acacia lifted her hands high and called out, "Flames! Come to my fingers!"

Instantly, two enormous fireballs, twice the size of beach balls, erupted in her palms. Closing her eyes for a moment, she took a deep breath and began waving her arms in tight circles. The fireballs expanded and stretched out horizontally until they merged into a sphere the size of three elephants. Acacia appeared to be a diminutive Atlas carrying the world in her little hands.

With her face tense and her lips pursed, she continued to swirl her arms, letting out high-pitched grunts every few seconds.

As the ball continued to grow, Clefspeare shuffled close to Billy. "I am concerned for her," Clefspeare said. "She is likely too weak to undertake such an enormous task."

"Yeah. Me, too. It hurts just to watch her."

Acacia slid her feet through the mud and again pressed her body on the window. Like a bursting bubble, the fireball broke apart. Flames spread across the glass, crawling in every direction. Acacia rubbed her palms on the surface in wide circles. As if propelled by her motions, the flames continued to spread up and around the cylinder.

"It is time to add more fire," Acacia called. "And fan it with your wings!"

Clefspeare raised up on his haunches. "Son, climb aboard and come with me. We will both add fire from the air."

Billy ran up his father's tail section and along his back, dodging the longer spines. As soon as he seated himself at the base of the neck, he shouted, "Let's do it!"

Beating his wings, Clefspeare rose into the air. The wing on the bruised side seemed to falter, making him tilt for a moment, but he soon righted himself and began an orbit around the transparent cylinder.

"You aim low," Clefspeare shouted, "and I will aim high."

Angling his neck toward the sky, he sprayed a flood of orange from his mouth and both nostrils. Billy joined in, bending over to strike the glass several feet lower. As soon as the flames met the partition, they spread out in the same way Acacia's did, and gusts from Clefspeare's wings added to the momentum.

It took a few minutes for Clefspeare to complete one orbit. When they passed Acacia, she was still leaning against the glass and still moving her hands in circles, though she seemed slower, and her eyes were now tightly shut.

Billy continued shooting fire into the storm. With each splash, the flames made a whooshing sound as they joined in with the rest of the fire. Breathing in cold air, then blowing out hot, he pressed on, though each barrage grew weaker.

Clefspeare's fire remained strong, but his flight angle tilted again. The bruise on his side was definitely taking its toll.

The glass shook. As if boring holes through the partition, fire spilled to the inside and dribbled downward. A slight dizziness swam through Billy's head, likely a touch of hyperventilation, but he couldn't stop now. Something was happening. Maybe it was working.

As they approached Acacia again, the entire wall dissolved, and the fire dropped to the ground like a burning curtain. Her flames ceased, and she stumbled through and fell into Shiloh's arms. Shiloh sat down and, cradling Acacia, called, "She's okay! Just exhausted, I think."

Clefspeare and Billy shut off their jets. As they glided toward the snow, Billy shouted, "Yes! She did it!" But before his final word passed through his lips, the village began to fade.

"Dad! Get on the ground! Quick!"

As soon as Clefspeare landed, Billy jumped down. Sliding in the snow, he dashed toward Shiloh and Acacia, but the scene vanished before he could get there. They were gone.

He stumbled forward and plowed into a drift. As he rolled, snow pushed into his mouth, cooling the sensitive skin inside. When he came to a stop, he looked up at the cloud-blanketed sky and rested for a moment. His heart thumped. His head pounded. Every part of his body ached.

"Son!" Clefspeare called. "Are you all right?"

"I think so." Slowly rising to a sitting position, he looked at his father. Now his heart pounded even harder. Tears came to his eyes, and the chilly wind pushed them back toward his temples. They had failed. Not only did they not rescue Shiloh, they lost Acacia, an Oracle of Fire, no less, probably a great asset in the battle if Abraham's protective wall should ever fail. She had the best chance of opening the portal at Mount Elijah. Now what would they do? Could a dragon open it? With no good place to land, it wasn't likely. And poor Shiloh. Within seconds of being rescued, her hopes were dashed.

He rose to his feet and batted the snow from his pants. Or maybe they weren't dashed after all. Could she have transported to a safe place, away from those who wanted to slice her into pieces? Maybe Shiloh's captors had no idea where she ended up.

Sighing deeply, he pushed through the drift until he worked his way back to the muddy section. He leaned against his father's side and draped an arm over his neck. "Now what're we going to do?"

Clefspeare picked up Acacia's cloak with his teeth and laid it over Billy's shoulders. "We will go back to the village. What choice do we have?"

"We could try to open it again. You know, create another circle of fire."

"We can, and we will, but not in my weakened state. I will return later with Hartanna, and we will see what we can do."

Nodding, Billy looked up into his father's eyes. "Any speculation?"

"If you mean their destination . . . no. When the firestorm toppled the Tower of Babel, the bottom third transported from Earth to Hades, so it seems that these portal jumps are unpredictable, at least for us who have no knowledge of the cross-dimensional paths."

Billy touched Clefspeare's bruise. "How does it feel? Going back will be mostly against a headwind."

Clefspeare bent his neck until his head hovered in front of the purple blotch. "I would not want to do battle for a while, but I am confident I can make it to Founder's Village."

"If we go another route, maybe it won't be so bad."

"I assume you mean that you still want to check on the wall of fire and deliver the supplies."

"Right. Do you think you could make it that far? I can go with Hartanna later."

"I see value in going now. The warrior chief will be glad to get a report, and the men could be hungry." Clefspeare shuffled to the large boulder. "But first, I want to create a landmark to ensure that we are able to find this place in the future." He heaved in a breath. Then, with a narrow, laserlike stream of fire, he chiseled into the boulder's surface. As he guided the stream, smoke shot out, veiling his mark, but after several seconds, he finished, and the breeze cleared the smoke, revealing a letter *X* about the size of a human head.

"*X* marks the spot?" Billy asked.

"Indeed. It is a simple but well-known symbol."

Billy laughed, "Mom used to put an *X* on maps when we played Treasure Island together. She would even put one on the ground at the place where she buried . . ." He let his voice dwindle away.

They stayed silent for a moment until Clefspeare breathed a sigh. "I know, Son. I miss her, too."

After resting for a few minutes, Billy remounted Clefspeare and the two rode southeast to the north side of the Valley of Shadows. A wall of flames stood before them, rising from the ground on the northern border of the valley, through the clouds and out of sight.

As they passed around to the northeastern side, Billy looked back at the river. Before the start of the season of death, one of Valiant's warriors tried to cross into the valley by diving into the cold water, a test to ensure that no one could come through from the other direction. Under the surface, the water boiled at that point, but most of the flow passed through, proving that this was a vulnerable spot. The same was true where the river exited the walled-in zone. So Valiant stationed armed guards at each point. Even if the enemy breached the wall, they wouldn't be able to get more than one soldier through at a time, making them easy prey for the guards.

Billy spotted two men wearing thick coats and huddling under a makeshift shelter, more of a lean-to than a hut. With a spear in hand, one faced the river while the other appeared to be sleeping under a pile of blankets.

After delivering a fresh supply of food and clothing to the guards, Clefspeare and Billy took off again and rounded the valley's eastern boundary. Billy looked down at the rugged terrain. Snow dressed the trees in skirts of white, though the depth whittled down with every inch closer to the wall, until only mud and scorched trees lined the area nearest the flames.

Several minutes later, Clefspeare flew around a bend and reached the south side just beyond Adam's Marsh. When the river came into sight, Billy patted his father's neck. "I see the guards."

His wing obviously faltering again, Clefspeare angled down and landed in a deep drift near the eastern side of the river. As he slowed, he toppled over, spilling Billy, and then slid into the water.

"Dad!" Billy jumped up and splashed into the chilly flow. His father's wings splayed over the surface, and his head had disappeared underneath. Chunks of ice bounced against Billy's thighs as he waded deeper, pumping his arms and churning his legs. Finally, in waist-deep water, he plunged in, hooked his arms around his father's neck, and hoisted his head above the surface.

Shivering, Billy listened. Was he breathing? The river's rush made it impossible to tell. But his father was definitely unconscious. How could he possibly drag him out?

Loud splashes sounded behind him, then a voice. "Hold on, Billy! Help is on the way!"

He twisted around. Two men waded in, a tall and hefty man in front carrying a rope. Billy heaved in a shaking breath and let it out through chattering teeth. "Thanks . . . uh . . . Sorry, I don't remember your name."

"Name's Stout." He threw the rope over Clefspeare's back, dove under the water, and resurfaced with the end in hand. After shaking away droplets from his hair, he tied the rope in place. "Just keep his head above water, and Frank and I will haul him out."

Billy looked at the other helper, a short, skinny man with a thick beard. "Frank" seemed like an odd choice for these folk who were usually given names based on their personalities.

The two men charged back and forth with the rope, looping and tying until they had fashioned a makeshift harness. Then, with each man pulling on an end, they began hauling Clefspeare to the river's western shore.

Still holding his father's head, Billy trudged along with them. For a few seconds, they moved into deeper water that rose to his neck, but soon they angled up and slid Clefspeare up to the snow.

Frank shook his body and shivered. "We'd better get a fire going here. The dragon is likely dead already, but until we're sure, we should do what we can."

"Just b-bring wood." Billy's teeth chattered so hard, he could barely spit out his words. "I c-can light it."

While the two men hustled to their camp, Billy knelt and set his ear close to his father's nostrils. A wheezing breath warmed his skin. It sounded awful, but it was still music to his ears.

After a few minutes, Stout and Frank had set piles of split logs around Clefspeare's body. Billy moved from pile to pile. The intense cold had chilled his belly, making his fire weak, but as he ran around, reigniting each log as it burned low, he managed to get them all blazing nicely.

With warmth now spreading all around, melting the snow underneath and around his father's body, Billy sat down and rested. His father's breathing had grown deeper and even, but he showed no signs of waking up.

Stout and Frank stood on the other side of one of the fires, Stout now holding a spear. "What brings you to this guard station?" he asked.

Billy pulled his wet clothes away from his skin. "We were checking the wall's security. I wanted to get a report to Elam."

Frank slapped Stout's arm with the back of his hand. "The warrior chief lacks trust in us."

"Lacks trust?" Billy untied the second box of supplies from Clefspeare's back and shoved it into Frank's chest. "Elam sent this for you."

Frank staggered back but regained his balance. "What is it?"

"Food, socks, clean underwear, compliments of your distrusting warrior chief, though they probably aren't dry now."

Stout took the box from Frank and set it on the ground. "I apologize for my partner's frivolous words. We are grateful for Elam's concern. Please let him know that all is well, and there have been no breaches."

"I also apologize," Frank said. "I fear that listening too often to the concerns of other villagers has skewed my thinking."

Billy squinted at him. "Concerns? Other villagers? What are you talking about?"

Stout nudged Frank with an elbow, but Frank didn't seem to notice as he rattled on. "Some believe that Elam is unqualified. First, he is a foreigner and does not understand our ways. Second, he seemed to force Angel to lie. Why would he do that? Third, he commanded the singing girl to change the words to her song, and that brought the giants and the evil dragon into our world. Quite a number of our people died as a result. Now our great prophet is gone, we have strange weather that paralyzes us, and a constant threat looms beyond this fiery wall. And it seems that each one of these problems can be attributed to—"

"Hush!" Stout batted Frank with his huge hand. "You have said far too much."

Frank stepped back, his eyes wide. "Oh, I do not believe this blather myself. Heaven forbid! I merely said that it skewed my thinking, and this noble knight asked me to explain."

Billy scowled at Frank. "Has anyone suggested to these doubters that Angel's lie, and not Elam's decisions, led to all these problems?"

Frank parted his lips to speak, but Stout clamped a hand over his mouth. "I have spoken to several, Billy. Most are merely frightened. Doubts do exist, to be sure, so we should be wary. If doubt is allowed to fester, idle talk can cause it to spread, and seditious talk can set it on fire. Fortunately, Flint has been the only seditious influence in our villages, and he is now on the other side of this wall, so we need concern ourselves only with idleness. Discipline and purposeful hard work will surely be of great benefit to everyone and will silence the mouths of the busybodies."

As soon as Stout lowered his hand, Frank added, "Including the dragons. People think they are not working hard enough."

Stout gave him another punch. "Remember what you said when you are eating the food this dragon nearly died to deliver to you."

Billy looked back at Clefspeare. His breathing was steady and strong. The firelight had to be helping his photoreceptors recharge, but was the bruise a sign of internal bleeding? Would his photoreceptors promote healing fast enough? Maybe a healer could get the process moving faster.

"If you don't mind," Billy said, "could one of you go back to the village and ask Thigocia to come out here? And one of the other dragons, like Hartanna, Legossi, or Firedda."

Frank pointed at himself. "I will go. Stout is stronger than I, but I am swifter. In these conditions, Stout might take until next week to arrive."

"He speaks the truth, as usual," Stout said, laughing as he delivered another punch to Frank's arm, "but he could learn a bit of diplomacy."

"Thank you." Billy reached back and touched Excalibur's hilt, but his arm felt stiff, and a hard shiver shook his body. "I can take Frank's place here till he gets back."

"You will need dry covering." Stout hurried to a tent, returned with a thick blanket, and draped it over Billy's shoulders. "Now you will be much more comfortable."

While waiting for the guard to return, Stout provided Billy with a long and eloquent account of the history of the two villages, at least what he could remember. Since he was only one hundred twenty years old, his recollections didn't reach as far back as some of the elders. Still, he recalled tales that Abraham had told, as well as some of Valiant's adventures. With Abraham gone, Valiant was now the oldest citizen in either village, but no one knew exactly how old he was, and he would never tell. Some said six hundred years, some said well over a thousand, but his physical vigor and mental acuity had not faded in the slightest.

During the stories, Clefspeare shifted his body from time to time and let out a low groan. The bruise spread farther across his scales, red giving way to purple from just above his right foreleg all the way back to the base of his tail. It looked bad, very bad.

After a few hours, a booming call sounded from above, a dragon's trumpet, then another. Billy looked up. Two dragons slashed through the lower layer of clouds and angled toward them. As they drew closer, their identities became clear, Thigocia and Legossi, both with wings folded in and diving fast.

The next few minutes seemed like a blur. With barely a word, Thigocia snuffed out the surrounding fires and covered Clefspeare with her body and wings while Legossi coated her with flames. Under the barrage, Thigocia's scales slowly turned from beige to reddish orange. Again and again Legossi applied new coats until Thigocia called out, "Enough!"

She lay motionless, save for the normal rise and fall of respiration. As her glow diminished, Clefspeare began to stir. Thigocia rose and stepped out of the way, giving him room.

"He will soon rise," she said.

Billy knelt at his father's side. The bruise had diminished to the size of a grapefruit, and even the color of his healthy scales seemed bolder and brighter than ever.

Soon, he blinked and lifted his head. His blazing red eyes shifted to each onlooker in turn. With a low rumble, he murmured, "It seems that I have taken a spill."

Billy patted him on the neck. "You just went for a swim in the river, that's all. You seemed kind of cold, so I called in a heating specialist."

Clefspeare draped a wing over Billy's back. "A healing?"

His throat tightening, Billy nodded. "It looked pretty bad for a while."

Clefspeare climbed to his haunches and spread out his wings. "I am still quite sore, but I think I will be able to fly back to the village."

"No riders for you," Thigocia said. "I will carry Billy."

Legossi shuffled close to Stout. "And I will remain with this guard until the other returns. Frank is not fond of riding dragons, so he chose to walk back."

"I welcome your presence," Stout said, bowing low. "As an amateur historian, I would like to learn more about dragonkind from your world."

After a minute or two of stretching and testing his wings, Clefspeare lifted into the sky and flew in a wide circle, apparently without difficulty. Billy climbed up Thigocia's tail and settled at the base of her neck.

Seconds later, she joined Clefspeare, and the two dragons headed back to the village, slowly but steadily.

As they ascended to just under the cloudbank, Billy watched his father's flight, his eyebeams aimed straight ahead. He seemed to be in deep thought. Was he thinking about his vulnerability? His relative weakness in this place of cold and so little sunlight? How long could these dragons maintain their power?

Billy's thoughts turned to his conversation with the two guards. Apparently, Elam had vulnerabilities of his own. Stout's words came back to mind. *If doubt is allowed to fester, idle talk can cause it to spread, and seditious talk can set it on fire.*

Sure, Flint was gone, but could there be another source of sedition? Semiramis definitely talked a good talk, but it seemed that everything she was involved in turned into a disaster. Because of her, a new plant was growing that was a spawn of Arramos, and they couldn't do anything to stop it. Her discovery of Shiloh's prison led to Acacia's disappearance. And even her help with healing Listener could be explained as a stealthy way of gaining trust rather than a truly caring gesture.

Billy lowered his head to get out of the stiff breeze. The coming weeks, months, and maybe even years would seem so long, especially without Bonnie around to talk to.

* * *

Bonnie stood near the waterfall in the Valley of Souls and looked into the pool. Her rippled reflection, a human-shaped statue of flames stared back at her. It was all so strange, good in a way, yet awful in another. It was like the passions in her heart burned on the outside of her body—love, faith, zeal—but was it always the best idea to show these feelings to everyone so plainly?

Two other flaming people joined her, one on each side. To Bonnie's right, The Maid's French-flavored voice sang out. "Do not fear." She dipped her toe in the water. Although the girl's skin and the outline of her foot clarified, the fire kept burning. "Nothing is able to extinguish your flame, unless you allow it."

Standing on Bonnie's left, Sapphira looked at the waterfall. "Can we try to go back through the portal?" She let her fire die away. "I can try it by myself and see what happens."

"Oh, please do not," The Maid said. "Abaddon has already warned me that this portal is closed at the other side by thick layers of rock. You would drown if you made the attempt. And if you wish to perish by water, the pool would be more efficient. It would be easier to retrieve your body."

"Thanks," Sapphira said, "but that's not exactly comforting."

The Maid withdrew a dagger and set it on the ground next to Bonnie. "Abaddon said you must take this."

Sapphira stared at it. "It's the staurolite dagger! How did you get it?"

"It washed down from your world, and Abaddon found it. I can only assume someone threw it into the portal."

"I did that," Sapphira said. "It's evil. It tried to get me to kill myself."

"I see." The Maid picked it up again and looked at it. "Perhaps its evil nature has been purged. Since Abaddon insisted that Bonnie keep it, the dagger must be safe. He is quite adept at exorcising an evil spirit."

Bonnie took it from The Maid. "I don't have a sheath for it."

"That is easily remedied. I think we will be here long enough to make one."

Sapphira pulled the ovulum from the pouch and stared at the clear glass.

"Still no Enoch?" Bonnie asked.

Sapphira pushed it back in place. "I think we're on our own."

"The heavenly viewer will work here," The Maid said. "There is likely a problem on the other side."

"That's not good news," Bonnie said. "If Enoch's in trouble, then everyone else is, too."

The Maid laughed. "There is no need to fear. An Oracle of Fire surely understands this."

Bonnie stared at her hands again. Somehow she could see the outline of her fingers a little better. It was almost like being in the candlestone. When she first dove into the stone, she was just a mass of energy, but over time her details grew clear.

She looked at The Maid. She, too, seemed to be clearer. Her eyes were sharp and piercing, and her hair flowed behind her, clearly blonde, even within her fiery shell.

Yet, The Maid had been there for years, so the reason for her clarity had to be a sharpening in Bonnie's vision. Would they soon be able to see each other plainly? Could The Maid already see every detail in Bonnie's face and form?

Bonnie sat down and dipped her feet in the water. Although it felt neither warm nor cool, it was refreshing. "How much warning will we have if we're about to be called?"

The Maid stooped beside her. "Abaddon receives word of possible callings at least an hour in advance, by Earth's reckoning, but with the will of man as part of the equation, it is rarely certain. He sometimes prepares, and the call does not occur. Only when the call is a fulfillment of prophecy is he ever certain."

After a pause, The Maid added, "But since you are an Oracle of Fire, I am sure you suspected this."

"Why do you keep saying I should know these things?" Bonnie asked. "I've been an Oracle of Fire for what? Three days?"

"Do you mean to say that you did not know these things?" The Maid cocked her head, a curious expression behind her flaming aura. "Do you not know that God would give you time to respond to a resurrection call? That there is no need to fear the future? If not, then how can you be an oracle?"

"Okay, I did know those things." Bonnie shook her head sadly. "Now I'm not sure why I thought I might not have known. I feel kind of foolish."

"It is because you have lived so long among people who love their slavery. Although the key to the lock has been provided, they refuse to employ it, even those who verbally profess the same faith. They hold on to the chains, because a faithless life seems easier to them than the sacrificial suffering that you and every other oracle is called to live. They even drag these chains and moan about their weight, yet they still refuse to let them go, even though they are told time and again that every lock has been rendered powerless by the Lord Christ. Such is the madness of this generation of mankind."

"And living among them," Bonnie said, "I guess I caught the mindset and got used to the language."

"Even though you threw away the chains long ago." The Maid's fiery hand touched Bonnie's. "Speak the truth. Live the truth. Be the truth. Never let the faithless ones change any of those three principles. Remember that you are an Oracle of Fire, as is every faithful follower of our Lord. For all true disciples possess the pure silver, purged of all dross, and the fire of God's love burns within, an everlasting flame that others, even those who give lip service to the truth, will never comprehend until you are able to pass along that fire from heart to heart.

"The essence of such an Oracle is spiritual in nature. After you leave this place, you will not create fire with your hands, yet fire will burn in your heart with far more boldness and passion than ever before. As an Oracle, you will look through portals to the hearts of those lost in shadows, you will feel the heavy sadness of their lonely and dark estates, and you will possess crystal-clear vision that will allow you to see what will bring them deliverance from their sorrows. In trying to bring this deliverance, you will say and do things that will make them shake their heads in pity. 'That poor girl,' they will say. 'Her passion has addled her brain.' Your confidence, they will call arrogance. Your faith, they will call wishful thinking. Your purity, they will call self-righteousness. Your firm standing, they will call pride. Yet you will know, because of that fire within, that they are the ones dwelling in darkness, and you must touch your lighted wick to their darkened lamps.

"While you are here, I will remind you of these things daily. Not only that, I will train you in the art of the sword, both the physical art and the spiritual."

Bonnie felt warmer all over. The Maid's touch seemed so real, so energizing. And her words made the inner flame burst into an inferno.

"Have no fear," The Maid continued. "For as long as you stay here, you will neither hunger nor thirst, and you will always walk in the light. Since Jehovah has called you to this place, you must believe that all is well."

Bonnie let every syllable sink in. They felt peaceful and good as they filtered through, like hot soup poured into a cold belly. After a few silent moments, she nodded. "I am an Oracle of Fire, so I know without a doubt that God will not forsake me in this place. I will rise again."

ACKNOWLEDGMENTS

The Dragons in our Midst/Oracles of Fire story world now includes more than a million words. It would be impossible to thank every person who offered a helpful hand in the creation and polishing of these works, so please forgive any omissions.

Thank you to my wife and children. You helped me in more ways than I can count, from conception, to gestation, to birth. This story would have remained a crazy dream without you.

This book, part one of the longest in all three series, required the editing prowess of many willing helpers, including some of my faithful readers, so I send my thanks to Peter Blaskiewicz, Connie Wolters, and Holli Herdeg for poring over the two hundred thousand words and offering their suggestions.

And most of all, thank you to my Lord and Savior, Jesus Christ. You implanted the flame within me that helped me understand what an Oracle of Fire is. Without You, I would be nothing.

For every Oracle of Fire who reads this, I pray that your heart's flame blazes once again as these words reignite a passion that can never be extinguished.

ABOUT THE AUTHOR

Bryan Davis is the author of fantasy/science-fiction novels for youth and adults, including the bestselling Dragons in Our Midst series. Other series include The Oculus Gate, Reapers, Dragons of Starlight, Tales of Starlight, Astral Alliance, Time Echoes, and Wanted: Superheroes, several of which have been bestsellers.

Bryan was born in 1958 and grew up in the eastern US. From the time he taught himself how to read before school age, through his seminary years and beyond, he has demonstrated a passion for the written word, reading and writing in many disciplines and genres, including theology, fiction, devotionals, poetry, and humor.

Bryan is a graduate of the University of Florida (BS in industrial engineering). In high school, he was valedictorian of his class and won various academic awards. He was also a member of the National Honor Society and voted Most Likely to Succeed.

He continues to expand his writing education by teaching at relevant writing conferences and conventions. Although he is now a full-time writer, Bryan was a computer professional for over twenty years.

Bryan and his wife, Susie, homeschooled their four girls and three boys, and they work together as an author/editor team.